A HISTORY OF THE BIG HOUSE

ALSO BY CHARIF MAJDALANI

Beirut 2020: Diary of the Collapse

Moving the Palace

A HISTORY OF THE BIG HOUSE

CHARIF MAJDALANI

TRANSLATED FROM THE FRENCH
BY RUTH DIVER

Other Press
New York

Originally published in French as *Histoire de la grande maison* in 2005
by Éditions du Seuil, Paris

Production editor: Yvonne E. Cárdenas
Text designer: Patrice Sheridan
This book was set in Arno Pro and Granjon by
Alpha Design & Composition of Pittsfield, NH

1 3 5 7 9 10 8 6 4 2

Library of Congress Cataloging-in-Publication Data
Names: Majdalani, Charif, 1960- author. | Diver, Ruth, translator.
Title: A history of the big house : a novel / Charif Majdalani ; translated from
the French by Ruth Diver.
Other titles: Histoire de la grande maison. English
Description: New York : Other Press, 2024.
Identifiers: LCCN 2024013824 (print) | LCCN 2024013825 (ebook) |
ISBN 9781635423402 (paperback) | ISBN 9781635423419 (ebook)
Subjects: LCGFT: Novels.
Classification: LCC PQ3979.3.M34 H5713 2024 (print) |
LCC PQ3979.3.M34 (ebook) | DDC 843/.914—dc23/eng/20240723
LC record available at https://lccn.loc.gov/2024013824
LC ebook record available at https://lccn.loc.gov/2024013825

Publisher's Note: This is a work of fiction. Names, characters, places, and incidents either are the product of the author's imagination or are used fictitiously, and any resemblance to actual persons, living or dead, events, or locales is entirely coincidental.

FOR NAYLA

Such is the way of the world and I have nothing but good to say of it.

SAINT-JOHN PERSE, *ANABASE*, IV

PART ONE

THE TIME OF HEROES

1

HE FELL QUIET again and slumped back into his armchair with a lost, faraway look in his eyes, muttering in protest that he would never ever talk about it, that it was a story from a bygone age, that nothing was worth waking the dead. Then he picked up the pack of cards again, and started shuffling them continuously to keep his hands busy, a pack that he had once used to play solitaire before he gave up on even that pointless activity, but that he was now happy simply to shuffle all day, then to set down on the tray next to him, beside the address book in which almost all the telephone numbers were of people long dead, all the names reminders of another time in his life, of a history that had collapsed, crumbled, disappeared, and been swept away, like everything else around him, while he stayed there, solid as a rock, a survivor of almost heroic eras, the last offspring of a huge family whose members had all died in turn, one after the other, leaving him all alone in a field of ruins, of memories, in a sea of stories whose inextricable tangles he now found himself less and less able to unravel, and so he would pick up the pack of cards again, and shuffle them once, twice, then put them down again, and stay silent until I asked him another question about someone else, about another incongruous or distant or implausible event. He would think for a while, muddle up a few dates or wars, then find the thread again and go back to the beginnings, to the initial exile, the orange groves, the fleeing deserters, the father's banishment, the destroyed village in Anatolia, then he would take a long stride through time, lunge over an entire decade, the very one I wanted him to talk about, and go to the Egyptian deserts, the fire stoker on the Suez Canal, the laughing Ethiopian soldier, then he would turn around again, slowly make his way backward, talk about the older branch of the family, about the famine, the Big House crumbling into ruins, the orchards liquidated for next to nothing, coming closer and closer in concentric circles to that mysterious story, to that unnamable thing, holding it close, almost touching it, as he spoke of a Panhard at the bottom of the front steps of the Big House. I would keep quiet, like someone holding their breath while watching a tightrope walker reach his goal, but he would always come to a final halt again at that unnamable thing, then breathe heavily for a while, bite his bottom lip, mutter an incantation and fall quiet, then pick up the pack of cards and swear that he would never ever speak of it.

And then suddenly, one day at noon, as he was eating lunch, seated in the same place as he always had been for the past forty years, at the huge table where no one besides himself ever sat anymore, except when we came to keep him company, as I had that day, and to have lunch with him (but always after him, because since my mother's death, he had started taking his meals imperceptibly earlier and earlier, so that he now had lunch almost when we would usually be having breakfast), so yes, one day at noon, or to be more accurate while he was having lunch, and I was distracting him by asking him the same questions over and over again, without him fully realizing that I already knew all the answers but one, instead of starting to go around in circles again, inexplicably, he uttered the fateful words, he revealed the final secret, he muttered that *they* had had *him* thrown into prison after setting *him* a shameful trap, and it was up to me to understand that *they* were the members of the older branch of the family, and that *he* was one of his brothers, one of my uncles.

I was dumbfounded for a split second, illuminated, as I gathered up these words that were more precious than gold to me, and held them in the purest silence I could find within myself in that instant. Then I realized that I had always imagined that things had happened in exactly that way, that, from the scraps of what he had let slip over the years, I had reconstituted the story precisely as he just told it to me, although I could not be sure whether he had cleverly suggested all of its elements to me without my realizing it, or whether everything he had ever told me, like a slope, inevitably led all the streams of story to flow toward the very one that I was missing and that I thought I had simply made up.

Whatever the case, it seemed to me at that moment that I held all the pieces in play at last, and that I could now re-create the history of the entire family, from the time of the Big House and the land covered in orange trees to the three brothers' exile in Egypt and their return, a history that would finally flow into my own story, after crossing paths with my mother's equally tormented family history. And it seemed to me also that I could easily imagine the bridges, the junctures, and all the dizzying lacework of details of the story, with the certainty I now had, that anything I might imagine might just as well have happened, that any distinctions between reality and invention are naturally blurred, and that truth becomes legend and legend acquires authenticity, all within the same edifice.

And as the moment of inner illumination passed, I heard my father add, as he looked right through me into the distance inside himself, that in any case all of that—the sons' wanderings, the exile in Egypt, and the rest—it was all to blame on an absence, the father's absence, his own father and the entire family's, a man who was too imposing, too powerful, and had died too soon, so that the entire universe he had created around himself had vanished along with him. That was something I already knew, but my father made this admission in a kind of absent, altered state, and the dreamy tone of his voice as he made it gave it the sense of an augury. That was when I realized it was time for me to start, and that I could only start from there. From his father's history.

All the legends and accounts of the father's life that his descendants have preserved and passed down are similar in beginning his story with his departure for exile, a minuscule exile in terms of distance, but one that would have incalculable consequences. They all start with this man's appearance, one spring morning in the last years of the nineteenth century, in the middle of the olive and mulberry groves of Ayn Chir, at the edge of the Pine Forest.

He has just crossed the border of the Beirut vilayet and arrived on the autonomous lands of Mount Lebanon. As far as he is concerned at this point, it is undoubtedly not an exile, just a matter of getting away for a few days, while things settle down in Marsad, the neighborhood where he was born. And in fact he is not alone. His younger brother is with him, and they are riding on their horses side by side: Wakim—as he will later appear in the photographs taken by Bonfils, the first photographer of Beirut—a taller-than-average man, with a wide forehead heightened by the tarbouche he wears straight, and his distinctively martial, slightly turned-up mustache that will later, when he becomes a father, make him look like a viceroy of India, and beside him his brother, Selim, still almost an adolescent, with no beard but a serious countenance, like Wakim wearing a European suit and riding boots. They are on horseback, riding abreast without speaking, perhaps musing about everything that happened in the previous days, about what compelled them to turn their backs on Marsad, to flee their own neighborhood, the one to which they would never return, but that they would continue—that we would all forever continue to claim as our own, like those South American farmers who even after five generations born in the colonies still consider themselves Castilians.

And yet, no. In fact, it is impossible to start like this. For the two men who have just ridden into the mulberry groves of Ayn Chir on this spring morning are only who they have been until now. They have a past, professions, daily lives, a house, they have just lived through a critical event, and they carry all this within themselves. This is what constitutes them, this is what they are thinking about in silence as they reach the edge of the Pine Forest, and I must take all this into account, if only so that everything that comes later makes sense. I cannot start this history without trying to imagine at least some of the mythical time before, without inventing a general ambience, a nebula from which I can then extract what comes next, starting with that moment when two men cross the abstract border between Beirut and the Mount Lebanon governorate, to arrive on horseback, one morning, at the edge of the mulberry groves of Ayn Chir.

To do this, I have at least one clue at my disposal: Wakim Nassar's profession before that inaugural escape. It is almost the only thing I know about him from those days, no doubt the only thing even his sons ever knew about that quasi-mythical time, and which my father, who learned it from his brothers, once whispered to me and then later confirmed, while shuffling his pack of cards, putting it down, picking it up again, as he picked up the main threads of his history. And what he told me was that his father, in that faraway time, was a middleman. A strange word, a strange trade, even more so in its Arabic syllables: *simsar*. It's a bizarre thing, and not particularly inspiring, especially as a beginning. But I will try to solve that riddle later.

For now, let us just take this fact as it is. And I must admit it is rather convenient. For Wakim might have been a retailer, and then I would have to invent a storefront, a specialty, some clients and employees. He might have been a government official, and then I would have to reconstitute the complex and archaic world of the Ottoman administration of the time. He might have been a farmer, and that would not match the image I have of him or the photographs from that time at all. He might have been independently wealthy, and then I would have to invent a whole world of futile activities to fill an idler's days in bygone Beirut. No, he is a simsar, and that is just as well, because he is the kind of man who owns nothing, has nothing, is always listening to the world around him, and his workplace is simply the outdoors, the city, the people.

When I try to imagine him before his exile, I can almost immediately see him in the lanes of Marsad, walking between the gardens and the low sandstone walls with the branches of lemon and loquat trees stretching over them. He is walking, and I have just decided that he is going down the lanes toward the city. That is where business takes place, that is undoubtedly where he belongs. He left home a few moments ago and is now passing through a smell of clean linen and boiled bay leaves, and there he is, stepping over a puddle of steaming laundry water flowing into the street. He passes through a smell of resin, and there he is, crunching wood shavings under his feet as he goes past a row of door panels that a carpenter has lined up on either side of his storefront against the walls of the neighboring gardens. He passes through a smell of warm bread, and there he is, breathing it in deeply and wondering where it is coming from, he is bound to have aunts and great-aunts all over the neighborhood where he could stop to visit and eat some warm bread. But he does not stop, he is walking down the lanes, no doubt swaggering a little, because women find him attractive and he knows it. Or rather, he is not the one swaggering. He lets his mustache and his tarbouche do it for him. For he has somber eyes and a particular gaze that always seems to skim over the surface of things. He is carrying a walking stick that gives him additional panache. It is not the ebony cane with the golden band with his father's initials. That one he keeps for special occasions or Sundays, it stands in the corner of the Normandy armoire, in his bedroom.

And, curiously, that Normandy armoire has now allowed me to step inside his house, to imagine something of the time *before,* although it will always be difficult for me to believe that he could ever have lived anywhere but in the Big House he will soon found at Ayn Chir. I can suddenly see a garden, with lemon and loquat trees, three steps, a high porch, and the floor inside covered in clay tiles with arabesque patterns, rooms opening onto each other, where the sweet spring air circulates freely, the smell of the trees, the fragrance of bay leaves scenting the clothes folded in the wardrobes, but also the simple sounds of daily home life, his younger brother's voice humming as he dresses in a neighboring room before he goes out to his office, let's say at Khan Antoun Bey, or his mother's voice as she greets her cousins and sisters-in-law who have come to visit in the early morning, and as she settles down with them in the armchairs on the porch—his mother, who also appears in a photograph by Bonfils, distant and dreamy in her corseted dress, so stiff and aloof that I will always have trouble imagining her in anything other than a Victorian outfit, almost as unreal, disincarnated, and majestic as ancient queens under their mortuary masks. And then I can also see that Normandy armoire, in front of which he stands up straight every morning before going out, as he opens one of its doors to inspect himself in the slightly tarnished mirror inside. He inspects his pants, his waistcoat, and his stiff detachable collar, smooths down his mustache, adjusts his tarbouche, stares darkly into his own somber eyes, then opens the other door, on which there is another mirror, and suddenly he sees his image reflected by the two facing mirrors, duplicated into infinity. I like to think that he amuses himself every morning with this multiplication of himself, before he goes out to scatter his presence throughout the world as he walks.

When he arrives on horseback in the olive groves of Ayn Chir, in the morning of his first day of exile, is Wakim Nassar thinking that at that very moment he could have been in the lanes of Marsad, walking with an assured, long, powerful, and yet lively stride, because it is springtime? It is always springtime when I think of Beirut in those distant times, and the warmth is swelling the stems of all the gardenias and jasmine vines in the lanes. The weather is pleasant as Wakim walks along the old garden walls, and his stick doesn't touch the ground so often, he keeps it up and occasionally hits the pommel with the palm of his other hand, or throws it over his shoulder a few times, then thrusts it eagerly forward: it is dancing, swaggering too, and that is surely because of the springtime. Now he is coming out onto the main road at Basta, the one that goes down into the city. Carriages pass by from time to time with elegant young ladies inside, dressed in European style, just as he is, and that gives him a quiver of pleasure. And yet the street is just beaten dirt, and the dust that is stirred up by the carriages, the hansom cabs, the carts, the horses, and the donkeys covers his shoes and the hems of his pants legs, and that should annoy him. But it doesn't annoy him, and when he enters the city, he is still in a good mood, as evidenced by the play of his walking stick. He arrives at Assour Square and crosses it, letting the hansom cabs and carriages go by. He smiles as he passes a group of idle porters laughing heartily among themselves. He goes into Grand-Rue, which leads up to Cannon Square, overtaking ladies in European dresses and an entirely veiled Muslim woman. He sees men in European suits and tarbouches, just like his, walks past a few storefronts on the left, and I'm wondering where he might be heading, what I'm going to do with him now.

He could continue onward, going up Grand-Rue, coming out onto Cannon Square, and then go on to the Hamidiye Public Garden and step inside, then sit down to watch the young ladies take their early morning strolls. Around the bandstand, at this hour, there must be only gentlemen wearing European suits like his, sitting on park benches reading last month's French gazettes. He might also take one of the little alleys leading off Grand-Rue to his right, and follow it down to the souks, where he could mingle in the dirty, noisy crowd, in the smell of dung and rotten vegetables, avoiding the muddy puddles that would do his shoes and pants legs no good. Then, after going past the Orthodox church, his own church so to speak, since he is Orthodox himself, he would come out for a moment into the Rue du Pas, where he would walk past the storefronts overflowing with all kinds of merchandise—baskets, tin wares, bric-a-brac, wrought iron—advancing with restrained haste among the veiled women, the porters, the licorice juice sellers, and the bear tamers, and then enter the relative peace of the El-Tawileh Souk, where he would calmly pass in front of the wooden stall fronts and the European-style store windows with their signs lettered in French. After which, exiting onto the seafront, he would head left with a lively gait toward Khan Antoun Bey, where the offices of the Ottoman administration are to be found.

But let us not forget that he is a simsar and that a simsar must have some kind of headquarters, a place toward which all the information about the business of the city must flow, and where he can be found without fail every morning. A public place amid the noise and hubbub of the city. A café, surely. And that's why I'll have him take the Grand-Rue toward Cannon Square. So now he is walking along the wall of the convent of the Sisters of Mercy, just a few steps behind two nuns in their cornette wimples, while being overtaken by a hansom cab, and now he is coming out onto Cannon Square, but instead of going toward the park he enters a café on the corner of the street and the square. There are men in suits there, just like him, and others in seroual pants. No one is playing tarot or backgammon yet, only smoking narghiles or drinking tea or coffee. He greets the assembled customers, and they all answer in chorus, distractedly, without moving, in a kind of long, gruff rumble. Then he sits down, alone, at a table on which he sets down his walking stick diagonally.

And this is undoubtedly what he does every morning, for this is where he carries out most of his business, this is where he hears other men talking about their deals—from a field for sale not far from the convent school of the Sisters of Nazareth, to a low-ranking dignitary from Zahlé looking for a house to buy in town, to a consignment of iron bars that a supplier to the Ottoman army has managed to appropriate and would like to sell on, to a magnificent purple roan horse that its owner wants to sell to pay off his debts, but only to a connoisseur. And this is where he steps in and offers his services: he finds a purchaser for the field (a pistachio seller from the Rue du Pas); he finds a house in Santieh for the dignitary from Zahlé; he finds someone to offload the iron bars to (the owner of a marble masonry over by the Saint Elias convent); he finds a buyer for the purple roan horse (a rich Muslim merchant from Sidon who has a small stud and wishes to increase his breeding stock). And he earns a commission every time, one that he sets in advance himself, according to his straightforward appraisal of the value of the merchandise being traded or of the research that he will have to conduct: a row of mulberry trees in the mountains, a cargo of saffron languishing at the customs office. His business is going well, he gathers together a little nest egg, and all this carries on until the incomprehensible day when he escapes me completely, that day when an event takes place that compels him to leave, to ride out of Marsad one fine morning, in silence, with his brother by his side, an event that no one will ever be able to tell me anything about, not even his older sons, my uncles, an event moreover that apparently must have been almost instantly transmuted or lost in the hazy limbo of rumor and hearsay, before it was reconstituted in the memory of his descendants in the form of implausible legends.

At the moment when the two brothers enter the jurisdiction of Mount Lebanon, when they are riding along the road lined with old mulberry trees, this is what is preoccupying them, what they are obsessed about, whatever happened the previous day and the ones before, which I will never be able to know. Was it a simple brawl after a game of dominoes, and did they, on a moonless night in Marsad, draw knives, wield sticks or even pistols, did someone die, were there calls for revenge, women screaming, vindictive burials? Or was it just something to do with women? With Muslim women passing by and casting mischievous enticing glances over their veils to listless young Christian men, who are then tormented by the desire to find out who those beautiful eyes belong to, and end up getting into trouble, scaling a garden wall by night, whistling a little tune behind a low fence, and then finding themselves face-to-face with a hostile brother, and then there's the fight, the knives, the sticks, and perhaps the dead. Or worse yet: climbing a wall for those beautiful eyes and suddenly it's a catastrophe, an unexpected encounter with women caught unawares in privacy without their veils, a frightful commotion in the house, other unveiled women appearing and disappearing in turn, servants running, but hesitating at the last minute for fear of seeing the women uncovered, and finally the appearance of the master of the house before the intruder who retreats in confusion into the garden, bumps into the central fountain that he didn't see in the darkness, somehow makes it over the wall and gives the signal to make a run for it. Then there is the pursuit, all the Muslims in the neighborhood roused by the cries, running on the heels of the fugitives, until they reach the first Christian houses, where they meet other young Christian men, and then there are shouts and blows and calls for revenge, and attempts by the neighborhood chiefs to bring the situation under control. Unless it is something else entirely that Wakim can't stop thinking about, as he urges his horse quietly forward through the mulberry and olive trees of Ayn Chir, something to do with his work as a simsar, a betrayal by one of his associates, a transaction gone wrong, with one of the owners refusing to pay his commission, or an outsider intervening without even striking a blow and making off with a promising deal behind his back. And in order for this to have finally turned out so strangely in the clan's imagination, in order for the rumors to have made the affair into a religious crime, that villainous associate or that sneaky outsider must have been Muslim.

It is therefore possible that everything started with a violent argument, let's say at the café on Cannon Square. I can imagine Wakim and his rival suddenly standing face-to-face, the latter composing his face into a scandalized expression, the former brandishing his accusatory cane, neither one listening to the other, each talking about different things, one about the shame of the offense to his besmirched honor, the other about treachery and betrayed confidence. And little by little, inevitably, the ghastly monster emerges and becomes more and more obvious—the Christian's contempt for the Muslim and the Muslim's contempt for the Christian—it shows its face and leaps out into the open, and even though the insults are indirect, the allusions sweep away in the blink of an eye any cordial familiarity, any customary courtesy in the relations between the two men. Finally, here are the waiters and the other customers that come running, in the tumult of chairs crashing down and tables shoved out of the way. They separate the protagonists, bundle one toward the door and the other to the back of the café, while the passersby and the onlookers in the street have already gathered, and some have even stepped inside to help separate the opponents, pulling one outside and pushing the other inside, and Wakim, trapped for a while in the crowd, ends up disappearing, only to reappear again an hour later in Marsad after having prepared an adequate response to his rival, who is also a resident of Marsad himself.

And it is this response, this revenge—whose substance would be forgotten, suppressed into the unconscious of the clan, the family, and the entire community—that leads to the necessity of exile. Either because the retaliation succeeded so completely, or because it failed so dismally, which both amount to the same thing. What is certain is that it was not a simple act of revenge—not acolytes sent to damage the trees in a mulberry grove, or a cartload of pitchers intercepted and destroyed on the Sidon road, or dogs' corpses thrown over the garden wall in the middle of the night. Nothing so petty, no. It was something that threatened civil peace, that almost set a spark to the powder keg, that almost reignited religious warfare. What would those two scraps of story mean otherwise—those vestiges of memory passed down from generation to generation without ever being understood again, like those snippets of ritual, those fragments of beliefs that men continue to repeat or perform long after their origins and their significance have been lost—namely the fact that, first of all, the day after the event, the Muslim residents of Marsad let it be known that if they ever saw so much as a cat belonging to Wakim or any of his relatives, they would slaughter it with no mercy, and then secondly, the fact that, the following day, Gerios Touwayni himself, in other words one of the most influential members of the Orthodox community in Beirut and one of the richest men of that time, came in person, in the name of the Majlis Millet, to ask Wakim to agree to make peace.

I can see him quite clearly, that Gerios Touwayni, arriving in his carriage, dressed in the latest Parisian fashion, crossing the garden, climbing up the steps to the porch, his gleaming shoes on the brown arabesque tiles, deferentially greeting the mother, who is dumbstruck to see such an important man in her house. And if he is putting on such respectful airs, it is not merely out of politeness but because he can tell from the mother's appearance—that appearance shown on the photograph by Bonfils—that the most respectable blood runs in her veins and that she is well bred. He then sits down in an armchair, with his ivory-pommeled cane on his knees, and talks to Wakim in a paternal tone, under the watchful eyes of Halim Nassar, Wakim's uncle, who approves everything the great worthy says and nods along while observing his nephew's reactions. And I would like to believe that Halim Nassar never understood a thing about his nephew, that Wakim's somber gaze, which constantly follows the contour of things from above, seeking the horizon on them, inspires him only with embarrassment. And yet he is ostensibly the guardian of his two nephews, but maybe he has something of a guilty conscience. Having been made responsible for their assets at his brother's death, he wasted no time, when the land surveys were first drawn up, in registering their properties in his own name. He continued to pay an allowance to his sister-in-law, but Wakim took his distance from him very quickly.

And here an image comes to me. When I think about Wakim's profession as a simsar, about this compulsion to deal in other people's assets, to seek his fortune by rendering his services to one man and then another, I realize that this was actually nothing other than a more modern way of living the life of younger knights, those nobles in the European Middle Ages who never came into their rank and fortune, who were always wandering from kingdom to kingdom to place themselves in the service of one prince after another in hopes of someday carving out a fiefdom of their own. And I realize that this strange comparison can be justified by the image of the two brothers riding slowly into exile one fine morning, unaware that they were in fact about to found a grand estate of their own at last.

But we are not there yet. We're only at the moment when Gerios Touwayni tries to convince Wakim to make peace. He has come on behalf of the bishop and also on Halim Nassar's request, for he knows that Halim, who is an elector in the assembly of the Orthodox community, votes for him on behalf of all the Nassars in the elections of the Majlis Millet. Gerios Touwayni tries to persuade Wakim, and I'd like to think that Wakim lets himself be persuaded.

So from now on, I will have to proceed like an archaeologist who has two shards of glass from which he must reconstitute the shape of a vase; I will have to revise the order of the two scraps of information that we possess about this event and reverse them so that the story becomes more consistent. I must therefore consider that it might be Gerios Touwayni's visit that comes first, that it bears fruit, that Wakim agrees to make peace. Gerios

Touwayni then brings the news to the bishop, who charges the priest of Marsad to bring it to the head of the Muslim neighborhood. And that is when the Muslims of Marsad declare, for their part, that they refuse to make peace and will skin the first cat belonging to the Nassars that strays onto their path. And the situation deteriorates from there. Stones are thrown against the wall of Wakim's house. His brother is caught in Basta one morning on his way to Khan Antoun Bey. He runs, they chase him, they almost catch up, and he finds safety only by forcing his way into the carriage belonging to the wife of the dragoman of the Austrian consul that was just passing by, the wife of the dragoman being very fortunately accompanied by her mother-in-law. That evening he goes home by the Damascus road, making a detour through the pines in the forest, and the next day there is a small family council meeting with Halim Nassar, Wakim, his brother, and his mother, as well as Costa Zreiq, the head of the Christian neighborhood, and the priest of Marsad, who all decide that Wakim would do well to disappear for a few days.

So there they are on horseback, the two of them, riding into the autonomous jurisdiction of Mount Lebanon, through the mulberry and olive groves of Ayn Chir. They are already deep into the orchards when between the wide leaves of the mulberry trees they see the belfry of Saint Michael, the Maronite church, and this is when Wakim halts his horse and says calmly:

"That's enough. I won't go any farther."

His brother, who is a little ahead of him, pulls on his horse's reins and turns it around without saying anything.

"I won't go any farther," Wakim repeats.

And he takes his tobacco pouch out of his pocket, rolls himself a cigarette, and lights it.

Without a word, Selim dismounts, lets go of the reins, enters the field on the right, takes a few steps between the hardened furrows, takes a handkerchief out of his pocket, a handkerchief embroidered with their father's initials, and sits down under a mulberry tree, in the position of someone who is prepared to wait for a century.

Wakim finishes his cigarette calmly as a woman riding sidesaddle on a donkey passes by, staring at them intently, and the sounds of children playing and of a carpet being beaten can be heard in the distance. He finally comes over on his horse and joins his brother.

"Do you really think Tanios Rached has been told we are coming?"

His brother nods.

"Of course he has," he adds. "But you don't expect him to come out to greet you with pipes and drums, do you?"

Wakim pushes his horse forward without answering. His brother stands up, picks up his reins placidly, swings up into the saddle, and starts riding off too, making sure he stays two paces behind Wakim. Five minutes later, two riders appear on the road in front of them, and when they come nearer Wakim recognizes Tanios Rached and his elder son.

So it is at this Tanios Rached's house that they will stay and start their curious life as fugitives. Tanios Rached is not a stranger to them, far from it, he is an old friend of their father's, and Wakim even helped him to sell his first production of olive oil the previous year. The two men treat each other as equals, despite their age difference, and despite the fact that Rached, like everyone else, has heard about Wakim's actions in the past few days. Like everyone else, he believes that Wakim got the better of the Muslims, and he therefore considers him as something of a hero. And so when the four men have ridden side by side and arrived at Rached's house, the boys, girls, and women welcome them in a silence full of respect and intrigued curiosity.

That said, of course, this is not the Wild West; we're in the countryside around Beirut at the end of the nineteenth century. Rached is a wealthy landowner, with mulberry orchards that start at Kfarshima and end at the foot of his house, and his home is not a luxurious ranch but a low house, built in the shape of a U around an open patio and a central fountain. The windows are a few inches off the ground and the wooden doors are open to the four winds, and to the cows, who sometimes wander into the large empty rooms with divans arranged around the sides, before they get chased out by the women shouting and the boys called in to help, cooing and rolling their tongues as the surprised and compliant beasts, like great ladies, step outside in front of them. And finally, the two men who have just arrived on horseback are not cowboys, not romantic, sweating, dusty, handsome heroes, but two city dwellers, one of whom has a gaze that flits insistently on the crest of things and the other a sober and well-bred demeanor. Neither is lacking in charm, which explains why from that point onward, they will spend all their days under the watchful eyes of the girls of the house. Under the girls' eyes, they dismount and first embrace Tanios Rached, then kiss Mother Rached. Surrounded by the girls' furtive glances into the house through the open windows and door, the brothers have their first discussion with their hosts, a discussion that lasts until midday. And finally, under the girls' attentive eyes, the brothers have lunch as the girls serve and then clear the table and bring coffee. And while the girls are busy with all this, they take stock of the older brother and the younger one, then make their choices, exchange amused remarks about them on returning to the kitchen, reappear in the main room, and glean a few more little details—Selim's tie in the latest fashion, Wakim's enigmatic eyes, which sometimes do stop ruffling the surface of things, to land instead on the bare shoulder or underarm of the oldest daughter—and finally, once the meal is over, the girls go sit behind the house to unpack their impressions and their long-suppressed desire to talk and laugh, while inside the house, the men have fallen silent at last.

2

THE DISTANCE BETWEEN Marsad and Ayn Chir is approximately two miles, and part of it is covered in the Pine Forest, which also marks the border between the vilayet of Beirut and the governorate of Mount Lebanon. The forest was apparently planted at the time of the first emirs of the mountain, to stop the sand dunes creeping from the seaside toward the arable lands of the interior, lands that were none other than the very olive groves of Ayn Chir. I don't know whether Ayn Chir is mentioned in the ancient war chronicles from the Middle Ages, the time of the Crusades or the reign of the emirs, but its olive trees with their knotted, hollow trunks would certainly already have borne the stigmata of great age in Wakim's time. The mulberry trees came later, around 1850 in fact, at the time of the general redevelopment of the economy of Mount Lebanon, which ambitiously interjected itself into the worldwide economic circuit by producing silk for the textile industry in Lyon.

At this time, Ayn Chir isn't even a village yet, nor would it ever actually become one, but an expanse of vast plantations, scattered here and there with isolated farms, most of them Maronite. The Shiites are settled only on the periphery, at the edge of the dunes, whose shifting sands they have tamed, and they are not often seen along the road that passes through the orchards and vegetable plots. During the daytime, this road is quite busy because it is the only one that leads from Beirut to Sidon. At night, the hyenas from the sand dunes come dangerously close to it, and to the houses as well, and it is not a rare occurrence to hear a shot ring out in the darkness. In the farms, if anyone is still awake, there is a moment of silence as they wait for the next shot, then they comment about where it came from, and that gets conversation going again, and all the old stories are told once more, like the one about that night when a strange booming sound was heard by all the inhabitants of the Rached house. So Tanios Rached grabs his gun and goes outside, thinking he will surprise a hyena, or even brigands, and he calls out in the darkness for them to show themselves, with his wife behind him holding the lantern high to throw light on the widest possible area around them. But there is nothing there. They go back inside, snuff the lantern, and are about to go back to bed when the same loud noise is heard in the darkness, a kind of questioning, frightening bellow, quite close, almost a human cry, like a man in agony or in rage. "It's a ghoul," Mother Rached says. "It's a ghoul, Tanios, don't go out there." "That's strange," Rached says. "The dogs didn't even wake up." "That's because the ghouls took them all down, Tanios, don't go out there," his wife begs. But Tanios makes her hold the lantern again, and out he goes, whistling for the dogs to get up, and he calls out in the darkness again, walks around the outside of the house, and just as he is passing by the stable, he hears rustling and whispering, he stops, he's got goose bumps, a trickle of icy cold slides down his spine, he calls out a third time and walks toward the stable, bangs on the door, goes inside holding his gun in front of him, and at that very moment one of the cows, who is having a bad dream, ruminating and grumbling in her sleep, makes the same bellowing cry without waking up, and Rached goes back to the house muttering that the cows will start sleepwalking next.

But that is nothing compared to the incredible story of Maroun Maroun, a neighboring farmer who goes out one night, foolishly forgetting to take his gun, because he hears a noise in his stable and thinks a horse has taken ill, and bumps into three brigands there with their faces unmasked. They put a gun to his head, threaten him, and promise to spare his life on the sole condition that he lets them leave with his horses. Maroun argues, negotiates, promises money, food, whatever they like, so long as they leave his animals, he raised them after all, he knows them and loves them, but the brigands remain intractable and suddenly he has a strange idea and asks: "These horses, you're going to sell them, right?" "Well we're not going to eat them, are we, old man?" says one of the brigands. "Well then, I'd like to buy them off you," says Maroun Maroun. And then the four of them start bargaining, Maroun trying to lower the price of his own horses by pointing out some of their flaws, their age, the faded color of the coat of one of them, the lame foot of another (and it pains him to slander his horses like this, and he promises himself to avenge them one day), but the brigands won't be moved (they fixed a price and that's that), and in the end they are the ones who prevail (they have the guns after all), they call out to Mother Maroun, who can't believe her eyes, is terrified, and has to go back into the house to get the money so that Maroun Maroun can buy his own horses.

Apart from the Sidon road, there was always another way of getting to Beirut from Ayn Chir. It was to go through the Pine Forest to the west and get onto the Damascus road at Furn el-Chebbak, half a mile away. From there, passing through the caravanserais of Djerid and then Berjawi, you could get to Cannon Square in around twenty minutes on foot, walking among the carriages, hansom cabs, and caravans coming from Damascus. That's how Selim goes to his office, starting from the day after their escape.

And that's how Wakim returns to Beirut too. But he doesn't go as far as Cannon Square, or venture into the markets. He stays at the edges, sits down in a café under a sycamore tree at Berjawi, a café where he knows not a soul, but he can be sure no Muslim from Marsad will come to quarrel with him. Then he goes as far as Rmeileh, stops to drink a julep from the cart of a traveling salesman, walks up the Damascus road past the Jesuit school, and is back at Ayn Chir at midday. Unless he had visitors in the morning before he left. Indeed there are quite a few people who come from Marsad on the very first day. His mother arrives in a portered chaise, as well as the priest of Marsad, and Costa Zreiq, and some of the Nassar cousins, in a show of solidarity and concern, and also Halim Nassar, on horseback with his son, Gebran, and then Gebran by himself, a young grandee of all of seventeen acting like a city slicker, striking flattering poses in front of Tanios Rached's daughters and making clever comments about the gun hanging at the door. And all of them, the uncle, the cousins, the priest, the mother, the head of the neighborhood, all remind Wakim of the infinite rewards of patience. Wakim sees them all home on horseback, crossing the Pine Forest with them, advancing inside the border of the vilayet, pushing forward to the first houses of Marsad despite their warnings, and it's only when he has stared into the astonished eyes of the first Muslim in the neighborhood that he unwillingly decides to turn back.

One morning he finally decides to go as far as Cannon Square, and even to return to the café at the end of

Grand-Rue. After all, Cannon Square is not Marsad, nor Basta for that matter. He goes down the Damascus road on horseback, leaves his horse at the caravanserai on the edge of the square, approaching it from the west, which feels very strange to him. He walks at a self-assured pace, passes in front of the row of hansom cabs stopped by the gates of the park, and enters the café as if nothing has happened. But just as he is offering his usual greeting to the assembled customers, he realizes that it's too soon, that it won't be taken the right way. And indeed, instead of the bass rumble of distracted answers that he is used to, the dumbstruck silence that greets him drills into his ears. Nevertheless, he advances toward a table near the window on the left, but this feels as if he is crossing an infinite, elastic space, where the least of his gestures bounces back, ricochets in an exaggerated way, as if the general immobility, the fifty pairs of eyes trained on him, the narghile mouthpieces stopped in midair at the edge of lips, the glasses of tea and coffee held up by motionless fingers created a kind of intolerable resonance chamber around him.

He reaches the table at last, puts down his walking stick, takes his seat, and calls over one of the waiters. At that very moment he sees a man wearing a kombaz stealthily slip out of the café. He turns around, looks for the café owner, a Muslim from Bab el-Derkeh whom he considers one of his friends, and sees him staring at him severely from the counter, making a hand gesture that Wakim takes some time to interpret. And just as the waiter he called over is approaching, Wakim's eyes meet those of a customer slowly setting down his narghile, pushing away a table to his right and a chair to his left, making empty space around himself, as one resolutely arranges the area for a sacrifice, or as one rolls up one's sleeves before starting on a dirty task.

The meaning of all this ceremony conducted in silence suddenly reminds Wakim of something, but his mind is stupefied, and he does not react. It's only when the waiter repeats that he is waiting for his order that Wakim wakes up, makes a decision, stands up slowly, sends the waiter away, takes up his cane, walks toward the exit, says "goodbye" to everyone, which resounds in his ears like another unintended provocation, and finally crosses the threshold safe and sound.

It is very probably after a day like that one that things take a different turn. Backed to the wall, facing the city of Beirut that is now closed to him, Wakim has to stop living in a state of impermanence and try to find something to do while waiting for better days. Except that's just it. Of all the things he might have done at that moment—from taking up his activities as a simsar again, this time in Ayn Chir and extending them to Mount Lebanon, to turning at last to the land and the mulberry orchards and finding a plot to tend, or even trying to establish some other kind of business—of all the things he might do, he does nothing. In Wakim Nassar's story, there was never anything about mulberry trees, not a single one was planted around the Big House, never was a mulberry tree so much as mentioned in any of the anecdotes throughout the entire family saga, as if that tree had remained incomprehensible to these Orthodox people settled on Maronite lands. As for a business of any kind, there is not the slightest allusion to one in all the annals of the Nassar family. It is to oranges and orange trees alone that the memory of Wakim Nassar is always connected, it was on orange trees that he founded his ephemeral greatness. But the question remains unanswered as to why he turned toward that tree from the very start, without even trying to do anything else, at a time when the mulberry reigned supreme. Intuition? A sudden whim? In jest, again?

There is in fact one fragment of history, not a very clear one, that came down through the century and that I often heard, to the effect that Wakim brought back the first orange trees from the area around Sidon. And there is also a mysterious name connected to this event, of a certain Ramez Amir. Of all the names that constitute the Nassar family's vast onomastic heritage—from the most ordinary to the most peculiar or rare, from those found in the old telephone notebooks, ephemeral, transient, with no depth or savor, to those, heavy as gold, that were entered in calligraphy with a quill on the pages of ancient documents, from those that I remember being mentioned once by one of my long-gone uncles, who were in possession of more intact details of some of the family mythology than my father was, to those that had made their way down to him, and that he would sometimes pronounce, and then be incapable of pronouncing again, and that would sometimes appear in his stumbling conversation like a reflex, a long-lost residue of an old set phrase that time had unraveled but whose trace was still perceptible in his speech, like a fossil or the memory of particles dissolved in water—among all those names that circulated or slept in the Nassar's vast family heritage, the name Ramez Amir was always a riddle, an odd one out, a precious, incomprehensible item that was preserved in memory out of habit and that came to be connected, also out of habit rather than through preserved knowledge, with the origin of the orange trees.

If you asked any member of the Nassar clan to tell you about the provenance of Wakim's first orange trees, they would invariably reply either that he brought them back from Sidon or, if they were more in the know, or involved in preserving the clan history, that he got them thanks to a man called Ramez Amir, and this Ramez Amir always seemed to me to be like one of those ancient kings who are nothing more than a word in the memory of men, who are remembered only as a name at the top of genealogical tables, without any real certainty that they ever actually existed, or about who they were or what they might have achieved.

In a rather uncanny way, however, that fragment about Sidon being the origin of the orange trees is corroborated by established historical facts, since apparently one of the first people to introduce the extensive cultivation of orange trees into Lebanon was the Druze prince Saïd Jumblatt, and he did so precisely in the area around Sidon, where he eventually had a palace built. But I will need to imagine what it was that made Wakim go to Sidon in the first place, and also to find a place in the story for the character of Ramez Amir, as the precious relic that he is.

Let us just suppose that the reason Wakim sets off for the south, only a few days after his arrival in Ayn Chir, is that there is something there connected with the original dispute, the one that forced him to escape into exile, something that remained unresolved and needed to be settled, something about land, a house bought or sold, a villainous owner and a betrayed intermediary, an affair that one morning, after his failed attempt to return to Beirut, Wakim decides to go sort out at Sidon himself.

So on the twelfth day after his flight from Marsad, he gets up at dawn, before his brother, before Rached, before the women and children but at the same time as the mother. The dawn is the color of apples and a scent of jasmine floats in the air. He drinks his coffee standing up, chatting quietly with the mother, who is sitting on a stool shelling peas. Then he leaves an oral message for his brother and sets off on horseback. The sound of galloping hooves wakes up Selim, who is dreaming about the wife of the dragoman of the Austrian consul, and who turns over in bed without noticing his brother's absence and goes back to sleep without remembering he is at Ayn Chir and not in his own bed, at Marsad.

Wakim takes the road heading south. As the sun rises, he is crossing Kfarshima. Around noon, he leaves the olive groves of Choueifat behind him and is galloping toward Damour, with the wide-open book of the sea on his right side. He has lunch, a plate of raw liver, at Damour. At Rmeileh, he lets his horse drink from a tank on the edge of a field, a tank that is an ancient sarcophagus decorated with garlands and a bacchic scene. Around two o'clock in the afternoon, he arrives in Sidon. He enters the town's dirty, winding alleyways on horseback, then comes back out again and heads for a caravanserai he noticed at the gates of the township, where he asks a porter about Ramez Amir. The porter knows nothing, he has never heard of our man, and just like him, no one else will be able to tell Wakim anything, not the storekeepers, nor the men in turbans and pantaloons sitting in front of the great mosque, nor the fishermen caulking their boats at the small port across from the castle. He learns nothing more that evening either, in the common room of the caravanserai, when he questions the stable boys and the boss too, and also—which is absurd in fact, but you never know—the Palestinian caravan drivers among whom he spends the night.

The next day he goes back into town to make the most of the marketplace, where he questions the fruit and vegetable sellers, the butchers and fishmongers, the children, and even, in a narrow passageway, two Muslim women veiled from head to foot and who look like those mysterious Venetian ladies leaving a palace ball covered in black capes that you see in Carpaccio paintings. Finally, he leaves Sidon and goes back up toward Aabra, crossing paths with a tinsmith, who knows nothing, a mule driver, same thing, and it goes on like this until he is somewhere near Jiyeh, where he rejoins the coastal road.

That evening he is back at Ayn Chir, exhausted and famished, and while Mother Rached prepares a meal for him, he talks to Tanios about Sidon and its mulberry groves, and when he goes into the bedroom, his younger brother, who is already half asleep and barely opens one eye, asks him with detachment:

"Did you find him?"

"No, but I'll go again tomorrow."

And Wakim does go again, and this time he does find him. Completely by chance, as a matter of fact. At around noon, when he has just gone past Rmeileh, he sees a horseman riding on the Joun road, beside the cypress trees at the edge of the terraced fields. Wakim is riding along the coast and the two men's paths finally join. Wakim greets him, and the man amiably returns this greeting. He is a young man with a thin mustache, who is wearing a waistcoat trimmed with ribbons and riding a fine sorrel horse. They ride side by side for a while in silence, then Wakim takes up the reins and rides away ahead of him, but then remembers all of a sudden that he forgot the essential question, pulls the bit back in the horse's mouth, waits for the man from Joun to catch up, starts riding beside him again, and asks him if he knows someone by the name of Ramez Amir, and to his amazement, the man from Joun says yes, of course he knows him, and the two men ride on at walking pace and start up a conversation.

The man from Joun is called Khiriati, he is a stonemason, a master craftsman, just like his father, who built the walls of Lady Stanhope's palace. He is heading for Bramiyeh, where he has some business, and he affirms in no uncertain terms that Ramez Amir will be there too.

"How can he be in Bramiyeh, when I have searched the whole area with a fine-toothed comb and nobody has even heard of him?" Wakim asks.

"He is arriving there today," says Khiriati. "With Nassib Jumblatt. The mountain is no longer big enough for all the Jumblatts. There are not enough mulberry trees for so many chiefs. So Nassib Jumblatt is going to try his luck in Bramiyeh. That's why he needs Ramez Amir."

"Ramez Amir is going to plant mulberry trees for him? Doesn't Nassib Jumblatt know enough about mulberries to look after them himself?"

"Not mulberries. He doesn't want to plant mulberries. Orange trees."

Wakim doesn't say anything. Khiriati adds:

"He is going to plant hundreds and hundreds of orange trees, just like in Turkey or Algeria. He reckons that oranges are the future. That they will replace mulberries."

Wakim purses his lips approvingly. Through his transactions as a simsar, maybe he has already heard of the extensive plantations of orange trees in North Africa and Turkey, which some people are trying to imitate locally. Wakim says nothing and Khiriati thinks his traveling companion is not interested in what he is telling him. He leaves him to his thoughts and starts singing a zajal. Ten minutes later, they arrive at the foot of the Bramiyeh hill, where a group of horsemen have come to a halt on the summit. Wakim and Khiriati can see them from the road, between the huge olive trees and the cypresses.

"That is Nassib Jumblatt's company," Khiriati says.

And those are the first words he says to Wakim since he told him about the orange trees.

Three minutes later, the two men ride through the olive grove and join Jumblatt's company. Druze men in seroual pants are pressed in a dense shrubbery of fierce bushy mustaches around Nassib Jumblatt, who is in the middle of a discussion with Ramez Amir. Khiriati dismounts but Wakim stays in the saddle and calls out to Amir without concerning himself with the presence of the Druze chief. Amir turns around, the shrubbery of mustaches parts for a moment, Nassib Jumblatt turns around as well.

"I have a serious complaint to make about you, Ramez Amir," Wakim says.

Amir says a word to Nassib Jumblatt and approaches Wakim, who is still on horseback.

"Wakim," he says, "I heard about everything that happened in Marsad. But I am not to blame."

Wakim remains on horseback, dominating Ramez Amir, as the whole company looks on. Ramez Amir is tall and, like Nassib Jumblatt, is wearing a wide silk abaya of which he holds one side folded over the other.

"Why did you sell your house to Tamer Attar without telling me, when you had asked me yourself to find you a buyer?" Wakim asks.

"Tamer Attar offered me a huge price, one I could not refuse. And as you know, I was in a hurry to move. I told you that."

"And it never occurred to you to ask Attar how he heard about the house?"

"I did ask him. He must have lied."

"Well then, Ramez Amir, you owe me some compensation."

"I recognize that, Wakim. I will pay your commission."

"I don't want money, Ramez Amir."

"What do you want, then?"

"Orange trees."

3

IN THE FOLLOWING days, Wakim continues his search, but this time it is for a piece of land where he can plant his orange trees. He is on horseback in the mulberry groves again, going from one farm to the next according to Rached's directions, asking about the boundaries of the sections, the tenancies, the owners, and he returns in the evening to discuss it all with his host, around a meal at which his brother is almost always absent. And when Wakim is getting ready for bed, Selim, who is still awake, asks him the same question in the dark, a question that has become so much of a ritual that Wakim eventually sees it as ironic: "Did you find it?" He gives an evasive answer each time and the next day, when Wakim wakes up, Selim is already gone. He gets up himself, has a wash in the basin, shaves in front of the mirror hanging on the window frame, while he mulls over the day ahead, turning his plans over and over a thousand times in his mind, and it is certainly at around this time, in other words very early on, that he starts thinking about settling in Ayn Chir.

One hundred years later, when I occasionally asked my father about the reasons that compelled his own father not to return to Marsad, he would reply vaguely that it must have been some deal that went sour, that it was all over for him, he had compromised himself back there. But that wasn't entirely the opinion of his brothers, who all claimed that it was oranges, quite simply, that had compelled their father to stay at Ayn Chir. The three brothers never agreed on this question, and I quickly realized that in fact all three of them were mistaken about the real reason, although it was quite clear and should have been the most blindingly obvious one to them, since it would repeat itself in their generation and be at the origin of their own wanderings, namely the absence of the father.

No one would ever be able to say exactly how Wakim Nassar and his brother lost their father, although everything leads me to the idea that it must have happened quite early on. A brawl, a bad flu, or an ambush in the Barbary fig trees of Ras-Beirut during a gallop to the seaside, one morning in 1872 or '73—whatever the case, the father is now dead, leaving behind two infant sons and a magnificent signet ring as mementos for the generations to come, as well as an ebony cane and the fact that he was one of the first men of Marsad to adopt European dress.

But he also leaves—and in fact this is the only certainty we can have—a large amount of land, since the registers preserved at the Orthodox bishopric, which I was somehow the first person to think of going to consult, mention that he paid taxes in sums that placed him among the richest men in Marsad. And it was that information that allowed me, very early on, to imagine the rest of the story. Because, for the elder son of the deceased to have become a simple simsar twenty years later, obliged to take flight because of some altercation around a commission on the sale of a house or a piece of land, something not very catholic must have taken place. And that something, I have concluded after deep reflection and lengthy comparisons of the lists of taxes paid by the deceased's brothers in the following years, notably by Halim Nassar, was quite simply a matter of despoliation.

So this is how we might imagine it happened: when the father dies, and after his widow's long mourning period that Halim Nassar scrupulously respects, visiting her every other day, in the afternoons, to see how she is doing, he arrives at his sister-in-law's very early one morning. This is the sign that he has come to talk about serious matters. She listens to him, sitting up in her bed, dressed all in black, her eyes dry but bulging and too fixed in their gaze to be those of a woman ready to think for herself. Halim Nassar makes the most of this, talks about the assets, their management, the children, and says that they now need to start thinking about the future, and she replies firmly, mechanically, almost without thinking, that she trusts his decisions. He falls silent then, once more adopting a tone of voice appropriate for the circumstances, offers to take care of the income from the land and the leases personally, to deposit the money in Wakim's and Selim's names in gold mejidiehs with Spoleto, a renowned Italian banker, and to pay them a monthly allowance for their expenses and the household upkeep until they are capable of looking after the properties themselves. All that the widow can think to ask him is whether Spoleto is trustworthy. Halim gestures that yes, of course he is, and from that day forward he does everything he promised, bringing the necessary money every month himself and providing a report every six months on the gold deposited with the banker. That goes on for four years, time enough for his role as guardian to become an unremarkable routine, for his reports on the state of the accounts to become less and less regular without this appearing questionable, then for him to fudge the numbers on the actual income without arousing suspicion. And finally, one morning, thanks to a compassionate administrative officer whose palm he generously greases, he has the land survey registers corrected so that the assets belonging to his brother go into his own name with a simple crossing-out, a light stroke of the pen, and the application of the seal of the complicit officer.

Fourteen months later, however, the widow hears word of this business, through a rumor that finally reaches her, or through a sister-in-law or a cousin confiding in her, or through an employee of the land survey office snitching on his colleague. She then has the carriage hitched to take her to visit her brother-in-law. She must look even more like that only photograph of her, with an even more somber expression, an anger turned inward that tints her eyes with a glow of contempt. She adopts the role of the outraged woman, betrayed in her good faith and, what's worse, in her widowhood. But she does not wish to get angry, for the actions she has come to demand an account of are all but unspeakable. And precisely, she does not speak of them directly. When she finds herself face-to-face with Halim Nassar, in his European-style drawing room, she demands to know whether *what she has heard* is true. Backed to the wall, Halim Nassar does not flinch, he has been expecting this, he knew that this explanation would have to take place one day. The time has come at last and he is ready, with all his arguments long since prepared. Sitting across from his sister-in-law on an Empire-style sofa, he holds forth in justifications and explanations that *this* is only temporary, that it was essential, that a serious dispute with the neighbors might well have led to a case coming before the courts and maybe even the authorities seizing the deceased's properties, confiscating them as a payment of the miri, and that it was essential to prove their ownership authoritatively, but that everything will be sorted out soon and then the property can be registered in the two children's names again, and anyway it's all the same, we're family, we're the same blood, it's in our common interest. Of course, the widow does not believe a word of all this, and demands to know why she wasn't told about it at the time. "Because I wanted to spare you the worry, I didn't want to frighten you," Halim Nassar replies, while the widow observes him with eyes full of contempt. Then she gets up, announces that she will think it over, and leaves without saying goodbye. She then has the carriage take her to see her other brother-in-law, Farid Nassar, and Farid Nassar listens to her without saying a word, only nodding in understanding. Then he promises to do something, while at the same time advising her not to say anything about the affair, but to let the Nassars solve their problems among themselves. And in conclusion he assures her that Halim is a generous man who only wants what's best for the whole family, and on that point he is the one who doesn't believe a word of what he is saying.

By the time she gets home, the widow has made a decision. Not only is she going to make the affair public, but she will also appeal to her own family. I have not the slightest idea about the family to which this ancestor belongs, but since she appears to have class in that ancient photograph, let's say that it is an old Beirut family, let's say one of the Fernaines. And so now we have a steady stream of Fernaine relatives visiting the house in Marsad, some of them in European suits, tarbouches, and gleaming shoes, others in seroual pants, but proud in their bearing, with their mustaches turned up and their boots polished. They go through the house, cuddle the children, come back to sit with the widow, their sister, and ponder the problem with her, keeping their indignation to themselves so as not to upset her, but with their eyes full of fury, they smooth down their mustaches and pace back and forth theatrically over the arabesques of the ceramic tiles while thinking the matter over. They are part of the Beirut establishment, they can intervene with the bishop, or even the Ottoman governor, but they know that Halim Nassar can do exactly the same thing, and that all that would lead to in the end would be a vendetta that would only harm the children. So finally, all they can do is advise the widow to be patient, and that's where the matter ends, and ends definitively.

Halim Nassar, knowing that the more time passes, the more everything will become irrevocable, continues playing the game and coming every month, without fail, to bring the usual sum to his sister-in-law. The widow glowers at him from head to toe and does not invite him to sit down, which he does anyway. She glares deep into his eyes, but he doesn't flinch and finally puts down the purse with the money on the little cabinet on his left. Of course, in the moment, the widow wants only to throw it in his face, but she reminds herself that this money is actually hers and her children's, that he owes it to her, and so she keeps it, and will continue to accept it, and will ask for more and more in fact, against the advice of her Fernaine brothers, who offer to help her themselves. Halim Nassar agrees to all her demands, knowing that nothing is worth more than the land that he has appropriated, and he pays for new furniture, new armoires, new dresses, a gardener, a cook, then the boys' European suits for Palm Sunday, for Easter, hats, gloves, school fees, doctors, whims and fancies, so that ten or twelve years later, the neighbors, the cousins, the Nassars, the Fernaines, all of them have forgotten the truth, and as far as everybody is concerned Halim Nassar is nothing but a loving uncle, a model guardian, and the money he pays out is a generous allowance, and not the interest on stolen assets. And the widow probably lets her children believe this illusion, hiding the truth from them, then making them believe, as they grow up, for example, that the Nassars are just one big family, that their wealth is indissociable, and that they all live off the income of jointly held assets.

Up until the moment when Wakim starts wanting to know more, bringing up the memory of his father, questioning his mother on the past, on the ebony cane and the monogrammed gold signet ring, and of course inevitably, in the end, wanting to know the reasons for the assets being jointly held. The mother first tries to evade his questions, then responds vaguely, and he feels there is some hidden mystery here, and makes it his business to find out all of its details, every single one, patiently, fending off the sighs, the ambiguous expressions, the diversions, summarizing the information each time in front of her, reconstituting the elements, positing the most outrageous hypotheses to incite her to react, observing her acutely, with his gaze that already swoops over the top of things, in fact doing exactly what I did a hundred years later with my own father, when I finally made him tell me the story of his scandalous brother. And she, just like the grandson she will never know, a hundred years later, opposes a passive resistance, doesn't deny anything but doesn't admit to anything either, brings her son to the edge of the solution and then draws back again, gets a grip on herself, and suddenly declares tenaciously that there is nothing to be concerned about, that everything is perfectly normal, that he mustn't worry, that God and the Virgin Mary provide for everything. However, just like her grandson a century later, she finally lets the truth slip, and the world seems to crumble around Wakim. He never really loved his uncle Halim Nassar, no doubt influenced by the distant relationship between his uncle and his mother, but now his whole universe is thrown out of orbit.

To begin with, out of pride, he shrugs and accepts the blow, but I tend to think that it is from this day forward that he becomes the distant and somberly pensive man who can be seen walking in the lanes of Marsad, always dressed to the nines in a three-piece suit with a stiff collar and tie, with his shoes polished to a high shine and a tarbouche set straight over his ephebic beardless face, or the one who, during family reunions at Easter, Palm Sunday, or Michaelmas, no longer speaks, but remains aloof, seeming to keep his distance from his cousins and his uncles, and whose gaze, once it stops sliding over the crest of things to burrow into the eyes of one of the guests, is like a sharpened blade trying to dissect their soul, to slip between the most imperceptible fibers of their thoughts, so that everyone ends up thinking he is arrogant. But in reality he is not arrogant, he is only observing everything in silence, quietly discovering the world in its new version, the one he was unaware of, a world in which he and his mother and brother survive only thanks to the unbelievable charity of Halim Nassar, a world where he owns nothing at all, where even the house he lives in belongs to his uncle, a world where some people can live a carefree life thanks to a stolen fortune, such as for example his cousin Gebran, that affected and disagreeable boy. In short, he discovers injustice, and especially the mysterious rules that allow the world to go on turning as usual despite these injustices.

Finally, when he is sufficiently familiar with the ways of the world, let's say at eighteen, he makes a decision. He is older now, his mustache has grown and makes him attractive, he sometimes goes out with the ebony walking stick, and he decides that he must work, he wants to become independent, to owe nothing to his uncle, and maybe he even dreams of being able to buy back the house one day and a few properties from his lost inheritance. But he cannot be a government official, for how could he hope to reconstitute his lost birthright with an official's salary? He cannot imitate the innumerable craftsmen of Marsad, start a carpentry or glassmaking business, nor seek a place for himself around the marble quarries near the Saint Elias convent, because for that he would need a sum of money to start out with, and he wishes to owe his uncle absolutely nothing. And so gradually, imperceptibly, without actually intending to at the start, he becomes involved in the profession of simsar, where you can make a few pennies without any starting capital, and remain your own boss, and which is probably one of the few professions in the world that can be practiced without being recognized as a profession.

And I tend to believe that this is precisely what he thinks about every morning, his profession, as he shaves in front of the mirror hanging from the window frame in the bedroom in Tanios Rached's house, one month after his escape to Ayn Chir. He muses, as he lifts up his mustache to pass the razor blade over the top of his cheeks, that after eight or nine years, he has had enough of sniffing around all over the city to find the next deal, of going from one transaction to another as if he were selling door to door, tacking among the fortunes of businessmen, traders, and craftsmen, instead of being the one whom people come to flatter for his own fortune. That is what he is thinking about as he wipes his face with his rough towel, and also—and this is the more serious part—about the fact that even after eight or nine years of samsara he still doesn't have a footing in Marsad, so that all it took was a brawl, albeit a violent one, but still just a brawl, to have him booted out. And this is what tints his pupils with a somber glint every morning as he sprays his body with eau de cologne, and what confirms his plans to stay in Ayn Chir, to buy some land, and to plant orange trees.

And so, for weeks on end, he runs from one farmer to the next. They tell him about an acre on the border of

Kfarshima, with a two-story cabin on it, then about an extended section at Furn el-Chebbak with a barn, then about three fine terraces at Baabda, at the foot of the governorate palace, with a water wheel and a shed. But each time his city slicker appearance and the reputation that precedes him everywhere he goes, namely the fact that he wants to plant orange trees, all that antagonizes the farmers, who end up fearing becoming neighbors with him and his fields of unpredictable citrus planted in the middle of their mulberry groves, and all the negotiations end in stalemates.

Finally, one morning, in the company of Tanios Rached and Maroun Maroun and without the slightest scruple, Wakim takes over the mouchaa lands bordering the Sidon road, lands that, from being commons and belonging to everyone for centuries, ended up belonging to nobody during the establishment of the first land surveys. Situated a few hundred yards away from the edge of the pines in the forest, they constitute at this time what one might call the marches of Ayn Chir. Over the course of one morning, he locates the abstract border markers that define its contours, an old sycamore tree here, a rock shaped like a wolf's jaws there. He rides over his sixty dunams at a gallop twenty times, dismounting here and there to pile up rocks as markers or to plant a stake in the ground, and the next day four plows, four pairs of oxen, and four farm boys borrowed from Tanios Rached come and turn over the soil.

The following week, they continue plowing, pull out the rotting stumps, prune the old olive and Barbary fig trees, clear out the wells, tamp down the ground around a cabin that Wakim has inherited along with everything else, and when they have finished, it is clear for all to see that this stretch of land now has a master.

4

IN THE BEGINNING of beginnings, there is always an explosion from which the world makes itself anew, and here it is the demographic explosion of Beirut, which was initially a large borough encompassed by its ramparts, compact and closed in on itself, and which around 1840 for various reasons (the expansion of the port and therefore of the bourgeoisie, its advantageous geopolitical location, the fertile surrounding countryside) sees its borders overflow and its children scattered throughout its environs like the seeds of an overripe pomegranate. The newly wealthy families are the first to move out of the morbid miasmas and overcrowding to go build their mansions on the high ground on either side of the city. The Greek Orthodox settle on the hills to the east, the Muslims on those to the west, thus replicating and magnifying, like a genetic code, the religious divisions that were already inscribed in the original layout of the city inside the ramparts. Almost at the same time, the overpopulation is absorbed into the development of the city to the south. First comes the colonization of Bachoura, a few cables away from the southern gate of the city, then Basta, and then finally Marsad. There is surely a Nassar among the settlers who leave Beirut for Bachoura in the 1850s, just as there are surely Nassars who settle in Marsad in the 1870s.

But what matters here is that each time the inhabitants settle outside Beirut, they push back the Bedouins who have lived on the outskirts of the city for centuries, camping for part of the year at the foot of its ramparts, in the middle of the ancient olive and Barbary fig groves, tending small plots of land, watching the caravans come and go, and contributing, in the city dwellers' fevered imagination, to the chronic insecurity of the entire area as soon as night falls. First pushed back from the immediate outskirts of Beirut, they make the area around Marsad their seasonal camping ground, before being moved on again in the early 1860s. From then onward, when they come down from the mountains at the beginning of winter, they develop the habit of stopping near the Saint Elias convent, or in the sand dunes to the south, or instead of going farther north to the vicinity of Marsad and Msaytbeh, they head east, to Ayn Chir, where a few tribes then settle on the last remaining mouchaa lands in the area, the ones to which Wakim Nassar lays claim one morning. Putting up their tents on this rough ground, first letting their goats graze among the old olive trees, then gradually letting them spread out to the edges of the first mulberry groves, they quickly become a nightmare for the farmers of Ayn Chir. For several months, bands of children run wild over the land and prowl near the houses, where everything must be kept under lock and key and the farmyards and liwan courtyards under constant watch, although some children do manage to get in nevertheless, while proudly tattooed women distract the inhabitants with offers of palm readings or goats' milk for sale. These women are actually under strong suspicion of abducting small children to sell them to Arab princes in Mount Hermon or the Hauran. They throw menacing glances and vengeful imprecations if they are told to go away too curtly, leaving behind a diffuse sense of impending doom.

It is this sense of chronic instability at their borders that must have compelled the farmers of Ayn Chir to allow Wakim Nassar to arbitrarily take possession of the mouchaa lands. They probably decided that the newcomer would have to overcome the Bedouins' disruptiveness, which could only be a good thing, or give up, which wouldn't be a bad one. I can see them gathered in the evening, those farmers, sitting cross-legged next to their guns, wrapped in their abayas, smoking narghiles of dry tobacco as they mull over thousands of conjectures about the orange trees, the imprecise borders of the mouchaa, the Bedouins, and the Shiites, while their dogs howl into the night and wake each other up, frightening away the hyenas approaching the borders of the lands of Ayn Chir from the seaside dunes. What I especially see, in the center of these gatherings, is the most important landowner of Ayn Chir at the time, old Baclini, whose name has remained very much alive in the mouths of the descendants of Wakim Nassar.

This Baclini will become Wakim's closest neighbor and carefully observes everything that happens along his boundaries. I don't know why I imagine him as a short man, slightly hunched, wearing seroual pants, and with a low, rasping voice. As far as I know, he is one of those old farmers who succeeded, when the land survey registers were established, in scrupulously putting his name to the assets he acquired through mugarasa, but also some mouchaa land on which he had been growing wheat or barley. Nothing particularly noteworthy, in fact, although it was enough to enlarge his holdings substantially. But his reputation as a cunning fief-holder comes especially from the circumstances by which he got his hands on the land of Hanna Malkoun, another curious farmer of Ayn Chir, who also attends these evening gatherings where they play dominoes and knucklebones and exchange opinions about Wakim Nassar.

I can imagine him quite well, that Malkoun, and I know for a fact that he is one of the most superstitious men ever to live not only in Ayn Chir or Beirut, but even in the whole of Mount Lebanon or Syria. He is famous for screaming in rage at his wife or daughters if they happen to sweep the floor in the evening in his presence, and he is often seen taking bizarre detours during his walks. He makes sure never to go straight home after a funeral, for fear of bringing back the spirit of death into his house, and doesn't even want to hear about making repairs to the family vault in the cemetery of Saint Michael's, because in his eyes that would be tantamount to preparing it for a new arrival. And it was precisely that kind of superstition that made him lose his land bordering on the property belonging to his neighbor Baclini. That mouchaa land was some that Malkoun was bold enough to appropriate even quicker than Baclini, when the surveys were made. Baclini held that against him, and two years later, when Malkoun was starting to plant mulberry trees, a heavily tattooed Bedouin woman of an impressive age, a fortune teller with a fearsome voice and eyes, and with all her teeth covered in gold, appears at Baclini's door. He immediately has a diabolical idea. The old woman is accompanied by two or three young girls with nubile bodies and wide pantaloons, who serve as her guides, like vestal virgins waiting on a great priestess. Instead of chasing them away with a rude word, Baclini invites them in, sits the old prophetess down on a mat in the middle of the main room, and has rose syrup brought to her. Then he patiently endures the ritual of having his palm read. He closes his hand on an herb, repeats incomprehensible phrases, gets out a matlic when ordered to, sees it magically disappear, gives another one, then a third, listens to his future without demurring, gives a half-mejidieh, waits for the old witch to pretend to emerge from a perfectly acted altered state, and receives her advice for his welfare and his family's. At last, when all of this is finally over, he asks the vestals seated behind their mistress to leave him alone with her for a moment.

You can easily imagine the rest: the next day, the Bedouin woman and her attendants appear at the Malkoun house, only to be chased away with contempt. They come back the following day, and the next, and Malkoun has them rudely sent away each time, up until the morning when the old lady with the gold teeth finally grabs him by the arm in the iron grip of her tattooed hand, stops him turning away from her, fixes him with her feverish eyes, and announces that she knows that he is starting a project and that he will die on the very day he finishes it. Having said that, she turns on her heel and leaves, never to be seen again. In the moment, Malkoun just shrugs, rubs his arm, and doesn't think about it again. But when night falls, a doubt starts to niggle him, and then doesn't stop tormenting him. He says nothing to anyone, but three days later he suddenly stops all work on the plot of land and delays planting the mulberry trees. After a month, he finds himself caught in the crossfire of questions from his sons, his wife, and his brothers. He doesn't give any answers, remains evasive, finds implausible excuses. His wife becomes more and more insistent, heaps recriminations and suspicions on his head, until he finally admits the truth to her. Instead of cursing the Bedouins and her husband's superstition, she gently, patiently tries to make him listen to reason. Two months later, when time is starting to run short and the memory of the Bedouin woman has faded a little, Malkoun starts looking wistfully at his uncultivated land and abandoned mulberry saplings, and finally admits that he was being ridiculous. But the evening of the day when work restarts, either because of his extreme irritability or simply by chance, he swallows the wrong way during dinner, chokes and coughs, cannot contain himself, feels like he is suffocating, and he needs assistance to go spit it all back up and lie down, and nothing can rid him of the idea that this is a warning. The next day, work is halted again. From his rooftop, Baclini checks every morning whether the work has stopped for good this time. He lets time pass so as not to arouse suspicion. Every once in a while he asks why the work is being interrupted, shows interest, then disappointment, then doubt, then finally, five months later, he comes to offer to buy the land, which Malkoun lets him have with relief, and with no comment at all from his wife, who doesn't dare interfere anymore.

No one would ever know anything about the whole affair until Baclini, on his deathbed, confesses everything to the priest come for the last rites, in the presence of his children, his wife, and a few neighbors who then spread the story far and wide. But at the time Wakim settles in Ayn Chir, the event is still fairly recent, and none of the farmers at the evening gatherings suspect anything is amiss. Malkoun believes he is Baclini's very good friend, and Baclini is happy to let him believe this, he gets on well enough with his mate Malkoun, but believes himself to be smarter, that's all, and in the conversations that circle endlessly around the orange trees, the Bedouins, and Wakim, he speaks very little and mostly listens, like an old fox on the prowl. Then the next day and for more than a month afterward, he goes up onto his rooftop and observes everything happening on the land that Wakim recently appropriated bordering on his own. And every once in a while, he ends up going over to see the new owner and spend some time with him. He looks on as the old cabin is being renovated or the well being cleaned. He gives advice, speaks from his own experience, makes quiet comments. But he often asks Wakim questions as well, in his low, rasping voice, his hands crossed behind his back, his shoulders hunched slightly forward. With an unconcerned air, he tries to find out about everything, the measurements of the cabin, the depth of the wells, the future layout of the orange grove, but Wakim, who has learned to observe men in silence and to find out their secret games, realizes that each of the answers he gives is filling in a blank square in a calculation that Baclini has long since discreetly prepared, and that once he has obtained all the information, filled in all the blanks, Baclini will be able to make his first move in his little game. Very quickly, Wakim realizes that his neighbor is preparing for the eventuality of the failure of the extensive cultivation of orange trees, and is stealthily trying to calculate the worth of buying up the land. From that moment on, Wakim starts giving ambiguous answers to all Baclini's questions, muddling up his ideas, giving unreliable measurements and prices, but Baclini, who didn't come down in the last rain shower, sees through his game, immediately stops asking questions, and then stops coming altogether. But he never stops scanning the horizon from his rooftop in the weeks and months following. And he probably sees the arrival of the hundreds of cuttings that Wakim buys and those sent by Ramez Amir. He can just make out Wakim Nassar in the distance, directing some twenty Maronite farm laborers, tirelessly going from one end of his land to the other, from dawn until mid-afternoon, on horseback when the land is dry, on foot with water up to his knees when it is being irrigated, always dressed in the same old, worn-out Ottoman army uniform and riding boots. From the end of that spring onward, Baclini never stops sizing up the dunams bristling with frail orange saplings as far as the eye can see, like thousands of egrets dancing in the slightest breeze, which he believes are highly unlikely to ever turn into a real plantation. And finally, one morning, what he sees, in the distance to the west, are the signs of the first Bedouin camps.

They appeared in the first days of fall. And if I say that they appeared, that is because I always had the sense that apparition was one of the modalities of their existence. On the lands where they settle, the plains, the outskirts of cities, around cultivated fields, they have the miraculous or skillful gift of never being announced or expected. The previous days, the land is bare, the view is boundless, there is nothing and nobody there; the next day, at dawn, there they are, suddenly materialized, apparently transported as is, set down by some djinn from an oil lamp, in the form of a couple of pitched tents with their goatskin door flaps stretched up high like canopies and, already lying all around them, the alluvial deposits of what appears to be a long period of sedentary life, basins and plates unpacked, laundry hung up to dry, goats in their pens.

In any case this is the kind of spectacle that Wakim Nassar discovers one morning in early fall, a few steps away from his land, where the orange trees are starting to take root: the vast disorder of the campsites, children playing with a goat kid, women moving from one tent to another, graciously coming and going, holding basins against their hips or pots on their heads, calling out to each other, singing and shouting without ever paying the slightest attention to anything outside the circle of their canvas dwellings, without taking the rest of humanity into account at all, as if their universe, which by nature was open, limitless, and boundless, was in fact perfectly enclosed, impermeable, and autarchic. And Wakim, on his horse, thinks that if this is what the Bedouins are like, then it's really nothing to worry about, while his laborers standing around him make nasty remarks about the Bedouins' patched tents, dented pots, and faded baskets, without noticing that their own ragged clothes are in an even more pitiful state.

But trouble starts the very next day. The abstract area in which the Bedouins are moving around seems mysteriously to expand, and young women start moving through the plantations without paying any attention to the orange saplings, spreading out their mattresses and their blankets in the furrows and coming to draw water from the well. When Wakim's daily laborers tell them that they are on private property, the women answer with incomprehensible words and laugh, showing their fine teeth and pulling their veils over their mouths. Then only their jet-black eyes can speak. They go away, with their basins and their jugs on their heads, soon to be relayed by others, and it's the same circus all over again. Wakim finally decides to let them draw water from the well, as long as they follow the same path between the young trees. But that is all in vain and for several days, no matter how hard the workers try to channel their comings and goings, it's like trying to direct bees toward artificially pollinated flowers: the Bedouin women with their deep eyes and complicated tattoos continue to follow their own trajectories. Then it's the men who appear, asking for work. Since there is none, they start wandering all over the fields, constantly passing through the new groves to get to the road.

Soon other tents appear on the borders of Wakim's land, and one morning a herd of goats invades the new plantation, uprooting the saplings, munching on the young leaves, and sowing panic among the laborers. For over an hour the men try to push the animals back with all sorts of cries and whistles and tongue-rolling, while Wakim and a foreman, on horseback, shout and gesticulate to try to stop the billy goats and dogs from going any farther.

After this last incident, Wakim decides that it is time to act. That same afternoon, he crosses the boundary of his new land and enters into the Bedouins' camp. As he passes among the women with their eyes shining over their veils and the children backing away from his horse, he has perhaps already decided to deal with these people once and for all with a show of strength. So there he is, dismounting in front of the tent that was shown to him. A man with a weather-beaten face and gleaming eyes, in a long robe, comes toward him and wishes him all sorts of good things, but with mistrust in his eyes. Wakim goes inside the tent, sits down on the ground, which must be covered with a large kilim, and immediately starts to talk. He explains that the neighboring land is his, that he has planted orange trees, that you can't come and go in them just like that, and especially not with goats. The Bedouin chief listens to him, nodding occasionally, then explains that ever since he was a child, his family has come to camp on this land in winter. That he planted radishes and cabbages there himself, and that, in some ways, the land is just as much his as anyone else's. Wakim replies that the land is mouchaa, that it belongs by right to the farmers of Ayn Chir, and that, if the tribes want to plant anything or graze their animals, there is space to the west, and he gestures vaguely in the direction of the Saint Elias convent. With his riding boots, his European suit, and his tarbouche that he has no doubt kept on his head, he must be sitting cross-legged, his back straight, his palms firmly set on his knees. When he stops speaking, coffee is served. He takes a cup, out of politeness. The Bedouin chief sips noisily from his and the dialogue is briefly halted. And in fact, it's not even a dialogue. Each of the men speaks without being interrupted, then listens to the other without interrupting him. Two monologues, taken up again when the empty cups are set down on the rug. The Bedouin chief is the first to speak:

"I don't want to cause you any trouble. I have authority over two or three tents. Those belonging to my brothers-in-law. I will tell them what you have told me. But I cannot get involved with what the others do."

"I have no intention of going from tent to tent to repeat the same thing," Wakim replies. "You certainly have the means to let all your neighbors know that, from now on, there are boundaries around here. I would be grateful if you would do that. It will avoid any conflict between us."

"There will be no conflict, if God wills it. We have always been the friends of the inhabitants of this region."

"Well then, warn your neighbors. I let men cross the land when they want to go to the road, even though they could reach it by going around my orchards. And I let your women draw water from the well. That was to show my goodwill toward you. But it needs to stop now."

"Everything is in God's hands."

Sixty years later, when my mother, recently married to my father, arrived at the Big House, there was still one

Bedouin woman, no doubt the last one to come to Ayn Chir, who brought milk in an iron jug every Monday in fall. She was expected, she was part of the rhythm of life in the house at the time of its last renaissance under my father's rule, and she was apparently fond of me; she used to fuss over me with her rough voice. I can't remember how, as a very young child, I reacted to her face, her gold teeth and the double line tattooed on her chin, I who had almost caused a scandal during my baptism by screaming bloody murder at the prophet's beard on the face of the priest who had come to wash me of original sin. And if a fortune teller from Mount Hermon leaned over my cradle like the fairies over the princesses in the folktales, you can be sure she would have been kept under strict watch, since even in those days Bedouin women still had the reputation of being baby snatchers. My mother and my aunts, my father's sisters, must have exchanged worried looks when the milk seller approached to fuss over me and say mysterious words in her abrupt, rasping tongue. Maybe my aunts were even frightened that she was pouring out vengeful curses on me, to make me the instrument of her father's revenge on their own father. For this Bedouin woman, according to what one of my aunts said to my mother, was the daughter of Abou Kharroub, one of the chiefs of the nomadic tribe that had once defied Wakim Nassar by pitching his tent under the windows of the Big House, under the big oak tree a few steps away from the well. My mother once told me about this again quite by chance, a long time afterward, when we spoke together about her own arrival in the Big House, after the most complicated saga you could wish for, full of exile, wars, noise, and fury. However, at the time when the Bedouins would have defied Wakim Nassar, the Big House was not yet built, nor even what was later usually called the Little House. What my aunt must have been talking about, without realizing it, was in fact the cabin that Wakim had restored when he took possession of the mouchaa lands. In that case, the story of Abou Kharroub would have taken place in the first seasons of the creation of the orange groves, when the Bedouins had just appeared in front of the plantations. And it is possible that the old tent that was suddenly pitched next to the well, in the middle of the new orange grove, was the catalyst for the war between Wakim and the Bedouins.

Anyway, the day after Wakim's visit to the chief of the tribe, everything continues just as before, the women's carefree wandering to the well, the orchards being used as a boulevard by the men heading for the farms of Ayn Chir, and a herd of goats entering once again, trampling the young trees and causing panic among the laborers, amid the volleys of insults exchanged between Wakim's men and the nomadic shepherds. All this must have given Wakim the idea of building a protective stone wall. It costs money but it has to be done, and then there are the workers for whom he needs to find something to do. He probably thinks about it that morning when that legendary tent suddenly appears in the middle of the orchard, next to the well. Wakim understands that the Bedouins are trying to test him, to gauge his determination and capacity for resistance. And so he presents himself in front of the tent, on horseback, and without dismounting asks for the man who must be Abou Kharroub, whom he hasn't yet met. Abou Kharroub makes him wait, then steps out of his tent, and the two men take stock of each other in a few terse words.

"This land is planted, as you can see," says Wakim. "Go settle somewhere else."

"These lands are mouchaa," Abou Kharroub replies, "and they belong to everyone. I have been drawing water from this well for fifteen years. I will continue to do so."

"These lands do not belong to everyone, they belong to the farmers of Ayn Chir, who let me plant trees on them. You have no right to be here anymore. Go camp somewhere else or I will have to chase you away by force."

"Do not threaten me. You know very well that I will be able to defend myself. And if you dare to touch my family or my flocks, it will cost you dearly."

"I repeat that your family and your flocks have no right to be here anymore. There is plenty of land to the west. All you have to do is move over a few yards."

"I will not move from here. If I had stayed here during the winter, you would not have been able to plant your orange trees."

"But they are planted now, and you know very well that the presence of men and goats is not doing them any good."

"I couldn't care less."

"That's what you say. But what I am saying is that you have until tomorrow to strike your camp. After that I can't answer for anything."

The next day, of course, the tent is still there, with a goat pen a few yards away. Wakim comes at dawn to confirm this, and for the rest of the day he rides over his property and those around him. But this time he is looking at them with new eyes, not those of a landowner assessing the lay of the ground, the direction of the ancient furrows and of the wind blowing over them, but as a strategist exploring the terrain of an imminent battle. He rides along his fields, gallops up to the edge of the Bedouin camp on their border to estimate the distance between it and his boundary lines, returns, rides around the cabin several times, goes back and forth between the well and Abou Kharroub's tent, under the indifferent gaze of the women working, squatting on their heels, and conversing in strident voices. He gallops like this for hours, riding away, then back again, reappearing, stopping, turning around to look behind him, his face shuttered in an air of profound concentration.

In the meantime, the Bedouins have taken possession of the new orange groves. The women come and go freely to the well, which they gather around as if it were the Bachoura fountain, while herds of goats shamelessly take over several areas of the orchard and lay waste to the young orange trees under the eyes of Wakim's laborers, who are finally overwhelmed and give up trying to control them. At midday, the whole plantation appears to be overrun. Abou Kharroub remains invisible. Baclini is on the rooftop of his house observing the situation and cursing Wakim's continuous and incomprehensible riding, and the farmers of Ayn Chir are starting to get worried. That the Bedouins should contest a landowner's right to his property can only constitute a dangerous precedent in their eyes, and their anger against Wakim rumbles all morning. But in the early afternoon, Wakim comes to see them. First he goes to Malkoun, then to Maroun Maroun, then to a couple of other farms where he knows there is a tradition of valor or young men ready to prove their mettle. Each time, he sits down and talks, explains the situation and what he plans to do, and asks for help. After his departure, there are long discussions in each farm because it's no small thing to go fight for someone else, for mouchaa lands, for orange trees with an uncertain future, and especially for the sake of a Greek Orthodox man to whom they graciously ceded a plot of land, but who will just have to fend for himself for everything else. From some of the evasive replies he receives, Wakim understands that he won't be able to count on many men, and when he comes back to the Rached house and sums up the situation with Tanios, it all seems hopeless. But he doesn't have a choice. He is backed to the wall.

At nightfall he rides out again, but in the direction of Beirut this time. He rides along the edge of his fields, which are momentarily under Abou Kharroub's control, enters the Pine Forest, and fifteen minutes later, without having met a soul, he arrives in Marsad. It's the first time he's been here for many months, and it obviously must feel strange to him, but he has no time for nostalgia. Without worrying about any unwanted encounters, he goes from one lane to the next, stopping in the houses of Elias and Tanios Nassar, then at Costa Zreiq's, then Gerios Nassar's, and finally at Youssef Halabi's. He doesn't spend more than fifteen minutes at each one. Then he heads for his mother's home. He approaches it like a marauder, makes sure everything is normal, then hides his horse and enters through a back door. He avoids waking his mother, doesn't bother looking around the house, and heads straight to his brother's room.

This brother, whom I have described, in accordance with family tradition, as Wakim's companion during the flight to Ayn Chir, is almost impossible to imagine as a mute and insignificant spectator of all the events that took place after the appropriation of the mouchaa lands. It goes without saying that I never met him, and everything I know about him relates to a much later period, when he was known for being a dandy, with a reserved and distractedly amiable personality.

At the time when this story begins, he may not yet have reached that point, but one can imagine that he was already a somber character, rigid and somewhat too attached to formalities, to the strict principles and code of honor, a whole lot of stuff attributable to the absence of his father and his status as a young man from a notable family struck down by ill fortune. This concern with formalities, along with his awkward rowdiness in late adolescence, gives him an extreme character, coldly capable of the worst excesses. In the first period of exile, he goes to Khan Antoun Bey every morning via the Damascus road and comes back the same way. In the evenings, he joins the company of Tanios Rached and his family, even when his brother is absent, and because he is handsome, with a wide forehead and candid eyes, he is constantly bathed in the gaze of the Rached sisters. But when he finds out that his brother is planning to stay in Ayn Chir for good, the cocktail of youthful pride, snobbery, and zealotry of clan and community that constitutes his personality reveals its explosive character. Not only does he refuse the idea of settling in the countryside and among Maronites, but he also refuses the idea that his older brother should have this intention, and he stops speaking to him, for fear of being asked his opinion on the matter. And when he is finally forced to give it, he brusquely replies that it doesn't concern him, that he is at Ayn Chir only for a few weeks, and that he will soon be returning to Beirut. And that is what he does. One morning he packs his clothes and personal effects and, with what is tantamount to discourtesy toward Tanios Rached, says his laconic goodbyes and announces that he will not be returning in the evening. And he never returns at all. Wakim, who does not appreciate his brother's cavalier attitude, pretends not to worry about him, and Rached, out of the greatness of his heart, never mentions it again. But when all of Wakim's plans are threatened by the Bedouins and he comes to seek help from the abadays of Marsad, Wakim feels the need of his brother's presence, and goes into his room, where Selim is lying in bed.

"You've come back?" asks Selim ironically, without getting up.

"Not only have I not come back," says Wakim, "but you are going to get up and come with me."

"I already told you I would not set foot in Ayn Chir again. I followed you once, that was enough."

"Stop spouting nonsense and listen to me," Wakim replies.

And in the middle of the night, he talks, he explains. In the room next door, their mother, who is sitting up in bed, listens to the tense whispers and the stifled shouts between her two boys.

"Your oranges are madness."

"Maybe, but you still have to help me with the Bedouins."

"If the Maronites didn't want to do anything, that means there's nothing to be done."

"Youssef Halabi and Costa Zreiq agreed to join me tonight, you think it's normal for you not to come, you, my own brother?" etcetera.

After which there is a long silence, and then the whispers start up again, more calmly this time, because Selim, who is probably not convinced, but cannot fail in his duty of brotherly solidarity, finally gets up and gets dressed with a somber air, and there he is again an hour later, riding with his brother through the Pine Forest toward Ayn Chir, along with five Greek Orthodox men from Marsad, brawlers ready for action with all the Bedouins in the world, even with the Maronites if they have to, or indeed with the whole of creation if need be, in order to bring triumph to the cause of one of their own.

Obviously, this march of seven men toward Ayn Chir resembles the ride of the Magnificent Seven, although these men are not mercenaries, as they were, far from it. Beside the two brothers are Gerios, Tanios, and Elias Nassar, three battlers from the plebeian branch of the family, all three of them indispensable in giving a hand, by fair means or foul, with anything required to uphold what they believe is the greatness of the Nassar clan. There is also Costa Zreiq, the neighborhood chief, a swashbuckling but respected man and the oldest of the seven, who agreed to come along in order to make sure that things don't go too far. And finally, there is the famous Youssef Halabi, one of the most fearsome abadays of Marsad in those days, whom I have included in the seven because he would later be linked by a peculiar friendship to Wakim, according to my uncles' and father's accounts. One day quite by chance I found a photograph of this Youssef Halabi—who was himself forced to flee Marsad at the beginning of the French Mandate—posing as an abaday in seroual pants, a rifle in his hand and a bandolier full of ammunition across his chest, like the Mexicans of Emiliano Zapata, who had the same kind of mustache. That is why, during the ride of the seven men, I imagine him with a sash of cartridges slung across his chest and the barrel of the gun pointing back over his shoulder. The other riders, who are galloping along, talking in lowered voices, have also brought their rifles with their interminable barrels, their pistols with mother-of-pearl handles, and their curved daggers sleeping in their marquetry scabbards.

In the middle of the night, they dismount in front of Tanios Rached's house, where seven other armed men are waiting for them: Rached and his son, Maroun Maroun and his two boys, and two of Wakim's laborers, originally from Kfarshima, who have been able to procure horses. At dawn, the fourteen horsemen ride abreast into Wakim's orchards and advance cautiously among the saplings toward Abou Kharroub's tent. When it is in sight, the signal is given and a huge clamor of shouts and constant shooting rises into the sky, waking up the farmers of Ayn Chir. Within ten minutes, Abou Kharroub's tent is in flames, his wives and children in flight, and he himself, unarmed and without his headdress, is pushed back outside of the orchard by the whirlwind of riders, who seem to number in the hundreds. Then Wakim's troop pours into the camp at the edge of the orchard, screaming and shooting into the air. Alerted by the ruckus of the first attack, the women and children are already out of the tents and the men have seized their weapons. Most of them don't have time to use them and are jostled, thrown over, their guns taken in flight by the horsemen arriving like arrows. But around the most distant tent, which Wakim and his companions reach last, the men have taken up their positions and open fire. One of Maroun Maroun's sons gets shot in the shoulder and stops, while Youssef Halabi, Gerios, and Wakim charge toward a group of four Bedouins standing up and shooting at close range. With one swoop of the butt of his gun, which he is using like a lasso, Halabi sends the first one to the ground, his face covered in blood. Wakim knocks over a second one while the third shoots at Gerios Nassar, who cries out, lets go of his horse's reins, and comes to a halt. The other riders quickly catch up and overtake him, routing the remaining shooters, pulling up stakes, beating down the tents, and scattering the Bedouins' belongings. The cavalcade, which lasts thirty minutes or so, finishes when the riders arrive at the edge of the Shiite village. That is where they stop, their horses champing at the bit, and everyone takes a moment to look around. The sun is not yet risen but the sky is rosy in the east. Abou Kharroub's tent is burning to the ground; there is not a single Bedouin to be seen anywhere around them and all the way to Wakim's orchards. But Maroun Maroun's son, who was splattered with lead, has blood on his arm and his shirt is in tatters, and, what's worse, Gerios is holding his wrist, showing the others his hand, where some of the fingers have turned to mush.

"He needs a doctor," says Wakim.

"We should take him to Alexaki," says Costa Zreiq, and Youssef Halabi approves.

"Alexaki looks after eyes and noses," says Wakim, while thinking about Calmette, the French doctor who has a house near Ayn Mreisseh.

As far as houses go, the one belonging to Doctor Calmette is one of those mansions of the Sunnite bourgeoisie that stands high facing the sea to the west of Beirut. The sun has been up for less than an hour when the panicked servants see Wakim arrive, with Youssef Halabi, Tanios Rached, and Costa Zreiq surrounding Gerios, whose hand is bound in a handkerchief with blood everywhere. With their boots and cartridge holders, their guns hanging from the belts of their seroual pants, and their wounded companion, the four men wait among the marble columns, the marquetry furniture, and the great princely divans in the drawing room. Doors slam, servants whisper, there are comings and goings and no doubt already murmurs spreading throughout the house, scenarios of massacres or religious conflicts, such as often erupt in the country, and which the sight of weapons and blood inevitably evokes. And then Calmette arrives, in a silk dressing gown with his mustaches pushed up, curious to see what is waiting for him, and he is probably not disappointed. He leads Gerios away, accepting that Wakim comes with him because he wants to understand what happened. Thirty minutes later, the three men waiting patiently in the drawing room, leaning against the columns or sitting on the cedarwood chairs, hear a scream and look at each other while biting the edges of their mustaches. An hour later, Gerios reappears, missing three fingers—his middle, ring, and little fingers—which will earn him a definitive entry into the history of the Nassars of Ayn Chir.

As a sign of gratitude or by way of compensation, Wakim takes him into his service and he will remain there until the end. Many stories but no photographs remain of this man, henceforth nicknamed Old Seven Fingers (which could be taken as teasing, were it not for the homonymy in the local Arabic dialect between the words for *seven* and *lion*, such that anyone daring to call Gerios by his nickname could do so with the clear conscience of also calling him Gerios the Lion). This means that I can never imagine him otherwise than with the appearance and features of his son, whom I did know and who much later married one of my aunts, one of Wakim's daughters. Let's imagine him as solidly built, with a large nose with flat nostrils, small eyes, and a slightly fixed and stubborn expression that makes him look like a wheezy old otter, but that all of this, which is heavy and devoid of grace, suddenly becomes animated when he starts to speak, in a kind of incomprehensible muttering that gradually turns into a loud grumbling and finally explodes into a cry of rage and indignation, a cry he will always use, even when speaking about the most mundane subjects, as if the state of things, the way of the world, were a permanent scandal for him, one that recomposes his face, when he speaks, into that of an inspired and vengeful prophet.

This behavior made Gerios famous at Ayn Chir, and as far as Baabda and Kfarshima. But he also owed his celebrity to his skill, despite his three missing fingers, with the rifle and the revolver and to the legendary way he had of walking through the orange groves with two sickles held in a cross behind his back by his belt. In fact he would very quickly be considered the manager of Wakim's properties. From the morning after the fight when he becomes an amputee, he joins Wakim, who has started to repair the damage to his trees caused by the Bedouins. He mutters as he takes off his jacket, or what serves as one, and his tarbouche, and puts them on a stone, and despite his bandage, he sets to work. And what is certain is that he is skillful, as if he had been planting orange trees all his life, such that after three or four days he is the one who takes on the management of operations, as if he was giving Wakim to understand that no one is better in helping a Nassar than another Nassar, that all the Tanios Racheds and sundry Maroun Marouns of this world can never be relied on in the end, that a Maronite will never help an Orthodox to prosper, but all this without a word, only by correcting an alignment here, having a few trees replanted there, like an old servant woman who comes back just for a visit to her old masters, after fifteen years, and suddenly decides to take charge again of the management of the house, which she knows better than anyone else and considers very poorly run by her successors. Wakim leaves Gerios to it, listens attentively to the advice and recommendations of the former abaday, follows everything to the letter, has everything carried out exactly as he says, and for his part Gerios perhaps recognizes, in that cold, definitive, wordless decision to put everything into the hands of a stranger, the firmness of a chief, for what is a chief if not someone who knows when and to whom to delegate important powers?

As for the immediate consequences of the battle, let's imagine that the very next day, while Wakim is riding over his land, he receives several visits. First of all, three horsemen arrive from the west, Shiites who come to assure Wakim of their neutrality in the previous day's altercations, of their goodwill and their desire to live in peace as neighbors. As a token of good faith, one of the horsemen drops a sack of walnuts at Wakim's feet, another a sack of figs, and the third a sack of still-green olives. Then four gendarmes from the Mount Lebanon administration arrive, the news of the fight having reached it with a day and a half's delay. The sergeant commanding the squad asks for explanations of the event, appears not to care about Wakim's responses, but seems more interested in the little orange trees stretching out as far as the eye can see all around him, which quickly become the topic of conversation. And finally, a Bedouin arrives on foot, cautiously introduces himself to the laborers, enters the orchard under their supervision, and asks for permission to speak to Wakim. When this request is granted, he declares that he comes on behalf of Abou Kharroub and pleads to have the goats he left in the pen restored to him. Wakim asks him whether Abou Kharroub is in a better disposition now, and the Bedouin swears that the two parties are at peace, and that Abou Kharroub is ready to call himself Wakim Nassar's servant for life. Without too many illusions, Wakim lets him take away the goats.

But the most important consequence of the battle is probably the decision that Wakim Nassar makes to move out of Tanios Rached's house and to live on his own land from then onward. This presents a problem, for at that moment there is only the little cabin to sleep, eat, and live in. But Wakim Nassar makes this decision as a security precaution, to keep an eye on his property and prevent any more nocturnal incursions by the Bedouins.

Everything starts with a bivouac. Wakim and Gerios, occasionally supported by Rached and his son, sleep in something like a campsite, relaying each other at night, carrying out guard rounds. And Selim is there too, although the day after the fighting, he considers that he has done his duty and returns to Marsad. But then one morning, maybe from remorse or the intuition that he is excluding himself from his own history, he leaves on horseback, crosses the Pine Forest into Ayn Chir, and appears on Wakim's land, where he dismounts and declares with slightly overwrought solemnity that he has come to participate in guarding the estate, and that if there is any work that he can do during the day, he is ready for it. He is given the responsibility of anything to do with stone. It is therefore he who, silently but efficiently, monitors the state of the boundary walls, who takes care of the wells, who will have an olive press built a little later on. It is especially he who takes on the task of enlarging the cabin, who has another room built, then two, then has a kitchen installed.

After three months, the camp has become a real settlement and the cabin a small house. In the middle of winter, the threat from the Bedouins is definitively removed, so that in springtime Wakim has a stonemason from Kfarshima add another story to the initial building, which makes it the first two-story construction in Ayn Chir, next to which would be built what would one day be called the Big House. And so, the origins of the property and the Big House where I was born would eventually resemble those of cities in Germany or northern Europe, which were first Roman military camps set up to oversee the borders of the empire under threat from barbarian incursions, before becoming facilities for military families, then little towns of settlers, and finally flourishing cities.

5

IT IS AROUND 1820 that eucalyptus trees first appear on the shores of the Mediterranean and in western Europe. One is noted in the outskirts of Nice that year and another one, of a different species, in the south of Italy around 1829. A few years later, some botanists discover an even older one in a garden in Caserta, Italy, one that had been confused, in the registers, with another tree. By the middle of the century, several species are being grown in southern Europe, but it is only from 1860 onward that the cultivation of eucalyptus is developed rationally and systematically, thanks to a Frenchman by the name of Ramel, who is on a business trip in Australia and sends the seeds for the new trees back to Europe. On his return to France, Ramel encourages the importation of seeds and conducts a lively correspondence with a German engineer settled in the antipodes, with whom he builds up a considerable business and scientific project around the exploitation of eucalyptus. In 1855, he is in Algeria, where he has had whole sacks of seeds sent, and where the cultivation of the trees has taken off, then he goes to Egypt, where his epistolary encouragement and dispatches of seeds to the French botanists in Cairo have led to the significant development of eucalyptus plantations.

During his stay in Algiers, Ramel has a chance encounter with a compatriot by the name of Émile Curiel, a Provençal man of independent means setting off from Algeria on a long journey of curiosity and aesthetic pleasure in the Orient. Obviously, the talk between him and Ramel soon turns to eucalyptus trees. Curiel listens to Ramel's adventures in Australia, questions him about the deserts and the indigenous people that are to be found there, and observes him over the following days as Ramel draws up a list of the eucalyptus trees in the botanical gardens of Algiers, where the two men have long conversations. Then they both go their separate ways until they find each other again, quite by chance, in Cairo in 1890 or 1891. In the meantime, Curiel has been through Tunisia, and even Libya, where he took note of the presence of eucalyptus trees. He thought about Ramel, and even took a close interest in the trees, examined their bark and checked the leaves, as he saw his onetime friend do. He also asked the inhabitants about the origins of the trees and discovered the fabulous possibility of the migration of pollen, and when he sees Ramel again, he is happy to be able to bring new information to his friend, and to be able to talk about eucalyptus as a connoisseur with the

French botanists in Cairo. One year later, he disembarks in Beirut, where his friend Doctor Calmette receives him in his mansion in Ayn Mreisseh.

The accounts of this Émile Curiel, who played a small part in the history of Lebanon, are relatively numerous. They tell us all kinds of things: that he was the sole heir of an impressive Provençal fortune, that his curious mind covered everything, that he was handsome, that he swore only by Ernest Renan, and that he almost made pointed beards, like Frédéric Mistral's, fashionable in Beirut. He rapidly becomes the darling of high society in the city, is often invited to dinner by the Bustros and Sursock families, where he drinks liqueurs and talks about poetry and travel with the ladies. And when he is with the men, he smokes cigars and talks about business, makes plans and proposes ideas for the region's industrial development. Following in Renan's footsteps, he undertakes a journey to Tyre for three days, then to Baalbek for a week, then tries to go as far as Damascus but doesn't make it there; he spends two days with Bedouins in the north of the Beqaa plain, and on another occasion, when he is hunting in the mountains with his city friends, he goes in search of Emperor Hadrian's forest boundary markers. In the end, he has such a fine time in the Levant that he decides to live there for part of the year from then onward.

At this juncture he receives a letter from Ramel, who proposes that he plant eucalyptus trees in Syria. Curiel then abandons his plans to buy a mansion like his friend Calmette's on the hillsides of Beirut and turns to the flat lands of Ayn Chir and Furn el-Chebbak, which he explores with a large retinue of translators and servants, as if he were conducting a royal progress. He pays very generously, so people rush to assist him, and after a few days he has acquired a considerable estate on which he immediately starts uprooting the mulberry trees and planting eucalyptus seeds and cuttings. Very soon he also starts construction on a peculiar residence, called Villa Eucalypta, which he has built according to his own plans. It appears on one of the famous postcards of the period that perfectly shows the eclectic style he gives it, a sort of Italo-Moorish look, with zigzagging arcades that set all his visitors' tongues wagging. For the interiors, Curiel has precious marquetry objects brought from Damascus, most notably the painted woodwork from a palace in Istanbul that he has taken apart piece by piece and reconstructed in his house, in what would paradoxically become the *Arabian* salon of Eucalypta, with a central basin and a little fountain.

In fact, Curiel eventually ends up spending the whole year in this villa, almost never leaving the country, conducting his business thanks to the European postal service of Beirut and to his diplomatic connections, who ensure the safe reception and dispatch of his mail. He keeps his shares in Suez, but quickly sniffs out a bad deal with his shares in Panama and sells them off through his power of attorney in Marseille. He invests in the Ottoman Bank, in the Port of Beirut Company, and in the Electricity Company, and becomes a member of the board of the Damascus Railway Company. But what will exercise his powers more than anything else is the cultivation of eucalyptus trees, and the huge estate at the heart of which stands Villa Eucalypta.

Wakim Nassar hears many a story about this man, his villa, and his eucalyptus trees. But I imagine he listens to them only distractedly to begin with, when the farmers of Ayn Chir talk about him during the long evening gatherings that now often take place at his house, in the living room of his new home, where they are happy to come play dominoes or smoke narghiles in the European décor, which they are not quite used to yet, and which gives them the feeling of being French gentlemen. From time to time the cry of a hyena disturbs the night over by the seashore, and the dogs go wild. The farmers fall silent for a moment. The bubbling of the narghiles is interrupted, ears are pricked up, a domino stays poised in the air held between two fingers, and finally someone, either old Baclini or Gerios Nassar or Maroun Maroun, declares that it's nothing, and since no shots are heard ringing out, everyone agrees, and the bubbling in the pipes starts up again, the domino game too, along with the discussions about Curiel. At first, the subject of conversation is mostly those uprooted mulberry trees that break everyone's hearts, then those strange trees that are supposed to replace them, then it's the villa that Curiel is starting to build that becomes the center of all conversations, because of the tales of marble on the floors, arabesques on the chimney, and plaster moldings on the ceilings—riches that prompt Wakim and Rached to tell the others about Calmette's palace, while Gerios grumbles that all he can remember about it are the three fingers he left there.

Then the farmers leave with their guns slung over their shoulders, and the next morning Wakim is in his orchard again. He inspects his orange trees, gives orders for the huge Barbary figs that mark his western boundary to be pruned, directs the work on irrigation, the repairs to a stone wall, the cleaning of the well. On the days when he really has nothing to do, he gets up a little later, takes a quick walk through his orchards, then toward mid-morning he goes back up into the house, changes his clothes, and goes to spend an hour at the café at Furn el-Chebbak, on the edge of the Damascus road. For the occasion, he dresses as he did when he was still in Marsad, in a three-piece suit and tie with his city shoes, his cane, and his tarbouche. To get to the café, he walks by the mulberry groves and the farms, passing through vegetable gardens, and the mountains on the horizon facing him are blue. He still has his slightly martial air and distant look, although he sometimes lets his cane dance around him and gaily lead his steps.

At the café, he is received with deference and admiration because he is both the abaday whose vengefulness is fearsome (he defeated the Bedouins, and there is already some unavoidable exaggeration creeping into the stories passed around about this event) and a gentleman who is respected for his social status (he is the son of a good family, you can tell from his manners). He always sits in the same place, and while his coffee is being prepared, he exchanges news with the boss and the customers. Then he rolls a cigarette, which sets him apart from the other customers smoking narghiles. Once he has finished his coffee, he crosses one leg over the other, balances his cane on his left knee, and chats with the customers some more. Then he leaves and I think he goes back to Ayn Chir by another route than the one he came on, to prolong his outing. And it is impossible that, either on his way there or the way back, he does not pass by Curiel's estate. As the weeks go by, he certainly sees the transformations of the land and the appearance of the frail eucalyptus trees swaying in the slightest breeze like grieving women. Then, at the end of the first year, he must be able to distinguish the contours of Curiel's villa in the distance. But he probably never sees Curiel himself, and for the first two years their estates seem destined to live side by side like two kingdoms that ignore each other. Up until the famous evening when their first encounter takes place.

The story of this evening is one of those that my father and uncles told me most often, having probably heard it from their own father, or more likely from some of the old farmers who experienced the event firsthand or heard about it later.

Let's say that everything starts one morning when a horseman unknown in the area presents himself at the bottom of Wakim's front steps, dismounts, goes up to the porch, and asks to speak to *Monsieur* Nassar. When he is in his presence, he announces that Émile Curiel is inviting him to dine the following Tuesday. The same horseman then goes from farm to farm and invites everyone who matters at Ayn Chir, Furn el-Chebbak, and Kfarshima. That evening at the gathering at Wakim's, this is obviously the only thing anyone talks about, especially the horseman who calls everyone *Monsieur*. They continue to talk about it over the following days, in fact every day until the appointed Tuesday, for I am not sure that the farmers of Ayn Chir at the time often had the opportunity to be invited to a dinner party. Even going out in the evening is no small undertaking, and some wonder whether they should take their guns. In the end they decide to go in small groups, and that is how they arrive at around eight o'clock at Curiel's villa, which many of them have not yet seen up close. Among the farmers from Kfarshima are some who arrive on horseback and hand their reins to a groom. Then they climb up the steps leading to the porch and enter one after the other into the lit-up house. Most of the farmers are wearing their Sunday best or their marriage outfits, well-ironed seroual pants, a new waistcoat, and flat shoes, which it feels strange for them to be wearing in the evening. And then there are the dignitaries who have donned sumptuous caftans or precious silk abayas. But all of them wear a tarbouche, and most have a finely groomed mustache, and each one has a proud look in his eyes and refuses to let himself be intimidated by Curiel's villa. Their host receives them one by one in the vestibule, with its small colonnade imitating those in the mansions of the Beirut bourgeoisie. He is sporting a midnight-blue suit and a magnificent lavaliere, and invites his guests one by one into the so-called Arabian salon. The farmers of Ayn Chir, Furn el-Chebbak, and Kfarshima sit down on the divans around the edges of the room, and each is provided with a narghile to smoke. Soon the hubbub of conversation drowns out the bubbling of the water in their pipes and the central fountain. The first dishes are served while the latecomers are still arriving. Through the intermediary of an interpreter, Curiel strikes up a conversation with a farmer from Furn el-Chebbak (seated to his left) and Michel Farhat, a rich farmer from Kfarshima in a vast caftan (seated to his right). From time to time he delights in the spectacle of his guests, who are conversing loudly and laughing as they reach out to the low tables set before them and covered in veal kebabs with onions, chicken with almonds, and beef brains with lemon. At that moment he feels like an oriental prince or an ancient king giving a banquet, even though the guests on this occasion are neither local satraps nor governors of distant provinces, but farmers and silkworm breeders.

Soon the arak begins to take effect. A farmer from Ayn Chir first raises his glass to toast Curiel's health while composing a short zajal to exalt the miraculous whiteness of the drink. Another guest imitates him, then a third, and then everyone has a couplet to deliver that invariably starts with "*Ya* Curiel! *Ya* Émile!" Curiel has his interpreter translate the essential words of each poem, waits for another sextet to be spoken, then replies in turn by improvising a short and finely rhythmical poem in French. When the interpreter finishes his translation, a clamor arises, the farmers are happy, they raise their glasses to him from their divans and laugh, they are delighted to have such a clever new neighbor, and the atmosphere warms up. The zajals, delivered ceaselessly one after the other, start singing the praises of the stuffed lamb being continuously passed around, the sausages with pine nuts, and the truffles with garlic. After listening to them all, Curiel stands up once more and replies, with a sly smile on his face, with these few improvised verses:

The curious and the gourmands
are of the same species.
When there is something to learn
you'll see the first arrive,
when there is something to savor
you'll see the second arrive.
About the world they understand
the first make treatises,
about the flavors they taste
the second make poems.
The first are scholars
but you are poets.
Eat up, gentlemen, eat your fill

so that by tomorrow
Poetry may be enriched
with a few new verses.

When Curiel finishes speaking, an attentive silence falls in the salon. The guests are all ears, their eyes riveted to the interpreter's lips. But when the interpreter finishes speaking, instead of an approving clamor, the silence is prolonged and then turns to ice. Curiel does not understand, thinks that the translation is not finished, then starts to worry, and stares insistently at his interpreter, who has just taken his seat again.

According to my father, it was the word *gourmand* that broke the evening in two, and caused the diplomatic incident that almost led to a permanent falling-out between Émile Curiel and his neighbors, the farmers of Ayn Chir, Kfarshima, and Furn el-Chebbak. However, I always found it hard to believe that things could have deteriorated and the farmers felt so insulted just by a simple word like that, and each time my father told this story with amusement, he would find me somewhat skeptical. But in fact he must have been right, because in the local Arabic, the word *gourmand* has particular connotations that give it a meaning close to *glutton* or *scrounger*. The whole affair must have arisen from a poor appreciation of the weight of words and of the fragility of their meaning on the part of the dragoman, a young man who was still studying and not yet accustomed to the subtleties of the lexicon. From the moment he chooses the fateful word by which he translated *gourmand*, the farmers of Ayn Chir, Kfarshima, and Furn el-Chebbak, so sensitive and punctilious on matters of hospitality and the traditions of dining, can hear only that unfortunate term in the zajal and refuse to consider the meaning of the rest of it. They consult each other with their eyes, looking highly offended, and when the moment of stupefaction passes, the main dignitaries wind up their narghile tubes and set down their glasses of arak one after the other. The murmurs get louder around Curiel, who is waiting for an explanation from his dragoman. But the young man only raises his eyebrows in a show of impotence. Then, after a few moments of silence and uncertainty, two dignitaries from Kfarshima rise solemnly to their feet, adjust their caftans on their shoulders, and leave without even a passing glance at Émile Curiel. A sudden bustle arises as the other farmers start getting up as well.

At that point, Curiel is already on his feet and rushing to the middle of the salon, trying to make them all stay with a "Messieurs, what is happening?" here and a "Messieurs, please, messieurs" there. Then he turns to his interpreter with thunder in his eyes. The young man stands up in turn and finally makes an attempt at an explanation, an exegesis of the poem, to show its true meaning and prove that it did not contain the slightest offense. But one after the other, the farmers pass by Curiel without so much as looking at him and head for the door. Some of them, the more badly off among them, say a few words of farewell to him, then leave with the rest. In three minutes, just as in a bad dream, Curiel realizes with dismay that his evening has turned to disaster. His dragoman at his side, impotent though he is, is trying to gauge how much he might be to blame in this. The servants, who all crowd around and watch the unhappy guests leave one by one, remain just as stunned into immobility as their master, and don't dare say a word. And when all this is over, the last person remaining in the room is Wakim Nassar, sitting on his divan on the south side. Faced with the spectacle of what has just occurred, he has a faintly amused smile that gives his Bengal lancer's mustache a slight sashay to the left side of his face. Leaning against the wooden panels with one shoulder, he is holding one knee in his crossed hands.

"Monsieur," says Émile Curiel as he approaches, "I am grateful that you stayed. But could you please explain what happened?"

Wakim, who I assume was educated at the Three Doctors' School or by the brothers of one of the Christian schools, certainly has a few words of French and Italian, maybe even Russian. In any case, he understands what Curiel is saying to him.

"You offended them, Monsieur Curiel," he replies, and this is immediately relayed by the interpreter.

Curiel sits down in an armchair to listen to Wakim's explanations, and when the interpreter has finished, he remains silent for a moment, his hands cupped together against his mouth.

"But you don't look offended yourself," he says finally, observing Wakim with curiosity.

Wakim shrugs slightly as if to say none of this is of any great importance.

"Don't worry, they will calm down. They felt the need to mark their displeasure. They've done that. Now you just have to wait a little and things will settle down all by themselves."

"I am not worried," says Curiel. "I just think it's a shame that things took this turn. And by my own fault. But you will certainly be able to help with the reconciliation, won't you, Monsieur?"

"You know, I am just as much of a stranger here as you are," Wakim says. "But let's just say that I know the moods of the local people. That may indeed be of some use here."

There is a moment of silence, during which Émile Curiel observes Wakim again with interest.

"I hear you planted orange trees," he says at last. "Doctor Calmette told me about you. I was curious to make your acquaintance."

"And I am also curious to meet your eucalyptus trees," says Wakim.

The two men laugh, and of course this dialogue is completely fictitious, but there is nothing to say that things didn't happen in exactly this way. Whatever the case, that is how I imagine them. And I can well imagine that the conversation went on for quite some time, that they spoke about orange trees and eucalyptus trees, about mulberries and the character of the local people, in the middle of the paneled salon and the scene of the brutally interrupted feast, between heavily carved tables piled high with plates of untouched food. After a while, Curiel gets up and comes back with two cigars that the French consul accepted to have sent to him by diplomatic pouch. The two men light them at the still-glowing embers of one of the braziers for the narghiles, while the servants start tidying up the salon.

"Congratulations for your zajals," says Wakim as he blows out the smoke of his cigar. "You make it seem like you have done this all your life."

"I had heard a few at dinner parties in Beirut. Their rhythm had trotted around in my head for days afterward. And since I had composed eclogues and epigrams when I was in France, it was easy enough. But it seems I need to learn more about the meaning that words have around here before trying again."

"Do not be concerned," says Wakim. "Let me repeat this, everything will turn out just fine. Let time do its work. And in the meantime, come and see my orange trees tomorrow."

This may well be how the friendship between Wakim Nassar and Émile Curiel was born, at the beginning of the period when they each settled in the area. The very next day, Curiel presents himself on horseback (with a different dragoman) in front of Wakim's house, and the two men later take a tour of the orchards. The day after that, it is Wakim who goes to Curiel's house, and the two men wander among the tender eucalyptus groves, between hundreds of lanky little trees that rustle in the slightest breeze, swishing and waving their branches as if they were trying to say something but couldn't quite find the right words. Then they go and drink a glass of liqueur in the European salon of Villa Eucalypta, while discussing the affairs of the Levant.

They do this again frequently thereafter. While on his way to the café on the side of the Damascus road, Wakim makes a detour to see Curiel. He joins him in the middle of his trees and from time to time, when Curiel is free, the two men go to the café together. And when I say that they go together, that also means that they get on well with each other, they are the same age, they are both more or less outsiders in the area, and they both are busy, each on his own lands, cultivating new species that will modify the physiognomy of the country sooner or later. When they enter the café on the side of the Damascus road, Wakim with his cane and Curiel with his lavaliere and both of them in city shoes, the regular customers stand halfway up, the waiters bustle around addressing Wakim as *khwaja* and Curiel as *missio*. Curiel orders a narghile and Wakim a simple coffee to go with his cigarette, and as they watch the hansom cabs pass by on the Damascus road, they tell all kinds of stories. Curiel talks about Provence, Algeria, and orange trees, Wakim about Marsad, samsara, and also probably about the altercation that made him flee his native neighborhood and that I know nothing about. Each man speaks his own language, sometimes using words from that of the other, who listens attentively, brows knitted in concentration, working out one by one the words coming from his friend's lips, finding his way as best he can in the meanders of grammar and syntax, navigating by sight thanks to the more familiar words, and making his best guess about the rest. Unless it's the other way around, and each one speaks the other's language, laboriously constructing sentences, impatiently stumbling along to try to forestall the help that he senses is just about to be offered by his friend. Sometimes they chat with the other customers and Wakim then becomes the interpreter for Curiel, and when they get up, after an hour or so, and all the customers farewell them, again with deference for the *khwaja* and the *missio,* Curiel reminds Wakim that he is responsible for his reconciliation with the farmers in the area, and that he is still waiting. Each time, Wakim shrugs or raises his eyebrows, as if none of this had any importance whatsoever, and answers nonchalantly that things will get better all by themselves, but that a little patience is required.

And indeed, he knows perfectly well that things will get better. He knows that the farmers of Ayn Chir and Kfarshima cannot stay on bad terms for long with a man who welcomes to his home the French consul, Doctor Calmette, and all the local dignitaries, Ibrahim B., Thérèse de F., and the dragoman of the Austrian consulate (in fact it is around this time that Wakim himself starts seeing these people, that Thérèse de F. starts making ambiguous hints at him, and that Habib Fayad becomes his investment adviser). And so each time Curiel speaks of the affair again, Wakim shrugs and repeats distractedly that it will just take a little time. For he notices signs from day to day of how the farmers' attitudes are changing, slowly but irreversibly.

To begin with, whenever Curiel is mentioned in their presence, they have a reaction of cold indifference and contempt. During the evening gatherings, for example, there are pointed remarks like "If he sings zajals like that when he goes to visit Ohannes Pasha, he'll get deported." To which the answer is obviously "Unless he calls the governor a gourmand. Then at least he'll be right, for once." And then everybody laughs at the double reference—to Curiel and to the governor's corruption—and the water in the narghiles bubbles all the more gaily. Then the irony gradually disappears, and if Alfred Sursock's coupé or a governorate minister's carriage should happen to pass by one morning, and then someone such as Baclini, that evening, or on leaving mass at Saint Michael's, says, "They're going to listen to zajals," then Malkoun or Rached cheerfully counters with: "That's enough now. Anybody can commit a blunder, we're not going to talk about it for a hundred years, are we?" To which Wakim adds, just to push things along in the right direction, "Of course not. And anyway it was just a matter of translation. I've told you so a thousand times." And if there are still some hotheads who refuse to give it up, the passing months see a slow and inescapable reversal occurring, such that when a farmer coming back from Furn el-Chebbak announces, "The Frenchman had a visit from Mansour Eddé this morning," it doesn't lead to any more jokes about rudeness or poetry, the event is taken seriously, and someone adds: "And yesterday, it was Nicholas Chehade." But some hesitation remains in letting it be known that the grudge is over, and the rather derogatory use of "the Frenchman" is the most obvious proof of this. And then one day that way of referring to Curiel also falls away, like a fruit that has ripened without anyone noticing it. No one says: "I saw the Frenchman coming out of his forest," but rather: "I ran into Émile Curiel outside his property." After which there are no scruples in admitting: "I came across Émile Curiel. He came toward me to shake my hand." And in that confession there is now a trace of pride, until the day when, to someone saying "Émile Curiel waved at me as he was passing by on the road just now," the reply is: "Yes, he's actually a decent man, that Curiel." That day, Wakim considers the deal is in the bag. But he still waits awhile. At last, one morning, he rides up to the Villa Eucalypta, dismounts, and goes into the salon, where Curiel is sitting at his writing desk dealing with his correspondence.

"Curiel, get up and go get dressed. We have a condolence visit to make to Michel Farhat, at Kfarshima. He has just lost his mother."

Wakim is speaking in Arabic, but Curiel understands. He sets down his quill and stands up.

"So this is it, we're going to make peace?"

"Yes, the time is ripe."

Two hours later, the two friends enter the main room of Michel Farhat's house, where several dozen men, mostly farmers from the area, are seated on chairs set out in rows around all four sides. The moment Wakim and Curiel appear, the murmur of whispered conversations is suddenly interrupted, and it is in complete silence that they walk toward Michel Farhat, Wakim imperceptibly pushing forward Émile Curiel, for whom this is his first condolence visit in the Levant. Michel Farhat rises to his feet, and when Curiel stretches out his hand, then embraces him, just as Wakim recommended, the thirty farmers also solemnly rise to their feet, and it's the beginning of reconciliation, which is sealed the following Sunday on the occasion of the mass. On the front steps of the church of Saint Michael of Ayn Chir, Curiel shakes the hands of everyone he didn't see at Farhat's, says a few words to the priest, and is then invited to sit in the front row for the service, among the notable dignitaries of the area, including Wakim Nassar, who is thinking about something else entirely during the mass.

For this whole affair with Curiel and the farmers of Ayn Chir and his new friendship with the owner of Villa Eucalypta are not the only things that have been occupying his mind for the past two years. There is also the work on the plantation, the monthly irrigation, the yearly pruning, and the legions of workers he needs to recruit, supervise, then pay. This is all causing him a problem because of his diminishing funds, which only the slow but sure growth of the trees allows him to confront with optimism. Wakim never takes his eyes off them, squeezing their leaves, checking their branches, looking for the first signs of new growth, until one day during the third spring season, the miracle at last occurs. One night when he is walking home from Tanios Rached's house, wearing his riding boots and a revolver in his belt, as he crosses the pathway that leads up to the bottom of the front steps of the house, Wakim smells it. The scent of flowers. Barely a hint, more like an allusion, but which his nostrils in high alert still capture with assurance. He stops, looks into the night, toward the dark shapes of the trees that are still no higher than he is. He remains motionless, like someone keeping watch on a hyena. And he breathes deeply. But he can't smell it anymore. He takes a couple of steps, cautiously, as if the scent might be frightened away by the movements of a man. Then he stops again, his whole body concentrated on interpreting the sensations that his nostrils are taking in. But all he can smell is earth, leaves, branches, the smell of night, and the slightly moist air coming from the seashore. He starts walking again and hasn't taken three steps before an imperceptible breeze rises, as if it were talking to him, as if it were trying to hold him back—like a child playing hide-and-seek who shows himself when you pretend not to be looking for his hiding place anymore—and he smells the scent of flowers again. He smells it, he breathes deep, and even though on the second inhalation it's already gone again, he is now sure that this is it. He strides toward the house, runs joyfully up the steps, and when he gets to the top, at the front door, the breeze rises again, and he can smell the scent once more. The next day, at dawn, even before Gerios arrives, he is walking through the trees looking for the first flowers. But he doesn't find a single one. And yet, that evening, and all the following evenings, the scent is there, fleeting, rare, precious, lifted up by the breeze, surprising him the very moment he gives up on trying to smell it. And one night, when a few farmers who spent the evening with him are on the front steps getting ready to leave, the soft, sweet scent is obvious to them all, not fleetingly, liberated by a faint breeze, but right there, present in the night air as if it were its very essence.

The following day, Wakim discovers the first flowers hiding behind the young leaves dancing in the morning air. Selim and Gerios discover more, then blossom appears all over the orchards, and a week later the whole plantation, as far as the eye can see, appears in the middle of springtime to be covered in snow.

6

ONE DUNAM IDEALLY holds twenty-five orange trees, and each tree should yield twenty forty-pound baskets of oranges per annum at its full yield. In other words, the one thousand two hundred and fifty trees planted on the fifty dunams that Wakim Nassar owned must have produced, at their apogee, around five hundred tons of oranges, which must have made quite a lot of money and justified my grandfather's huge expenses yet to come. But to begin with, things are generally less opulent. There are fewer trees, and of course they are still young. In other words, they produce only three or four baskets each, their yield doubling every year until the trees reach maturity. Whatever the case, from the very beginning, it is Muslim wholesalers who come to visit the orchard, and who buy up the harvest, and will continue to do so up until the Great War, in the days of Sabri Bey and Amer Bey, those all-powerful masters of the wholesale markets of Beirut, whose story is yet to come. And it seems that, even at the start, the Muslim wholesalers were prepared to pay top prices. Oranges are as valuable as gold, that's for sure, otherwise how could success have been achieved so quickly—and it came very quickly indeed, according to all the tallies and accounts—how could it all have been achieved, the Big House, the abduction of Helene, the wedding, the lifestyle of the Nassar family, which, from the first child onward, was that of landowners and members of the upper bourgeoisie? The Muslim wholesalers pay a high price—and probably a higher price each year, because the production increases and reaches its full yield only around 1905 or 1906—and thanks to that, the old dreams and desires left fallow for so many years are remembered and can be fulfilled in one fell swoop. The last debts are paid off, new wells are dug, of course, but especially new French cravats are bought, and American hunting rifles, and sorrel horses, and then finally things get serious and the decision is made to give the Nassar family a residence worthy of its ancient name.

Whereas no one can remember the exact date of construction of the Big House—the family home around which the clan's life was organized for a hundred years—what has remained vivid in everyone's recollection are the mind-boggling twists and turns of its creation. In fact, the memories of these events were preserved and passed down not only by Wakim's descendants, but also by those of the farmers of Ayn Chir.

Let us imagine, to begin with, that thirty orange trees are transplanted to make space for it. Let us also imagine the three or four master stonemasons in seroual pants, coming to take measurements and talk about money and materials, master stonemasons whose names were not recorded by history; we shall soon see why. Let us next imagine Wakim and his brother in shirtsleeves and boots, standing at the top of the steps of the Little House and, from there, making wide gestures and deliberating, tracing abstract lines above the orchards and pondering the issues, as they rub their earlobes like two generals before a battle. Let us further imagine how the future house takes shape in Wakim's mind during his daily walks to Curiel's and then to the café at the side of the Damascus road, walks during which his thoughts are expansive, when he is proud to be participating in the ways of the world and can see in his mind's eye sumptuous acroteria rising in the sunshine and cool, wide vestibules opening onto terraces filled with birdsong and the murmur of leaves. When he arrives at Curiel's, he stands back to look at the facade of Villa Eucalypta, its bizarre turrets and its zigzagging Moorish arcades, which are to Arab or Venetian arches what a grimace is to a smile. Then he shrugs and mutters to himself, starts walking again, and, when he enters the house, Curiel knows that he will spend the whole time looking at the marble flooring, discreetly detailing the moldings on the ceiling, mentally measuring up the dimensions of the rooms, and Curiel laughs and leaves him to it.

Let us imagine all that, then, but more than anything, let us imagine the huge building site that is about to be created, thirty yards away from the Little House, and which no doubt resembles all the building sites of the world at that time, a parking lot for donkeys and carts, with sand and mortar lying in heaps everywhere, workmen's sheds, a pile of stones that the masons come and carve on the spot, in other words, a scene of chaos from which an increasingly impressive scaffolding at last starts to emerge, growing higher and higher month after month, along with the different stages of the house as it is being built.

After three months, Wakim orders the ironwork for the balconies, the woodwork for the windows, the marble for the floors, and in the history of the Nassar clan, the provenance of these materials has been passed down from one generation to the next, like an inheritance, to become familiar words in the family members' language, part of their common culture. This is how I have always known, as if it were taught to me like the first words of my childhood vocabulary, that the ironwork of the Big House, in which I lived only for the first five years of my life, came from the Dutilleux firm in Lyon, the roof tiles from Masse Frères in Marseille, and the marble from Carrara. I take pleasure in imagining all these materials deposited on the docks of the port of Genoa, stroked by great gusts of Mistral on the port of Marseille, or in the bottom of the holds of ships passing off the coast of Stromboli blazing in the night.

When at last they arrive in Beirut, and are taken up from the port on donkeys' backs through all the alleyways of the city, then on the Damascus road to Furn el-Chebbak, and from there to Ayn Chir, the house has already grown, it is enclosed now in an enormous mantle of beams and scaffolding protecting its growth while hiding the gestation of its miraculous beauty from the eyes of mere mortals, like a pearl inside an oyster. The evenings in the farmhouses of Ayn Chir are soon haunted by it, the admiring discussions about it flow freely, and this lasts at least four months, until the long-awaited day when the first scaffolding is taken down. The house appears, but slowly, very slowly, so that first the tile roof, then the cornices, then the windows, then the balcony, then the front staircase with its railing going down to the foot of the house are revealed one after the other like a woman being undressed. Its imposing stature rends sighs of satisfaction from the master stonemasons and their assistants, from the carpenters, and from all the farmers of Ayn Chir who come to see it up close. Wakim himself seems satisfied, he acknowledges the congratulations from his neighbors, he receives Curiel, whom he takes on a tour of the house, although it is still only an empty shell, and everything seems to be going well, up until the moment when a devastating mechanism is triggered in his mind.

Everything undoubtedly starts with a terrible realization. It doesn't come to him abruptly, all at once, but slowly, gradually, like a doubt that steadily becomes a horrifying certainty. Just as a novelist who thought he was satisfied with the last few pages he wrote realizes, on rereading them, that they are not at all what he wanted, nor what he believed them to be, and becomes terrifyingly conscious that they are actually even dreadful, that their rhythm sounds stunted, the sentences lack expansiveness, and the turns of phrase have no flavor, Wakim discovers little by little that the house does not please him, that it gives him nothing like joy or delight or pride, but rather a vague feeling of moroseness. He regains his distant pensive air, his gaze that looks down upon the crest of the world and all beings in it, giving you the constant feeling he is looking at something just behind you. At the café, he is distracted and aloof, people avoid disturbing him, and when he leaves, he says goodbye distantly, as if he knew no one there. In the evenings, at the gatherings, he gives evasive answers to the questions he is asked, and when anyone inquires whether all is well, he pulls his lower lip over his upper lip in an expression that signifies that he knows nothing about anything. It is only when he is within sight of the house, examining it from the road or from the other side of the orchards, walking around it in silence, observing each element separately, it is only in these moments that he loses his distracted air for one of intense concentration, absorption, and determined reflection, and little by little, very gradually, he comes to understand everything he dislikes about his new house, the Venetian windows whose curves are too heavy, falling like sad eyebrows, the narrowness of the area between the tops of the windows and the cornice, which gives the house a kind of stubborn frown, the roof whose pitch is so low it looks as if the house has a receding hairline.

Once he has come to this realization himself, he calls together the master stonemasons, who are already preparing to work on the interior, and explains that he wants to change the facade and the shape of the windows. Then he calls for the master carpenter and announces that he wants the roof to have a steeper, more lofty pitch. The four men protest, explain themselves, all talk at once, justify their work, try to reason with their employer, then admit that what he is asking for is all but impossible unless they rebuild the whole house. And Wakim Nassar, impassible, simply replies:

"Fine. Tear it down. We'll start all over again."

Of course, one might well wonder whether this episode, which became famous in the history of the family and of the whole area, might have been subject to the process of lyrical amplification and exaggeration that mythologists always detect in the genesis of great legends. I believe however that this is not the case here. For when I started getting seriously interested in the history of Wakim Nassar and wondering whether the basis of the unassailable myth of the destruction and reconstruction of the Big House wasn't a simple matter of a few touch-ups of details here or there—the rebuilding of a door frame, or a wall, or a patch of the roof—touch-ups that might have become, in the imagination of the locals and in the oral transmission of the facts, a reconstruction from the ground up, and when I said a few words about this to my father, he affirmed that Wakim not only had the first house destroyed to its foundations, but also took charge personally of its reconstruction. As my father was speaking, without getting up from his couch, he pointed at the picture that a White Russian artist had painted of the Big House in the 1950s that was hanging on the wall across from him, on the other side of the living room where he habitually spent most of his days shuffling cards. And as he pointed it out, as if I had never noticed it before, he explained that his father had turned the house around like a toy and had rebuilt it with the facade facing the Pine Forest and Beirut, whereas the first version looked out at the mountains. And he made a gesture with his fingers like a cube pivoting on itself. That strange detail, which he told me only that one single time, appeared like a lightning flash of lucidity from the depths of his memory, and its dazzling suddenness confirmed my faith in the story of the reconstruction of the house, for I had become used to giving more credence to the old memories that appeared abruptly and then vanished in his mind, and that thus had a greater purity and authenticity than those relating to more recent events, which I suspected might contain traces of his current preoccupations.

I therefore hold this episode to be definitely creditable: once the decision is made and announced, Wakim starts the work of deconstructing the house, under the incredulous eyes of the two project managers, of all the farmers of Ayn Chir, and the passersby on the road. On his rooftop, Baclini is speechless, and during the evening gatherings in the farmhouses there is talk of a crack in Wakim's brain. After three days, the two project managers abandon the site. But that doesn't stop Wakim from persevering and the house from undoing itself from the top, first the roof, from which the tiles are taken down, with as much care as in the inventory of a Limoges porcelain store, then the upper walls, then the windows, then all the rest of the edifice, along with the central stairway and balcony, whose ironwork is dismantled with a thousand precautions. Forty days later, the Shiite farmers, the Bedouins whose tents are prudently pitched to the west, the daily passersby on the Sidon road, who had all seen the house go up, and then go down, discover the horizon where the house once stood as empty and undisturbed as it was a year earlier. However, all around its site are the stones that served to build it, spread out over the ground in a rigorous order, with a few of them, such as the cornerstones, the window frames, the balcony, and the stairway marked and numbered.

When the reconstruction starts, it is Wakim who directs operations, in his faded military uniform and riding boots, seconded by his brother, Selim, and his foremen, who all have their opinion to give about every little thing: "This should be done like this and not like that, Khwaja," or "This should go here instead," or "The master stonemasons did this like so and not like so." He listens to them all distractedly and then does just as he pleases. He climbs up the ladders with the workmen, supervises the work from the tops of the walls, and once a day, he takes stock at home, on an old wooden table installed in the main room of the Little House, which has suddenly become something of a headquarters for the workers, who come in like soldiers to take their orders, soiling the floors and furniture with dirt and mortar, leaving their trowels and hammers lying around all over the place, more often than not forgetting their caps on the table where they set them down to listen to Wakim's orders more comfortably. When things don't need close supervision, Wakim sets out on horseback for Baabda or Kfarshima. At the foot of the houses that serve as models to him, he mentally redraws the shapes of his windows and the pitch of his roof, the spacing of the columns, the curves of the arches, and the boldness of the stone egrets on the acroteria, then he comes home with his head full of shapes and designs that he tries to make good use of, as if he were leafing through a sketchbook, in the directions he gives to his masons and carpenters.

Four months later, Baclini on his rooftop, the other farmers, the passersby on the road, the Shiites and the Bedouins, everybody sees the house rise up once more, in the middle of the ladders and scaffolding. As the contours of the three windows now turned toward Beirut are redesigned, and the little columns are replaced by taller ones, and the front of the house is raised up, Wakim brings in new carpenters to make the fretwork at the windows, and new stonecutters to touch up and refine the scrolls on the cornices. Fourteen months later, the exterior of the house is finished. Before taking down the scaffolding, Wakim wants to finish the interior as well. The marble from Carrara is finally brought out, then come the painters and plasterers to make understated moldings on the ceilings, wandering around nonchalantly with their ladders, their stepstools, and their goatskins full of paint, such that hides need to be put down everywhere to protect the new flooring.

Five months later, the work is at last completely finished. For the second time, the house is relieved of its raiment, gradually revealed, slowly disrobed to reappear in its entirety. The passersby on the road wonder what to think about this new version, while the farmers of Ayn Chir can't tell the difference between the two. "If he rebuilt the whole thing just so he can see the forest from the windows of his living room, he really is cracked," they murmur. But when Curiel arrives to see the house finished at last, he observes its new forms in silence, and feels that it now possesses the untranslatable beauty of a creation set down where it is, in the full manifestation of its essence, then he whispers to himself with satisfaction:

"Well, obviously, that's something else!"

Soon visitors from Marsad arrive as well, and among the first are Halim Nassar and his son Gebran, riding up on two fine stallions. When he sees the house from a distance, with its three windows rising up like pennants borne aloft, and where there has been no concession, as there is in many other bourgeois houses, to an excess of Venetian or Moresque style, Halim Nassar is surprised to be agreeably surprised. But as he enters the still empty house, whose walls and marble floors resound with every footfall, he doesn't make the slightest compliment—that's not his way. On the contrary:

"With all the marble businesses in Marsad, you had to go and get your marble overseas," he says to his nephew with a frown as he paces around the large living room. "Wasn't the marble from here good enough for you?"

"Judge for yourself, uncle," Wakim replies, having decided to remain polite. "And tell me what you think."

Halim Nassar grumbles something and the three men continue the tour of the house. Unusually, it is then Gebran Nassar, come down from the heights from which he believes it is his right to deal with other men, who is the one now asking Wakim about every detail of the construction and the materials used, taking a sudden interest in his cousin's life, in the orange trees that he had considered nothing more than a whim, and who even asks for news of Selim, all this as if he had last seen Wakim only the day before. In fact, from the moment Gebran realizes, on looking around the house with an expert eye, that there has been quite a lot of money spent there, this rather haughty and contemptuous character changes his attitude and opinion of Wakim, and suddenly becomes particularly friendly with his cousin, who until then had just been a relative with little to recommend him. During the entire visit, he peppers his conversation with familiar expressions such as "Tell me, cousin," or "The way I know you, I bet you did." Faced with this circus act, Wakim remains icy, replying with little offhand phrases, and offering a deliberately annoyed and impatient expression to his cousin's long, inquisitive stares. Finally, when the three men are back in the main living room, Halim throws a circular, summarizing glance around the room and tells his nephew, with the magnanimous expression of a man concerned for the welfare of the members of his clan:

"That's good. Now you will be able to give a home to your mother. She will be looked after like a queen here. The loneliness must be hard for her."

Wakim soon relays this comment to his mother, the day she comes herself to visit the house—which she calls "my two sons' house." She arrives with a sister or a niece, a Fernaine in any case. Both of them are in crinoline dresses with hats and parasols, which doesn't seem right in the austere, impoverished countryside of Ayn Chir, although it suits the house perfectly. Their dresses are the first to sweep across the marble floors, which they take care not to scratch with the tips of their parasols. They wander all over the house, exchanging circumspect remarks. The mother especially remains prudent in her enthusiasm. Not that all this doesn't please her. On the contrary, she is proud of everything she sees, moving from one room to another as if she were in her own home, and already considering the placement of a sideboard or the size of the rugs required. But if she lets none of this show, that is because it is not her habit, reserve has become her way of being in the world, one that she shares with the Nassars and that has also been sharpened by her bitter experience with men. She therefore feigns a serene, poised, and steady attitude, and it is only immense curiosity that finally compels her to ask, but without batting an eyelid as she continues to walk one step ahead of her son, and as if the answer were perfectly indifferent to her anyway:

"So what did your uncle Halim have to say about all this?"

And when Wakim tells her what Halim said, she stops, turns around, looks at her son in stupefaction, holds back her anger, and, taking her cousin, sister, or niece, or whichever relative is accompanying her, as a witness, she smiles and retorts in an ironic tone:

"That's right. He has already done the sums. He can already see me turned out of my own home. That doesn't surprise me. I bet he has even made plans already to sell my house. But I will show him how mistaken he is to be in such a hurry. Not only is it out of the question that I should come and live here, but he will have to take me out of my house dead in a coffin to be able to appropriate it for himself."

From the next day onward, she starts her new war against her brother-in-law. She has painters come to redecorate the interior of her house, and masons to plaster the exterior. She has her furniture restored, buys a new sideboard, and has four magnificent orange trees from her son's orchard planted in the garden. Halim Nassar gets the message but tries to take revenge on another front. A few months after Halim's visit to his nephew, he sends him a delegation of his wife, her cousin, and the cousin's daughter. The three women arrive in an open carriage, in silk and lace dresses and little hats. The house is barely furnished but they cheerfully agree to be seated on three chairs in the middle of the large empty living room as if they were camping. Then Halim Nassar's wife sweeps her cousin off for a tour of the house, hoping to leave Wakim and the young woman alone together. But Wakim, who has suspected this stratagem, rushes along with them to conduct the tour. Two days later, when she hears about this, Wakim's mother declares coldly that there is no question of such a thing ever happening, that none of her sons will marry a Nassar, she will make quite sure of it. And she launches immediately into her final battle with her brother-in-law. Every week or every month she arrives without fail with a relative of her generation and a young woman of marriageable age, first a Fernaine, then more distant relatives, but always from her own side of the family. Halim Nassar, who intends to keep his nephew in his own clan, counters by sending his wife with a young woman from the Trad clan, along with her mother of course, who is a Nassar. Then he tries to make him yield by having a young beauty from the Fayyad clan presented to him. The widow does not let herself be beaten and in return brings an ally of the Fernaines, a timid and delicate girl whose mother speaks loudly in her stead, then a young woman from the Chehade clan, who remains distant and mostly silent during the whole visit, as if to make it clear that she has no desire to get married.

To begin with, Wakim patiently accepts this little game and politely receives the rival delegations in his half-empty rooms. The women find this highly amusing. All the marble, the moldings, the ironwork, in their eyes all this is a promise that the furnishings to come will be nothing but sumptuous, just like Wakim's suits, which have become increasingly luxurious and impeccably cut. After a few months, Wakim ends up becoming rather expeditious about it all, receiving everyone without carefully choosing his outfit and without asking the Rached daughters to come take care of the coffee and cakes. Then one day, to mark his impatience, he receives his mother and some women of the Mattar clan wearing nothing but the military uniform he puts on when he is working in the fields, and with his boots on, and no tarbouche. When they are seated on the chairs, having unfurled their dresses around themselves with all their drapery and flounces, having set down their parasols and taken up their embroidery hoops, he makes his excuses on the pretext that he must go direct an urgent task in the orchards, and leaves them dumbfounded in the company of Gerios Nassar, who mutters a few things that only the widow manages to understand, having long ago gotten used to this man who was on good terms with her late husband. The news of this boorish behavior makes the rounds of Marsad but does nothing to dampen everyone's enthusiasm. Wakim's somber and haughty look has something that pleases young women, who all swear to train him properly should the chance arise. And so the visits continue, with one visit from the Nassar clan for two from the Fernaine clan, until the day that Wakim puts a stop to the parade by announcing to his mother's face, his uncles, and all the ladies of Marsad continuously traipsing through his house, and to the stupefaction of all the Orthodox Christians of Beirut, that he will marry neither a Nassar, nor a Fernaine, nor a Trad, nor a Fayyad, but—scandal and consternation—a Maronite woman from the Keserwan district.

7

ACCORDING TO A scrap of story that resisted oblivion or disfiguration with surprising tenacity, the first and decisive meeting between Wakim and Helene Callas took place in Michel Farhat's house in Kfarshima. As for Youssef Callas's initial refusal to give his daughter to Wakim, which led to her abduction, the Nassars always imputed it to the notorious character of old Callas, who was madly attached to his two daughters and consistently refused to remarry so as not to impose the presence of a stranger in their home, but who was also so possessive of them that he put huge obstacles in the way of their getting married themselves.

Whenever I tried to get my father and his brothers to give me some kind of information about their grandfather Youssef Callas, they answered without hesitation that he was a peasant. It was something of an automatic response from them, one that they always used rather abruptly, as if they were wondering what else a man might be, in those days, in the Keserwan district. But I was aware, somewhat confusedly, that this was a sort of affectionate teasing on their part, a tender lack of respect, such as when a quality is euphemized to make it stand out all the more while praising someone, or in the same way that Napoleon's soldiers called him the "little corporal." For in truth, I think my father and his brothers knew very well that, despite his appearance (their memory of him is of a man from the mountains, dressed in seroual pants and high boots), their grandfather was actually more of a landowner, one of those men who had benefited from the peasant revolts and agrarian reforms of the mountain lands in the middle of the nineteenth century. He owned mulberry orchards around the village of Qattine, wheat fields on the uplands of Ghineh, and even a mill he bought at the same time as some walnut plantations in the depths of Wadi Ghazir, in the aspens and sycamore woods.

Two accounts attest to the fact that he was a wealthy peasant. The first is a fine but fleeting memory that one of my uncles had of Wakim and Youssef (after their reconciliation) going on horseback to visit the Ghineh plateau, and pushing on to the spring that is at the foot of Jabal Moussa, then at last toward the hamlet of Machta. And when I think about it now, it is clear that such a journey on horseback could be undertaken only by rich men in those days, since mules were by far the most frequent means of locomotion for the peasants and goatherds in those mountains, with their steep, winding tracks. The second account is one by a man from the mountains who let me taste some grapes from his climbing vines when I was at that very spring at the foot of Jabal Moussa one day. On learning who I was, he told me that the Callas family once owned the farmland in the area around Machta, and that the rents had never been collected for eons, and that the land was finally sold to the farmer.

In short, Youssef Callas was undoubtedly a man who was able to make his daughters' daily life a happy one, and he did so, but without thinking about their future. He thought only about his own, and his rather monstrous selfishness is the reason why Helene's sister had to wait five years before her father agreed to give her away to the man she wanted to marry, because she would be going to Jezzine to live with him, and Jezzine was too far away from Qattine. Helene nearly knew an even more dire fate because he was fond of her, she was his favorite, the apple of his eye, as my father would often repeat to me. And in a way, he was not wrong, that Youssef Callas. What allows me to say this is my grandparents' wedding photograph, one that I have examined in detail, often and at great length, in order to try to distinguish a few traits of the bride's and groom's character from their general appearance. Helene is in a loose dress that doesn't show anything of the shape of her body. But it is her expression that is interesting. Standing arm in arm with her husband, with a gloved hand on his forearm, a light veil over her hair, she has a little mischievous air and something in her eyes like an imperceptible preparedness for a reversal of attitude—like a shift from the serious demeanor that is proper for these kinds of formal photographs to hilarity, like a sky starting to change and become stormy, or the light in autumn—which appears also in a very slight smile that makes her chin deliciously jut out. All of this is rather unusual in these photographs from the end of the nineteenth century, for which the subjects had to hold long and serious poses, to the point that it could become tiresome and give them an artificial or almost fixed look, as is in fact the case for Wakim, who in the photograph, despite his extreme elegance, has the look of a rooster caused by the need to keep his eyes fixed on the lens without moving. I've also often imagined that at the moment this photograph was taken inside the Big House, Helene started making jokes, or could not contain a burst of giggles, which seems to point to a rather unconventional turn of mind, not given to letting itself be overawed by the pomp of the event. And so this is how I have always imagined her at the time of her marriage, carefree and as if sun showers were constantly passing through her eyes, and how I imagine she first appeared to Wakim Nassar, and why he fell in love with her.

When I started taking an interest in the story of Wakim, and asked my father what Helene had to do with Michel Farhat such that she was at his house on the same day as Wakim, he replied evasively that the Callas and Farhat families were relatives long ago. But he obstinately refused to make the effort to untangle those relations, which I therefore never really understood. And when I wanted to know exactly what Helene was doing in Kfarshima, when all the versions of her story concurred that she lived in Qattine at the time, and because Qattine is not exactly three steps away from Kfarshima, and at the end of the nineteenth century it would have taken a day at least, and an exhausting one at that, to make the journey, he grumbled in reply that all these questions of mine were beyond his competence, and that was when he asked me, rather maliciously, whether or not I was writing the family history. I told him that if I was, I would need a few details, including that one.

I ended up convincing myself that there was no way I would ever find out, and had resigned myself to having to start imagining a scenario of my own devising, when we received a visit from one of my cousins one morning. She was a very elderly lady, and although she was my father's niece, she was much older than he was, although she still called him *uncle,* all this because of a general disorder in the lines of descent and the levels of the generations in the family that meant that my father had nieces ten years older than him and I had cousins who were already great-grandmothers. This niece, who came to visit my father twice a year, never gave notice of her arrival, so that she often arrived at her uncle's implausible mealtimes and amused herself by teasing him about eating so early. However, once she arrived in front of our building, she would send her chauffeur in first, to check with the caretaker that the elevator was working properly, that there were no electricity cuts or mechanical problems or other misfortunes that might interrupt his mistress's ascension up the floors, then he would ring my father's doorbell to make sure that he was at home. My father hardly left the house anymore, but the ritual was inescapable. Fifteen minutes later, my very old cousin would come out of the elevator, supported by her chauffeur and the caretaker, one on each side, helping her to cautiously make her way into the apartment, where she would enter while finishing her brief conversation with the one, or giving a list of instructions for the rest of the day to the other. My father, who would wait for her at his front door, would slowly accompany the little group crossing his living room, and it was only when he was sure that his old niece was safely deposited in her armchair that he would respond to her greeting by scolding her about gadding about like a young social butterfly when she could barely stand up. She would retort by asking him why he never went out himself, when he could walk perfectly, knowing full well that this question would annoy him even more than her remarks about the times of his meals, and their conversation would continue in this vein, in a series of affectionate jabs and remarks full of calculated irony. She was always very richly dressed, would flutter around in her chair, changing the position of her cane, first to the right, then to the left, then down on the carpet, as she gave news of her grandchildren and great-grandchildren, who were also the great-great-grandnieces and -nephews of my father. He would invariably get lost in the genealogies, forget the names, the relationships, and in the end would listen only distractedly to his excessively voluble niece's stories.

And so that day when I was there during her visit, hoping to make the most of what remained of her lucidity, after getting her started with anecdotes about the past that she loved to tell, I asked her, by the way, whether by chance she knew why Helene Callas, who was in fact just as much her grandmother as mine, used to come to the Farhat house in the period before her marriage. Without the slightest hesitation, as if she had been thinking about this that very morning or talking about it just the day before with her chauffeur, she replied that Helene used to come to Beirut twice a year with her father to go shopping and update her wardrobe. And she turned to my father for confirmation of this fact. But he didn't even look at her, and replied sullenly, in the way you do when someone is awkwardly questioning you about an event of which you have very unpleasant memories—his usual way of talking to anyone who tried to remind him of old stories—by muttering:

"No, my dear, I knew nothing of all that."

As for me, needless to say that marvelous little detail of my grandmother's life before her marriage gave rise to an almost aesthetic emotion, the kind of jubilation that an archaeologist feels on discovering a kitchen utensil or a makeup vial from the first millennium before Christ—insignificant objects that provide much more information on the ambience of the distant epoch he is studying than any accounts of battles, mythologies, or lists of kings. But that was all there was, because despite her goodwill, that was all my cousin knew about the situation. And since at the time she was the only person, along with my father, who was likely to know anything at all, it became clear to me that I was left to my own devices again and would have to make everything up.

The details of this first encounter must therefore be imagined from scratch. The number of possible stories is almost infinite. Wakim and Helene might have met at a small gathering in the Farhat drawing room, one afternoon or one morning (she sits down beside him, because the armchair is comfortable, then he engages her in conversation). It might also have occurred in Mother Farhat's bedroom, where Wakim had come to pay his respects, and where he finds Helene (and at one point he makes a witticism, she laughs, and complicity is born, or she is the one who makes a joke and he is the one who laughs). It might have been at the front door, as he was arriving and she was leaving to go shopping or go for a walk (she sees him and blushes in surprise), or at the bottom of the steps, as he was leaving and she was arriving (she drops a ribbon unawares, and he leans down to pick it up), or in the hallway (there is a crowd of people and he is pressed against her involuntarily). All of those would do, all of them could be the start of an infinite multiplication, and what I am going to choose, arbitrarily, is another version entirely. Here goes. We are at Michel Farhat's house one day in the spring of 1896, on one of those mornings when the Kfarshima dignitary is receiving visitors. In the drawing room, the floor is covered with an enormous carpet with a central medallion and maroon patterns that match the color of the tarbouches, there are visitors sitting in the massive armchairs set around the edges of the room, farmers from the area in seroual pants, dignitaries from Baabda in European suits. Maybe a captain of the gendarmerie of Mount Lebanon is also there, sitting next to Michel Farhat, noisily sipping the coffee that has just been served to him. And maybe all these people, who are continuously coming and going, are there due to the presence of two envoys from the great silk factories in Lyon, who are visiting Mount Lebanon, and whose presence in Michel Farhat's house can be explained because he is an important intermediary between the silkworm breeders in the region and the French dealers. The two envoys, one wearing a lavaliere and one a stiff detachable collar that straightens his spine, are accompanied by a dragoman who explains approximately who is coming into the drawing room, who is leaving, and what is being said around the room. Sometimes Michel Farhat himself addresses a few words to them, which are immediately translated for them, and they nod and continue looking at all the people around them as if their host were giving them a running commentary. Sometimes they have a little chat with one of the dignitaries through the intermediary of their dragoman, and then they are leaning forward, with their elbows on their knees so as to be closer to the dignitary and to hear the translation of his words at the same time, as if they were having an important conversation on the side. It is possible to imagine that this is the reason for Youssef Callas's presence there this morning. Youssef Callas, who owns mulberry orchards, may wish to be acquainted with the latest fluctuations in the price of silk and its industry politics in Lyon, unless he and Farhat are partners in the business—either Farhat has a role in selling Callas's production of silk, or Callas himself is Farhat's agent for the sale of cocoons in the Ghazir region.

In any case, let us imagine that Youssef Callas, sitting between the captain of the gendarmerie and Michel Farhat, is making a skeptical comment to his cousin about a machine developed by French industrialists that empties cocoons, when Wakim Nassar enters the living room with his impeccable European suit and fluffy tie, his tarbouche set slightly forward, his stiff mustache, and his jubilatory cane. He greets the assembled gathering with a wide gesture, and several farmers rise to their feet as he approaches and sit down again as he passes by them, in a sign of respect for the orange groves that make so much money, the house that must have cost a fortune, and his eligible status that all the wealthy young women in Beirut are fighting over. At the sight of him, Michel Farhat interrupts Youssef Callas, rises from his armchair, and folds his abaya around himself, only to spread it wide again as he welcomes Wakim with open arms. After they have embraced, Wakim politely greets the captain of the gendarmerie, and also Youssef Callas, distractedly, because he happens to be seated between them. Then Michel Farhat draws him toward the two Frenchmen and laughs as he presents him as the only grower in the region who will be of no interest to them. And so a conversation about orange trees starts. Wakim sits next to the two envoys from Lyon, with his cane on his knees, and is happy to discuss his harvest and the citrus market. He has just finished the construction of the second version of his house, which is already being called the Big House, either in reference to the Small one where he lived beforehand, or because it is in fact the largest one in the area. For a few weeks now, he has had a camp bed set up there and is living in one of the vast empty bedrooms. The previous day he had Gerios Nassar receive the visit of a hopeful young woman. He also sold his next harvest of oranges at an excellent price, and he is talking about precisely this with the two men from Lyon when Helene Callas enters the room.

She first hesitates on the threshold, turns around to speak with her cousin, the daughter of Michel Farhat, with whom she has just been shopping, then, with a firm step, she enters the living room alone. She is wearing a voluminous sky-blue dress and a hat on her hair tied back in a chignon that reveals the delicious insolence of her neck and shoulders. She is holding a little box that she probably didn't want to leave outside, passes it to the hand that is already holding the parasol, and walks past all the guests, greeting them without stopping, sliding like a cat through a pleasant silence. Seeing her arrive near him, and understanding that she is the daughter of Youssef Callas, the captain of the gendarmerie would like to stand up and offer her his seat next to her father, but the seat on the other side is occupied by a farmer from Kfarshima who is lost in admiration of Helene, and there is not a single other seat free. The captain of the gendarmerie stands up nevertheless, then is trapped, and, not wanting to appear awkward, he decides to leave, not without first inviting Helene to sit down. Helene is embarrassed and looks him in the eye as she tells him she doesn't want to sit down, but he insists and manages to be gauche, so she doesn't want to make matters worse and finally accepts and sits down next to her father.

Flattered by the success of the apparition of his daughter but uneasy at her incongruous presence in this room full of men, Youssef Callas takes her hand, squeezes it tenderly, and says:

"Allow me to present my elder daughter, Helene, a wonderful young woman but one who obstinately refuses to get married."

Then he turns to his daughter, his face all but covered up with a huge mustache, and asks her to translate that into French, for the delegates from Lyon. Without looking at her father, she says in French:

"He is introducing you to his wife: me."

"That's not what he said," protests one of the two men from Lyon, who knows a little of the local language for having lived there for a few years and helped a man from Marseille to build a silk factory in the mountains.

"What did you tell them?" asks Callas, looking at his daughter with an amused air.

"I told them that you refused to let me marry anyone but you," says Helene.

"Nonsense, I introduced you to ten idiots, and you didn't want any of them," Callas replies grumpily.

"If you really wanted me to get married, you would have introduced me to someone who is not an idiot."

The gathered men laugh heartily, every one of them looking at Helene with curiosity, reviewing what she said in his mind, putting himself into the situation, wondering whether he had been one of the idiots, whether he is the kind of man that women make fun of once he leaves the room. Then little by little their minds clear, they move on to other things and soon start talking about mulberries again, and silkworms, and exchange rates, whispering little calculations and noisily sipping coffee. And as the room once again fills with talk of bygone harvests, of fickle cocoon buyers, and tree diseases, Helene Callas, pretending to listen patiently but barely hearing the conversation around her, discreetly glances at all the guests of the Farhat household, as if she were observing them without being seen from behind a mashrabiya. What she sees, on the whole, is not very different from what she is used to seeing at home, at Qattine. But along with all those farmers in seroual pants with their big mustaches, who could be peas in a pod with the farmers from Keserwan, there are those two Frenchmen, and Wakim Nassar, and a few dignitaries in European suits, and there is the son of a raw-silk merchant from Baabda who is not badlooking, and it is their presence that proves that this is Beirut and not the mountains. She observes them one after the other, as if they were also part of the atmosphere in the city's European markets, where she has been enjoying herself all morning with her cousin, seeing gentlemen with monocles and young men in European pants. She notes a pensive air here, a way of smiling there, a hooked nose on the son of the raw-silk merchant, a sensuous habit of nibbling his upper lip on the younger of the two Frenchmen, the feminine hands of the other one when an impressively huge cocoon, being passed around as a curiosity, is put into his hands and he takes it up carefully, squeezes it gently, pulls off a few threads, which he examines by holding them up to the light like a diamond dealer with a stone whose clarity intrigues him. And then she gets to Wakim, that's inevitable, and judging from what we know happens next, we can assume that she looks at him for quite some time, but cautiously, intermittently, skillfully letting her eyes slide between him and another guest, then yet another, before coming back to him again, slowly, methodically, back and forth. And it is certain that he too, like all the men in this room, occasionally throws curious glances her way. But let us imagine that their eyes do not meet, not a single time. Wakim continues to talk to the two Frenchmen about this and that, up until the decisive moment when this appears to him: the armchair next to Helene, who is at this precise instant exchanging a few words with her father, is now empty. On the other side of it is a petty dignitary from Baabda whom Wakim met when he was looking for land to buy but hasn't seen since. He doesn't know whether it is a predatory instinct, or the challenge, or simple curiosity that pushes him to act. But what he does know is that this is urgent. For the empty seat is under threat. The petty dignitary from Baabda might move over into that armchair, and then all would be lost. To say nothing of that little merchant from Choueifat who has just entered the drawing room, putting his hand first to his heart and then to his forehead in greeting the assembly, but who finally, instead of walking toward the empty armchair, slides along the wall to the left of the doorway and stays there for a moment, like someone standing just inside the church door waiting for mass to be over.

Seeing the danger thus averted this first time, but knowing it won't be the second, Wakim rises without thinking, behaving almost discourteously toward the two Frenchmen, and walks over to the empty armchair with his cane under his arm, and sits down next to the petty dignitary, greeting him amiably. Helene by his side has not reacted and is still leaning toward her father, whispering something that looks like gossip. Wakim starts a conversation with the dignitary, waiting for Helene to straighten up in her chair. When she does this at last, because Michel Farhat says something to her father from the other side, Wakim can no longer get out of his conversation with the dignitary, who is telling him all the details about a scandal that occurred in his clan the previous week. Wakim listens to him without comment, without even blinking for fear that the least reaction will encourage him to expand on his story, while fuming internally at the idea that Helene might get up and leave without his having said a single word to her. But Helene remains seated, motionless, distractedly staring into the distance, probably waiting for him to speak to her. Which finally happens when the dignitary at last falls silent. Wakim lets a few seconds pass, out of politeness and so as to not appear too eager, while praying that the dignitary will not start talking again and that Helene will not get up, and finally he turns slowly toward her and engages in some kind of conversation, such as: "You speak perfect French, allow me to congratulate you." "Thank you. I learned it with the Sisters of Charity, at Ghazir." "Do you often come to Kfarshima?" "Once or twice a year." "But you know all there is to know about Parisian fashion. You are just as elegant as a city woman." "Thank you." And so on and so forth, not that I have the slightest idea if this is the kind of conversation that might have taken place in the drawing room of a dignitary from Kfarshima at the end of the nineteenth century. But let us assume it is, and that the two guests chat like this for a few minutes, until Helene leans down, picks up the box she had set down on the carpet next to her, puts it on her knee, opens it up, and takes out a hat with ribbons that she shows to Wakim and then to her father. The two men and the young woman comment on the purchase and laugh, after which Helene puts the hat back in the box, shuts it, puts it back down at her feet, and turns toward Wakim and the conversation starts up again, but this time in the other direction: "And what about you? Are you from the area?" "Of course." "You don't look like you are." "Why don't I?" And so on and so forth, until he tells her about his house and invites her to pay a visit, even though the house is as naked as it was when it was first built. Unless it is she who tells him that she is planning to go shopping the next day at the El-Jamil Souk, and she asks him to join her and her cousin there.

So she comes one afternoon, with her cousin, in a portered chaise, and Wakim gives her a tour of the house. Or it is he who indeed joins them at the El-Jamil Souk, the next day, wearing a navy-blue suit. If they are at his house, the three of them wander through the vast empty rooms and utter little shouts so that the echo answers them. If they are in town, they wander cheerfully from one store to the next and exchange little winks or funny faces as they pass by the fat man in the tarbouche and the skinny man whose nose leans to the right. If they are at his house, in his bedroom there are two opposing mirrors in which they play at seeing themselves multiplied a hundred times. If they are in town, the women try on hats with feathers and ribbons at a milliner's, and he gives them advice, pretending that both women are his cousins. If they are at his house, Helene gives him an expressive look in the dining room and his heart burns to ash, and if they are in town, he wants to buy them embroidered handkerchiefs, but since the cousin doesn't dare accept, Helene also refuses, but with a gaze full of allusions. And finally, whether it is at the bottom of the front steps of his house as he sees them to their chaise, or at Kfarshima as they are preparing to alight from a hansom cab, in either case, or in any other case, the cousin pretends to be distracted by this or that, and leaves them a few minutes alone, and at that moment Wakim proposes marriage to Helene, and she looks at him straight in the eyes and laughs inscrutably:

"Ask my father."

Which is almost a provocation.

8

THE STORY OF Helene's abduction, after Youssef Callas refused to let her get married, was always told in one of two versions, both of which are more akin to speculation than authentic memories passed down through the generations. This uncertainty around a crucial moment in Wakim's life can be explained only by the even greater importance, in the memory of the Nassar family, given to the immediately subsequent events, which ended up overshadowing the one that was their original cause. Both versions have it that Helene was abducted, in one from Qattine, in the other from Kfarshima itself.

For a long time, I considered myself as an adherent of the "Qattine version," because I must have been seduced by the drama of the story—the horsemen galloping in the mountains, the young woman kidnapped from her family home in the midst of a huge ruckus, etcetera. If this is the version we retain, let us imagine that, to begin with at least, everything happens in due form: the marriage proposal is preceded by a letter from Michel Farhat, then is presented by Wakim himself, at Qattine, where he arrives with his brother only ten days or so after the first encounter, at the house with its thick walls and deep window casings, where the braziers are still glowing and giving out a gentle scented warmth, whereas on the coast the weather is already hot. After listening with an absorbed and almost absent expression, smoothing down his mustache, old Callas straightens up on the divan where he is sitting cross-legged in his big boots, nods, and asks for a small delay to think about it, let's say until the next day, and orders narghiles to be served, after which he is cheerful and affable all evening, so that Wakim thinks it's all set, it's in the bag. The next day, Youssef Callas takes Wakim out by himself on horseback under the pretext of showing him around his properties, and while he is riding through his mulberry orchards near the village of Qattine, his wheat fields on the uplands of Ghineh, and even to the mill at the end of the Ghazir wadi, he asks Wakim a thousand questions about his land, his oranges, his income, and mentally tallies it all up to see what his daughter might expect in the way of daily material comforts, and by this time Wakim is full of confidence. But when they get home, and coffee is served, and Wakim impatiently asks his host whether he has come to a decision about the business between them, old Callas, as if he had just remembered that he does in fact need to give an answer, hesitates and then declares that, as far as marriage is concerned, of course it's out of the question, Helene cannot possibly live so far away from her family and her father, Beirut is just too far away from Qattine, and it's a pity, but what can you do, that's the way it is, life doesn't always go the way you want. After which he moves on to a question about the orange trees. An hour later, when Wakim is leaving, with Selim by his side saying nothing and waiting for his brother to be the first to speak, he has already decided everything. At Jounieh, in the dusty main street, he rents a carriage and rides ahead of it back toward Qattine.

No, that's absurd. Qattine in those days is of course still a village of sparse houses, scattered up the mountainsides, but none of them can escape the sight of the others, and nobody on the road through the Ghazir wadi can pass by them unobserved. It is obvious that Wakim and his carriage would thus quickly be discovered, at least after Ghazir, where there are market stalls, and people sitting in front of those stalls all day long, smoking, or reading the local rags, or getting a shave from the barbers. To say nothing of the mule tracks in the area that are also busy with goatherds, peasants on foot, or women in long dresses and headscarves constantly passing by, and all these people would of course have seen Wakim arriving with his companions and the carriage, and would have brought the news or had it delivered by all the shortcuts weaving through the mountains, such that the strangers arriving at the house would have received a "warm welcome" and their plans would be thwarted. And even if they had reached the house, and Helene had climbed into the carriage without arguing, it is certain that they would have been caught a few minutes later, and no doubt things would have taken quite a different turn.

No, all this is just impossible. The "Qattine version" is of no use, so I will have to work from the "Kfarshima version," which seems more pragmatic to me. Let's try that one out. Let's say it happens the day after the second encounter. Wakim arrives that morning at Michel Farhat's. After a short consultation with the master of the house, he is introduced into the presence of Youssef Callas. Farhat speaks first, singing Wakim's praises, and old Callas, who understands exactly what is going on because he has seen it all before, listens while staring straight down at a motif in the drawing room carpet and smoothing down his mustache. Then it is Wakim who speaks, announcing his intention to marry Helene. This is followed by a moment of silence that Callas enjoys stretching out, continuing to smooth down his mustache and appearing to be considering the matter. Wakim doesn't falter but waits unperturbed, sitting back in his armchair, his cane between his legs, his hands crossed on the pommel. After one or two minutes, Callas finally speaks. He asks Wakim a few questions about his financial situation, his income, his land, his house, what kind of security he can offer his bride. Wakim calmly answers all these questions, and Callas nods each time and seems to be thinking about it. He is probably worried, because it is obvious that the man being presented to him with a request to marry his daughter clearly has everything one could wish for, that's a fact, and now the old man from the mountains is looking only for a way out. He understands that Wakim is Greek Orthodox, he can't stop thinking about it as the ultimate argument in his disfavor, but he hesitates to use it and finally decides not to, but announces instead that he is going to consider the matter, that he'll think about it, that a day of reflection is necessary, and that Helene will also have to be asked for her opinion.

The next day when the three men are gathered together again, Youssef Callas is more affable, his eyes are sparkling, he welcomes Wakim with an amusing word, and everything seems to be going just fine. But this is only a ploy, for after a few minutes, as if this were just a detail to be sorted out and not the main purpose of the meeting, Callas announces that his daughter left for Qattine this morning and that (let's use the same scenario) as far as marriage is concerned, of course it's out of the question, Helene cannot possibly live so far from her family and her father, Beirut is just too far away from Qattine, and it's a pity, but what can you do, that's the way it is, life doesn't always go the way you want. After which (same thing) he changes the subject to a question about orange trees and Wakim, who is hardly listening to him anymore, answers only in monosyllables, which Callas doesn't mind but which he eventually takes as a pretext to talk to Michel Farhat about something else. But Farhat is dreadfully embarrassed by this turn of events and also replies only distractedly to his cousin. When at last Wakim stands up to take his leave without even a glance at Callas, Michel Farhat sees him to the porch and tries to soften the blow, because he is not at all happy that this all took place at his house when he was vouching for the whole thing.

"Don't be angry with him. Remember what Helene said in front of everyone the other day. And if he won't give her to you, he won't ever give her to anyone else. Poor girl."

"How long has she been gone?"

"Two hours."

Of course, we might also imagine that Helene has not yet left, that she is still at Farhat's house, and that Wakim abducts her from there. We could imagine servant girls being jostled, furniture thrown over, startled women screaming, but none of this is plausible because the consequences would have been disastrous for the relationship between Farhat and Wakim, which is not what happened. So the abduction probably takes place on the coast road by which Helene and her escort are returning home, and in that scenario we still get the wonderful cavalcade, with Wakim, Gerios, and Selim galloping along, followed by a closed carriage they intercepted on the Baabda road. They charge ahead, shouting through the dust, and an hour later find Helene's company at Antelias, or maybe Nahr el-Kalb, in front of the Assyrian kings sculpted into the rock face, who have been making the same grand gestures at passersby for the past three thousand years. In the midst of the confusion, the cries, and the hubbub, Wakim talks to Helene, who pulls back the curtain of the chaise. ("Helene, I asked your father for your hand in marriage yesterday, he refused. You can come with me now, and in two hours we will be married. Make up your mind, quickly.") Helene looks at him with her eyes full of terror, or maybe gratitude, or admiration, but what is certain is that after a moment of reflection that briefly darkens her pupils and makes her appear distant and fearsome, she finally opens up the curtain of the chaise all the way and steps up into the carriage without hesitation, after which the Nassars turn around and set off at a gallop, taking the three horses loaded with baggage with them as well. Once they get to Beirut, the group doesn't head toward Ayn Chir, where there is not yet an Orthodox church, nor toward Marsad, because Wakim would probably not be able to barge in and get married there without reviving old animosities, so let's say it's to Saint Demitrios, where they dismount. Wakim helps Helene out of the carriage while Selim rushes to get the priest. When the priest arrives, looking as ruffled as his beard, Wakim takes him behind the iconostasis, introduces himself, makes sure the man of God hears the fine ring of the Nassar family name, and adds to that sound the sweet clinking of a few large gold coins. The priest is a little disoriented, because people from *good families* normally don't get married like this, unless there's something suspicious going on. Wakim hurriedly explains the whole affair to him, but then the priest rebuffs him, and the fine family name and the gold pieces lose their powers, because you can't marry an Orthodox to a Maronite just like that, the Maronite would have to be baptized first.

"But she is already baptized!" Wakim says. "What's the point of washing linen that is already clean?"

The priest smiles into his beard, but Wakim has already pulled him by the sleeve and they both walk back to the main space of the church, where Selim and Helene are talking in low voices. Wakim tells them what he has just heard, is quietly furious, and tries to apologize for this absurdity, but Helene shrugs serenely and says she doesn't mind, it's actually a privilege to be baptized several times.

"Alright then," Wakim says, thinking that it will be a quick matter of the priest dribbling two drops of holy water onto Helene's hair.

He is forgetting that the baptism obviously will have to be consecrated according to the Orthodox rite, which entails the full immersion of the body in the baptismal water. That's what the priest mutters into his fluffy white beard as he readjusts the Greek cross hanging from his neck and that has turned itself around against his soutane.

"And in any case this will all require the authorization of the bishop," he adds, reluctantly no doubt, as he sees the gold pieces disappear.

And indeed, they disappear along with the Nassars and Helene, who get back into the saddle and the carriage respectively, and ride off in the direction of Ayn Chir.

Obviously things start to get complicated from here, because the Nassars cannot take Helene home before she is married, for that would constitute a breach of the most elementary rules of propriety and be deplorable for her reputation. But there is a solution. When they arrive at Ayn Chir, Helene is settled into the Little House, while Wakim and Selim share the Big House. And so that honor can be saved in the eyes of the entire world, the Rached sisters move in with her, and a messenger is sent in haste to the Farhats in Kfarshima, the Farhats, who send one emissary after another to see Helene from that moment onward, and thus discover that she has consented and is happy to be a prisoner of the Nassars, to defy Wakim, to try to understand, to ask for a consultation. But each time the emissary is sent away with the answer that Wakim is not at home, and in order to avoid nasty surprises, a state of siege is declared. Selim posts himself on the balcony of the Big House with a gun, and Gerios at the entrance gate to the property with two pistols in his belt.

As for Wakim, as a matter of fact, he is not at home. He is in Marsad, where he is asking the priest to obtain a special dispensation from the bishop for the next day at the very latest. And after that, because he has time to spare, he goes to Beirut, where he wanders through the European markets and buys, all at once, all the presents he should have given Helene over several months of engagement—cloth for her dresses, shoes, belts, scarves, dozens of purses, dozens of hats, hundreds of handkerchiefs, fans, pairs of gloves, vials of perfume, music boxes, bonbonnieres, and also a wide China-blue porcelain basin whose use it is not difficult to guess. Then he spends an hour at Medawar Bros. in the El-Jamil Souk, where he is shown all the Parisian catalogues with designs for wedding dresses. He orders a dozen so that Helene can choose, because he has decided to give her a real ceremony, as if to beg forgiveness for the situation with the baptism. Then when all that is done, he returns home to Ayn Chir, where he finally receives an emissary from the Callas family, whose demands for explanations and justifications, whose orders and threats, he answers with a single statement: he is going to marry Helene. Period.

And indeed, the very next day, the priest of Marsad sets out with two deacons on the road to Ayn Chir to prepare for the baptism. Let us imagine him walking in long strides, with a solemn, preoccupied expression, on the road through the Pine Forest, occasionally picking up the hem of his soutane or raising an arm as if to greet someone, but in fact only to let his wide sleeve fall down a little so that he can free up his hand to finger his cross or adjust his soutane on his shoulders. The two deacons are almost running behind him, one carrying the thurible and the psalter, the other the vestments for mass, which are hanging down either side of his right forearm. After around twenty minutes, the little group comes out onto the lands of Ayn Chir, and just as the priest is walking past Wakim's orange groves, about a hundred yards from the entrance to the property, he catches sight of a line of horsemen coming toward him. A few more steps and he can distinguish the shaven faces, headdresses, and boots of Maronite men from the mountains, and their weapons—guns slung over shoulders, pistols tucked in belts, daggers held at the ready against the horses' withers—and he thinks this is it, everything has gone wrong, and even though he knows that his status as a priest protects him, he still touches the cross hanging from his neck and mutters a few words of imploration while continuing to stride firmly forward, without turning to check on his deacons, who themselves are wondering, as they imperceptibly slow their pace behind the priest, whether what they are seeing is real, or whether it could be an illusion, a mirage.

But it is not a mirage, it is the inevitable result of everything that preceded this moment: these are the famous horsemen from Keserwan who are coming to the rescue of old Callas, and who would later enter the chronicles of the Nassar family and thus be remembered in perpetuity. It took me quite some time to figure out exactly who they were, but I finally did, notably because all of those men would end up becoming friends with Wakim, then, after his death, consider themselves the protectors of his children. There is of course Camille Callas, Helene's brother, and his two cousins, Chaker and Fadel, along with Ramez and Farid Chahine, the direct nephews of the leader of the peasant revolt of 1860, and Sakr and Ghaleb Chehab, two brothers and princes, direct descendants of the last emir of Mount Lebanon, and finally Elias Helou, an abaday from the region of Antelias. I imagine them in their turbans, with one end of the cloth falling onto their chests, making them look like Muslim horsemen from the desert. They wear wide belts to hold their pistols and short embroidered jackets that they don't know were introduced into their mountains by the Shiite tribes from Baalbek, while they all have an icon of the Virgin or a piece of the real Cross sewn into the inside of their shirts.

When they see the Orthodox priest of Marsad appear in the distance on the road, they advance toward him, lightly pulling in their reins, without consulting each other, without saying a single word. He also continues walking, and when he is at last in front of them, he greets them and attempts to continue on his way, while the two deacons, one of whom has the ceremonial vestments hanging from his arm, have already stopped. But the horsemen do not let the priest pass, and firmly restrain their horses, then turn them sideways so that they are not agitated by having a man in black standing so close to their muzzles. The priest then demands to be let through, and Camille Callas asks him if he is the one charged with going to baptize Helene. The priest, standing quite still now, solemnly declares that if he is talking to Christians, then they must know that one can only be baptized in a church and that consequently he is not going to baptize anyone. On saying this, he makes the sign of the cross internally, because he is shamelessly lying. But the horsemen don't know this. However they do start to have some scruples about picking a quarrel with a man of God. Ramez Chahine is the first one to push his horse to one side, and soon his brother and then all the other men do the same, so that the priest passes through what looks like a guard of honor, followed by his two deacons, who are almost running now, for fear of being left behind in such dire circumstances.

It matters little after that to know how the inhabitants of Marsad were made aware of this grave event. We might imagine a farm boy secretly sent off, or one of the deacons returning for some reason or other, or quite simply a passerby witnessing the scene. The main thing is that, an hour later, the rumor spreads throughout Marsad that the Orthodox priest was threatened. Youssef Halabi and Habib Qasan hear it at Merched Saliba's café, just across from the church, then roll up their narghile tubes and rise to their feet without a word. On their way, they meet Baz Baz, who is playing checkers with a carpenter from Msaytbeh in front of Youssef Choueiri's store. Baz hears their story, stops concentrating on the move he was just about to make, advances a pawn, considers the carpenter's response, plays another move, queens all his adversary's remaining pawns, and stands up to go and get his weapons. On his way, he passes the house of Costa Zreiq, who is in the garden planting loquat trees, and

Costa Zreiq immediately leaves his trees, goes inside to get changed, and as he comes out meets Mitri and Nicholas Chehade, who have just returned from Ayn Mreisseh, where they sold the skin of a magnificent bear they killed during a hunt in the Hermon valley. Half an hour later, as tradition would have it, these are the six men—who are already Wakim's friends and will also be his children's protectors—who are galloping toward Ayn Chir to come to his aid, and let's say that after they ride through the middle of the Pine Forest, and reach the boundary of Wakim's property, they find themselves eyeball to eyeball with Camille Callas and his companions.

For of course, in the meantime, that group has started what they came down from their mountains to do. After making a show of strength by riding around the boundaries of the Nassar property at full gallop while shouting and making an infernal racket, a racket that eventually irritates all the passersby and the farmers in the area, they are on the point of penetrating onto Wakim's land to wrest Helene away from him, and are at the front gate when the horsemen from Marsad appear. After a quick conferral, they change their plans. They cannot allow themselves to be attacked from behind, and decide to deal with the new arrivals first. From the balcony of the Big House, Selim Nassar sees the Maronite horsemen block the whole width of the road. He also sees the horsemen arriving from Marsad. He sees them slow down, stand still for a moment, then slowly walk toward the Maronites. He signals to Gerios, who is still guarding the front gate, and is just about to run to warn Wakim, but then decides not to, because he knows that at this very moment Helene's baptism is well underway. Which means that just a few minutes ago, in the bedroom of the Little House, the Orthodox priest started singing his hymns in a resounding throat voice, holding his psalter high above his eyes, while his deacons hold the censer smoking at the end of its chain and the silver chalice. Which also means that Helene Callas, standing with her hair undone in a simple white dress under which she is completely naked, is getting ready to step into the large enamel tub where the warm bathwater that was poured into it a moment ago is now, by virtue of the priest's prayers, being transformed into the waters of the River Jordan. Which finally means that Wakim, sitting on a chair as the only congregant, is starting to feel impatient. And because he cannot sit still, he gets up to open a window so that the smell of incense is not so overpowering, and at the same time to lean out and listen.

But he doesn't hear a thing, although at that precise moment, on the road, in front of the entrance to the property, the Orthodox horsemen are only a step away from the Maronite horsemen. They are all starting to get a good look at each other, eyeball to eyeball, in complete silence, and Selim from his balcony is wondering whether one group will stop or the other one back up. But none of them stop and none of them back up. Left hands keep a firm grasp on reins while right hands start caressing the butts of pistols and the handles of knives. Soon the two lines of horsemen meet. Costa Zreiq, one of whose descendants will marry the grandson of Ghaleb Chehab, stares into the prince's eyes. Youssef Habibi looks defiantly at Elias Helou, who will, twenty years later, give him shelter when he has to flee the French Mandate police. Baz Baz, whose legs are almost touching Camille Callas's, appears to be about to slam into him with his shoulder to get past, unaware that fifteen years later, he will save him from a charging boar during a hunt in Keserwan. Their mustaches quiver, their eyes darken, the horses pace on the spot, imperceptibly turning round in circles. Alba and Rome are about to go to war, unaware that they will one day be Alba and Rome. The least misplaced gesture, a hand sliding too swiftly over a hip, a chest puffing out too suddenly, and it will be a massacre, a bloodbath that all the waters of the Jordan, the Lycus, or the Dog River will not be able to wash away, all this precisely at the moment when on the property, in the Little House, in the bedroom, Helene Callas has just put her bare foot into the water in the blue enamel tub while the priest leans down, takes some water from this diminutive River Jordan into a porringer, and pours it over her head, once, twice, three times, so that Helene's white dress is soon soaked through and dripping and her hair sticking to her forehead and neck. But then, just as Mitri Chehade is about to grasp his pistol and Ramez Chahine to seize the knife at his hip, Camille Callas receives an unexpected gift of grace. Something inside him suddenly gives way, all his male conceitedness, petulance, and foolhardiness, all of that suddenly falls away like scales from the eyes of the heathen, and Camille sees, all at once. He sees *himself*, as if in a mirror where he is surprised by his own image and doesn't recognize it at all. He sees himself in this absurd melee, he becomes aware that he is the one who bears the primary responsibility for it, and that what he is preparing himself to defend is not the honor of the Callas family but the tyrannical stubbornness of his father, and that in doing so, he is stupidly destroying his sister's chosen happiness, destroying the one chance she has of getting married, all that to please his despotic father, who has sworn to keep his daughters for himself, his father, who like Saturn would rather devour his own children than see them abandon him, and then, in that moment so brief that Ramez Chahine doesn't even have time to grasp his dagger, nor Mitri Chehade to close his hand on the butt of his revolver, in that instant, Camille Callas chooses his sister over his father, and moves backward away from Baz Baz, jostling Ramez Chahine, who lets go of his knife, and now Baz Baz crosses the cordon, soon followed by Mitri Chehade, whom Ramez Chahine must now give way to and let pass, then by Costa Zreiq, to whom Sakr Chehab can no longer offer any resistance, and finally the horsemen from Keserwan completely open up the road all the way and it becomes clear that the Trojan War will not take place.

PART TWO

THE TIME OF ZAYMS

9

THE MEMBERS OF the Nassar clan have always told the story—without really knowing its origin—of the wish that Wakim, their common ancestor, made on the evening of the birth of his first son, namely to populate the whole earth with his progeniture. As absurd as this promise may be, made no doubt in the enthusiasm of first-time fatherhood (let us imagine a classic scene: basins, cloths and towels, a midwife with bloodied arms, and finally the parcel of flesh closed in on itself and wailing—it's a boy!—while being passed from one person to another, then given to his father, who then shivers with joy and emotion, and makes this peculiar vow), Wakim's wish was nevertheless almost fulfilled, for his sons did spread throughout the world. One left for North America, another for Brazil, three others were exiled into Egypt, while the daughters were scattered to Sudan, India, and as far as the Philippines.

But before that, Wakim's children all lived in Ayn Chir at least until they were twenty years old, and thus their original landscape, their common heritage of memories, was the Big House with the huge furniture made especially for it by Berouti the cabinetmaker, the orange groves, the land adjoining the seasonal Bedouin camps, the mulberry groves all around, and also Gerios Nassar with his seven fingers muttering like a prophet, and Selim with his distant, finicky aloofness that some of them inherited. They also all lived among the farmers of Ayn Chir, who would often come to visit, and for whom they always felt a particular affection. They knew the wide Provençal hats Curiel used to wear and the soutanes of the Jesuits of Ghazir. And even though they didn't live through exactly the same events or the same eras—the elder children having known the house in the time of its splendor, Curiel in his prime, and the orchards at their full yield, the younger ones remembering only an aging Curiel, the orchards going wild, and the house falling apart—from the accounts they gave of it, we can nevertheless compile a general picture of the life of the Nassar family in the years 1896 to 1914, the period of its heyday, almost a sublime apex, when the elder sons are already young men attached to the house and the younger ones (with the notable exception of my father, who will be born precisely at the time when that whole universe is about to fall apart) were still little boys, albeit already starting to be marked by memories.

Among those memories there is, for example, the time when Wakim and Helene set off in the carriage for Aley and its Grand Hotel (let us imagine them, him in his navy-blue pinstripe silk suit and tarbouche, with his cane under one arm, and her in an ivory gown, a hat set atop her chignon and a parasol in one hand, leaving the property in the hands of Selim without a care in the world, and taking several trunks of dresses, white, lilac, royal blue, with trains and flounces, leg-of-mutton sleeves and Medici collars, or maybe hoopskirts and bustles, as well as fifteen pairs of long gloves, eight pairs of lace-up boots, twelve fans, six parasols, all that for her, while for him there are straight pants pressed down the middle, dozens of shirts, eight jackets, ten waistcoats, six tarbouches, four pairs of pointed boots with and without buttons, patent leather low boots with square toes, dozens of ties, lavalieres, and even a boater); there is the time when Wakim came home from hunting in Keserwan, where he shot foxes around the Ghineh plateau and boar in the Moussa Jabal with his brother-in-law, Camille Callas (let us imagine the remains of the defeated beasts piled up in the kitchen of the Big House under the children's fascinated eyes, the doubtful look of the boars, the almost smiling faces of the fox cubs, but also the roe deer, the wood pigeons, the grouse, a sumptuous booty that is later distributed to the local farmers); there are the times Helene received visits from the Orthodox women of Marsad and Msaytbeh (these are *ladies* who arrive in carriages or in portered chaises, and let's imagine them wearing dresses with short trains and spinning parasols in their gloved hands, lifting up the flounces on their skirts to go up the steps to the house, where they throw off their hats as they enter and drink tea or rose cordial or orange juice from the Nassar trees, sitting in the living room with its huge furniture or on the balcony where they can watch the children play, the coachmen chat, and the farm laborers appear from between the trees in their dreadfully ragged clothes to ask for water and then disappear just as quickly, like wood creatures lost in the human world).

And there are also the individual memories of each of the children, memories that have now come into the public domain, like the one from Elias, the first son, hunting with his father and his uncle in Keserwan and shooting his first boar (the story remained famous: it was in the mountains around the Ghineh plateau, Wakim and Elias are a little distance away from the other hunters, and suddenly, there it is, an old male boar backed up against a hedge, snorting and getting ready to charge to force his way through, like a bull in an arena. Wakim doesn't move, his gun is laid across his saddle, he looks at the boar, then at his son, who is waiting, he is barely fifteen, has shot a few quail, a few partridges, a fox cub, but never such a huge boar with its russet coat, and never point-blank, up close, face-to-face, like a duel. He can feel his horse is impatient, alarmed. He holds it firmly, glances at his father, who is looking back at him placidly, as you do when you want someone to know you are waiting and prepared to wait as long as it takes, when in fact there is no time to wait, the boar is grunting, stamping, and obviously preparing to charge. Suddenly realizing that this really is his baptism of fire, that his father will do nothing and would rather let the beast charge than shoot it himself, and that he now has no choice, Elias raises his gun just as the boar is springing forward. The shot resounds throughout the wadi, and continues to echo throughout the mountains long after the struck boar has been thrown back by the blast). Or the memory about Catherine, the oldest daughter, who announces to Wakim one day in the middle of mass that she loves the Farhat son (everyone will always wonder why she did this in the middle of mass, and I think it was to take him unaware, so that he couldn't react too impulsively, as if she had waited for him to have his mouth full at lunchtime to announce she had done something silly in the garden, and so I imagine her, not yet sixteen, proudly going to mass with her father at Saint Michael's, the Maronite church, in a cream-colored dress with a wide belt and a little hat, laughing mischievously, knowing she is Wakim's favorite. Once she gets inside the church, she leads her father to the front row, jostling the peasants in their seroual pants and Sunday jackets, and carves out a place for herself and her father, whose passage sets off a soft roll of whispered salutations, which he responds to with a movement of his lips but no sound, so as not to disturb the service. When they take their places just in front of the altar, she waits, goes through the motions of worship while thinking about something entirely different, opens and shuts her Maronite breviary, even though she is Orthodox, let us not forget that, and finally, when the priest has intoned a recitation from the Gospels and started his sermon, all the while glancing over at Wakim, whose presence so near is an honor, which means that Wakim feels bound hand and foot, unable to react without causing a small scandal, she leans against him, stretches her neck to reach his ear, and announces that she loves George Farhat, and her father, without turning a hair, without so much as blinking, but continuing to stare at the priest as if he were absorbed in the pointless things he was saying, whispers: "Well then, marry him"). Or the memory about the third son, Farid, not yet eight years old, going to Beirut in a buggy one day with Wakim, and witnessing a scene he will never forget (on Cannon Square, in front of the gate of the Hamidiye Garden where the hansom cabs for hire are lined up, a few feet away from the café where Wakim caused his famous fight fifteen or twenty years earlier. The horses are champing at the bit and stamping on the beaten earth of the square. The coachmen are chatting while waiting for their next customer, and then they start making fun of a little julep seller in a skullcap, who had the bad idea of walking past them. One of them grabs the cap, throws it to a second, who throws it to a third, and they keep on teasing him this way while Wakim and his son, who have left their buggy and are on foot, have almost reached the line of cabs. At that point Wakim makes a quarter turn and inexplicably heads toward the carriages. All of the coachmen, abandoning the little julep seller, rush toward him, because he is an extremely elegant gentleman swinging his cane. But he pays no attention to their loud *salaams* and gets into the first cab, then, when the coachman is on his seat, gets back out again and chooses another cab, waits for the coachman to be settled, then gets out again, amid the shouts and invitations from all the others, with his son following him without understanding what is going on, and gets into a third cab. Again, just as the coachman is about to let his horses go, he gets out with his son and cuts all the coachmen's joking short by dramatically rolling a gold mejidieh between his fingers, settles himself and his son into a fourth cab, and waits to see the coachman is seated before getting out again. But this time a crowd has formed around him, the gold piece rolling around and around in his fingers has transformed the laughing banter into cries of allegiance. He gets into a fifth cab that has been graciously brought forward to him, and it is only after the sixth or the seventh time that he gets out for good, puts the gold piece back into his hip pocket, and starts walking toward the gardens under the stifled insults of the coachmen, with his son at his side, his son who has finally understood, and who turns around, sees the triumphant smile of the julep seller, and feels proud).

These are the memories, among others, among many others, that marked the life of the family during that time, such as Gerios Nassar's wedding (yes, Gerios Nassar, with his never-ending muttering and his seven fingers, who comes to Wakim one day to confide something incredible, and Wakim frowns in disbelief and it's clear why, when Gerios brings him his intended, a very pretty woman, and still quite young, a widow who had the weakness to make one or two missteps after the death of her first husband, and to whom Gerios is generously offering a safe haven now that she is chastened, or supposedly chastened, for in fact Gerios is the only one who is convinced that she is in fact, while the rest of the world looks at her dubiously and is sure that she will make a fool out of him, poor man. But not at all, she will never leave the straight and narrow path again, will love Gerios despite—or maybe because of—his seven fingers and his demeanor of a wrathful preacher, and especially because he is generous, brave, and also probably an accomplished lover, and she will give him three children who will grow up with Wakim and Helene's youngest, and Wakim's elder daughters will joyously agree to be bridesmaids at his wedding). Or such as the death of the widow, their grandmother (let us imagine her one last time, regularly coming to see her grandchildren, being received with infinite grace by Helene, whom she loves and who loves her. They are both sitting in the living room, or on the balcony, in the middle of the fabric of their dresses spread out all over the space around them, showing each other their embroidery or crochet, or walking toward the Little House to see Selim while confiding in each other, the mother one day going so far as to tell the whole story about the business with Halim Nassar—a story that has not given her a moment's peace all her life, but now she has her revenge, her son is Halim's equal, his house is even more magnificent, and especially she has grandchildren, and favorites among those grandchildren, the girls of course, the ones she never had herself, who are now her goddaughters, and whom she spoils with little presents and sometimes even big ones, beautiful dresses or jewelry that she buys with the money she obstinately continues to receive from Halim, and receives up until her dying day, a day she is in no hurry to see—let's imagine her being present at the birth of eight out of ten of her grandchildren, starting to feel severe back pain after the birth of the fifth, and leg pain after the birth of the sixth, being brought to see her sons despite her walking sticks and the staircase of the Big House, which is impossible to climb, resisting valiantly, violently, even refusing the very idea of death as long as her brother-in-law Halim is still alive, so as not to give him the pleasure of laying his hands on the house in Marsad, and since Halim is hale and hearty, she battles on, her feet swell, her back tortures her, she gets breathless, but she is tough, toughened by spite, she bends but does not break, until the day when, returning home from Halim's funeral, she gives up the fight on the spot. Within two months, she cedes all the terrain she managed to gain from death over many years with no further resistance, and her eldest grandsons attend her funeral in suits and tarbouches and solemnly follow her coffin). These are the memories, along with many other similar ones that allow me to reconstitute the warp and weft of daily life, the unchanging ways of the world, the long, quiet river of days whose sparkle leaves simple but vivid images in the children's memories—the carpets being beaten at the end of winter, a boy falling into a well and the commotion in the property and all of Ayn Chir, the games with the foals, the days spent among the olive trees, the thorns of the Barbary figs in their fingers, the cicadas they tie up by one leg, the owner's share of the oranges that is distributed to the surrounding farms, the Bedouins bringing goat milk every morning, a wolf that has the audacity to come right up to the foot of the house one winter's night, the horses' screeches from the stables, and the men going out with their guns and lanterns—an entire epoch of which I have always somewhat forlornly tried to distill the essence from the faces, the poses, the clothes, the bearing, and the chosen place of each of the members of the family in the only two photographs where they all appear gathered together around Wakim and Helene.

In the first, there are only eight of them, all in their Sunday best, the boys standing stiffly in tight starched collars, except for the two elder ones, who look more at ease, one of whom has his hand on the shoulder of one of his sisters sitting on a stool. Wakim and Helene are at the back, as in a school photo where the teachers are standing behind the class, with him in a dark suit with a straight mustache, and her in a dress open at the top over a frothy lace blouse. In the second one there are nine of them, in other words the entire family except for Catherine, the eldest daughter, who must be already married, standing around Wakim and Helene, who are sitting in large wicker armchairs, him in an almost white suit and laced boots, his mustache freshly trimmed and slightly turned up, her with a large chignon and in a floral dress billowing all around her. The eldest boy has the assured air of someone who believes he is a lady-killer, the youngest is in a little sailor suit, the girls are in light dresses and stare at the camera lens as if this were a long-acquired habit. But one of them is looking mischievously at the youngest child, the one who will become my father, sitting on Helene's lap, and whose presence shows that this is the beginning of a difficult period, that the time of carefree grandeur is about to come to an end.

Which also means that the great events that marked the history of the Nassar clan at that time have already taken place, events that are part of its mythology as much as everything that preceded them, and which we will need to say a word or two about.

10

WE ARE AT present in the European dining room of Émile Curiel's Villa Eucalypta. Beneath a huge enameled copper chandelier, the table is set with silver soup tureens and large serving dishes of moghrabieh, vine leaves with mutton cutlets, and more kebabs with tomatoes. The wine has been poured into crystal carafes. On the cedarwood sideboard, which is also enameled, there are other silver platters waiting to be served. Seated at the table to honor this spread are Calmette and his wife, the French consul and his dragoman, a Jesuit whose identity has been the subject of controversy for the past hundred years, and a minister of the Mount Lebanon governorate, who might be Tamer Bey, the minister for roads. All these fine people are here dining and talking about eucalyptus trees, the possibility of planting them along the roadsides, the recently discovered antiseptic properties of their leaves, the collapse of the Venice campanile, or the renewal of the Triple Alliance. At around eleven o'clock, the sofragis in white suits clear the last of the silver platters. The guests are waiting for dessert, their napkins on the table, their glasses half empty. Calmette is making his glass tinkle almost imperceptibly with the blade of his silver knife, while his other arm is idly thrown over the back of his chair. The French consul, while playing with his dessert fork, is trying to extort some information from Tamer Bey about the concession obtained by the Germans for the construction of the railway in Baghdad. At that moment the doorbell rings. Two minutes later, Wakim Nassar enters the dining room. He was invited to dinner but announced that he would come only for dessert. He knows Curiel's habits and is right on time. He greets the guests, engages in banter and jokes. He is wearing a light-colored suit and a patterned tie, and is holding a plate covered with a large cloth, as a priest would hold a paten covered with a napkin. He sets it down in the middle of the table, pulls off the cloth like a magician making something miraculous appear, and in fact it is a bit like that, even though no one realizes it just yet. On the plate is a pyramid of small fruits, like oranges, but no bigger than plums. Similar to mandarins, one might say, but with a very smooth peel. They are pretty to look at, these miniature oranges, with their peel gleaming as if it were polished with olive oil, as you do with colored Easter eggs, and their arrangement is very pleasing. Wakim says nothing about what they might be or what they are called, so there is nothing for it but to taste them. The first one to serve himself is the Jesuit, who takes the fruit crowning the pyramid, then Calmette stands up, reaches out, and topples the whole edifice, and the miniature citrus roll all over the table. But that's for the best, since everyone can now pick up whichever one rolls in front of their plate, while the sofragis lean down to rescue those that fall on the Persian carpet. Wakim is sitting on the edge of his seat. With his arms crossed on the tabletop, he observes the guests like a cook waiting for an opinion of a sauce he has just invented to go with meat prepared in the most traditional way. He sees them struggling to remove the peel sticking to the fruit, tells them that it is easier to do it with one's fingers, and demonstrates this, gently separating the segments from each other. Everyone imitates him, bringing the succulent flesh to their mouths, and then a palate revolution takes place, acidity bursts out, immediately balanced by a sweet note, and then there is a slow exhalation of something fragrant, in other words the fruit is stunning and can be enjoyed effortlessly, without the annoyance of any pips, which in oranges and mandarins might release a bitterness that would spoil everything. The Jesuit nods in concentration like an oenologist trying to discern all the subtleties of the bouquet, the consul mutters something and takes a second fruit, and Wakim throws an amused glance at Curiel, like a card player who has just won a good trick, although he has no idea yet of the success that this odd little citrus he has invented will soon have.

One of the features of the new fruit that the Nassar descendants would never brook any disagreement about was the fact that it was a hybrid of the mandarin and the bitter orange, in other words the equivalent of the clementine. That clementines were invented in Ayn Chir, before their so-called official discovery in the garden of an orphanage in Oran by the French Jesuit Clément Rodier, was one of the two or three pillars of faith that all the members of the clan embraced. Some went even further: since the relationships of Émile Curiel and, initially, of Wakim himself with the Jesuits of the Ghazir seminary were excellent, the more informed chroniclers of the Nassar clan decided that the Jesuit who was present that evening at the dinner in Ayn Chir, when the fruit was first presented, was none other than Clément Rodier himself, and that (let's say, on the basis of this snippet of information) he might have met Curiel in Oran, then would inevitably have been invited to Curiel's house during a journey to the Levant, and might have been there exactly on the right evening in order to commit his misdeed.

Unfortunately, I have not found the slightest trace of Rodier in Lebanon. There was, however, a Jesuit in Wakim's entourage at the turn of the century, but his name was Barthélemy. This name, Barthélemy, is part of the onomastic heritage of the Nassar clan. I even remember that my uncles referred to him as Bartélémé, with a strange old-fashioned inflection surviving there in their speech, like those that might have allowed an archaeologist of phonetics to make conjectures about the accent of the inhabitants of Beirut in bygone days, just as historians did about the Romans based on the spelling mistakes in the graffiti in Pompey. When I tried to find out more about this man, my uncles were already dead, and my father could provide no help. Fortunately, my curiosity was satisfied, and in a most unexpected way. It was one evening when I was at a dinner party seated next to a jolly Jesuit father, who spent the whole meal telling morbid or comical anecdotes, like the one about a woman who emigrated to marry a wealthy farmer of Madhya Pradesh and regularly sent tea from their harvest back to her relatives at home, until the day when, in a package of the same kind, her family received her ashes—for she had died and been cremated—which they took to be a new kind of tea and drank a few spoonfuls of infused in boiling water; or the story of the day when he was required to reorganize the cemetery of the Jesuit fathers in Ghazir, and he had gathered together the bones that the earth had mixed up, and reconstituted all the good fathers piece by piece. That was when I stopped laughing and asked him if he knew of a Jesuit from the old days at Ghazir called Father Barthélemy. And this guest, in whom the sugar from dessert was gradually amplifying the effect of the alcohol he had drunk in vast quantities, in the form of an excellent wine from Ksara, set to explaining to me, in a voice a little louder than necessary since I was sitting right beside him, that not only had there been a Father Barthélemy, but he was in fact one of the superiors of the seminary whose bones he had himself carefully gathered together and buried a little distance away from the others, under the clementine trees in the orchard, because Barthélemy was a pharmacologist and botanist, and had taken a particular interest in developing the seminary gardens, and had in fact planted those very clementine trees.

Some time later, I paid a visit to the seminary at Ghazir. I walked through the cool, wide corridors where footsteps echo, I heard doors slam, breezes whisper, and the cries of goatherds rise from the valley. I smelled the soap wafting from the laundries, crossed paths with a Jesuit who nodded without appearing to be troubled by the sight of a civilian in the convent, and finally reached the gardens, where I found orange trees, lemon trees, and two or three magnificent clementine trees, but of the common variety that cannot be proven to be the one Wakim invented. But that was enough to prompt me to take an interest in this Barthélemy, who would in any case become one of Wakim's acquaintances.

It's possible that, the day after the dinner at Villa Eucalypta, he goes with Curiel to visit Wakim. I imagine him as a tall, strong man, like the Jesuit father who told me about the bones, with his neck shrunk into his shoulders, and affected by a gait that gives the impression of a slow meandering, of a permanent struggle to walk straight, which has nothing to do with inebriation, but rather with such a strong focus on things that have nothing to do with the environment of the body, so that his own body seems to follow an itinerary independent of the lines of pathways, tracks, or roads. In the Nassar orange groves, Wakim and Curiel are constantly just about to grab him by the arm for fear of seeing him fall, or they meander along with him, adjusting their pace to his, until Wakim shows them a pathway among the trees and brings the group to a wider furrow, while the Jesuit continues to talk, digressing in his words just as he does in his walk. They finally stop in the middle of the clementine trees, whose size and leaf color stand out in the ocean of orange trees, where they talk, touch, pick, taste, then walk again, and after a detour among the lemons and the abouserras, they come out of the orchard right in front of the Big House, where Barthélemy will soon become a regular guest. He comes back there often, on foot, walking between the mulberry groves and the vegetable gardens, framed by the vast blue mountains behind him, and greeting the tinsmiths and the shoemakers who stop politely on the roadside to watch him pass in his long soutane and inordinately wide-brimmed hat. Sometimes a farmer goes up to him and kisses his hand, bringing it up to his forehead, and sometimes it's a hansom cab heading up to Baabda, and carrying *gentlemen* in suits, that slows down as it goes by him, so as not to drown him in a cloud of dust, and the *gentlemen* doff their tarbouches as they pass. Often, in the evenings, he comes with Curiel. They both stay for dinner, and after dessert, clementines are served, which are tasted and discussed as you would discuss a cognac. Barthélemy makes suggestions about grafting, Wakim offers him cuttings for the seminary garden, they talk about the orange groves in Algeria, after which, while the peelings are spread all over the tablecloth around the dessert plates, each of the men brings out a Havana cigar, which the fragrant acid taste of the clementines irresistibly calls for, and the conversation continues about the nomination of a new mutasarrif, or the inauguration of the first railway station in Beirut, or the assassination of King Alexander of Serbia. After that, the possibility can be entertained that Barthélemy had the idea of writing to his compere Clément Rodier in Oran one day, telling him about the new fruit, then sent him cuttings that would allow the tree and the fruit to spread throughout the world, and therefore the possibility can also be entertained that the origin of the clementine was indeed at Ayn Chir and nowhere else.

Whatever the case, before it was eclipsed by Rodier's clementine, the Ayn Chir clementine knew an uncontestable glory. According to the clan's annals, it was served at the tables of the most upper-class families of Beirut. The mutasarrif of Mount Lebanon was supplied directly by the Nassars for his personal consumption, and the pasha of Acre sent them to his mistress, a married woman from the Haifa bourgeoisie. The khedive of Egypt himself is said to have demanded some from the Syrian officers on his staff, and the sultan to have had some sent to Istanbul for his private dinner receptions, and while I always wondered where one of my aunts got this information, which she always stood by, they were apparently also served at the table of Prince Novarina in Venice. I don't know if this Prince Novarina ever existed, or if my father's sister wasn't confusing Venice with Prague, but it was a clever way to express the wide success of Ayn Chir's new fruit. In any case, I was always firmly convinced that commercializing the fruit was not what was on Wakim Nassar's mind to begin with. Much like an author who writes a little short story of no consequence to amuse himself, and then the thing becomes a novel that everyone wants to get hold of. Let's imagine that everything started with a friendly gesture on his part: the day after the dinner party when the fruit was first presented, he sends a basket of carefully chosen clementines to the French consul and the governorate minster. And it is an instant success. For as soon as there is something on the table of the French consul, it is immediately also on the tables of the consuls of England, Austria, and Russia, who are rivals in everything in this country. And when there is something on the tables of the consuls, it is then found on the tables of the dragomans, who are also influential people, and whatever is on the tables of the dragomans must also be on the tables of the ladies of the Orthodox bourgeoisie, and whatever is on the tables of the Orthodox bourgeoisie, in the mansions on the hill to the east of the city, must also be on the tables of the Sunnite bourgeoisie, in the mansions on the hill to the west of the city, and then it's all set. After which, in accordance with the pyramid structure of the Ottoman administration, clementines appear at the receptions of the mutasarrif, and the following year at those of the pashas, who send some to the sultan. Unless it is a Muslim wholesaler who takes charge of the whole harvest and sells part of it in Egypt and the other part in Constantinople.

Whatever the case, within three years the demand is so strong, even though the fruit is expensive, that new trees must be planted. To make room for them, Wakim buys land at Ayn Chir for the first time, and plants new orange trees there to replace those he tore out to make room for the clementines. He buys one hundred dunams over by Saint Michael's church and two hundred at Furn el-Chebbak, not far from Curiel's eucalyptus plantation. Around 1910, a particularly good harvest brings in huge resources, and it is possible that it was thanks to this income that Wakim was able to build the famous Orthodox church at Ayn Chir, the first in the whole region, and especially that he was able to buy several dozen dunams on the edge of the Damascus road.

But the most resounding result of the invention of the clementine is probably the visit made by the mutasarrif in person. The images of that visit that always come to me are of military boots and side-carried sabers, of insignia and gold braid on puffed chests, of horses lined up in an honor guard all the way to the steps of the Big House, and of a mutasarrif whose vague figure looks more like the emperor of Germany than an Ottoman governor of

Mount Lebanon. In reality, it must have been much more prosaic, so let's imagine the mutasarrif's convoy (it must have been Youssef Pasha or Ohannes Pasha) passing through Ayn Chir one morning, raising a hellish cloud of dust, throwing walkers to the sides of the road and hansom cabs into the ditches. Tamer Bey, seated next to the governor, leans over to say a few words about the Nassar plantations and reminds him of the famous clementines, and three minutes later it's panic stations all over Wakim's property. There are gendarmes everywhere, ministers in black dismounting with folders in their hands, horses shuddering, mustachioed officers shouting orders. Gerios rushes out in alarm to the orchard to find Wakim. Inside the house, Helene runs to the kitchen, comes back to the living room, doesn't know where to put herself, and finally whispers a few instructions to her elder daughters, while onlookers, farm laborers, and passersby are already crowded at the roadside. Finally, Wakim arrives, plucked out from his trees somewhere, and climbs up the front steps with the mutasarrif, a little bearded man in formal dress (not parade dress, no saber, no gold braid, just gold thread at the collar of his jacket, and square-toed shoes) and wearing a kalpak. There is no honor guard but something like a train all the way down the steps behind the two men—of ministers, civil servants, and officers with stiff mustaches—and all these people gather in the large living room of the house. Soon there are men in black suits in all the armchairs, and behind each armchair a civil servant is standing, while a crowd of officers, secretaries, but also of farmers from Ayn Chir who have rushed there for the occasion, is pressed together all the way to the front door, the porch, and the steps. And in the midst of all this, there is Wakim in his work clothes and Helene in a simple dress, her hair barely tied up, and between the two of them the mutasarrif with his gold thread. And all this hullabaloo for what? To talk about clementines. It seems bizarre, but this is how tradition has it, and I must respect that. So they talk about clementines, but the mutasarrif does not speak the local language well (whether it's Youssef Pasha or Ohannes Pasha makes no difference), but speaks Turkish and adds in a few Arabic words here and there, and Wakim does exactly the opposite, and all this doesn't get them very far. The members of the mutasarrif's suite bide their time, talking discreetly among themselves, or observing the living room with its enormous pieces of furniture, and the vast, almost palatial carpet on which they are standing, whispering to each other until this is all over. Finally, something happens at the epicenter of the event, which is communicated to the entire assembly as the mutasarrif straightens up in his armchair and Wakim does too. An imperceptible current flows through the room, everyone moves and is preparing to get up, but then, as if a silent order to the contrary has been given from nowhere and passed along through looks, raised eyebrows, or pinched lips, the movement halts, and the ministers, officers, and civil servants who were extracting themselves from their armchairs finally do not stand up, but remain on the edge of their seats, while the mutasarrif and Wakim do stand up, and walk over together toward the balcony, where Wakim shows the governor his orchards, explains one way or another about the distribution of the different varieties, indicates the boundaries of his property, the line on the horizon where the Pine Forest appears. The mutasarrif nods and smooths his little beard, makes promises and assurances about releasing funds to support agriculture and encourage the production of citrus, but Wakim doesn't believe a word of it, he knows all about the governorate's debts to the Ottoman treasury, just as everyone does, and also all about the venality and the corruption by power of governors. But he expresses his gratitude, then they come back inside, and this time everyone does stand up, and everything happens in reverse motion, they move back from the living room into the garden, and as the convoy leaves the property in a flurry of shouts, barked orders, and martially stamping hooves, it passes through an even greater crowd of people pressed together on the road, some of whom are so impressed by the pomp and ceremony that they start clapping, and one or two tarbouches are raised, and one or two caps thrown in the air, and soon the convoy starts up again at a gallop and disappears into the dust.

As for Wakim, let's be novelistic about this, or better yet, let us dabble in antiquity, and have him return directly to his clementines.

11

FOR A NUMBER of reasons, linked both to the farmers' high levels of indebtedness and to their involvement in a vast and traditional system from which it is never easy to extricate oneself, Ayn Chir placed its trust in the cultivation of mulberry trees up until the very last moment, and fully converted to orange trees only from 1920 onward. And yet it is certain that as early as 1910 or 1911 some farmers started extensively planting orange trees, tearing out the old mulberry trees or making space for them in their olive or fig plantations, taking their inspiration from the model presented by Wakim Nassar, whose success they could see and probably envied for the material comforts and prosperity it brought. Wakim Nassar, without any possible doubt, became a sort of capital contemporary man in the eyes of the inhabitants of Ayn Chir. I tend to believe that he may have even been considered a capital contemporary man at the Topkapi Palace, when a royal concubine peeled one of his clementines, or at the Abdeen Palace in Cairo on a similar occasion, or even in that Novarina palace in Venice or Prague. But in any case, let us stay in Ayn Chir. And in Ayn Chir, Wakim is the object of admiration and envy of all the inhabitants. He has one of the grandest houses in the surrounding area, a luxurious lifestyle, and a wife who dresses so elegantly. The farmers sigh in his huge living room as they admire the carpets, which they consider so fine that a king of Persia would have hung them on the walls rather than let them be trampled underfoot. He has a buggy in which he goes to Beirut every morning with one or other of his children, his shoes are from France, his hunting rifles from America, his children go to the Zahret El-Ihsan School, he has shares in a project for a paper factory with Curiel, stocks in the Ottoman Bank and the Beirut Tramway Company, he lends money to his friends with no interest, he gave money to Rached for him to buy a plot of land at Baabda, he helped Malkoun buy his first twenty orange trees, and paid off the debts of a farmer at Furn el-Chebbak. He is a man about whom people say with pride that they shook his hand when they met him on the road in the morning. Some are convinced, but wrongly, that he has become a close ally of the mutasarrif, and friends with the French consul. When he enters a farm where condolences are being received, all the men present stand up, and when anyone passes by on the road near his house, they try to see if there is anyone on the balcony or the front steps, and then make up all sorts of stories from these minute details of daily life on the property. It is to be expected that a man with all this harvest gathered up would want to turn it into something exceptional, and that Wakim Nassar has started looking further, higher, in other words why not, for example, to the Majlis Millet and a seat next to the bishop. Everything that he has achieved until now, quietly, slowly, is like those deposits of black oil, slowly accumulated over the course of millennia, that men transform into energy and burn in an instant for their greater glory.

To achieve this goal, Wakim soon has a golden opportunity: the battle for the succession of his uncle Halim on the majlis. This battle, however, is not one that he participates in, no doubt because he thinks that it is too soon, that his position is not yet strong enough. This must be around 1908, and you might think, why not, that certain influential members of the family are considering him as a candidate and coming to make their case to him about it. But he doesn't budge, and lets Gebran Nassar be elected. Unless he has a plan. At his mother's death, Wakim freely lets Gebran have all the last possessions that the widow actually no longer owned, and thus completely disengages himself from Marsad, calculating that, from now on, he will wage his battle from Ayn Chir. Ayn Chir is in Mount Lebanon and even though there are not many Orthodox inhabitants there, there are still quite a few of them, and their affairs are managed by the Beirut members of the majlis. Maybe his idea was to demand a seat for Mount Lebanon from the bishop, then claim it for himself, after which he would set out on the conquest of the traditional Nassar seat. At least that's how I always imagined it went. And that would actually explain why in 1907 or 1908 he started spending insane amounts of money, playing the philanthropist and major donor in the Orthodox community, which all led to the construction of the famous Orthodox church at Ayn Chir.

However, let's be honest, that's not exactly how the annals of the clan record the origin of the construction of that church. But the memory of the Nassar clan is cluttered with stories and anecdotes that are only secondary facts, to which the causes of serious events are nevertheless attributed, in the exact same way that, in mythology, the abduction of a woman is recorded as the cause of the ten years of war between Troy and Greece. The imagination of the members of the Nassar clan, which often tended to record and understand anecdotic facts rather than the play of slowly working forces, forever imputed the construction of the Orthodox church to an insult inflicted on Wakim Nassar by the Maronite priest of Ayn Chir. It is not the accuracy of the fact that I am contesting here, but only its significance, in the same way that, without casting any doubt on the assassination of Franz-Ferdinand, one is not necessarily compelled to see it as the underlying cause of the First World War.

According to the annals of the clan, it is on a Sunday when Helene and Blanche, her second daughter, are attending mass that this priest gives a sermon where he makes disagreeable remarks about *our Orthodox brothers,* citing one or two criticisms on points of dogma that no one understands, maybe not even he himself. Nobody could ever give the slightest explanation for his attitude. It may have been religious zeal, he may have had a dream about the Virgin or Saint Thecla, who told him some nonsense about the Orthodox people, or he may have read a few books on the nastiness of the Byzantine empire toward the Maronites in the year 1000, and decided to exact revenge. It may have been entirely personal, maybe he had a sore back that day and was angry at all of creation, or Helene had smiled or whispered to her daughter during his sermon, which had annoyed him. Or maybe it was something more important, such as revenge for the fact that Wakim had gotten a piece of land for a good price, one that he, the priest, had his eye on for his nephew. Whatever the case, after the sermon he refuses to give Communion to the two Nassar women, who have walked up humbly, with their embroidered scarves delicately covering their hair, to the foot of the chalice he is holding. This is talked about in all the farmhouses for the rest of that Sunday, and Helene tells Wakim about it. According to official historiography, Wakim immediately buys a piece of land at an exorbitant price and with no further ado has an Orthodox church built on it, the first one in Ayn Chir and one of very few in Mount Lebanon, just so that his wife can go pray undisturbed. It sounds a little abrupt, but that is how the chronicles of the clan record the fact, and it was always understood that the church was built in the snap of a finger and thumb: snap, there it is, a little thickset, almost square, with its feet in its Maronite neighbors' vegetable gardens, which are immediately also bought up to make a fine esplanade. There is a little onion dome on top of the bell tower and a stone cupola covering part of the esplanade. Wakim has a Russian icon painter come and paint some marvelous icons for him, he spends a fortune on the iconostasis, and after that Helene and her daughters can go pray there in peace.

It all sounds rather idyllic, wonderfully fine and chivalrous, but it doesn't make any sense, because you can't just build a church as you would a bakery or a forge. You have to get involved in a whole complex universe of dioceses and eparchies and hierarchies, of land to be consecrated and priests to be nominated, and in any case all of that depends on the authority of one person in particular, namely the bishop. Precisely. Therefore, if the whole story about the Maronite priest is true, it was only what provided the first impetus. And so now we have Wakim engaging in negotiations with the bishopric, with the priests and archimandrites who are treasurers, assistant secretaries, and general secretaries of everything you can imagine in a civil hierarchy, but with great big Byzantine crosses hanging down around their necks and their hair tied up in buns under their headgear. After which Wakim at last meets the bishop himself, with the pendant icons, crosses, and imperial insignia making a delicate little metallic tinkling music on his chest, and it is a well-known fact that the two of them are soon on close terms. Let us also not forget the majlis, the council for the management of the community's civil affairs, whose members are the most eminent representatives of the Orthodox bourgeoisie, the richest men in the country, and to whom Wakim's donation is officially presented. It is likely that the majlis seriously considered the risk of irritating the Maronites by building an Orthodox church at Ayn Chir, and that they finally charged the committee for relationships with other religions with the task of carrying out a survey. At the next council meeting, these gentlemen listen to a report given by an archimandrite, an eparch, or by one of the members, and this is how they come to the discovery—as if it were of the survival of a population believed to have disappeared in an unknown corner of the world—that there are indeed Orthodox people in Kfarshima, Furn el-Chebbak, Dekwaneh, and Baabda, not very many of them, to be sure, but who do need to be taken into account, and who have no church in which to congregate, which obliges them to attend Maronite or Greek-Catholic churches. Once it is put to the vote, Wakim's donation is then accepted *with gratitude,* and from then onward, okay of course, we get the construction of the church, the assembly of the iconostasis, and the invoice for the icons. But after that, and before Helene can go there to pray, there is still the inauguration to come, in the presence of the bishop and the entire majlis, whose members all come out in force, determined to prove that Mount Lebanon is part of its jurisdiction. And once again, we must imagine a whole to-do, with a procession, three knocks on the door of the church by the bishop, hymns, the smell of incense, ribbons on the mulberry trees lining the pathway, the Orthodox bell ringing for the first time above the Maronite vegetable gardens and mulberry orchards of Ayn Chir, and there in the midst of all that, Wakim, who is now incontestably very much in the public eye. The expenses incurred for the church are such that the members of the majlis, the bishop, and the crowd look at Wakim with a mixture of curiosity and admiration.

To say that he is now very much in the public eye is something that we can therefore take literally: he has made himself *visible*. He already was, for the people of Ayn Chir, for the Nassars and the Orthodox community of Marsad, but now he has become noteworthy for people with far more influence, and in a way he will now never cease to be in the public eye; he will be drawn into a spiral of *visibility* such that it will be considered by his descendants as the principal cause of his premature end.

But we are not at that point yet. According to the archives of the bishopric of Beirut, the church of Saint George at Ayn Chir was inaugurated in the spring of 1912. That autumn, the Italian navy bombs Beirut. There is no obvious relationship between these two events, but in the Nassar history, it is quite clear: the business with the Italian warships enhances Wakim's visibility. For when King Victor-Emmanuel's vessels open fire on Beirut, the salvos of shells that hit the Ottoman Bank, the Orosdi-Back department store, and a whole series of other buildings, taking down entire facades, sections of walls, and whole stalls in the souks (and the booming can be heard at Ayn Chir, the windows of the Big House imperceptibly vibrate, and Gerios Nassar, who is in his vegetable garden, says to himself, "Here comes an earthquake," while the passersby on the road stop and turn to look toward the Pine Forest, above which slowly rise first one, then two, then three long, lazy clouds of smoke, like indecipherable signs of what is happening in Beirut), so when the Italian ships launch their successive salvos, and inevitably after that the Muslim crowds, once they have recovered from the shock and the near paralysis of impotence and the desire for revenge, rush to the European stores in the city, then go after the Christians in Western dress, then Christians in general, and when the inhabitants of Marsad and Msaytbeh, faced with their age-old enemies, take up arms and their men climb up onto the rooftops of the houses to shoot anyone on sight and discourage any attempt at trespass (and the whole city is in chaos, the shots can soon be heard in Ayn Chir, and Wakim, who is on his way home from Curiel's house, can make out the bangs but cannot determine where they came from), when all this degenerates, then, the first refugees appear on the road to Ayn Chir, at the edge of the Pine Forest. And this is where Wakim Nassar, despite himself, will move his pawns forward on the board. He is obviously not the kind of man to profit from others' misfortunes—his story and his end show that well enough—quite the contrary, nor to flourish on the ground of misery. But let us just say that the events worked in his favor.

When the refugees arrive, on foot, on horseback, in carts, haggard and loaded with bundles, they settle all over the fields and on the roadsides as if they were there for a picnic, or as if it were only a question of a few hours before they can return home. But night falls and the gunshots are still ringing out, the people are still coming on foot from Marsad or Msaytbeh and telling of deserted streets, of pillaging and shootings, and soon it becomes clear that they will need to spend the night out of doors. And that is where the Nassars intervene. Not because the overwhelming majority of refugees are Orthodox, but because you can't just stand there doing nothing while there are improvised camps being set up beside the mulberry groves and the vegetable gardens. At the start of the evening, Wakim and his two elder sons launch a campaign with Selim and Gerios. The property is opened up for the families. The women and young children are welcomed into the Big House and the Little House, Helene gives up her bed to a pregnant woman, and the bedroom of her elder sons to two slightly bewildered old men. All of the reserves from the kitchens are brought out and distributed, it's action stations everywhere, a state of emergency on Wakim's land, while he has gone to Saint George to have it opened up by the priest, who is more or less at his command, to shelter a few families there. All of this continues the following day, when the wounded start arriving from Marsad. A doctor is called to the Big

House, Wakim makes the rounds of the refugees taken in by the Maronite farmers and promises to take care of all the expenses involved. A distribution of food and supplies is carried out by the Nassars, who have all rolled up their sleeves, and Wakim's elder daughters, my oldest aunts whom I hardly knew, retained a strong memory of these three days of mobilization, of bustling activity and exalted agitation, of which they passed down an account to their descendants.

But what they didn't realize at the time was that this compassionate battle that they were waging alongside their father would be ten times more useful than any electoral campaign for his ambition to serve on the majlis. For when it is all over and done with, when the Turkish troops finally decide to intervene to reestablish order, when the refugees finally return home, the people of Marsad, Msaytbeh, and Bachoura feel enormous gratitude toward Wakim. His name starts to sound like the snap of a hoisted flag in all their conversations, haloed with respect and reverence. I myself often heard my father and his brothers tell each other with emotion forty years later how they met such and such an old man from Marsad who suddenly took great affection to them when he found out that they were the sons of Wakim Nassar. The very existence of Wakim, in his house with the high windows, became like a gold coin on a stony path, a lighthouse in the midst of the rocks. During the two years that followed, hurtling toward the disaster of the Great War like a blindman's bluff player toward an abyss, people from Marsad and thereabouts would often go find him at Ayn Chir for anything and everything, a favor, a helping hand with the bureaucracy, for one thing or another. And that is how Wakim, by agreeing to listen to all requests without balking, by working to obtain a place for one man in the waqf, or a consultation with Calmette at his own cost for another, widens the ever-growing circle of his allies, and steps with both feet onto his cousin Gebran's territory. Obviously two people are never too many to help others, but not two Nassars. It's a question of principle. There can be only one head on the body of the clan. If there are two, then there is one too many, and that means war.

This Gebran Nassar, whom we abandoned fairly early on in this account, when he was still a snobbish young man living in the shadow of his father, Halim, and blithely taking advantage of his fortune, riding in his coupé, indulging his passion for fine horses, hunting, and women, was generally disliked by the inhabitants of Marsad for his haughty tone of voice and his way of treating all the other Nassars as his vassals. He might now appear to have been softened by life's pleasures, were it not for a streak of violence in his character that sometimes shows itself, albeit intermittently, notably when he is charged with certain tasks by Halim, such as calling in debts or share payments of farm tenancies. He then shows himself to be pitiless, calling on some of those plebian Nassars who have put themselves in his father's service to go teach a lesson to an indocile tenant or to ransack the home of an insolvent creditor. According to the Nassar chronicles, these actions were always disapproved of by Halim, who, while being no more lenient, was in favor of less abrupt methods except in extreme circumstances. However, around 1906 or 1907, Halim retires and leaves the management of all his assets to his son. Gebran in the meantime has married a Fayyad, who brought him the support of part of that family of wealthy traders, whose assets he will also start managing with the same firmness.

As the years go by, he adopts less summary methods in his dealings with people, which doesn't mean he becomes any gentler. But he takes care of his reputation, his father is getting older, and he has the succession on the majlis in his sights. His character seems to lose its sharp edges, he is more affable and patient, he greets the people he meets on the roads, and stops from time to time to say a few kind words to a craftsman at Marsad sitting in his doorway. But of course, all this has its price. When he lends money, he increases the interest, and if he is patient with his tenant farmers, it is only to extract a greater share from them later, or, if their dues have accumulated, to evict them, but legally, under the serene cover of the law, in other words not through the intermediary of Hanna or Nicholas Nassar but that of the Ottoman gendarmerie. Accordingly, when his father dies and the battle is waged for succession on the majlis, he is surprised to see his right to the seat contested by his uncle Farid Nassar. He reacts with violence, although I've never been able to find out exactly what happened that led to such an irremediable rift between the two branches of the family. Maybe it was threats, or blackmail, or the partisans of Gebran armed with sticks and knives coming to make their adversaries listen to reason, after which Gebran intervenes to bring back calm and thus passes as the champion of family peace. Once that is accomplished, he becomes a member of the majlis, then a little later, in around 1912, he is nominated to the city council, which manages Beirut's affairs alongside the pasha, and this gives him even more power. On a photograph preserved by his descendants, you can see Gebran Nassar standing wearing a light suit, a lavaliere, and square-toed boots. He is leaning on his elbow against a studio tree trunk and holding a cane in his hand. His whole person seems to exude an inflexible strength of character. When you look more closely, however, there is also something in his eyes and his smile that is imperceptibly intolerant, some kind of impatience—perhaps directed at the photographer, who might have had to try twice to get the shot right—that is reflected in his expression, like a wave that spread for a few seconds and was caught by the photograph, giving his whole face a disturbing, even rather cruel aspect.

According to Gebran Nassar's descendants, this photograph dates from 1913. That is approximately the date I am giving to the beginning of the conflict between Gebran and Wakim that ends up becoming an open war. The two men have known each other since childhood but never been able to stand each other. Gebran has long despised Wakim, whom he considered a poor cousin, but then he starts treating him with more consideration when he sees his situation improving. But Wakim stays firm, which ends up making Gebran more rigid toward him, and up until the start of the conflict that's how things stay, immobilized in a kind of non-bellicose status quo. Which never prevents the two men from meeting at family gatherings in Marsad, at weddings or funerals, from talking or conferring sometimes as the recognized clan chiefs, but without going so far as to become friendly. When the inauguration of the church of Saint George at Ayn Chir takes place, Gebran comes along with all the other members of the majlis and walks beside Wakim throughout all the processions, whispering comments to his cousin during the mass, while his wife does the same with Helene, as if the Nassars were allied and united in everything. And yet, at that moment Gebran must have sensed the danger. He must have felt the erosion of his influence as his followers left him and started to turn to Ayn Chir. My father and his brothers always recalled how the Big House was invaded by people from Marsad and Msaytbeh, but also from Baabda and Kfarshima, coming to ask for an intervention to decrease the tax for exemption from military service, or a position in the civil service for an unemployed son, or this or that.

After a while this all starts to get on Gebran Nassar's nerves. He becomes bitter when Wakim is mentioned to him, he picks fights with his cousin's friends at the meetings of the majlis or the city council. When Gebran meets Wakim at family gatherings or weddings, he treats him with disdain, makes nasty remarks in passing, and leaves without saying goodbye to him. Soon it is Wakim who leaves without saying goodbye and it becomes a real falling-out. In response, Gebran Nassar starts threatening the Orthodox people of Marsad and Msaytbeh who turn to his cousin for help rather than to him. He comes to present his condolences without a sorrowful or compassionate smile at the funeral reception of a family that he knows had recourse to Wakim to place one of their sons in the Damascus Road Company, and leaves without even drinking the bitter coffee, in an obvious show of displeasure. During the Easter celebrations, he refuses to receive a visit from members of the Nassar clan who went to ask Wakim for help to pay for a barn or to find work for a member of their family. And then, one day, he opens the hostilities. His thugs, led by Hanna Nassar, collar an inhabitant of Marsad for whom Wakim had obtained a loan at the Ottoman Bank the previous day, slam him up against a wall in a lane, and give him a serious beating, without providing any explanation or answering any of his questions. All of Marsad is disturbed by this, although no one understands what it is all about; there is talk of a settling of scores over unpaid debts or women. Wakim, to whom this is reported, is dubious for he knows his man, who has neither debts nor a bad reputation. Then three days later it is Gerios Nassar himself who is ambushed by Gebran's men one evening as he is returning from Ayn Chir. They wait for him at the edge of the Pine Forest, pounce on him, and although he struggles and fights back, thumping one in the eye, emasculating the other, breaking the nose of a third, he succumbs under the numbers, and as he falls, he hears Hanna Nassar advise him not to set foot in Marsad again but to stay in Ayn Chir if he loves Maronite peasants so much.

The next day, Wakim goes to see Gerios, in Marsad. He finds neighbors there, Nassar clan members and allies, who have all come for news of the wounded man and fall quiet when Wakim enters the room. When he comes out of Gerios's bedroom and sits down with the visitors, who all have shocked or solemn expressions, he calls over one or two Nassars whom he knows he can trust, asks questions about the ambush laid for Gerios, listens to their account, and nods. Then he reflects while nibbling at his upper lip or holding his cane by both ends, folding it and unfolding it and watching the wood straighten and bend. And what he says to himself is that he cannot stand idly by, because to do so would be to show unpardonable weakness, and anyhow leaving this unpunished would be a failure of solidarity and friendship toward Gerios. Perhaps he thinks about the Ottoman gendarmes, but that makes him laugh to himself. Then he sighs, stands up, and just as someone rushes to bring him his tarbouche, one of the two Nassars that he called over, let's say it is Mitri Nassar, asks him in a whisper what he wants them to do. And Wakim, setting his tarbouche on his head, replies:

"You know perfectly well what you have to do, Mitri."

And when Mitri, to be quite sure that he has understood, and to avoid any disastrous misinterpretations, asks whether they need to make sure that Hanna and his friends know they are not the sole masters at Marsad, "That's right, isn't it, Wakim?," Wakim doesn't answer, goes out onto the front porch, and, before going down the few steps toward his buggy, turns around and says to Mitri:

"That's right, unless you want Hanna and his friends to start ruling your lives."

Three days later, Hanna Nassar is stopped on a path in Bachoura going up to Marsad. In full view of several passersby and a veiled Muslim woman, he gets beaten up, tries to defend himself, recognizes his attackers, shouts oaths and promises of terrible revenge, and ends up in the dust, just as badly off as Gerios was a few days earlier. Two days later, before Hanna's friends have the time to react, Nicholas Nassar, Gebran's other thug, is encircled by four men right in the middle of a lane in Marsad and unceremoniously given a thrashing. In the following days, all the Orthodox men of Marsad seem to be jubilating under their mustaches, their faces widen in pleasure, they exchange news discreetly but could almost dance for joy, since Hanna and Nicholas are known as dreadful bullies.

Just as Wakim did a week earlier, Gebran Nassar comes to visit the wounded, and as he leaves Nicholas's house, he comes up with a plan. The very next day, he starts working on a proposal to impose taxes on fruit coming from the mutasarrifate, notably those that transit through the port of Beirut or its warehouses before leaving for Egypt or Damascus. The goal is clear. By raising unsurmountable customs barriers to the trade in oranges, he hopes to strike at the very roots of Wakim's fortune. Of course, things are not that simple, but he works toward this goal with the wali Hazim Bey and his own colleagues at the city council. Every time he meets the wali at a dinner party, he talks to him about money, about the inherent rights of the vilayet of Beirut, about the share of their common interests that he, the wali, should receive—their common interests being, for his part, putting that insolent relative in his place, and for the wali's, seeing his personal fortune grow—etcetera. Hazim Bey, who became the wali of Beirut only in order to enrich himself while waiting to be nominated, once his fortune is made, as ambassador in Paris or Vienna, or Berlin, or even as a minister in Istanbul, in short, the wali ends up letting Gebran Nassar know that all this is very fine, that one could take the appropriate steps, but, in the end, what would you, Gebran Nassar, give me in return for doing you this favor, for in fact, let us be clear (and we must imagine the wali, resplendent in his tailcoat embroidered with gold thread, at a formal dinner given by Selim Bustros, telling Gebran all his thoughts about this), when all is said and done, dear Gebran (which he pronounces "Gibron," closing all the vowels of his interlocutor's name), when all is said and done, let us be clear (and he drags this out on purpose, lengthening his sentence, keeping Gebran in suspense as he walks along beside him to seek a little more discretion, while the pasha takes a petit four from a platter held out by a servant, greets a lady whose hand he kisses, then comes back to the subject at hand), when all is said and done, let us be clear, there is still some risk involved, there are people who will not like this (and he knows there will also be whispers, and side conversations, and visits and gifts from those who won't like it, and that is just fine with him, but he pretends not to know this, and to be trying to run with the hare and hunt with the hounds, whereas he actually has both the hare and the hounds in his pocket, and it's just a question of who will offer him more than the other), so you understand, I need to know, don't I, just what is in it for me, because (more petits fours, more hand kissing, with a *good evening* here, and a *how are you dear Monsieur So-and-so* there) because, you know, I would not like this to provoke any conflict among the members of the city council.

And of course, Gebran is prepared for all of this. He listens to the wali, smiles, takes a petit four himself, also kisses a lady's hand, and is feeling calm, then three days later, a magnificent little padlocked coffer containing five thousand gold mejidiehs hidden in a fruit basket leaves his house in Marsad for the governor's palace. It is carried there by Ramez Nassar, one of his right-hand men, and as Gebran Nassar gets dressed in the morning, adjusting the knot in his tie over his detachable collar, smoothing down his mustache, and attaching the buckles of his suspenders to his pants before the mirror in his bedroom, he imagines Ramez speaking haughtily to the wali's soldiers on guard duty and to his majordomos, then him entering Hazim Bey's apartments, and he imagines the look on Hazim Bey's face as he sees the basket of fruit, then as he discovers the coffer, and finally Ramez's shining eyes as he hopes for a gratuity. He imagines all this as he puts on his jacket, then his tarbouche. Then he adjusts his watch in his fob pocket, rings a bell for his carriage to be prepared, and goes out, for he has a council meeting. But he is greatly surprised, when he arrives at the palace, not to be more warmly received by the wali, who does not stand up from his armchair when he enters the room, and who doesn't mention the customs tax even once during the whole meeting. At one point when the council is discussing an issue to do with the cultivation and transportation of watermelons, Gebran Nassar, making the most of the analogy between the two topics, asks for permission to speak, but the wali does not allow him to do so, and when the meeting is adjourned, Gebran is convinced that Hazim Bey did not receive the coffer. He rushes home and has Ramez Nassar sent for from his house in Msaytbeh. But when he is told that no one has seen Ramez since that morning, he goes into a terrible rage that no one can understand, not his children, nor his wife, nor his staff, and he is convinced that his right-hand man has made off with the money.

But that would be too easy. Ramez Nassar didn't steal anything at all, he was merely the victim of a secret war he knew nothing about. For, from the very moment Gebran tried to destroy his cousin Wakim by attacking the orange trade, he was also facing Wakim's allies, those dealers who bought his oranges and clementines every year at exorbitant prices. Let us imagine them, those two Muslim gentlemen, one of whom is called Sabri Bey and the other Amer Bey. They come from two ancient Sunnite families, and like many of their coreligionists from the upper classes, they dress in European fashion. Sabri Bey even has a monocle that he always drops at the opportune moment. Amer Bey has a short mustache that doesn't cover all of his upper lip and gives his mouth an air of disdain and constant contempt that he makes up for by often laughing heartily. Each of them owns a palace on the western hills; their wives invite their Orthodox friends to afternoon tea and cakes on the terraces of their houses looking out over the sea. They are members of the Sunnite community assemblies, are close to the mufti of the city, and accompany him when he makes courtesy calls on the bishop. They have tenanted farms at the end of the Beirut peninsula, and some of them border on Gebran Nassar's land, which should bring them closer to each other. And then the two men, besides their shares in the Ottoman Bank, the Tramway Company, and the Electricity Company, are also important wholesalers. Every year, they collectively buy up the harvests from the large landowners of the Beqaa and Sidon regions, and their hired men keep a stranglehold on the Beirut market halls, terrorize all the stallholders in the old town, and are able to mobilize the entire population inside the city walls, and then to calm it down again, at the mere snap of their fingers. Or at least that's how I see things, and if we allow this, then we must also allow that Sabri Bey and Amer Bey are no small players; quite the contrary. And those fearsome players, who have spies all the way into the wali's palace, have heard of Gebran Nassar's dealings, and this is a very serious matter for them, because by trying to destroy Wakim, Gebran would place huge restrictions on the whole trade in fruit and vegetables.

And so, the day before Ramez Nassar disappears, Sabri Bey arrives at Ayn Chir in his carriage and asks to speak to Wakim privately. The two men sit down together in a corner of the living room and Sabri Bey explains the situation to Wakim. He is calm but is constantly dropping his monocle. He is so well dressed that Wakim, in a brief moment of distraction, searches his memory for the name of the tailor where Sabri Bey has his suits made. Finally, in response to one of Wakim's questions, Sabri Bey explains that it takes at least ten thousand gold mejidiehs to win over the wali:

"I'll give a third, Amer Bey another third, and you have to give a third for it to be equal. Otherwise Gebran will win. And then all we can hope for is a new wali. And that would just be wishful thinking."

After an hour of counting and recounting, Wakim agrees and brings out the money, then after another hour, when he is showing Sabri Bey to the bottom of the front steps as he climbs back into his carriage, Wakim hears him ask:

"If things turn sour and we need to settle scores with men on the ground, you'll be with us, won't you?"

"What settling of scores are you talking about?" Wakim asks. "We are buying off the wali, and that's that."

"Wakim, you know your cousin Gebran. He is capable of starting street warfare."

Wakim thinks for a moment, then smiles at the thought that Hanna and Nicholas Nassar are out of action.

"Nothing will happen. Do not be concerned, Sabri Bey."

"Answer my question, Wakim. If anything should happen, are you with us or against us?"

It is obviously difficult for an Orthodox man to declare himself an ally of a Sunnite against another Orthodox man, especially if that Orthodox man is in fact his cousin. But in the split second after that challenge, Wakim thinks of his own interests first. And he replies, as he slams the door of the carriage shut:

"I am with you, Sabri Bey."

When Sabri Bey returns home, he calls up all his most faithful men, the chiefs of the vegetable market and the wholesale warehouses, as well as two neighborhood chiefs, to whom he gives strict orders. The next day, Ramez Nassar falls into an ambush set by their men. When Sabri Bey arrives at the council meeting, he has already been informed about this. During the meeting he has an idea that makes him shudder in horror and he no longer dares to look at Gebran Nassar. Two hours later, when Gebran is at home fulminating against his right-hand man, he is told that a cart loaded with watermelons is at the foot of the porch with a demand that it be unloaded. Gebran is so stunned by the stupidity of the request that he regains his calm, then he is suddenly overcome by grave misgivings, and he goes out onto the porch, where to everyone's astonishment, he orders for the cart to be unloaded, right there and then, in front of him. And there, standing on his front porch, his face fixed, his eyes black, surrounded by his confused servants, he sees the workmen from the market hall tip up the cart, and in the middle of the enormous watermelons tumbling down, rolling around, bumping into each other, some splitting open and splashing others with their flesh, in the middle of the watermelons rolling on the ground in front of his three front steps, along with hundreds of gold mejidieh coins that are thus being returned to sender, Gebran sees, also rolling to his feet, the bloodied head of Ramez Nassar.

12

FOR ALL OF Wakim's children, without exception, the decisive moment in his history is the time when the conscription dodgers and deserters from the Ottoman army started arriving on the family property in Ayn Chir. According to the most well-known version of these events, the deserters always arrived at night. They would appear in the orchards like haggard ghosts, chased by the Ottoman soldiers and announced by the dogs' howling and occasionally by gunshots, then they would climb the steps of the Big House or the Little House, and go inside to ask for shelter. All of Wakim's children told this memory to their descendants, such that it became one of the elements of the family heritage that was most shared by the members of the clan, even between distant cousins and descendants who knew nothing of each other, exactly as the different populations of a great race dispersed over several continents are unaware that they are all still telling the same stories of the same gods and the same heroes. Of course, among the different versions, variations would appear, an unknown detail here, a slight divergence there. One such detail that always fascinated me, but which doesn't figure in all the versions, is the fact that Wakim, as soon as he heard the dogs and the gunshots in the night, would rush out to the orchards with a rifle on his shoulder to meet the fugitive, accompanied by Gerios, Selim, and sometimes one of his sons carrying a lantern. However, one of the details that all the versions share is the fact that as soon as the fugitive was found (whether this was in the middle of the orchards plunged in uncanny darkness, full of cracking twigs, rustling wings, and rallying cries, or in the house once the fugitive had entered), Wakim would put him under his protection and have him whisked away to a hiding place before setting about giving the yuzbashi a good dressing-down, reminding him in no uncertain terms that his troops were standing on Nassar land, that this land was inside the boundaries of Mount Lebanon, that Mount Lebanon was an autonomous region, and that their presence there was therefore supremely illegal.

Long before I started to take a serious interest in Wakim's life, but when I already knew these stories just like everyone else, and asked the one of my uncles who was most likely to remember them about some of their details, he explained that the residents of the city of Beirut had been exempted from military service in the Ottoman army for fifty years, but that when the empire entered the war in 1914 and mobilized its troops, the exemption was lifted and Arab, Christian, or Muslim subjects were enrolled in the sultan's army for the first time. According to that uncle, it was during the short period from the date of the mobilization (late 1914) to the date of the entry of the Turkish troops of Generalissimo Djemal Pasha into Mount Lebanon (early 1915) that these well-known events took place. Until its occupation, Mount Lebanon had benefited from considerable autonomy and served as a safe haven for conscription dodgers. My uncle Farid, with whom I discussed all this at some length, was the one who told me the episode of the carriages that he witnessed one day as he accompanied his father to Beirut. He would later be known as the scandalous uncle, whose story is yet to come. At the time when I talked to him about this, he was already very old, but still solid, temperamental, extremely obstinate, and incapable of changing any of his ideas. He was still incredibly handsome, refined, and elegant, even when wearing his dressing gown, and it was his elegance that inspired me when talking about Wakim's. Despite having impulses that made me think of him as being similar to the character of the Baron de Charlus from my reading, he adulated me less as an uncle and more like a grandfather, and I could push hard in my arguments with him without him ever getting upset, which my father always considered rather suspiciously, as if he wondered why his brother, who could be so friendly and loving, wasn't like that more often, and why not with everyone. In any case I regret not having been more insistent that day when we talked about what happened with the fugitives, for I didn't get another chance to discuss it with him, and when I started writing Wakim's story, he was already dead. I do in fact have a few reservations about his version of the events, notably about the relatively short span of time in which he set them, which does not agree with the insistence, repeated in all the other versions preserved by the clan, that these events all lasted until Wakim Nassar was arrested by the Turks. For it is common knowledge, and of course my uncle was well placed to know this, that this arrest took place toward the middle of 1916.

And there is another thing, which may be less significant, but which seems to me to be more important than everything else, namely the earliest reference, in the history of the Nassar clan, to the existence of my father. My father, the youngest sibling of the family, was born at the end of 1914. And almost all the versions of the story, at one point or another and in an almost identical way, include an episode featuring him: one night when a fugitive had to be precipitously hidden in a trunk in the hallway of the Big House, while Wakim was arguing with the Ottoman officer who had been chasing him, my (future) father went over to the trunk (I imagine him toddling over as a child does who is still in diapers, with the deliciously clumsy gait of a bear or an astronaut), and he started talking to the trunk, in a very serious-sounding babble, all the while fiddling with the padlock, to the absolute consternation but simulated indifference of his older brothers and his mother. This account reveals an essential element: that if there were still conscription dodgers and deserters at a time when my father was already walking, this means that they were still arriving at the end of 1915 or the beginning of 1916. The theory constructed by my uncle about the autonomous status of Mount Lebanon therefore doesn't hold up.

All this led me one day to abandon the official version of the story and to consider that these so-called deserters were in fact nothing more than the generic name given in the Nassar history to anyone who, in the first two years of the state of emergency installed by the Turks in Syria and Mount Lebanon, for whatever reason, needed to escape from Djemal Pasha's soldiers. This would in fact confirm and extend Wakim Nassar's role in the clan and the wider Orthodox community, from initially being a zaym and protector to becoming, when the occupation began, a resistance fighter and patriot.

But before the time would come when everything was undone, there were a few happy events. Selim Nassar's marriage, for example, which, if I have my dates right, must have taken place at the end of the summer of 1913. My father told me several times about how his brother went about choosing a wife. Selim conducts long negotiations with a branch of the Chehade family, one of whose young and elegant daughters he finds attractive. He sees her often, gives her discreet but expensive little presents, and everything seems to be leading up to a marriage proposal, when, one fine morning, he catches sight of the sister of his future fiancée. Contrary to the usual fictional stories, in this case the sister is older and apparently less pretty. Which doesn't mean not pretty. No, she is even beautiful—fair complexion, pouty lips, slightly mischievous eyes—and if she is not yet married, it is only because she is picky, she sends her suitors packing with very little ceremony under the pretext that one has ears like this and the other has a gait like that. With the passage of time, she is getting dangerously close to the age when young women are considered too old for marriage, in other words she must be around twenty-four or twenty-five, whereas her sister is barely seventeen. That Selim should have preferred the older sister to the younger one remained an unexplained fact, except of course that love is blind. But we might also imagine that Selim, who is already over thirty-five years old himself, sees something of the younger sister in the older one, but in a more delectable version, like a ripe fruit next to one that is still green. He recognizes, in every detail, a creation still in progress here, but already accomplished there, already reaching its full fruition—the same gaze, but less fleeting, eager to be sought out, more assured, settling into his own as if pouring out warm honey, the same poise but less stiff, more rounded, more fluid. Whatever the case, he decides that she is the one he wants and not her younger sister, and she, divine surprise, accepts. The wedding is celebrated at Saint George of Ayn Chir and, one year later, Selim's wife is pregnant. This occurs at around the same time as Helene's last pregnancy, and also, I believe, as Gerios Nassar's wife's. The three women, heavily laden but joyful, spend their days together, sitting in the middle of the fabric of their dresses, soon joined by Helene's eldest daughter, who is pregnant as well (it's the baby boom before the war), being served by a vast retinue of maids, working on their embroidery, reading the gazettes, discussing the impending conflict, receiving visits from their friends and relatives from Marsad, Msaytbeh, or Qattine, moving according to their whims between the Big House and the Little House, then from the Little House (which is not so little anymore, since Selim improved and expanded it to welcome his bride, but it will always be called that anyway) to the Big House, then separating, going to pay their own calls in the buggy or the coupé—for there are all sorts of options now on the property—and getting together again the next day to report back and share the gossip, all this as their bellies swell and the danger increases.

At the beginning of July, Wakim and Helene go to Sofar to spend two weeks at the Grand Hotel, where the last lights of the Belle Époque, extinguished in Europe by the beginning of the war, are still belatedly glowing, like stars whose light continues to be visible even though they have been dead for eons. In the mornings, Wakim plays whist with Selim Bustros, Ibrahim de Tarazi, and a high functionary of the Ottoman Empire from whom they try to ascertain whether it will enter the war before the winter. In the evenings, Wakim plays roulette among the women in hobble skirts, high-necked lace blouses, and feathered hats, more often than not with Habib Fayyad at his side, with whom he amuses himself by giving each bid the name of an army engaged in the war in Europe. These bets rapidly take on the quality of predictions and are accompanied by hoots and cheers when the three, red, and pass, which is Joffre's third French army, gives them a win of two hundred mejidiehs, or when the twenty, black, and miss, which represents the fourth army of Germany, has them losing twenty mejidiehs. That story is one that a descendant of Habib Fayyad told my father once when I was there. It didn't seem to fit very well with Wakim's character as I had always imagined it, but since my father didn't find it implausible, I decided to keep it. Plausible or not, in any case it does show that, up until the very last moment, the war appeared to be a mirage, something that could happen only to others, something that the guests at the Grand Hotel would exchange news about as they greeted each other on entering the dining room for breakfast, or as they ate praline gateaux in the vast lounge after their siestas.

And then, at the end of the summer of 1914, as the babies are born one after the other, joy abounds in the Nassar clan, there are celebrations, receptions, baptisms, and then Turkey enters the war. But even then, it doesn't seem like the end of the world. Except that Émile Curiel, like all French nationals, is required to leave. Over several days he packs his trunks, tidies his paperwork and library, walks through his gardens with Wakim, and makes a long list of recommendations—for it is Wakim who is left with the task of looking after everything in his absence. He keeps his domestics and laborers on, and is so convinced that the war won't last that he gives orders and instructions for his return. When all the farmers of Ayn Chir and Furn el-Chebbak gather at the front steps of Villa Eucalypta to say their goodbyes and see him off, anyone would think that he was leaving for a six-month vacation at home in Marseille, from which he plans to return at a prearranged date.

The departure of the French is disastrous for the economy of Mount Lebanon, which sells all its silk to France. But to begin with, the concern is muted, and the belief in a real war is not anchored firmly in everyone's minds. To the point that Wakim manages to sell his harvest at a reasonable price, not the best, but still, it's difficult to argue with a wholesaler who reminds you that he is buying the whole harvest even though there's a war on. For a while, like an automobile that continues to roll after its motor has stopped running, normal life continues. Up until the end of the fall, everything follows the perfectly established routine. Wakim receives a few requests for assistance in the mornings and accords a few favors. This is when, for example, he receives the Shiite farmers of Ayn Chir and intercedes with Tamer Bey for a pathway to be dug from the Ayn Chir road toward their farms. Then he sets off for Beirut in his buggy, makes a few calls, let's say to Habib Fayyad or the Fernaines, his cousins on his mother's side, or to Sabri Bey, and there is always talk of business and the war, of the blockades on the coast, of the value of stock in the companies with European capital in which all of them, Wakim, Habib Fayyad, the Fernaines, and Sabri Bey, have invested. Sometimes the tailors come to Ayn Chir, with new suits or with dresses for Helene and the girls, or milliners with their hats adorned with huge feathers or eccentric little vegetable gardens, or an armorer who comes to demonstrate a new hunting rifle. And it is obvious that each and every one of them wants to know Wakim's opinion about the war, particularly about the possibility that everyone is talking about, of a bombardment of Beirut by the Allies' navies. And Wakim, as he tries on a new tarbouche, or watches the tailor move around him as he lifts up one arm for him to adjust the sleeves of a jacket or straightens his neck to button up a detachable collar, takes on a slightly sardonic air and replies that of course no one can ever imagine a new war except according to the last one they went through, which is not very reasonable. The tailor mutters something in agreement, with his pins stuck in his mouth, and makes Wakim turn around as he placidly continues by saying that one thing is certain, and that is that the high command of the Allies won't have broadcast their campaign plans over the telegraph, which makes the tailor laugh heartily and spit out his pins into his hand. Unless the previous exchange took place as Wakim was sitting in an armchair while his wife was having a fitting, and the tailor was on his knees adjusting the hem of one of Helene's new dresses and he bursts out laughing just as he stands up, then Helene cuts him off by pointing out a defect in the sleeves.

But all this changes from the winter of 1915 onward, when the generalissimo of the fourth Turkish army based in Damascus, Djemal Pasha, puts an end to the autonomy of the mutasarrifate of Mount Lebanon, in view of the operation against Suez. From then onward, he has troops based in the country. At Ayn Chir the Turkish troops force their way onto the farms of Rached, Baclini, Malkoun, and the others. They take the wheat, the seed, the fodder, and even the cows. Within a few weeks there is not a single donkey, horse, or mule left in the entire area, and the dogs are finally let loose, since they have nothing to guard anymore and nothing to eat, and they start roaming the roads, attacking passersby and howling in the night as if the world were about to end. And then finally, the Turks take away Malkoun's older sons, Baclini's youngest, and other young men from the area. Within a few weeks, there is not a single laborer left at Villa Eucalypta, where Wakim goes twice a week for an inspection. There are no waiters at the café on the Damascus road, where he continues to go whenever he can. It is here and now that the story of the deserters so dear to the memory of the Nassars should therefore start. And deserters do start to arrive, that is without a doubt. But not right away. We have to imagine how the great houses and the families of dignitaries are not affected to begin with, according to a process that applies in all times and places, so the Ottoman soldiers at first spare Wakim and his family.

Otherwise, of course, the Big House would not have been a reliable refuge. The long, smooth river of life seems to continue flowing almost normally on the Nassar property. It's as if there were the house on the one hand and the world on the other, both living in different reigns, according to different speeds, or different rhythms. While the carts full of soldiers and wagons full of supplies get bogged down in the mud caused by the rain, as they come and go on the road from Baabda, while the infantrymen are floundering, exactly as the generalissimo's offensive on Suez floundered, and while the farmers of Ayn Chir are all wondering what will become of their silk harvest, the women on the Nassar property are still getting together to gossip over their embroidery hoops and the babies in their cradles, making grand theatrical gestures. Wakim works in the orchards in the mornings, even if he has nothing much to do there. He can always find a tree to stake up, a water channel to consolidate, and he can be seen walking home at ten o'clock to get changed. And twice a week, if it's not raining, he goes out and heads for Villa Eucalypta. He enters the villa, opens the windows to air it out, to bring in the fresh, moist scent of the eucalyptus trees, and to replace the old smell that seems to remain suspended in the still air of the closed house. He wanders through the European drawing rooms and the dining room where he first presented his clementines. All the furniture is covered in white dust sheets under which the arms of the chairs and the backs of the sofas can just be made out. He quietly inspects these legions of silent ghosts, then turns back to make his tour in reverse, closing the shutters and the windows, leaving the house without seeing any of the butlers or servants whose recent presence he can nevertheless discern from a detail or two in the central avenue or on the front porch.

But two months later, he can no longer take this regular walk, in other words from the moment when someone rushes over to warn him that the Turks have taken over Villa Eucalypta. When Wakim arrives there on horseback and dressed for town, he finds soldiers and a cart full of victuals in the main avenue. He realizes that Villa Eucalypta is about to become a military post or a barracks, according to orders given by the generalissimo and Reda Pasha, the commander of the Turkish troops in Beirut. When he dismounts in front of the villa, an officer in a kalpak receives him curtly on the porch. They have a brief discussion, which Wakim cannot prolong without coming under suspicion. With a dark countenance and pursed lips, his cane tucked under his armpit like a sheathed sword, as if to show that he has no intention of fighting because it would not be an equal match, he does an about-face without saying goodbye, gets back on his horse, and, to register his bad temper and disapproval in principle, he goes to take another long tour of the property and leaves in no hurry an hour later.

From that day onward, when he comes back from his orchards, he gets dressed and settles into the living room with Helene, who wears a wide shawl, and with the children, and also Selim and his wife. They stoke the fires in the braziers, talk about the Suez campaign, or the defeat of the Russians at Tannenberg. I take great pleasure in imagining this family life, with the house like a cliff around which the waves are ominously whispering and not quite yet crashing. The visitors still keep coming, Nassars or other Orthodox residents of Marsad or Msaytbeh, as well as Maronite farmers from Ayn Chir or Furn el-Chebbak. They unwind their woolen scarves but keep their long European jackets on, which serve as coats over their waistcoats and seroual pants, as they set out their business. Wakim listens to them all and offers a few coins to grease the palms of the Turks, so that one man can keep his horse, and another prevent his woods from being cut down. Wakim's children have always been adamant in maintaining that their father spent considerable sums in 1915, even though precisely that year's harvest did not sell at a high price, and the following year's did not sell at all. It was out of something like solidarity that he spent the money, gave it away, threw it out the windows, but also, no doubt, out of a need to be forgiven for still having his own horses, his trees, and his children. And for continuing to live a normal life, a much too normal life, for continuing to go to receptions in high society in the drawing rooms of the bourgeoisie in Beirut, where he has been invited increasingly frequently since 1912. In fact, he uses these evening occasions to further some of his business. In the lit-up reception rooms with views over the sea, where they can watch the French and

English ships blockading their country's coastline, between a discussion of the Russian defeats and another about the new urban planning of Beirut that the new wali has in mind, he skillfully manages to achieve difficult goals. One evening at Émile de F.'s, for instance, when he is sitting on the sofa next to Thérèse de F. (she has a boa wrapped around her shoulders, waves a slim cigarette holder, laughs and flutters her eyelashes as she sets him salacious riddles, and is determined to have him say that no, Helene—who is distracted over there by a conversation with gentlemen wearing monocles—would not be jealous to hear her being so familiar with him), so yes, sitting next to Thérèse, who, he knows, is a great friend of the generalissimo and would, he feels, be prepared to gratify any of his requests, he asks her, as a challenge, with his eyes on hers (after in turn laughing and assuring himself that her husband would not be jealous if she accorded him a favor), to obtain the leniency of a military tribunal in Aley for the son of a peasant of Ayn Chir who tried to evade conscription. Another evening, at Selim de Tarazi's, during a game of whist with the master of the house and an Ottoman general, when his clementines are being praised to the skies, he responds flippantly to the general's request for him to send him some of this incredible fruit, that he will gladly do so if in return the general promises to suspend the sentence for a salesman from Kfarshima. The quid pro quo is so disproportionate that the players and the women watching the game while waving their interminable cigarette holders all laugh out loud. But as Wakim is leaving, and while the general is kissing Helene's hand, he reminds him of his offer and the general, as if in jest also, responds that it's a deal, it's settled, he is waiting for the name of the salesman.

"I'll send it to you at the same time as the clementines," Wakim says as he puts on his coat.

Then as they go outside and wait for their coupé, he winks knowingly at Helene and murmurs:

"It'll all work out for poor old Checri, you'll see."

In fact, Helene is in on the game as well. One evening, a German diplomat who speaks Arabic with a terribly guttural accent amuses himself by flirting with her at Habib Fayyad's. She laughs and plays along, tastes all the dishes he offers her and the desserts he wants her opinion of. Then to flatter him even further, she makes him admit that he has some influence with the generalissimo, and therefore with his colonels, so that he promises, as if to prove it to her, to have the sentence remitted for a Nassar who opposed the seizing of his cows a week earlier and wounded a Turkish soldier with a pitchfork. After which the peasant from Ayn Chir, "poor old Checri," and the Nassar despoiled of his cows come to the Big House to give their thanks and appreciation. The petitioners become more and more frequent and finally, one evening, the first fugitive conscription dodger appears. When he arrives normally, through the front gates of the property, and climbs the steps to knock at the door of the Big House, he is taken at first for a visitor coming to ask for a favor. But then Wakim recognizes him, he's a young man from Marsad who was supposed to be in the army. Wearing seroual pants with a European suit jacket, he is brought inside and seated across from Wakim in a secluded corner of the living room. He is feverish and wiggles his legs nervously during the whole conversation, which means that his tarbouche, which he has placed on his knee, is constantly on the point of falling to the floor. He catches it every time this happens and puts it back on his knee. Wakim observes him while he is speaking, and thinks there is something strange about him, then finally realizes it is because he has shaved off his mustache, no doubt in order to appear younger than he is.

"I thought you had been called up," Wakim says. "That's what your father told me a month ago."

"That's what we're saying so that the neighbors don't snitch on me. But actually I was hiding out at a cousin's place, he's a porter at the old bishopric. But he moved out of his house because it is going to be demolished. There was an evacuation order. As if this was the time to be beautifying the city! I'm quite sure it is just to flush out the young men hiding there. It's a trap. They don't want to beautify anything at all."

"Yes they do, they're going to demolish the Bab el-Derkeh neighborhood and the El-Toujjar Souk to build a European city. But what are you going to do now?"

"If the Turks catch me, I'm done for."

"I know."

"Wakim Bey, you have to help me."

"And what am I supposed to do?"

"Hide me at your house for a few days."

"And after that?"

"After that, I'm going to try to get to Hasbaya. I have cousins there. And it will be a lot harder for the Turks to find me at Hasbaya."

"You do realize that Hasbaya is a long way away, don't you?"

"Yes, but that's the only option I've got now."

This dialogue is absolutely plausible, and it's easy to imagine how Wakim arranges to hide the young man after that. They put him in the cellar of the Big House and give him food in secret for four days, keeping the smallest of the children away from him and carrying out a whole song and dance in front of any unexpected visitors who happen to arrive when someone is coming up from the cellar, and finally, on the fourth day, they dress him up as a Bedouin and he leaves with a bear tamer heading south.

The same day as this clandestine departure, Wakim attends the ceremony to launch the construction work for the modernization of the old town of Beirut. On the podium where he is sitting in the second row, and while a brass band is playing military marches, while the generalissimo and the new wali are whispering something that gets passed from one ear to the next along the first row, while the dignitary seated next to him is arranging the rose in his buttonhole, Wakim suddenly thinks that he should have instructed the deserter to pretend he was mute and to express himself only in gestures and grunts if he was asked for his identity. And that makes him smile, but internally, for his face remains placid. He watches a sheikh lean toward Gebran Nassar and whisper the thing passed on by the generalissimo into his ear. Then he thinks that once the ceremony is over, he should go pay a visit to the deserter's father, at Marsad, to give him the news. He is wondering how easy it will be to get his coupé out, having parked it on Cannon Square, where it was gradually surrounded by dozens of carriages, buggies, and coupés as the other guests arrived. There were even two automobiles there, the only two in Beirut apart from the generalissimo's. And he is just thinking about the automobiles when the brass band suddenly stops and the applause starts. He claps along with everyone else. Sabri Bey turns around and says a word he doesn't catch and at that moment the wali stands up to deliver a speech. Will he speak in Turkish or Arabic? Wakim wonders. He looks right and left, quite certain that everyone is wondering the same thing, and that is when he sees it, on the collar of the man sitting in front of him next to Sabri Bey.

He sees it but he doesn't understand at first what it is, it only appears to him slowly, although he has been looking at it for a few seconds: a grasshopper, moving clumsily with a tiny swagger and something like scrupulous hesitation, on the blue-gray silk of the dignitary's suit, toward the back of his shoulder. Wakim is stupefied and realizes that he is the only one to have seen this incongruous thing. He remains immobile, his eyes fixed on the insect, which is hesitating, its antennae raised, its body stiff on its N-shaped legs, inert but very much alive, and while the entire audience is waiting for the wali to open his mouth at last, Wakim wants to send the grasshopper packing with a quick slap, and just as he is leaning toward the dignitary to warn him of what he is doing, the wali pronounces the first words of his speech in Turkish and Wakim sits up straight without following through on his irrepressible urge.

Two hours later, in the fugitive's family home, where he has come to bring news, he learns that clouds of grasshoppers are moving up from Palestine. When he arrives at Ayn Chir, Gerios tells him the same thing. He replies that he is aware of this and is even acquainted with the advance guard of these new arrivals. Gerios looks at him dumbfounded, scratches his head with the two remaining fingers of his right hand, mutters something or other, and the next day the grasshoppers arrive.

In the morning, a cloud passes over the sun, then like a terrible hailstorm falling on the earth, buffeting the windows and roofs, thousands of bugs with ferocious appetites drop from the sky like a biblical plague and attack anything green as well as anything dry. On the road, the walkers stop, look at what is happening in stupefaction, then suddenly, under the hard showers of insects, cover their heads with the flaps of their kombaz or their jackets and make a run for whatever shelter they can find. Everyone is running around inside the Big House too, everyone is agitated, they finally shut all the windows and doors, the skylights, and all the other openings, but it is too late, and for a week there will be grasshoppers everywhere, under the pillows and between the plates in the huge sideboard. In the meantime, the men have been running through the orchards, shaking the trees, stomping on the grasshoppers on the ground (and it must be a horrible orgy of tiny cracks and crunches), and my oldest aunts and uncles kept a vivid memory of the horror of that day.

Among their stories, which I regret not paying greater attention to because they disgusted me and I didn't know that I would need to retell them one day, I especially remember one an uncle told me about the children of Ayn Chir picking up live grasshoppers by the shovelful and taking them in sacks to the Turkish army post, where they were given one matlic per sack. They were apparently burned afterward in the sand dunes, and I can imagine that the whole area must have smelled of burning flesh for days, instead of Wakim's orange trees that were flowering at the time.

But other methods of battling the bugs are said to be effective. A rumor circulates that a farmer from Kfarshima who happened to let his geese loose on the grasshoppers saw them feasting on the bugs. Everybody then lets their geese out, their ducks and chickens. But there are not many of them and the results are unconvincing. The Baclini son burns a few of his mulberry trees in the hope that the smoke will chase the gluttonous insects away, but nothing comes of it. The Rached son sacrifices his reserve of olive oil and spreads it all over his land and sets it alight, which roasts quantities of the bugs but doesn't prevent the next clouds from attacking his harvest.

This is where Émile Curiel's eucalyptus trees come in. During the many years that Curiel's name was retained in the memory of the people of the region, he was always associated with the miraculous powers of his trees during the sinister year that was 1915. For while all the harvests on the whole coastline are shredded in a matter of ten days, while all that is left of the great mulberry groves of Kfarshima, Baabda, and Ayn Chir is nothing but spectral lace, while all the cocoons are ravaged, while the fig and olive trees are in tatters, Curiel's huge garden with its five hundred different species remains intact, rustling away peacefully in the April breezes as if it were in a completely different geographical area, hidden from the grasshoppers' voracity like the heroes that the Olympian gods hide from the sight of their enemies, and spreading its immunity in a kind of incomprehensible generosity to the closest lands around it. When I asked my father one day for an explanation of this phenomenon, he compared the effect of eucalyptus on grasshoppers to that of geraniums on mosquitoes:

"If you have a window and plant geraniums along the whole width of it, the mosquitoes won't come in anymore. Geraniums are a barrier that they can't get through. It's the same for eucalyptus and grasshoppers."

Whatever the case may be, the memory passed down through the generations of farmers at Ayn Chir was of clouds of insects literally flying around the perimeter of the property, or rising high up into the air above it as they approached, before swooping down all around it, but always at a distance of at least five hundred yards away, which allowed some of the farms neighboring the plantation to be partially spared from the calamity, and everyone instantly calls it a miracle.

But it is not a miracle, and as soon as the first shock has passed, the farmers recover their common sense. They recall the inhalations of eucalyptus that Curiel and Barthélemy recommended to treat asthma and lung complaints, or the branches of eucalyptus that they suggested be burnt to purify the air in houses where someone had been sick with a fever. The farmers therefore attribute the miracle to an additional beneficial property of the tree. And all at once, to fumigate the grasshoppers, they start cutting down all the isolated eucalyptus trees in the countryside, all the trees that, thanks to their extraordinary powers of propagation, have grown on the roadsides of Ayn Chir and Furn el-Chebbak for the past twenty-five years. Within three days, all the wild eucalyptus trees have been trimmed, cut back, then chopped down, and bonfires are smoking everywhere. The farmers of Baabda, Kfarshima, and Dekwaneh follow this example and then, having demolished all the trees that have come to grow in their area, they try to attack those in Ayn Chir and Furn el-Chebbak. But the farmers of Ayn Chir are keeping watch, fights break out, knives and sticks are brandished, and soon there is not a single eucalyptus left standing in a ten-mile radius, which means that everyone ends up turning to the holy of holies, to Villa Eucalypta itself. Peasants from the area start by sneaking into Curiel's property to gather up sackfuls of fallen leaves and branches. Then they climb the eucalyptus trees on the property's boundaries and cut off branches that others gather up on the ground, until the day when a few of them are discovered, and shots ring out, and soldiers start mounting guard and sending patrols around the perimeter. Three days go by, and on the morning of the fourth, a delegation comes to visit Wakim Nassar to ask him to intervene. One hour later, he rides through the gates of Villa Eucalypta, accompanied by the Rached son, the Baclini son, and Fayez Maroun, the son of Maroun Maroun. The three farmers are riding horses that he loaned them, for theirs have been requisitioned or are hidden. They dismount in front of Curiel's villa, over which the Turkish flag is now flying. On the porch, a soldier makes them wait, then they are received by the officer who requisitioned the property. Let's say that he is a colonel and that his name is Rassim. He is sitting in Curiel's office and Wakim's heart sinks at the sight of his friend's library turned topsy-turvy, as if someone has opened all the books one by one to try to find secret messages hidden inside them, and then replaced them in complete disorder and with no respect at all. Rassim does not rise and receives the four men from his seat behind the desk. Refusing to speak standing up, Wakim pulls up a chair (a chair that is familiar to him but that he has trouble recognizing in this new context, just as it is difficult to recognize a person one knows in an unexpected outfit or environment) and he sits down facing the colonel, who puts both elbows on the desk, and his chin in his hands, and avoids remonstrating with the visitor, whose suit, cane, and demeanor indicate that he is a dignitary who may have contacts in the city and in the salons frequented by Reda Pasha. He says nothing while Wakim is the one talking, without pleasantries, but not brusquely either, in order to give their enterprise a possibility of success. He explains the necessity for the farmers to cut the branches and gather the eucalyptus leaves, and also the usefulness for the entire region of lighting bonfires with the wood.

"All the books that are behind you, Colonel," he adds, waving his cane at Émile Curiel's bookcases behind Rassim, "contain information about the benefits of these trees and confirm what I am telling you."

Rassim does not react but lowers his forearms so his arms lie across the desktop. He remains extremely polite but firm.

"I do not read French, sir," he says with an expression of mild reproach. "And as for your proposition, I would gladly have accepted it, but I have orders. This property will be transformed into a sanatorium and hospital for soldiers in the army. And therefore, for the very reasons you mention, we cannot allow the trees to be touched. Of course we must help the farmers. But at this time it is more useful to help the soldiers. You would agree, wouldn't you?"

Wakim feels the silence and immobility of his three companions behind his back become heavier, more dense. Hope has vanished. Without replying to Rassim's question, to which there is obviously only one possible answer, and knowing that it is pointless to argue, Wakim stands up, just as he did the first time, and heads for the door without saying goodbye. Rached's son and Fayez Maroun step back to let him pass, but at that moment Rassim calls out to him politely ("Sir!"), walks toward him, steps in front of him, opens the door, and asks Wakim's three companions to let them have a few moments alone, just the two of them. The three men leave with intrigued but weary expressions. Rassim closes the door behind him and returns to his desk, which he leans against.

"I have a proposition to make to you," he says calmly, with that Turkish accent that renders the Arabic language effeminate and treacherous, and which also gives it something pointy that doesn't ring true with its strong and rough sounds. "I could let you gather some of the trees and branches off the property. But I would be taking a huge risk. At least a court martial." (You liar, Wakim thinks.) "So therefore I need to receive something in exchange. The eucalyptus leaves would sell at a high price. Send your men to cut whatever you need, and we will set a price for it. Even if we share it, that will be a lot of money. The farmers would pay almost anything for them."

Wakim manages to take the blow without flinching. He knows that he must not antagonize the colonel, who might turn vicious now that he has shown his cards. Wakim remains absolutely still, making an effort to not even blink, knowing that Rassim is observing him with his scalpel eyes, and now he approaches the chair where he was sitting a moment before, and pulls it toward himself with one hand, and puts his square-toed boot on it, and while Rassim is observing the boot and the hem of the European pants leg whose seam reveals the work of an expert tailor, and Wakim himself notices that Rassim is looking at his boot, he thinks briefly about what he might do. He thinks, for example, but only fleetingly, that he could accept, then tell everyone at Ayn Chir, take the money, and then redistribute at least his share to the farmers. But all of this is ridiculous and only serves the purpose of letting some time pass so that Rassim believes that he is seriously considering the offer. The colonel senses that the moment of danger is past. He straightens up, goes around to the back of the desk, sits down, and is about to say something when Wakim interrupts him:

"No," he says, as if he had just come to the end of his thought. "And anyway I have no men of my own. Those three you saw are farmers, friends of mine. I can't see myself selling them eucalyptus branches."

"We could sell them to others, a long way away. At Baabda, or Dekwaneh, or Antelias."

This insistence is starting to give Wakim a strange feeling of suffocation. He straightens up too and, suppressing his urge to throw his cane at the colonel's face, concludes:

"No, I couldn't do that."

And because he needs to behave as cautiously as if he were in a lion's cage, even until the very last minute, Wakim adds:

"Goodbye, Colonel."

Then he leaves, and during the following days, the boundless rage of having to utter that "Goodbye, Colonel" makes him forget his friends' troubles, his own, those of Ayn Chir and the whole of Lebanon. When he gets a grip on himself again, he understands that the danger would now be for Colonel Rassim to ally himself with any random hustler to set up his trafficking business in eucalyptus wood. And that is exactly what happens. A pharmacist by the name of George Baydar starts coming regularly to Villa Eucalypta in a little buggy, supposedly to discuss the project of the first sanatorium. Everybody sees him, he even stops sometimes on the road to talk about the grasshoppers with the passersby or the farmers, he wears a top hat and an amiable, almost timid expression. Meanwhile, and until the beginning of summer, carts covered in tarpaulins and escorted by soldiers regularly roll out of the property and head for the coast road. Bonfires of eucalyptus are found burning in Antelias and Zalka, as well as in Matn. At Ayn Chir, the farmers are starting to get restless. When a few of them are gathered at Wakim's house, they desperately discuss ways of seizing control of Villa Eucalypta or of forcing Rassim to share the trees. Little by little, they mention the weapons they have hidden in the farms, they plot possible nocturnal expeditions into Curiel's property, the Baclini son reports on his observations of the sentries and their guard patrols, and a farmer from Furn el-Chebbak talks about a whole side of Villa Eucalypta that is extremely poorly protected, the one to the east. Wakim listens to all this without intervening, he knows that the least action against the Turkish military will be taken as a revolt and that this is a situation best avoided, even in their thoughts. And yet, he may be thinking right now about what is being whispered in the salons of Beirut, a possible defeat of the Turks, and a landing by Allied troops. British planes have been regularly flying over Ayn Chir, strange birds whose motors seem to fart as they leave streams of white smoke behind them. Whenever they appear, everybody goes out onto the rooftops to cheer and throw their tarbouches or caps in the air, and the peasants on the roads stop walking and shade their eyes with their hands to look up at the sky for a long time, pivoting around to follow the flight path of the planes from the south to the north, or from the west toward the interior, and all of this, together with the new setbacks faced by the Ottoman army and the regular incursions of French ships in the coastal waters, offers hope of better days to come. So yes, he thinks about it, and maybe he sees a role for himself as a war chief and lets the visiting farmers talk. Then he takes his turn to speak, but only to curb everyone's enthusiasm, explaining that they can't blindly throw themselves into that kind of adventure, and the farmers listen to him with worried faces.

However, even though he succeeds in getting them to be patient, he obviously cannot stop them from expressing their views. And at Ayn Chir, Furn el-Chebbak, and as far as Kfarshima and Baabda, the farmers can't keep their tongues from wagging. To begin with, when one of them says something like: "The grasshoppers have finished what the Turks started," during an evening gathering, it is not unheard of for someone else to reply:

"And our salvation could have come from a Frenchman." And then it is not long before that general sentiment is summarized by the priest at Saint George of Ayn Chir, in a sermon one Sunday morning:

"My brothers, it is easy to say that the grasshoppers are carrying out the same depredations in our fields as the Turks. And, as you know, there is a remedy for these depredations. The fact that it is of French origin is something that I see, and that you also must see, as a great sign of hope in the future."

The allusion is so transparent and so serious that the priest himself has a little moment of hesitation and throws a glance toward Wakim, who is attending mass with Helene and two of his daughters along with thirty or so farmers. Helene also looks discreetly at Wakim, no doubt as do all the other congregants and farmers. But Wakim shows no sign of reacting. As they come out of the church, Helene remarks that the priest has gone too far, but he just shrugs. One hour later, all of Ayn Chir has heard about the sermon, and a week later, during a dinner party at Ibrahim B.'s house at Aley, where the Beirut bourgeoisie has relocated to spend the summer in the cool of the mountains, and in the presence of the generalissimo himself, who is staying at the Grand Hotel, Sabri Bey takes Wakim to one side and asks him what this story of pro-French propaganda that he is encouraging at Ayn Chir is all about.

"I have no idea what you are talking about, Sabri Bey," Wakim replies, with little conviction.

"There are rumors circulating. A peasant told Colonel Rassim something about it, and he reported it to Reda Pasha."

Wakim remains silent, staring fixedly at the foot of a bronze cupid on a marble pedestal, behind which they have retreated to talk in private.

"Be careful, please, Wakim. That is the kind of accusation that can lead a man to the scaffold."

Wakim says nothing about this little exchange to Helene. Four days later, French ships bomb the coast from Chekka to Jounieh, and dinghies full of soldiers approach the beaches with the apparent intention of making a landing there. The news arrives at Ayn Chir slightly deformed and more optimistic than is reasonable. At the Nassar home, and in every other farm, everyone thinks this is it. They get their guns out of the cupboards and whet their knives and daggers. But nothing happens, the French don't disembark, the takeover plans for Villa Eucalypta have to be deferred, and meanwhile, as the summer arrives and the grasshoppers finally disappear, leaving the country in ruins and the prospect of famine behind them, there are more and more fugitives coming to seek shelter on Wakim's land. There are those who were meant to be in the army and who, one day, appear on the edges of the orchards and explain that they can't bear having to hide anymore. There are those who were indeed in the army and made the most of a moonless night to flee. And then there are the victims of a denunciation or those who had bad dealings with the authorities. To begin with, they arrive at any time of day, incognito or disguised in some way. Then, gradually, they no longer dare to go into the property in broad daylight. Some hide until nightfall and then jump the wall under cover of darkness and rush to the Big House. Others go into the orchards and stay there in hiding for a day or two, like wolves, then one night they come out at last, hesitate for a moment at the foot of the house with its three arched windows blazing like beacons in the middle of a storm, furtively climb up the front steps, and knock at the door.

And every time a huge commotion starts in the house. Wakim stuffs a pistol into his belt and goes to open the door, while his eldest son stands behind him, with a charged rifle close at hand. Helene and her daughters stay in their rooms, but keep their ears pricked. Sometimes, in the Little House, Selim is alerted by the noise and muffled shouts that make him bound out of bed. When he arrives at the Big House, with a weapon in his belt too, the fugitive has already been brought inside and is sitting in the corner of the living room telling his story, and Selim, by the light of three or four candles, can then recognize, under a beard of several days, under the drawn features and the pallid complexion, a face that is familiar to him. It can be a boy from Marsad whom everyone believed to be fighting in the war, but who in fact has remained hidden in his parents' house until the day he can no longer stand it and goes for a stroll but then bumps into a patrol. He escapes but can no longer go home. He hides in barns and mills, then one night he crosses the Pine Forest, meets a hyena that he frightens away by bellowing at it, then enters the Nassar orchards, where he roams for two days without daring to show himself. It can also be a young man from Msaytbeh or Bachoura who was denounced to the Turks by an uncharitable soul for sending signals to the French ships from the shack he owns near Ayn Mreisseh. The soldiers come to pick him up at his home. But he escapes through a window, hides for a few days at his brother's place in Marsad, but, fearing that he might compromise him, leaves one morning in the direction of Matn, can't cross the bridge over the river because of an identity check, turns back toward Furn el-Chebbak, hides for a night in the mulberry groves, and finally reaches the Nassar property. The fugitive can also be a deserter, a guy from Ayn Chir or Furn el-Chebbak who doesn't dare show his face at his father's farm for fear of being recognized and denounced. But he might also be, why not, a guy from Qattine, and then it is Helene who recognizes him before everyone else when he comes through the door with his uniform in tatters. She is the one who greets him, reassures him, has him sit down and tell his story. And he, in the dancing light of the candles, tells (for example) how his unit was camping around the Saint Elias convent and had been ordered to dig trenches for weeks on end until they were exhausted and morale was at rock bottom. And when he realized that Ayn Chir wasn't far away, he discreetly found out where the Nassar house was, and one evening, worn out but full of hope, he deserted without telling anyone, but then got lost in the mulberry groves, thought he was being followed, hid at the edge of the orange orchard for part of a night without knowing where he was, and then, once he had recovered a bit from his fright, finally realized what kind of trees were all around him, and that they were orange trees and not mulberries.

Once the man has told his story, and Wakim has carefully interrogated him about everything, and he has been served some food, and been shown a place to sleep somewhere (let's say in one of the rooms next to the stables), Wakim, Selim, and Helene hold a council. While they are talking, the rosy light of dawn rises to make the candles superfluous. Soon they can hear Gerios coming in from Marsad, and thanks to his infallible sixth sense and subtle interpretation of imperceptible signs, instead of going straight to his vegetable patch, as he does every day, he goes up to the house, having guessed that there is a fugitive on the property. In the morning, Wakim has another conversation with the fugitive in his hiding place, and comes to an agreement with him about how to resolve the situation, and then for a few days afterward, the property seems to fall into slumber over its secret. Even the farmers who are most familiar with the place, those who come to spend their customary hour talking to Wakim, even their wives who come to have a little visit with *Sitt Hileni* (as my grandmother was always called by the locals, who strangely gave her name a Greek accent), even they, who know exactly how the Nassars live, what happens at daybreak and at noon, what is cooking today and what will be cooking tomorrow, what is in the wheat barn and what is in the storehouse, they who know who comes to visit in the mornings and what Helene does in the afternoons, do not suspect a thing. And in fact, mostly, life on the property doesn't change. It is only from microscopic details that anyone could guess that there was some kind of clandestine activity going on. In the choice of a sheet that Helene casually makes while sorting through the recently laundered linen, a sheet that will be most useful to hide the fugitive on his departure; in the little detour that Wakim makes as he comes back from Marsad on horseback and that allows him to find out that the Turks have lifted the control post at Berjawi, which will facilitate the passage of the buggy; in Gerios taking out an old trunk from the cellar of the Little House, which will be used to hide the hidden guest. And one morning, Wakim's buggy leaves the property as usual, heads along the road to Furn el-Chebbak at a trot, goes past a Turkish patrol at Dekwaneh without being harassed, and then rushes along the coastal road to Nahr el-Mott, where it stops in the shelter of a little stand of sycamore trees. Wakim dismounts, opens the trunk, helps the fugitive get out, and, after giving him a couple of pieces of sound advice, lets him set off for Antelias or Jounieh.

Even if nobody sees anything, especially strangers to the property, it is nevertheless certain that everybody *knows*. Among the inhabitants of Marsad, there are those who have sent their son to take refuge with Wakim. For a while afterward they have no news, then, one fine morning, they receive a little message from the lips of a traveler: "Father, Mother, everything went well, I am doing fine, I am at our cousin's at Marjayoun." Not a word about Wakim, of course, out of caution, but the father and mother understand and give thanks. Likewise, there are deserters originally from Ayn Chir whom Wakim takes to their cousins in Matn or Keserwan. After letting them off at Nahr el-Mott or a little farther along, he returns to Ayn Chir and goes directly to their parents. He sits for a while on the doorstep, accepts a glass of mulberry cordial, then waits to be alone with the father and mother to announce that there is news of their son, who is in good health and will be arriving at his uncle's at Beit Chabab or Rayfoun. "You saw him, then?" the mother asks. "No, but I have reliable information." The reply is coded but the parents can easily decrypt it. Soon the news spreads and the Nassar house starts giving the impression of leading a mysterious double life. The curious become even more curious, but things are too dangerous to be the subject of gossip, and everyone holds their tongue. Only the children are incapable of doing so, and inevitably one or other of the farmers' sons who come to play with Wakim's children goes home one day and proudly tells his family that "there is a man sleeping in the basement at the Nassars'." He is told to keep quiet, which doesn't improve anything, or everyone shrugs and laughs at him, which makes it much worse, because then the child tries to prove what he is saying. But when he goes back to play in the next few days, the man has been evacuated and everything is fine again.

What is certain, in any case, is that the trouble didn't arise because of the children. It didn't really come by way of spies or informants either, although they were numerous and it is unthinkable that they would not have caught wind of something going on and reported it to the occupying authorities. I imagine that the famous Colonel Rassim, who was in command of the area at the time, must have been in the know fairly early on. But that's the thing: Rassim cannot believe a word of it. For how is it possible that a man who dines in the homes where the generalissimo and the German high command are invited, who knows Reda Pasha personally, and who seems to be on friendly terms with all the members of the requisition committee could be at the same time a dangerous protector of the enemies of the empire? Rassim certainly has no love lost for Wakim Nassar because of their meeting about the eucalyptus trees. But, in fact precisely because of that meeting, he refuses to accuse Wakim. Because that would entail a substantial risk for himself. Imagine Rassim ordering a search of the Nassar property. And now imagine that the search comes up with nothing. Wakim, to take revenge, might then report the shady propositions Rassim made about Curiel's trees to his high-placed friends. And so, Rassim prefers to convince himself that Wakim Nassar cannot be an enemy of the empire. He avoids picking a quarrel with him, and that lasts until a night when one of his patrols discovers a deserter entering the Nassar property. Ten minutes later, the colonel is at the Big House, and when he arrives, he finds Wakim sitting in an armchair beside the yuzbashi who is the commander of the patrol. Wakim is wearing his shirt and trousers and boots, which means that he must have gone out in a rush. A pistol is lying on a chair, which no one is trying to hide. Rassim thinks that this fact in itself is a serious offense. But he says nothing. Wakim asks him to sit down. Elias is there too, the eldest Nassar son. At one moment, Selim comes in and Helene herself arrives too, with her frightened youngest child nestled in her arms. Rassim sits down and, rather than listening to the explanations of his yuzbashi, listens to those of the master of the house. Wakim talks about the gunshots, the agitation, the rather disgraceful incursion of the patrol on his land, and mentions that he even gave the soldiers the authorization to search the property. Rassim nods and smiles, to calm everyone down, and explains that they must be on their guard and that deserters are hiding everywhere, even on farms and in orchards, where they think they are safe. Wakim mutters something in response. Selim sits down. Elias shifts in his armchair. Helene, who is now also seated, puts her youngest down on his feet on the carpet next to her, and that is how the child who would become my father makes his first appearance in this story. He is a pint-sized toddler, of course, and starts padding forward, babbling incomprehensible words. He heads toward Elias, who tries to pick him up. But the little boy struggles away, starts his determined and very important toddling again, advancing straight toward the large mahogany trunk on which a snuffed oil lamp is standing, one that must have been used when the men went out to meet the patrol. He heads toward it, burbling words that are not quite clear but that sound like a monologue, when in fact it is a dialogue, either with the padlock on the trunk or with the man hiding inside it. His mother and father, his uncle and his brother, all hold their breath, and that is when Rassim, who thinks that the atmosphere is tense only because of his presence, calls the little boy over to him and stretches out his hand to pull him gently toward him, making amusing little clicking noises with his tongue.

13

NOBODY IN THE Nassar clan ever expressed the least doubt about the fact that Wakim was arrested by the Turks not because of the fugitives he hid on his property, but because of his French friendships from before the war, and subsequently, because of his attitude in the Villa Eucalypta affair. The deserters he hid would only have been the straw that broke the camel's back, the tangible and irrefutable proof of his disloyal attitude toward the Ottoman Empire. And besides, there was never any doubt in Wakim's descendants' view, nor in History's, that he was not caught in the act of protecting deserters from the Ottoman army. For one thing is clear: if he had been caught doing so, he would not have been banished, but well and truly put to death.

What remained rather obscure to me for a long time in all this story is the reason why the Turks delayed their persecution of Wakim, as they did for all the friends of France, who met the same fate as he did, or worse. For the French were at war with the Ottoman Empire from the very first day, whereas the arrests of French sympathizers started only in April 1916. I talked about this several times with my father and my uncles. Their response was invariably the same and had to do with the notion that the repression was stronger from 1916 onward because of the military defeats—and the resulting anger—of the generalissimo Djemal Pasha. But that argument never really convinced me, and the solution came to me from the place I least expected it, for it was only when I took an interest in the fate of my other grandfather, my mother's father, that I at last understood all the complexities of the affair, an affair linked to the fickle personality of Djemal Pasha himself.

It is indeed highly probable that the famous generalissimo, who was the commander of the Fourth Ottoman Army posted in Syria during the Great War, was in fact, at least until 1916, what I would call a "crypto-Frenchman," a sort of secret friend of France. Acting with perfect independence from the high command of the sultan's armies, leading his own campaign in Suez and the occupation of Lebanon and the Syrian provinces as he saw fit, Djemal Pasha was quite quickly nicknamed the "Viceroy of Syria." And it is entirely possible that he may, at one time or another, have dreamed of a real throne in the manner of the old viceroys of Egypt, and that, in order to succeed in this enterprise, he sought assistance from the French. I would even go so far as to posit that he made this curious proposition to the French, explaining how his success would allow them to gain a foothold in Syria and, by the same blow, to outstrip the British by short-circuiting their alliance with the Arabs, who had just risen up under the command of Prince Faisal and T. E. Lawrence.

This incredible poker game is precisely what my other grandfather would contribute to thwarting. I will not speak of this here. But what I will say is that the defeat of this explosive alliance between Djemal Pasha and France became evident from the beginning of 1916, which was when the persecutions of the friends of France in Lebanon and Syria started. It therefore seems plausible to consider these persecutions as the generalissimo's violent reaction to the French refusal of his advances. In April, his police discover the famous "secret papers" in the former offices of the French consulate, papers in which some Lebanese patriots demanded the support of the French against the Turks. At the beginning of May, sixteen of these patriots are arrested and hanged. From then onward, everything and everyone who has or had the least connection with France becomes suspect, and Wakim Nassar's situation starts to change. Along with his family, the zaym of Ayn Chir now becomes one of the outcasts and undesirables.

However, this brutal about-face in the generalissimo's policy did not have any immediate significant effects on the lives of the Nassar family. It was followed by a reorganization of the leadership of the troops in the Syrian provinces, which included the replacement of Colonel Rassim with Colonel Omer Bey, who figures as a bitter memory in the clan history. More radical than Rassim, coming from the generalissimo's inner circle and the Young Turks movement, this Omer Bey—whose average build but decided pose and icy gaze can be seen in the photographs of Djemal Pasha's chiefs of staff conserved at the Istanbul War Museum—is charged with tightening the surveillance of the population in the whole area of Ayn Chir, Kfarshima, and the outposts of the Druze country. He takes up his headquarters at Villa Eucalypta in Rassim's place, and his first act is to install himself in the dining room, where he has some of the books from Curiel's library brought in—the historical and archaeological books—and he leafs through them one by one, distractedly, whenever he is alone, notably at night. Then he summons all his spies and informants in the area, and receives them discreetly in the little Arabian salon, where he turns on the fountain, so that the murmur of the water covers their whispered conversations. To the delicate sounds of water dripping on marble, then alone in his office, he mentally draws up a whole series of files on the principal suspects of the area, and on the first among them, Wakim Nassar. But he does not act straightaway. He waits, in seclusion, going through the historical books in Curiel's library, making a note of the passages that interest him on a piece of paper that he throws away after finishing his distracted reading, then he reviews his troops, but he never leaves the grounds of Villa Eucalypta. Which means that Wakim hears about him only when someone tells him that Rassim has been replaced, and he is completely indifferent to the news. But when, one morning, some visiting farmers talk about how Omer Bey spends his time reading through all of Curiel's library (they know this, they say with amusement, from an Arab soldier who told Malkoun's son, and they exaggerate, claiming that he tears off all the covers of the books to check that their boards aren't concealing any compromising papers), it is Helene who suddenly feels ill and stands up without listening to the rest. For the affair of the secret papers in the French consulate has been making the rounds for three days now. Helene is tormented with dread, and even though she keeps repeating to herself that there is nothing at Curiel's that would compromise them, that Curiel is not the consul, this banal story of an officer maniacally searching through the botanical treatises still ties her stomach in knots every time she thinks of it. But she says nothing about it. She tries to drown her premonitions in hard work.

And at the moment there is plenty of it. It is April. The winter was terrible, and bands of famished peasants are arriving from Beqaa and the villages high in the mountains. Attracted by the measly distributions of the Provisioning Commission, and especially by the aid given by the American evangelical missions, which the Turks are still tolerating, they descend on Beirut in whole families. In rags, already starved, some of them pass through Ayn Chir, which is on the road to Kfarshima, where there is a branch of the Commission. And on the way they inevitably stop in front of the Nassar property, go in, climb the steps up to the porch, and beg for something to eat. And they are given something, mostly bread, but also olives and milk for the children sometimes, which doesn't mean that they don't have to be stopped from going into the orchards and pillaging the oranges as well. Or at least what is left of them, for the grasshoppers have ruined the harvest and what remains of it is pitiful, except the second crop, those that ripen in April or May. Wakim manages to find a wholesaler to buy that crop, a speculator from the Provisioning Commission who has enriched himself by selling wheat at astronomical prices. Wakim sells his oranges to him without a second thought because it is clear that the man is not going to resell them to the starving poor, and take their houses for three pounds of abouserras, but that he will sell them for four times the price to Djemal Pasha, his German colonels, and all the profiteers, speculators, and war magnates who are suddenly proliferating everywhere.

Soon, then, the laborers start picking the fruit, and they have to defend themselves against the bands of famished people invading the orchards. The situation is about to turn into a riot when the Nassars intervene by distributing the oranges salvaged from the winter harvest. The farmers of Furn el-Chebbak and Baabda, who don't have much left to eat, rush in to receive a share of the harvest, along with Shiite farmers and Bedouins, and while Helene thus becomes a forerunner in humanitarian work, she keeps repeating to herself that you can't help people like this and then end up in prison, no, that's just not possible, there is such a thing as justice, God and the Virgin see everything. But this doesn't entirely convince her. A feeling of dread slowly rises up within her and turns into panic when, in the middle of the night, the front door of the house is violently shaken. For although the fugitives are still invading the property, Helene is now afraid, she tries to dissuade Wakim from going and opening the door, and when the fugitive is in the living room, she listens carefully to find out whether the Turks are after him or not. One night when Selim is alerted and arrives and scratches at the door as usual to come in, she cries out in panic and wakes up her daughters and the younger children. And finally, what she feared would happen does. One night, the knocking on the door is not anxious or nervous taps, but an imperious banging that resounds like a summons, along with shouts that fill the darkness all around the house. When Wakim opens up, with his eldest son behind him standing three steps back from the door and holding a lamp and pistol, he finds himself face-to-face with a man with a cold, amiable gaze and a distant smile, wearing a uniform with the insignia of a colonel. Then he understands that Omer Bey has come out of his lair.

He has not come out alone, in fact. Behind him, looking almost unreal caught between the shadows and the wavering light shed by Elias's lamp, are a yuzbashi and a junior officer. As for the shouts that are still filling the darkness outside, they indicate that the property is well and truly invaded. But Wakim does not move from his front door.

"What can I do for you, Colonel? This is no time to be waking people up."

"A deserter has taken refuge on your land, sir," Omer Bey replies.

"And how can I help you?"

"Let us come in while my men track him down."

"Impossible at this hour, Colonel. I have a wife and daughters to think of. But I can arrange for some chairs and a lamp to be brought to the front of the house."

"We will wait inside, sir."

"You are forcing my hand, Colonel."

"You are the one who is not cooperating, sir."

Omer Bey speaks perfect Arabic but with a deliberate touch of contempt for the language, a contempt manifested by a kind of monotone delivery, a total absence of modulation in his voice, as if he were pronouncing his words under duress. As for the word for "sir," pronounced in Turkish (*effendum*), with which he punctuates each of his replies, it has the effect of seriously annoying Wakim, and making him more stubborn every time. But in a flash Wakim realizes that this must be part of the officer's strategy, and that if he continues to refuse to let him in, he will be offering Omer Bey the perfect opportunity to suspect him overtly, and to have his house searched.

He finally allows the three military men inside, sits down with them in the living room with Elias as company, and for twenty minutes he gives laconic answers to all the questions asked by Omer Bey, who is pretending to be interested in the rugs, the furniture, and the clementines that he has heard so much about. Then a long silence falls. Wakim stands up and goes to post himself at the French doors leading onto the balcony where he showed the governor his orchards fifteen years previously, conspicuously turning his back to Omer Bey so that he doesn't have to answer any more of his questions. And also to make it clear that this is all going on far too long and he is getting impatient. Then he comes back to the middle of the living room and paces back and forth, with his hand in his belt. He looks at the points of his boots as he walks slowly over the carpets with their complex, meandering floral patterns. In the meantime, Omer Bey has settled into his armchair, one leg crossed over the other. As Wakim passes in front of him, he turns to his yuzbashi and asks him questions in Turkish, and Wakim understands that he is growing impatient too. The yuzbashi is about to stand up when a noise is heard in the hallway. Soon a junior officer appears, clacks his boots together, and says something that Wakim doesn't catch. He just has time to wonder whether there really is a fugitive on the property, or if this is just a performance. And all at once he understands that it is in fact both, for Omer Bey stands up and announces that he is going to have the house searched. Elias looks at his father impassively. Wakim remains motionless and, for the space of an instant, anyone who knew him in his youth would have recognized that curious way of his of looking down onto the surface of things, of looking at his interlocutor as if he were a genus, a species, and not an individual.

Omer Bey is disconcerted, and has the sense that Wakim is looking at something behind him. He is about to turn around but gets a grip on himself, his eyes meet those of his yuzbashi, to whom he addresses a sign. The yuzbashi takes a step forward but Wakim stops him by grabbing his shirt. The man puts his hand to his weapon.

"Don't touch your gun, it's no use," Wakim says to him in Arabic. "But think about this. I have daughters. There is my wife. Are you really going to enter their bedrooms at this hour of the night?"

Under the gaze of Omer Bey, who does not say a word or move a muscle, the yuzbashi replies in Turkish:

"Well then, get them all out and bring them here, into this living room."

Ten minutes later, in the middle of the living room, this is the scene: Helene sitting in an armchair, her eyes fixed as she tries to remain strong; on her lap is her youngest and at her side, clutching the arms of the chair, are the smallest of her children, those who will become my most familiar aunts and uncles and who are either staring at their parents to find out how to calm their own fear, or observing the soldiers with stupefied wide eyes as they brutally busy themselves around them; behind Helene, the two eldest daughters are standing up, leaning against each other with their hands on their mother's shoulders; facing this group is Wakim, his hand on the knee of his second son, Michel, who is fourteen years old and trying to look firm, sitting sidesaddle on the arm of his father's chair; Farid, the third son, my future uncle Charlus, who is twelve, is also sitting sidesaddle, but on the arm of the chair occupied by his older brother, who has an air of profound contempt; Omer Bey is in a fourth armchair, as if he were part of the family. Nobody is looking at him except one or other of the little ones who surreptitiously stare at him from time to time, with suppressed terror and the clear sense that he is the cause of all this distressing commotion.

As for the rest, we have to imagine the soldiers in the bedrooms, the bathrooms, the kitchens, the upturned beds, the emptied wardrobes, the sideboards and cupboards sounded with bayonets. We must also imagine, as they go, the silk dresses crumpled, the lace fingered with jubilation, the embroidered handkerchiefs and the ties discreetly filched and stuffed into the pockets of uniforms, the porcelain plates smashed, the rugs lifted up, the drawers turned upside down, and at the sight of all this, inevitably, the question Wakim asks:

"You really think you'll find a deserter under the carpet?" To which Omer Bey's response is:

"Anything can constitute a threat to the empire today. A deserter as much as a little note hidden in a drawer." To which Helene throws a dark look at Wakim.

We might consider this scene as the final one of the happy period in the Nassars' family life. The next day, the news spreads throughout Ayn Chir and the farmers come to show their support. They sit down on the edge of the armchairs while the family is busy putting things to right again. They whisper news to each other, notably about the arrests in Baabda and Kfarshima. Around midday, Rached's son, sitting down in turn, announces that the priest of Saint George at Ayn Chir has been arrested as well. On hearing this news, Wakim jumps on his horse. He rides to Saint George and finds the priest's house shuttered up, which means that the whole family has been taken away. An hour later, he is at the bishopric, where the powerlessness of the bishop is made patently obvious to him. There are Turkish soldiers at the door and an officer vetting the people who come for an audience. To his great surprise, Wakim is still received, but it is of no use, since the bishop himself is suspected of sympathizing with the Russians. On his return to Ayn Chir, Wakim gathers together Gerios and George Farhat, who is his son-in-law, and gives them his instructions about the orchards and the house in the months to come.

The next day, at dawn, the Turks are there, with Omer Bey at their head. A Turkish officer reads out a statement of indictment in Arabic (sympathy with the enemy, disloyalty to the sultan), which applies to Wakim and Selim as well, then the Nassars are given one hour to pack a trunk or two of things, for they are all being deported. Helene is incapable of restraining a light shaking of her hands, which she tries to hide from her children, as she throws together a random assortment of clothes. Her older daughters help her and try to be less frantic, and it is at that moment that an event occurs that has remained legendary for all the members of the Nassar clan.

Wakim, who initially tried to figure out where he would be taken and then talked for ten minutes with his son-in-law, announces to his daughters that they will stay where they are. Caught between her husband's praiseworthy firmness and her own horror at the prospect of a separation of undetermined duration, Helene is petrified and says nothing. The daughters balk at this prospect and continue packing their things. But when the moment of departure arrives, Wakim announces to Omer Bey that his daughters are staying. Paradoxically, the daughters are counting on Omer Bey's firmness, and indeed he declares that the whole family is banished.

"My daughters will remain here, Colonel," Wakim retorts as he puts on his jacket. "And that is that."

Then, as Omer Bey finally shrugs disdainfully, Wakim turns to his eldest daughter, the one married to George Farhat:

"Catherine, you are now entirely responsible for your sisters, you and your husband."

And then he turns to his two other daughters next in age:

"Blanche, Linda, you will take care of your younger sisters."

And then—let us once again paint this as a grand scene from antiquity—he takes his youngest son, my future father, into his arms and declares that the Nassars are ready.

14

IT ALL STARTS in army carts and the dust they cast up to the sky, then continues at the Beirut train station, where other families are waiting, then in the train, and more of the train, and still in the train. To begin with, Wakim carries his youngest and a large bag. Elias takes care of the trunk and his two younger brothers. Helene holds her second-youngest boy. When he gets tired, she carries him, or Wakim does, leaving the youngest to her. Selim carries his only son on one side and a suitcase on the other, and his wife has a shoulder bag. In the train, everyone can breathe again. But the farther they go, the more overwhelming the heat gets. The next day, at Aleppo, they change trains and are joined by more banished families arriving from Damascus. Two days later, on a platform in the middle of nowhere, there are more, from Baghdad.

During this whole time, Catherine, Blanche, and Linda do everything they can to find out any information at all about the fate of their family members. They go to the seraglio, to the bishopric, to Ibrahim B., who still has some influence; they even go to see Gebran Nassar, who is now hand in glove with the generalissimo (and he welcomes them, and listens to them, is kindly toward them, asks if they need anything, and finally answers that he will try to find out). They either go all together, the three of them, with Gerios driving the buggy, or in chaises, or even sometimes on foot, a terrible ordeal for them, since they are not at all accustomed to this and perspire despite their parasols and the handkerchiefs tucked into their belts. After a week has gone by, they have still not made much progress. The only information they have acquired, always the same thing, is that the banished are sent to Anatolia. They start mulling over this vague idea, over and over, "They are taken to Anatolia," like a coin in a pocket that one endlessly fiddles with, out of nervousness, while waiting for something that never comes. But that is like trying to light the darkness with a snuffed candle. And then one day Baclini's son's wife, who has a nephew in the army, pronounces the name *Dirkeker*. Gerios works out that this badly pronounced word must be the name of the town of Diyarbekir. Even though that is not much, it is better than total darkness.

"Is it a long way to Diyarbekir?" asks Margot, the youngest daughter.

"It takes days and days of travel to get there," Catherine replies.

"Even on a train?"

"On foot or on horseback it would be weeks and weeks," Blanche says.

The older daughters take turns answering the young ones' questions.

"And how will we know whether they've arrived?"

"God is great."

The families arrive at the end of the fourth day, defeated, exhausted, with puffy eyes, and the youngest boys whining at the slightest thing. They cannot see the town or perceive its still-open wounds. The following days, carts replace trains and jostle them on the appalling roads through the bald mountains of the Anatolian province of Diyarkebir, and Helene tells her daughters about this journey in her first letter to them: *My dear girls I send you heartfelt embraces I miss your affection and I am always thinking about you we are all doing well do not worry about us we have all been well treated even though the journey was tiring we had four days in trains and two days in carts your brothers behaved admirably and your father is doing very well and sends you warm embraces we are all settled now in a house with no comfort but thanks be to God it is better than nothing especially since the climate here is very pleasant and makes me think of Qattine which we are missing dreadfully and Ayn Chir but do not worry the people in the village where we are staying are kind and we are with two other families from Zahlé and Hasbaya who are all good people we talk with them about our country where we hope to return soon in the meantime we hope you are well we miss you terribly.*

The letters from Anatolia that tell of the exile of the Nassar family between 1916 and 1918 always seemed to me to be a myth, for I first heard about them in my earliest childhood, without ever seeing them or knowing where they were hidden. To begin with, or in other words, a long time ago, I thought that these letters would be somewhere in the disorderly archives of the Nassars, with one of my uncles or among the papers of the descendants of one of my aunts. But when I asked to see them, first my father, then my uncles, then the other descendants of Wakim with whom I talked about them gave only vague answers or passed off the responsibility for the preservation of these significant documents to each other, documents whose importance I thought was considerable not only to the Nassar clan itself but also to the region and the country as a whole. I went through several frames of mind, from certainty that these letters must have disappeared sometime in the stormy history of the Nassars to doubt about their very existence. One day, my uncle Charlus, in a kind of sudden illumination, seemed to recollect that they were at his house. He often had bursts of interest in his family heritage and would exert himself to dig out a photograph from an album or a name from a tangled genealogical line. He carried out a serious search for them that convinced me that any previous attempts had been only cursory. But actually, he was mistaken. The letters were not at his house. Another time, a descendant of one of my aunts thought he remembered (and this time with certainty) that he had once seen the letters among the effects belonging to his mother, who was one of those nieces of my father who was ten years older than he was. I had to follow the itinerary those effects had taken since the time that the great-nephew had first seen them. But in between times there had been the civil war and the diaspora, and the aunt's effects had been dispersed. My father interceded on my behalf, and I was able to arrange appointments with great-grand-nephews I had never met, but I did not find anything. There was also another rumor, the last and most improbable one, that the letters had been taken by one of Wakim's sons who immigrated to Brazil in the 1920s. I decided that I had had enough and that the letters must be taken to be lost, with *lost* being something of a euphemism in my jaded mind. I didn't speak to anyone about them again, until the day when I was tidying up our house after my father's death and found two forgotten boxes in the attic in which, among an incalculable number of letters, invoices, receipts, photographs, and the plans for the restoration of the Big House that my father undertook after his return from Egypt in 1950 and the deeds of sale of thousands of acres of land at Ayn Chir, I discovered the famous correspondence. My thought at that time, when all of Wakim's children were already dead, was that I must be holding a veritable treasure, one that would put a seal on all of the accounts, the one document that would erase all the uncertainties about the Nassars and their exile, the instrument that would perhaps even render the telling of the Nassar history pointless. But that was not the case. Helene's letters were in fact the most perfect nonevent in my long quest for fragments of the clan's history.

The whole of this correspondence is made up of six letters sent by Helene through the intermediary of the Ottoman military postal service and four letters from Catherine or Blanche sent from Ayn Chir. It took me several months to reconstitute their contents, which were worn away by time, the advanced fading of the ink and the sometimes irreparable decomposition of the old paper on the fold lines. Helene's handwriting in particular, febrile and with no real punctuation, gave me a lot of trouble. When I finally managed to work it all out, I expected to find out about an important part of that fatal moment in the Nassars' history, with indelible (and indubitable) evidence. But it was not to be. First because a large part of the letters is taken up by words of affection, stereotyped formulas, and strings of salutations. And especially because Helene omits a considerable number of facts. For instance, she never gives the name of the village where she and the family were billeted. Maybe she did so in a letter that is now lost, but I doubt it. But the name of the village was in fact always part of the memory of the clan, and I myself have tried on many occasions to find a trace of it on current maps of Turkey, without the slightest success. I also tried to find hamlets with names that approximated it, for I am almost certain today that the name of Kalaajek that subsisted in the memory of the Nassars must have been a deformation, or have been altered, or mispronounced by the exiles themselves, from the very beginning.

All of these points would have been clarified if Helene had only mentioned the name in her correspondence. But she didn't, just as she never mentioned, from the very beginning, one of the most important details, namely that Kalaajek had originally been a mixed village, populated by Kurds and Armenians, and that all the Armenians had no doubt been massacred there, and that it was in their half-destroyed houses that she and her family were forced to live.

The points Helene also doesn't mention are all the hassles, vexations, and finally the open conflict between the Kurdish villagers and the exiles, under the amused gaze of the Turkish gendarmes, a conflict that might have turned out very badly, as evidenced by the memorable injury of one of Wakim's sons. And finally, what she never talks about are the tribulations they endured because of the hard winters, and how their daily life was woven through with uncertainty and insecurity, and finally the fear—which was constantly stoked by the Turks as the war approached its conclusion and their defeats became irremediable—of a possible physical extermination of all the exiles.

What the letters do mostly talk about, however, is their daily life in all its little details: *My darling girls, I send you heartfelt embraces I miss you terribly and your brothers do too I hope you are doing well that everything around you is fine that dear George is in good health and our dear Gerios too and that you are looking after each other do write to us to reassure us about your health and the state of our poor dear country we are all well here your father sends you his most heartfelt kisses as do your brothers who miss you so much your little brother is being very good and I am sure that he misses you too especially you my dear Blanche who looked after him so well as I said we are settled reasonably well the roof of the house was a little damaged and we were able to get some help and fix it thanks to the village chief who is an obliging man two houses away from ours is where the other families live with whom we spend time talking about our dear country we cook together it was hard to find kitchen equipment but we had cauldrons and jugs and for the rest God provides it is starting to get cold the winters must be hard here but we are used to Qattine and so it will surely be alright your brothers have gathered wood in the area and they caught a weasel the other day we also got some military blankets because the nights are starting to be frosty but you mustn't worry for we are all in good health and we are very impatient to see you all again along with Gerios and George and all our friends of Ayn Chir and Qattine to whom we all send heartfelt greetings and with the help of God and the Virgin we will be together again soon my darlings look after yourselves and take care of your younger sisters see you soon your mother who loves you Helene.*

Of course, we could just take all this at face value and be led to the view that, apart from a few difficulties to do with comfort, exile was easy enough to manage after all. But in fact over the course of all six missives, apart from a few rare passages, Helene seems to be showing an extraordinary sense of diversion. I never really took any notice of it before, but as soon as I tried to compare those letters with the living testimonies and also with the more obvious realities, I realized that her repetitive, relentless style, this insistence with no regard for rules, this wavering structure with no backbone was like a purring voice designed to salve the distress and anxiety of her daughters, to anesthetize the least tendency to worry, whereas in fact, the real situation must have been something quite different. I never had the opportunity to talk to my oldest aunts about this, for I didn't know them well and they were dead when I started to take an interest in all this, but I would love to know whether they had been duped.

Of course, this correspondence reflects the way letters were written in our countries until about twenty years ago, in an irritating manner where affectionate greetings are repeated at every line and at every mention of a person's name, and the sentimental effusions are the equivalent of the salaams that are scattered throughout the spoken language. They are also the expression of a conception of language as an instrument designed to put on a good show, to make itself shine and glisten rather than to set out the facts. And yet Helene gives a few accounts of little incidents, and even talks about trivialities such as cooking and cutting wood, which is contrary to epistolary rhetoric, while she fails to mention more serious things. There is also undoubtedly something like self-censorship at play, not military censorship, which she seems to care very little about, but censorship out of maternal devotion, which pushes her to select the most ordinary events, the most banal ones, and to serve them up in a package of local color designed to allay her daughters' worry rather than any Turkish officer's concern. Unless of course all this was just a way of fighting back, of showing oneself to be bigger than the vicissitudes of life, of treating them with the most perfect disdain by turning away from them, as if they were nothing at all, and of concerning herself only with matters of neighborly events, the taste of figs, the creation of a checkerboard, or the discovery in an abandoned house of an absolutely spectacular wedding dress.

From now on, then, we will have to work our way backward, or in opposition to the principal document surviving from that era, which seems rather preposterous. After unraveling the fabric of events as Helene relates them, we will have to weave them back together another way, starting again from the beginning.

So here we have the exiles landing in Kalaajek, which is (let's say) a group of around twenty low mud brick houses, spread over a few terraced fields of wheat and fig trees. The Nassars and their fellow countrymen, the Batal family (from Zahlé) and the Hayeks (from Hasbaya), are standing together in the central square, in front of all the locals who have gathered there to see the spectacle. The gendarmes take a roll call, the village chief shows each family of exiles the house that they will occupy: the Nassars here, the people from Zahlé a little farther away, those from Hasbaya a little higher up. It's like being shown one's assigned bed in a dormitory. Let's not say anything about their mental and psychological state in the days that follow. Let us not think. No sentimentalism. Let's go straight to the facts. The houses are dilapidated, they smell mildewy inside. It has rained on what was left of their rudimentary furnishings and utensils, and the wood in the sheds has rotted. The families clear it all out and air everything, sort through it all, throw away this, keep that, make an inhabitable space out of the ruins of a world that must have once been happy but then brutally came to an end, right there, one day, just like that, and now there is not a trace of it left because of the pillaging afterward, and then the rain and the snow that disfigured everything, just as death makes a human face hideous to see.

Of course the first few nights, Helene doesn't get any sleep at all, and if she does, she dreams of corpses, or she sees the owners of the houses coming back to claim them, and they look either like Omer Bey or like Gebran Nassar. She then wonders with a start why it is Gebran she is dreaming of, and is taken with a terrible worry for her daughters. And her sleepless nights go on like this for weeks, until she almost collapses with exhaustion. Nobody is sleeping in fact, or only very badly, for their pallets are made of straw, there are holes in the roof, the walls are crumbling down in places. And for the moment there is no talk of repairs. They are all paralyzed by the brutal change, the misery of the place, and especially by the suffocating prospect of the future. Which explains Helene's anxiety attacks, her irrepressible tears when she goes out into the sunshine in the square in front of the house, appearing to the local villagers like a woman in mourning, her moist eyes staring into the distance. For obviously the locals have only one preoccupation now, which is to observe the families of exiles, whose children sometimes stand on the threshold of their houses, dumbfounded by this unfamiliar and pitiful spectacle of poverty, of snot-nosed half-naked children approaching them and speaking Kurdish. The men, for their part, walk through the streets of the village. They are still wearing their city clothes, which are not ironed and look slightly disheveled. They throw their jackets over their shoulders and leave their ties undone. Wakim walks without his cane, his shoes are covered in mud. But even like that, they all seem to have fallen from the moon when they pass in front of the local men in turbans, rags, and bare feet. During their walks, they think about the future, but especially about the present, about the possibility of conciliation with the locals, of gaining the favor of the village chief, of getting the better of the highly problematic vigilance of the gendarmes. They also worry about the women (the Batals and the Hayeks have daughters), the fate of their children, and consider joint security measures and alarm systems so they can come to each other's aid should things turn out badly. And then one morning, as they are attempting to go beyond the last houses in the village, they hear shouts, children running toward them, women calling to each other from one rooftop to the next, and soon the chief and two villagers arrive armed with guns and order them back the way they came.

After some discussion, it transpires that they are not allowed out of the village. And so they understand that all of the villagers are also keeping an eye on them. Wakim says nothing of this to Helene but she has already understood it, she read it on their prying, inquisitive faces when she went for a short walk with Wakim. Which doesn't stop her from going out alone one day. Then, at the end of the first month, she takes the initiative. This is the episode of the roof that she talks about in her second letter. It has collapsed, and she decides that it needs to be fixed.

"If we are supposed to stay here until the end of the war, and it doesn't end before winter comes, we'll have to protect ourselves somehow," she announces to Regina Hayek, who also decides that a wall that is about to crumble down must be fixed too.

Since they cannot repair the roof by themselves, Wakim talks to the village chief, who points out two men who will be able to help him for a few matlics. But when Wakim offers them work, they refuse:

"We don't repair Armenian houses."

Wakim talks to the village chief again, who, this time, like Pontius Pilate, shrugs and washes his hands of the situation:

"It's true, they are right. In fact, the gendarmes will stop us."

"But when the gendarmes come, the work will be finished."

"I cannot force anyone to work for you."

That episode remained vivid in my uncles' memories, although I never could figure out whether they actually remembered it or whether it was only secondhand. The main thing is that, in the version of events preserved in their memory, the role of the village chief is much less ideal than it is in Helene's letters. In fact, he was always talked about as a man full of duplicity, even though my uncle Charlus once tempered this a little:

"He was caught in the firing line from both sides. He was reasonable enough, but he had to deal with the gendarmes, the military, his own villagers, and the Tatars."

I didn't pursue this mention of the Tatars, for I knew that my uncles and my father, out of incredible obstinacy, always called the Turkmen horsemen who harassed the exiles Tatars, even though they were perfectly willing to admit that they weren't actually Tatars. (So much so that when anyone was surprised and asked them about it: "What do you mean, Tatars?," they would correct themselves without batting an eyelid, "Turkmens, you know," such that I finally convinced myself that this strange use of language was just a habit they had formed when they were in exile, when they must have heard the Turkmens being called Tatars, either by mistake or metaphorically, and were never able to let go of the habit.) So I didn't pursue the mention of the Tatars, but I did ask for explanations about the villagers.

"Were they really completely hostile toward the exiles?"

"Not exactly," my uncle replied. "They were also caught between a kind of fascination and genuine hostility. Don't forget that we were supposedly enemies and that we were Christians, which they confused with Armenians."

Khalil, my other uncle, added: "In fact, we caused them something of a Cornelian dilemma. They loved us as much as they felt they had to hate us."

That uncle was undoubtedly the best educated of Wakim's sons, but for someone who started work at the age of sixteen selling sewing machines, his definition of a Cornelian dilemma was rather fine. I swore to myself to use it one day. Now that's done we can get back to the matter at hand. After the village chief's refusal, Wakim rolls up his sleeves, calls his boys together, gets help from the Batal and Hayek sons, and the roof is fixed within the week, with all the possible logistical difficulties—the villagers refusing to lend any equipment (they make their own or use other items they adapt to new uses), the impossibility of cutting wood for the pillars and beams (they reuse the old ones or those from abandoned houses)—and after that, they help the Hayeks with the wall and the Batals with goodness knows what and all is going fine until the day when the gendarmes arrive for their inspection. According to the most familiar account in the Nassar family, a snitch from the village attracts the gendarmes' attention to these developments, and then they come along to inspect, take note of the repairs, and declare that they are forbidden.

"It's not for you to rebuild the houses of Armenian traitors," the shawish declares.

"Winter is coming," Wakim replies. "What are we supposed to do with the rain and snow?"

"You can do what you like, but you don't rebuild traitors' houses," the guy insists.

And Wakim understands what this is all about and returns with a mejidieh. But before he gives it, he hesitates for a moment, for when I think about this, I realize that these are not actual gendarmes, they are army auxiliary troops, brutal, unscrupulous men who were employed to exterminate the Armenians. Slipping them a mejidieh might be seen as a humiliating act and therefore fatal. Wakim hesitates for a moment, then ends up going ahead, and I often wondered whether it wouldn't have been far simpler for the auxiliaries to have searched the exiles and taken all their money in one fell swoop. But in that case the money would be considered "confiscated" and would thus need to be restituted to the Ottoman treasury, whereas this way it goes straight into the gendarmes' pockets. And plenty of it does, for after completing the same inspection of the Batal and Hayek houses, the gendarmes come back and do the same thing every month, and thus receive what amounts to a real salary for the simple business of fixing a roof, and then they make the exiles pay for the right to burn wood in winter, or eat figs in the fall, or drink water at any time of the year, to say nothing of leasing them a plot of land or selling them wool blankets in winter, blankets that are originally meant to be simply distributed. They will even charge for delivering the letters that arrive from Lebanon, of which the first, written by Blanche, has been preserved: *Dear mother, dear father, dear all of you, our darling brothers, we send you heartfelt embraces. Since your departure all four of us have been staying with Catherine and George who send their love. We lived through terrible days before receiving your letter and hearing your news but thank goodness you are all in good health that's the main thing. Lots of people here have tried to help us to get news of you, notably Ibrahim B. and Thérèse de F., and even his holiness the bishop. All of them are now glad to hear that you are doing well. However the country is not doing so well rationing is more and more disastrous there are shortages of wheat and what does get distributed is rotten but we are alright because there are still plenty of reserves and Gerios is still looking after the vegetable garden. Unfortunately the day of your departure the Turks took away the wheat that Father had bought a few days earlier and then the soldiers came and requisitioned the horses including Ambar but we stopped them from taking the provisions of olive oil from last year and the fig jam which we took to Catherine's. The house is being guarded by Gerios who sleeps there. He brought his family with him and intruders no longer dare go into the property. Uncle Camille came and spent three days there with him. We took the opportunity to go stay in the house and to clean up a bit. That's all the news. George sends his love as do the children and Gerios and his family. The Callases are going to write to you separately and we all send our love Blanche, Catherine.*

Dated in August, this letter probably arrives in Kalaajek in the middle of winter, a freezing winter, when the snow is so thick on the ground that one morning, as the children are going outside, one of them thinks that the village has disappeared, which is enchanting to him: "We are all alone, we are all alone." But in fact there is nothing enchanting about it. The cold is stinging and while the exiles can burn the remainder of the wood left by the former owners of their houses, they need to save what they can and use the rough blankets sold by the gendarmes. Moreover, there is almost no food left and they have to buy it from the villagers. But the problem is that, to begin with, the locals are keen to sell some of their provisions, especially since they have never seen so much money as since the exiles arrived. But then after a few weeks they start to get reluctant because they don't have huge reserves themselves. My uncles used to tell the story of how Helene would visit her neighbors, wearing a dress over two blankets that she strapped around her silk girdle with two belts, one at her waist, the other under her bust. The villagers receive her with great respect, even though they do not want to sell her anything anymore. But she offers them so much money, proposing what seem like astronomical sums to them for a rotl of flour or two ounces of dried meat, that they finally give in, and this adds a little tasty extra to the Nassars' daily meals, which are essentially thin soups. Of course, the rumors spread and the villagers sometimes bring out whatever surpluses they have in their reserves, a piece of cheese, some dried figs, or a few eggs, and come themselves to sell them to the exiles. And because of this, a few visitors now come to the Nassars. They sit around the fireplace and exchange pleasantries in Turkish, which is the common language that no one speaks very well. They make scraps of sentences with lots of holes that no one can fill in. There are silences while they observe each other, and then finally the negotiations start. Everybody knows the numbers in Turkish, and that is always the simplest part of the conversation.

One day the village chief himself comes along with a piece of smoked beef shank which he hopes to get a good price for. They talk more with him because his Turkish is better and complements what the Nassars already know. They pay him what he wants for his beef shank and also for the vague news he brings of the war, such that he comes back often, maybe he even plays checkers with Wakim or Selim, in the presence of other men from the village, why not, since Helene writes about this in her letters. But it is also possible, despite what she says, that she doesn't enjoy his visits, for the chief's eyes dart everywhere and she is convinced that the news he brings is not reliable because it is always news in favor of Turkey, the empire counterattacking here, the *Roums* getting a beating there, the *Inglisi* losing this, and the *Fransawi* that. Apart from the fact that this is all terribly depressing for the exiles, Helene perceives in the chief a kind of enthusiasm for making those he knows to be sympathizers with the Allies suffer.

Wakim sees this too and it makes him all the more furious that, out of a concern to protect his family, he must nod along, which makes him feel doubly trapped.

Nevertheless, these visits and the relationships with some of the villagers do allow the Nassars and their compatriots to figure out who is with them and who is hostile. For there are some people who are hostile, and this is something that left an enduring trace in the memories of exile, of which the famous story of the spit is only an anecdotic detail. The story has it that Helene, one morning, goes out with one of her sons. As she heads for the Batals, she passes in front of a group of young peasants who say something unkind to her. She doesn't respond, obviously, and one of the young men, seeing in her what he considers to be a haughty expression, spits on the ground. Helene, who can't stand it any longer, because the man must have said something vulgar about Christianity, ends up muttering something but doesn't stop walking. But that is precisely what the youth wanted, and he leaves his group and walks behind her while calling out to her. But since she continues walking and he doesn't quite know what to do anyway, he heads back to his group, shouting all the while, and that's when he slips on his own spit, which has frozen in the meantime. This gives the Nassars, the Batals, and the Hayeks something to laugh about, and also some of the villagers who are not too hostile toward the exiles.

But then there is worse to come, including the story of the deer. This story features Elias, the oldest son, who tries to do something to help with provisioning during the winter and makes up rudimentary hunting weapons, slingshots or bows and arrows. That entertains him and also occupies his younger brothers, who have nothing else to do except play in the snow. When the occasion presents itself, he leaves the house, goes some distance away from the village, hiding from the sight of the locals, passes far away from the frozen orchards where there might be a villager visiting his trees, in the hopes of finding an animal. In the meantime, his brothers are playing at hunting in front of the houses, shooting at imaginary wolves, foxes, and even bears, following what they have heard about the hunting parties in Keserwan. And one day their older brother takes them with him, and it seems this brings him luck, for that day he finds a young deer. Let us not dwell on the tracking, on the fascinated boys stuck in the snow up to their hips, but who are very good at keeping quiet and forgetting they are freezing, or on the wounded animal and the blood staining the snow. Let us not dwell either on how they carried the deer, one leg each, with its head bobbing against the snow, but let's get straight to the point. The catch does not go unnoticed by the villagers, despite the Nassars' care to hide it. But they do have to cut up the animal and empty the blood; in short, take care of all the butchering. They try to do it at night, in the shed, but it still attracts flies, namely the village chief and a few youths who arrive the next morning with their guns to get an explanation. Since they don't have a choice, Wakim and Selim tell them what happened, show them the bow and arrows, offer them a share of the bounty. But no, the chief and his men want everything, it's confiscated, the exiles are not allowed to hunt, it's forbidden, and they take away all the meat, the skin, and even the offal from the deer. As they leave, they also demand the bows. The Nassars protest, the armed men force their way through, there is pushing and shoving, threats, guns brandished under the noses of Wakim, Selim, and Elias, who are ordered to not move a muscle. And then, to the women's consternation, Wakim's three youngest sons get between them and start shouting. In the scuffle that follows, Wakim and his brother push back the guns, but the blows from the butts start raining down and that is when Farid, my future uncle Charlus, receives a rather severe blow that will make the family fear for his life. We must imagine the boy remaining knocked out for several hours, the panic, the bandages on his head, the prayers, the old wives' remedies offered by the Batals and the Hayeks. And after that, at the first sign of the thaw, the gendarmes reappear and start an inspection of the exiles' houses, and notably the Nassars', where everything is turned upside down, thrown carelessly on the ground or out the windows, as a punishment for the incident with the deer.

Of course that foreshadows a rather unpleasant spring, when everything seems to repeat itself desperately, over and over again, when the villagers are sometimes friendly and sometimes hostile, without there being any discernable logic to their behavior, when the future still incomprehensible and disheartening with so little news, or what news there is so deformed that the exiles no longer pay any attention to it. Whenever they do try to figure it all out, this leads to long discussions, as if they were trying to work out a riddle or a charade as a group. And then there are more negotiations about provisions, about the lease of a little plot of land abandoned by the Armenians where they plant vegetables and fruit for the winter, hoping that once winter comes they can send the whole lot to the thousand devils and be safely back in Ayn Chir, Zahlé, or Hasbaya. There is also the authorization Wakim manages to extract with a handful of gold mejidiehs for the gendarmes, to cut firewood for the winter. All that keeps them busy until the summer, despite the presence of the famous Turkmen horsemen, who settle near Kalaajek from the spring to the fall and harass the exiles, galloping through the village and stopping in front of the Nassars' house, where Helene and Selim's wife are busy preserving grape leaves. They demand the bracelet that one of them is wearing on her wrist or the scarf the other has on her head, or else money. If they meet any resistance, without even dismounting from their horses, they smash the finished preserves with the barrels of their guns, trample those that are waiting to be prepared, make their horses kick, then issue warnings that they will return later. Which is what they do, and then Wakim receives them and tries to parley and keep his composure before giving bits and pieces of what little is left of the gold or the clothing from Ayn Chir that nobody wears anymore. The Turkmen horsemen also appear in the exiles' vegetable gardens, and declare that the land is their sheep's pasture, and make it clear that they are demanding a tribute, and so they are given some cabbages, or potatoes, or that wonderful harvest of corn that my uncles never forgot they were forced to hand over to them after working on it all summer long.

There is nothing that can be done against these Turkmens except hunker down and wait for fall, when they finally leave, and Helene says not a word about any of this in her letters: *My darling daughters I send you my heartfelt embraces you have no idea how much we miss you we are all doing well your father and your brothers send their love how are you doing and dear George here we are finding that time drags by very slowly so far away from you and our dear country but we can't complain the winter was very cold but we lived through it with no difficulties thanks to the presence of the families from Zahlé and Hasbaya to say nothing of the people here who are very friendly there was lots of snow which forced us to stay inside and there is really nothing to do except the cooking and the evening gatherings your father who misses you dearly created a beautiful checkerboard but it was your oldest brother who always beat him your brothers are doing well and send their love they miss everything but do not complain and thank God for everything he does they sometimes go hunting when the weather permits they caught a fine deer and other things as well your little brother is talking very well now and he is the local people's darling he goes out with me all bundled up which is an amusing sight to see apart from that we get some news of the situation and the war but we can't be sure that it is very reliable do write to us to tell us how you are doing here we hope that it will all be over by the summer and we can all be together again at Ayn Chir if God wills it.* Or another one, always in the form of that incredible purring, that implausible thread of banalities woven like a veil to hide the reality of the situation, but which is sometimes interrupted by a singular and unexpected motif: *My beloved darling daughters I embrace you with indescribable affection as does your father who is constantly talking about you as do your brothers who miss you how are you and dear George and Gerios and his family are they still at Ayn Chir and still living in the house I hope you lack for nothing and that the situation is a little better we are very worried about you we are all doing well everyone is in good health the spring was very warm the country is pleasant and the people are good we leased some land where we are growing all sorts of things like Gerios in his vegetable garden this allows us to pass the time and to find it less long a few days ago something happened that will surprise you in an abandoned house in the village we found a wedding dress a magnificent dress in colored fabric with lace and braiding and gold pieces sewn into it no one knows how it got there maybe a wall collapsed under the rain and snow and was hiding a wardrobe of party dresses the dress was in excellent condition it was your brothers who found it playing near the house in this sad situation I saw it as a very happy sign especially since it appeared in the springtime at the same time as the fields and meadows were in flower and you will understand why it makes me think about you all the time my dear beloved daughters.* And of course these letters receive replies that prove that the contact, even though it was very intermittent, was not broken before 1918: *Dear Mommy, dear Daddy, dear all of you, we received your letter which brought us immense joy. We praise God that you are in good health and that everyone around you is well. We miss you terribly and everyone here sends you warm embraces George and Gerios and their families and the Callases who wrote to you and are all in good health. Unfortunately the situation in the country is not good more and more people are going hungry and there are more people dying you find them sometimes on the roadside and it is really dreadful but thanks to God we lack for nothing even though we have to ration things a little just like everyone else. The reserves are exhausted but we have been able to buy provisions although they were very expensive, and the Callas family send us wheat from Qattine and Gerios looks after the vegetable garden. Unfortunately the orange harvest was entirely requisitioned this year. Gerios did everything he could to stop this, but in vain. But he says that it was not a good harvest anyway, that the orchard is full of weeds, and some trees have dried up because of the grasshoppers the lack of watering and care and that won't bring much profit to the speculators but on your return God willing we can put all this to rights and have beautiful big oranges like we used to. We all tell ourselves the same thing, all five of us, and we dream of the day when we will all be together again. We miss you more than is possible and are waiting for the blessed day when we will be able to embrace you again.*

Contrary to Helene, it's noticeable that her daughters don't embellish anything, but say things as they are without trying to spare anyone's feelings, and this cannot have contributed much to raising the exiles' spirits. For one can easily imagine how the prospect of another winter must have made them despair. In fact, that catastrophic winter would probably be the fatal season for the Nassars.

It is at that point, according to all accounts, that the gendarmes decide not to come and conduct their inspections anymore. Since the fall their racketeering has not been very profitable, and they decide that trudging through the snow for some potatoes and pear jam is not worth it anymore. The heads of the exiled families must now come and report to the barracks themselves. When this new iron law is announced, it is received with contempt, and in the first week no one moves. But three days later the gendarmes appear in the village one morning, force the doors of the exiles' houses, undertake another furious and pointless search where they trample on all the provisions and preserves and throw all the clothes and bedding out into the snow, and then take the three family heads away amid the cries and entreaties of the women and the screaming of the little children. According to all accounts, the three men were held for two hours in a cell before being released, and they had to return to the village on foot. I try to imagine them during this journey, walking at a swift pace so as not to freeze, following the footsteps of the horses and those they themselves left on the way there, forcing themselves to talk to keep their spirits up and without worrying about the clouds of thick steam coming from their mouths like feathers on a hat, or like the speech bubbles in old comics, then finally falling silent and walking straight on without turning around. I imagine Wakim in his big boots, his mustache frozen, with his usual somber expression on his pursed lips and his steps still firm and solid. From time to time, he stops to look at the landscape and make a mental note of various details in case the families might have to flee one day. He notices that ruined farm, that stand of pine trees, he tries to memorize the topographical features, and after three or four hours he is surprised to be thinking almost fondly about Kalaajek, which has still not appeared. But after four hours the village does at last appear and it is almost like a homecoming, the warmth of the houses, the women rubbing their feet and then soaking them in a basin of hot water. The following week the men resolve after long discussions to go and make their stupid report. Elias proposes to go instead of Wakim or to accompany him.

"Stay with your mother and brothers," Wakim replies. "That will be more useful."

This time they are more warmly dressed, they have provisions, but from now on the families will live in dread of these departures. As the year goes by, the days get shorter. They leave earlier to avoid being caught by darkness. On the return trips they start hearing the howling of wolves before nightfall, and the men hurry along the road, but their feet sink into the snow that has frozen over and cracks, and in the houses the women put their hands on their hearts and whisper prayers. As the weather gets colder and colder, the blankets are no longer warm enough. Helene, who has sewn them into something resembling a woolen coat, realizes that even this won't do. In any case, Wakim refuses to wear it.

"The children need it more than I do," he says.

"We can still use it for the children, even if you sometimes wear it."

But he still refuses, and whereas walking keeps him warm during their journeys, when he has to stop to wait for one of his companions to catch his breath or tighten his bootstraps or take a leak, he feels as if he is turning into an ice statue and that nothing will ever warm him up ever again. Soon he starts to cough, he feels something like solid, pointy chunks cutting through his chest, and all this terrorizes Helene. But he laughs and declares:

"Don't worry, Helene, I have no intention of giving them that pleasure. For that is what they are hoping for, I'm sure of it. But they won't get me. And we will all leave here in good health."

However, the time of departure does not come, and would not come for almost a year, during which time Wakim manages to overcome his illness, but it has only settled down to sleep inside him, like those poisons that are deposited in the body and forgotten until an unknown catalyst wakes them up. I never knew for certain what the illness was, untreated bronchitis, rampant pneumonia, or something more sinister, for in a kind of anger and revolt against fate, my father and my uncles always refused to say the name of what would eventually take their father. When I started getting interested in all the details of this story, I thought it would be easy to get one or other of my father's old nieces or one of the descendants of his sisters to tell me, but whenever I spoke about it with them they all looked at me with incredulous eyes, and I understood that a kind of collective repression had occurred, a revenge by silence, a refusal to acknowledge the illness and its nature, which reflected the desire that Wakim's children obviously all had to keep the image of their father, and to pass it down to their descendants, only as a healthy man who up and dies just like that, with no real cause, on a whim, one fine morning, which in a way then also prevented me from ever being able to imagine him in any other way than standing up, walking with a decided step, always strong and reassuring, on the roads of Marsad, of Ayn Chir and Beirut, as well as on the snowy paths of eastern Anatolia.

In any case, the illness falls asleep, spring comes, and there is still no departure on the horizon, and it won't come for almost another year. A year in which the vexations and hostility are clearly attenuated. In the spring, the gendarmes come back to carry out their inspections themselves, but the Turkmens do not come at all, which leads everyone to believe that the migrations of pastoral nomads have been upset by the new mobility of the fronts. All this constitutes a series of clues they must decipher in order to guess a little of the progress of the war, and the exiles spend whole days doing so. But they are so far away, so terribly far away. The war and the state of the world for the exiles of Kalaajek are like the movements of tectonic plates for seismologists, movements that reach the surface only as distant and often barely perceptible effects. Sometimes, however, more concrete information arrives and provides the subject for speculations in the evening gatherings or in the meetings the men hold among themselves. Such as the village chief proudly announcing the end of tsarism one day. The Nassars, who have always avoided openly admitting to the villagers that they are Orthodox, take the blow without reacting. Or the salvo of gunshots to celebrate the accession to the throne of the new sultan, news brought by a traveling salesman and later confirmed by the gendarmes. Like astrologers who attribute events to the conjunction of two planetary influences, both the exiles and the villagers see this conjunction of the fall of one emperor and the arrival of another as the cause of the victory of the Turks over the Armenians and the Georgians north of Anatolia at the beginning of the summer. The meetings among the Nassar, Hayek, and Batal families become more somber. They feel as if it will never end. The women are in despair. The men hide theirs.

If none of the exiles are considering the possibility of a Turkish defeat at this point, that is simply because the information at their disposal is distorted by the partial and filtered news that is supplied to them. Like mariners whose navigation calculations are made with a compass dysregulated by the proximity of an unexpected magnetic field, they make conjectures while unaware of the essential component of the problem, namely the defeats of the Turks in Iraq and Palestine between the end of 1917 and the beginning of 1918, defeats that were much more significant than their victories in the Caucasus and that heralded the end of the Ottoman Empire. When I spoke to my father about this, he explained that this demoralizing illusion under which the exiles lived was probably salutary:

"If we had found out about the Turkish defeats at the beginning of 1918, we might have been afraid of retaliations, and we might have had the bad idea of leaving. And that's when things could have gone terribly wrong. But in fact, when we did decide to leave, it was really all over for Turkey and there was nothing for us to fear anymore."

This departure is recorded in the annals of the clan as being prompted by a slipup made by the village chief, who told Selim Nassar about the armistice of Mudros. This might have happened during a chance encounter in the village streets, or during a visit to the Nassars when Wakim was absent, or in a field where they were working side by side. Whatever the case, the chief gives the game away, probably without saying the word *Mudros,* which he probably doesn't know about, or even using the term *armistice,* but more likely muttering something like: "It's all over, we capitulated to your friends the *Fransawi,*" or "You must be proud now that we have capitulated, etcetera." The annals did not retain the circumstances or the exact words of the admission but that doesn't matter. What does matter is that Selim, who is overwhelmed and can't believe his ears, immediately tells the news to Wakim, who is just as dumbfounded and delighted, but keeps it quiet for half a day and then tells Helene about it, who can no longer sleep at night. The next day, the adults at the Hayeks and the Batals are told, and they all decide that if they must leave before any reprisals take place, then they should do so quickly because winter is upon them. Selim and a member of the Batal family set out on a reconnaissance mission. As they are about to leave the village, they are stopped by armed villagers, but the chief ends up just shrugging and letting them go. There is one more day of preparations and reconnaissance, and then, two days later, all three families of exiles leave the village of Kalaajek as a group.

This is where the episode begins of Wakim Nassar's family's departure from Anatolia and return to Lebanon, an episode about which I have a whole bunch of disordered accounts, all of them precise and succinct, which I will try to summarize. To begin with, they leave on foot, with the older children taking turns carrying the smallest ones. There are no trunks, but bundles carried on shoulders. They need to travel light and keep moving. To begin with as well, the roads are bad and stay that way for a long time. And then also to begin with, they sleep under a thicket, in an abandoned barn, and even in the ruins of an Armenian hamlet. During the first week, the men are constantly scanning the horizon to make sure they are not being followed. Whenever they meet a peasant on the road, they greet him in Turkish and the dread of being pursued intensifies. They avoid any farms that appear to be inhabited. On the sixth day, there is an alert, with soldiers appearing on the horizon. They all take cover so as not to be seen. The soldiers pass and they start walking again. By the eighth day, they reach Diyarbekir. Elias Nassar and a Batal son go ahead on reconnaissance and then they all enter the town, where there are soldiers everywhere—but they are not at all belligerent—as well as civilians and families of Syrian, Iraqi, and Lebanese exiles. The news that the new arrivals hear is good. The Ottoman army is no more. More than a week ago, the troops disbanded, the officers left, everyone went home, and no one has any concern about the former exiles anymore. For two nights, the Nassars, the Batals, and the Hayeks sleep on the train station platform along with dozens of other exiles waiting for trains that might take them home. It is cold and raining, and they make fires in whatever they can find to make braziers, with wood pulled off from old train cars, while they avidly listen to news of the end of the war. Trains pass through, returning from Aleppo and heading north, packed with demobilized soldiers. And then, on the third day, a train stops on its way south. There is certainly a bit of a commotion, some pushing and shoving, but somehow they manage to get on board and finally settle into a railcar, and one of the memories preserved by the Nassars is that it was the railcar of the high command, with imperial insignia and armchairs for the officers. It is almost comfortable, and I can imagine the women in rags sitting in the velvet chairs with their bundles piled up on the rosewood tables. At Aleppo there are thousands of soldiers on the platform, and the former exiles have difficulty getting down off the train. They carry the children so they don't get trampled, they hang on to each other, they lose a bundle that is carried off in the crowd as if by a receding wave, and then there are still two hundred miles to travel on foot to get to Zahlé, for there are no more trains going farther south. The Nassars and their compatriots cover the distance in four days. When they walk through villages, the peasants come running to watch them pass, and they are happy at last to be able to speak their own language again and to be looked at with friendship and even sympathy. Sometimes they even feel proud. At Homs, on the second day, they sleep in a caravanserai. The next day, they find a cart abandoned on the roadside. It has a broken axle. They fix it up, and the women and children take turns sitting in it while the men push and pull it, until the evening, when it breaks again and can no longer be repaired. They set out on foot again, and at that point Wakim starts coughing and Helene looks at him with alarm. An abyss opens up in her eyes, but he holds her close and reassures her:

"Don't worry, Helene, I'm fine."

And to prove it to her, he takes one of his sons, not the smallest one but probably Khalil, my future uncle of the Cornelian definitions, puts him up on his shoulders, and sets out at the head of the group, chatting away with him all the while. The next day, in other words four days after leaving Aleppo, he is the first to see the snowy peaks of Lebanon just as they appear, on the high sea, to the watchmen on ships. The former exiles look as if they have been shipwrecked themselves, they are in a pitiful state, dressed in bits and pieces, with their bundles and their children in their arms, but when one after another they see the snow-covered mountain, their eyes are dazzled by the sight. They approach it, then head south alongside it, feeling as if they are now accompanied by a pure force, benevolent and friendly. They are soon within sight of Baalbek and observe the citadel as pilgrims must have done in ancient times, and the last night they sleep in a convent. The following day, they arrive at Zahlé, and the last image of this episode of exile, the image that will remain the everlasting symbol of this dark page of history in the memory of the clan, is the one that is imprinted on the retina of Gerios Nassar, who has come to meet them at Zahlé and who, from a distance, over the crowd in the main street, recognizes Wakim's stature and wide forehead and, sitting on his shoulders with one leg on either side, his youngest son, who would become my father and the only one of all the exiles to retain almost no memories of this whole story, and who will not remember entering Zahlé like a little king borne aloft on a shield.

15

WHAT NOW REMAINS to be told of Wakim's story covers less than three years. With the perspective of hindsight and having untangled the facts, I came to the view a while ago that those three years could be seen as the dawn of a new era, one for which Wakim had waited a long time, and for which, directly or not, he had been exiled. But he died without really seeing it, and in that sense, he might be like a mariner who manages to survive a shipwreck only to die on the beach after the storm. Or like a soldier forced to cross enemy lines only to collapse as soon as he reaches the other side. These little comparisons were not something I could ever share with anyone, not even with my father, who had just died himself when they came to me. In any case, for Wakim, who was always considered a Francophile and who fought against Ottoman power during the war and was deported for doing so, to die in 1921, at the very moment when the French had just established their power in the country, is a rather bitter, bleak irony of fate.

But it is what it is, and according to all of his descendants, it was indeed exile that led to Wakim's demise, in particular the illness that he contracted in Anatolia and that no one would ever agree to tell me what it was exactly, tuberculosis, untreated pneumonia, recurring bronchitis, or something else along the same lines. But what everyone did agree on is that exile marked the end of Wakim's story because, after his return, nothing was as it had been before his departure.

When he gets back to Ayn Chir, Wakim is broke, and the orange orchards are in a pitiful state. Even though no description of them has been retained, I can easily imagine the groves as a shadow of their former selves, the weeds growing up to the height of a man's hips and half the trees invaded by dry wood and giving only scrawny fruit. The shipwreck affects the Big House as well, of course, and there are a few snatches of memories of this, of carpets having been stolen, the huge Berouti furniture smashed, and the contents pillaged. In short, it is certain that on the family's return they had to start all over again from next to nothing, and that they did start over. But in order to do so, according to the Nassar chronicles, Wakim had to go into debt, and give his first harvests as collateral, and sell his shares in the railways, the Ottoman Bank, and the Damascus Road Company. The situation was put to rights again, obviously, otherwise where would the last lights blazing from the Big House have come from, or the means to satisfy the demands of the petitioners, who, according to all of Wakim's sons, reappeared at Ayn Chir at almost exactly the same time as he did? And yet, the Nassar chronicles are categorical: this success was not to last. The end was in the air right from the beginning, just as it was for the Hundred Days. Everything that was remade was immediately unmade, everything that was taken in hand again immediately escaped the hand that was holding it. In order to restore the orchards, Wakim has to go into debt, but the harvest doesn't cover the amount he borrowed. Wakim sells two pieces of land that are outside the perimeter of the property, then one on the edge of the Damascus road. That gets rid of damaged trees, so he can concentrate on his fittest battalions of orange trees and his personal guard, the clementines. The snows of 1920 are a magnificent sight, but torrential rain the following spring washes away all the flowers and it's a disaster again. Two months later, Wakim comes home from his famous walk and dies within a few days.

If Wakim's return from deportation was like the Hundred Days for him, we can at least console ourselves with the thought that those hundred days actually lasted almost three years, which didn't include only bad times. But what interests me especially in those three years is that they allowed Wakim to be present, even fleetingly, at the beginnings of French power in the Levant and the first unsteady steps of the new Lebanon. It's like saying to oneself with relief, when thinking about an émigré returning home, that at least he had the time and the pleasure of living two or three years with his mother before she died. I don't know how Wakim felt, on his return, about having left under the Ottomans and come back under the French, but it must surely have filled him with satisfaction. If power is never visible with the naked eye, or not immediately, it does have its manifestations, it materializes itself to human eyes under degraded forms, just as the human form of the angel is a manifestation of a principle of light. Here the materialization of the new power to men's eyes, the proof that it does in fact exist, are the soldiers of the French oriental army that Wakim undoubtedly meets on the road to Ayn Chir and also in town, on Cannon Square, or in the middle of the vast demolished open spaces where he certainly goes for walks as soon as he returns. And we can imagine that when he passes a group of French soldiers, he doesn't understand a word of what they are saying, quite simply because they are speaking in their own dialect, but that he doesn't care and smiles under his mustache as he brushes past them. And then at Ayn Chir, on the potholed roads that lead to Baabda, there are military trucks that sway and pitch dangerously, like little sailboats on a rough sea. He sees them too, just as he sees the now more frequent motorcars, especially on the road to Ayn Chir, where one goes past every two or three days, bellowing so that everyone in the Big House thinks it's a sick cow being taken to the vet on Damascus Street. And then, without a doubt, he also sees the impending new times in the unbelievable stigmata on Beirut itself. I can imagine him walking in the city as a slightly dumbstruck spectator, with his cane under his arm or his hands behind his back, down the middle of the vast open spaces fringed with half-demolished buildings that used to be caravanserais or souks, mosques or churches, and which are now no more than ruins, not as a result of any bombings but of the notorious folly of the Ottoman urban planning authorities, who dreamed of re-creating the city in the midst of a war but in the end only had time to destroy whole neighborhoods and brutally open up wide vistas, then left everything as it was and ceded the ruins and the plans for the future to their successors. And there, in his strolls down the middle of what would become Weygand Street, but for now is nothing more than a long, wide gap in the buildings, looking like a main street of a bombed city where the rubble has been swept to the sides, or when he passes through what will become Maarad Street and stops to buy a kaak bread or to chat with a julep seller, there, in the crowd of merchants and porters, of messieurs in European suits, of veiled women and French soldiers, there is the place where Wakim is as happy as an emigrant returning home after thirty years of absence. He breathes in deep the smell of horse dung, dust, and sea salt that he realizes is his favorite in all the world, and he sometimes takes one of his sons with him to share his joy, especially Khalil, my future uncle of the Cornelian definitions, who told me one day that his only clear memory of his father was of a morning in Beirut where, either on Cannon Square or in the El-Jamil Souk, they had both stopped, Wakim and him, to eat broad beans with lemon.

But Wakim didn't just see the secondary proofs of the birth of a new world. He also was close to its source and, according to a few accounts, might even have taken part in its blossoming. In the large collection of scraps of stories that I have preserved about the life of the clan, of bits and pieces of memories, of odds and ends of chronicles, of scattered fragments that I dust off every time to see if they are of any use, like an archaeologist reconstituting a shattered pot and trying to place a shard here or there, there are a few elements that incontestably belong to this era. They are only fragments, but they have the gleam and solidity (to extend the metaphor) of ancient ceramic shards that finally, if one doesn't find the vase they belong to, can sometimes be considered works of art in themselves.

The most appealing piece of this collection is the famous episode of Helene having her hand kissed by General Gouraud, the giant one-armed man whom France delegated to the Levant to create a new Lebanon. That fragment is one with a long history; I even think it is part of the essential heritage of the Nassar family, one of the gold bars in its central bank of memories, one that was often recounted in the old days, and which I heard one last time from my uncle Charlus shortly before his death. But if the Nassars were able to get that close to the one-armed general, that must mean that they had already found their feet again in the city's drawing rooms, where, after having acclaimed the Turkish army and its leaders, everyone was now acclaiming the French army and its leaders. And so Wakim and Helene are back for a dinner party at the home of Thérèse de F. or Ibrahim B. They are amused by the negotiations about the upcoming reconstitution of the old assemblies, of the mutasarrifate, and of the Beirut city council, without realizing that this is all ancient history by now, that they are vainly trying to revive old specters, and that the one-armed general will soon get rid of the whole lot. And at each dinner party they have to give their account of their deportation again, as if it was a pleasure cruise sprinkled with hilarious anecdotes ("Helene darling, do tell us that story again, the one about the Turk slipping on his own spittle") or unexpected anthropological discoveries ("Wakim, is it really possible that they massacred the people who had owned the houses where you were living?"). And it is highly probable that one evening (let's say it's at Habib Fayyad's) they are introduced to Samuel A., the personal advisor of General Allenby, with whom Wakim exchanges pleasantries for a moment, unaware that indefectible blood ties will link his descendants to those of this extremely elegant and rather portly man, and that they will both become my grandfathers. And then finally, one evening at Edwige B.'s, just as they are coming into the drawing room (Wakim must have kept the stigmata of the past few years, a weary expression, an impatient look, his mustache drooping a little more, a few wrinkles and gray hairs), they are shown to the one-armed general, a huge man with a goatee like those worn ten years previously, but so tall, this man, that he appears to be hoisted to the ceiling by his shoulders, creating a gap of a few inches between the bottom of his pants legs and his shoes. He is not very elegant, that's a fact, there are the photographs to prove it, but he famously kisses Helene's hand and says a few polite words (on this point the annals of the clan are categorical) that sound to Helene's ears like the most beautiful lines of Racine's poetry, and thus he becomes part of the family heritage.

This fragment of a story about the hand kiss always sparkled like a little diamond for me (perhaps because of all the splendor of the chandeliers, crystal stemware, and jewels implicitly associated with it, and which is its hidden feature, illuminating it from the inside and giving it consistency and color). And, as if my imagination associated a diamond with a beautiful piece of fabric, that fragment of memory remains indissociable from another one that always comes to my mind as black and velvety (perhaps because of the color of men's suits that it reflects, along with the muted tones of their discussions). This other fragment is of the story of the delegations of messieurs who frequently come to visit Wakim, all dressed to the nines and with fine mustaches and stiff canes. According to my father and my uncles, these were supporters of France who were looking for an Orthodox Francophile close to the bishop to fill out their overwhelmingly Maronite ranks. Among them may have been the inventors of the new nation: Émile Eddé, an impatient and choleric man but one who knew how to keep himself in check and produce charming smiles when he had to, and Daoud Amoun, with his languorous eyes and aristocratic manners, who always seemed to agree to everything although no one ever knew whether this was just courtesy or politics. These famous men may have sat in the majestic armchairs made by Berouti and drank the Nassars' orange juice. I can imagine them assembled around Wakim in interminable conferrals, their eyebrows raised, their lips pouting in reflection, their chests supported by their elbows and their elbows leaning on the arms of the chairs, their canes on the dense pile of the patterned carpet or held tight between their knees, and of course I have no idea what these conferrals were about. And as a matter of fact, they ended up leading nowhere, either because Wakim never followed through with what was being proposed or because he died prematurely. But their importance to me is similar to that of the sewing machines and phonographs that I am sure Wakim must have admired at the Beirut trade fair in 1920, in that they attest to the fact that he did live to see the beginnings of the new Lebanon, and that despite the short time he had left to live, he was in fact the contemporary of the San Remo conference and the battle of Maysalun, of Émile Eddé's rages and the impatience of François Georges-Picot.

So he did indeed live to see those new times, and among the fragments of memories that attest to that brief period there is the one about the visitors and the petitioners of all kinds that start to haunt the Big House again, almost from the moment of the Nassars' return from exile. They come back, and there they are again, sitting on the edge of the living room armchairs, telling their sad stories and asking for what they need. And of course the sad stories and the needs are still the same: here a stable wall that needs repairs (and Wakim, who no longer has the same financial resources but doesn't know how to live without being generous, gives him ten mejidiehs), there an unemployed son (he finds him a position with the new customs office or in the new railroad company). As he hears them all speak about their families, their land, their harvests, their difficulties with their trades, Wakim has started listening to the great rumor of the world again, of his own world, that of the peasants of Ayn Chir and the craftsmen of Marsad, of the Orthodox and the Shiites. But what really matters here is that he is starting to hear things that he hasn't heard before, things that will become the daily concerns of the men of this new time. Peasants and men from the mountains come and tell him how they were despoiled of their lands by speculators during the war and ask for his help to get them back. I heard a hundred such stories of peasants forced to sell their land for a little wheat, or of farmers abandoning their houses for a sack of lentils, to say nothing of the stories of cunning arrangements between Ottoman officers and speculators determined to take possession of the farmers' assets. Wakim listens to all these stories as if they were new variations of his own story—of the spoliation he was a victim of before even starting out in life—and he feels a curious sense of solidarity with these men sitting with their seroual pants between their legs and making grand pathetic gestures as they tell the details of their woes. Maybe he shudders every time someone comes to talk to him about George Baydar, whom the farmers call the Ogre of Ayn Chir, or about Halim A., whom the peasants from Keserwan call the Sausage Bey because of that delicious meat that he would exchange a pound of for a mulberry orchard, or even more so about Gebran Nassar, who was nicknamed Monsieur Lentil Soup because he bought dozens of houses in Beirut for a few sacks of lentils each. Of course there isn't very much Wakim can actually do about any of this, but he whispers a few words and forlorn promises as his guests stand to leave ("We'll come up with a solution, ya Fawzi," or "I don't know what to say, ya Gebran, but I will do my best to help you"). And then, with a sense of despair because there is no solution, he gives them money, to lease a new plot of land here, to pay the deposit on a new orchard there, and thus fritters away the last of his own pennies. Maybe he even dreams about setting out, like Don Quixote or Saint George, on a harebrained adventure where he would sacrifice everything, firmly believing in those moments of exaltation that he has accrued such power only in order to measure himself at last against the Great Demon, the Prince of Evil, incarnated in his eyes in the person of the Despoiler, whoever he may be. But he doesn't do that. He has time only to deplete the last of the Nassars' savings, as if he were responsible for compensating for all the injustices of the war, and then dies shortly after that.

For of course, during this whole time, the interior enemy, the illness Wakim contracted in Anatolia, does not leave him for a second. It regularly wakes up in his chest and sends him dire warnings, like a volcano before an eruption. It can happen anywhere, in the orchards in the morning, or while he is walking on the roads of Ayn Chir or in Beirut, or while he is listening to the complaints of his visitors. Or when he is sitting with Helene on the balcony, chatting quietly in the two large wicker armchairs. He coughs and Helene, worried and attentive, looks at him pointedly. But he recovers himself. She turns away so that he doesn't see the abyss that has just opened up in her eyes and takes up her embroidery again. But she is filled with the darkest foreboding. One day it is Curiel (for Curiel returns, obviously, since he died in Lebanon at the end of the 1930s: let's say that Wakim finds a letter from him on coming home from one of his walks to Beirut in which Émile announces his impending arrival. As Wakim rereads it to Helene ten minutes later, he realizes with stupefaction that the date Curiel gives is imminent, "Let's see, what date is it today? But of course, yes, that was yesterday!" He runs to Villa Eucalypta but there is no one in the villa, which he himself has recently arranged to be cleaned and shuttered up. He goes to the port, where he finds out that the ship is two days late, and Curiel does indeed disembark the next day, stays with the Nassars while Villa Eucalypta is being refurbished, and a few months later they are back smoking their cigars on the verandah that still bears traces of the presence of the army, or taking their walks together again), so indeed it is Curiel who ends up talking to Wakim about it during one of their strolls in Beirut. And Wakim laughs and gives him the same answer as to everyone else:

"Don't worry, Émile, I'm fine. It's obvious, isn't it?"

Curiel says nothing more but resolves to talk to Calmette and Barthélemy about him. But in the meantime, Wakim stops coughing and everyone forgets about it, unaware that the inner enemy is probably still in there, lying in wait inside him, camouflaged, working away slowly, nibbling and gnawing at his lungs or I don't know what, until they are in an irrecoverable state. No one could know about it yet, except for Wakim perhaps, and he doesn't care. Unless he is only pretending not to care. Maybe he feels an iron file working away inside his chest, or a blade slicing through his innards when he gets breathless. But he turns away from it, he has other things to think about, the orange groves are in a pitiful state, they need to be pruned, cut, grafted, replanted, there are still more visitors coming to talk about their stolen lands, and all this lasts until the famous walk after which he will no longer get up again.

But before we get to that point, there were those three years with their vast fresco of days, the memories of which have been lost but can still be imagined and whose colors and flavors I have often tried to recompose for myself. The details that constitute them are like those background scenes that painters include in pictures of the Bible stories, a fishmonger behind a depiction of Mary at the Temple, or peasants tilling their fields behind the flight into Egypt. And so, behind or next to the scene of Helene's hand being kissed or of the delegations of men in tarbouches, there were all the other little things in life, the work in the orchards (shoes covered in mud, a laborer singing a zajal, one of last year's oranges still hanging on a tree in blossom); Wakim's walks along the roads of Ayn Chir (there he is, lifting his cane in a distant greeting to Baclini's son or stepping to the side of the road between the trees to have a word with Rached's son); the mornings at Curiel's (when they go for strolls, they laugh as they imagine scenarios where they take revenge on George Baydar and his depredations, then they wander through the eucalyptus trees and play like children, crushing the minuscule buds); the evenings where the farmers talk politics as they smoke their narghiles (and of course they talk about San Remo, which the farmers call Sarremo, and Maysalun, which an old farmer who is hard of hearing calls Nayzalum). And then, next to those well-known motifs, there are also life's little incongruities and surprises, a swallow that comes in and flies around inside the house (it gets in through a window and can't find its way out again, unless it doesn't want to leave and has come for a friendly visit with the inhabitants, and it cheeps away, whether out of joy or panic no one knows, and bangs into the walls, unless perhaps this is a dance ritual, then it flits into the living room, flies around in extraordinary loops, causes a commotion in the household, refuses to fly out of the windows and doors everyone opens for it, and then finally leaves by the same window it came in by); or a fox cub that trips up Elias one day in the orange groves (the oldest son often wonders whether an animal is scampering away between the trees in the orchard, when it is actually just a fruit falling and making a long, furtive rustling sound in the leaves on its way down, and then one day it really is an animal, only he doesn't believe it, and then a little fox comes out of hiding from behind a bush and, in panic, can't deviate from its course and runs between Elias's legs, tripping him up so he falls flat on his bottom on the ground); or a thief pilfering the Barbary figs from the boundaries of the property (Gerios decides to lie in wait for him with a gun, which he does, and one afternoon there are gunshots, everyone comes running, only to discover that Gerios has saved the thief's life by shooting a snake he was about to step on). And alongside all that, there is that whole fabric of the thousand sensations of life and days, the infinite palette of the small pleasures and emotions of each instant, the air smelling of apples in the mornings, the thick greenery of the trees sinking into darkness at sundown while the last light still clings to the fruit and makes thousands of little sunsets glow between the leaves, the maddening exaltation of the scent of orange blossom in the springtime, and then the moment it suddenly becomes too sweet and sickening, the blue bonfires of the jacaranda trees and the blood of the flame trees flowering in May, the deafening racket of the cicadas in the Pine Forest, the autumnal skies washed of all their faded summer whiteness, the snow of 1920, just as heavy as it was twenty years earlier, settling on the pine trees and mulberries, and for three days the oranges are all covered in little white nightcaps and the children wear mittens. And then, accompanying the cycle of seasons and its eternal and exhausting beauty, there is all the rest, the girls playing hopscotch, the sound of the buggy coming home, the Bedouins bringing fresh milk at dawn, Gerios proudly showing off his squash, Helene standing up and calling one of her daughters from the balcony where she is sitting with one of her cousins, an automobile passing on the road, a donkey protesting, and also the endless slamming of doors, air flowing this way and that, and cheerful shouts from one or other of the children saying things you can't make out from a distance.

And then comes the morning of Wakim's famous stroll, which will not be like every other stroll. That morning, however, is just an ordinary morning, and after spending an hour or so in the orchards, Wakim gets dressed and goes out. He heads to Marsad, maybe to make a few impromptu visits to some craftsmen, or to say hello to the regulars at the Saliba café, or quite simply to think about things, for he undoubtedly established long ago that real thought comes only through walking. So he goes for a walk, and there he is now, coming back to Ayn

Chir through the Pine Forest. About a hundred yards from what was once the boundary of the governorate, three individuals come out from behind the trees. They are dressed in European style, with three-piece suits and pointed shoes, and sport fine mustaches like Arsène Lupin. This new gangster fashion makes Wakim smile, and he is about to say something amusing to himself, when he realizes that the men are coming toward him, and it is not to talk to him, but to stop him from going any farther. He perceives this unfriendly attitude in their way of walking forward without looking at each other, as if they were concentrating on a prey, and that prey were him. He slows his pace, squeezes his cane under his arm, and prepares himself to say a word, but the word stays stuck in his mind, unpronounced, pinned onto one or two images that now leap violently into his eyes, and which he perceives in a flash but with spectacular acuity (a cudgel in one hand, a foot kicking away a stone as if getting rid of an obstacle, a small section of a cheek being rubbed cynically by the back of a finger). And then, in a kind of fulminating indignation, and as if his reflexes and instinct were leaping ahead of his rational mind, he relaxes, grabs his cane firmly in one hand, and whips one of the men, who starts to scream, then he throws a punch at the second one, sending him to the ground, then he receives a violent blow on the back of his neck, turns around, grabs the third ruffian by the throat and throws him to the ground, then goes back to the first one, and he lets loose like this without stopping, with vengeful punches and contemptuous kicks, accompanying his blows with shouts of "Take that, you dog," and "There you go, you bastard," and it is all over in a few seconds, the three men flee while the passersby who come running to give Wakim a hand are offering him words of sympathy, picking up his tarbouche, bringing back his cane, and making indignant comments to each other.

The annals of the Nassar family always recorded this fight as caused by brigands or petty ruffians, and there is no reason not to believe this: the Pine Forest was not a safe place, even in the first years of the Mandate. But that's not what really matters. What does matter is that this event was offered to Wakim, almost providentially, as an opportunity to take his final bow with an act worthy of the vigor of his youth. On his return home, while the news of the incident is immediately spread throughout Marsad and Ayn Chir by the onlookers, he suffers coughing fits. That evening and the following day, as the scandalized visitors follow each other to offer their support, he has a heavy barking cough that often forces him to retire. His chest feels like a furnace, boiling and burning, he says so to Curiel, but adds to play it down:

"It's like an old furnace, whistling and banging like cracked old pipes."

All the visitors think this is connected to the attack in the Pine Forest, while Curiel, who knows this has nothing to do with it, and Helene, who can hardly contain the shaking of her whole body, sends for Calmette and old Barthélemy. But it is useless, the internal enemy has made a feast of Wakim's windpipe and his lungs, it is strong enough now to resist the eucalyptus vapors and the quinine, and to finish its demolition work in all of two days.

But those facts are not the ones the Nassar descendants wished to retain. For them, Wakim died like the hero of old tales and epic poems, cleanly, with no ill humor or bloody spit, with no sweat and no agony, and the same goes for me too, in fact, which means that we will stay here at the threshold to his bedroom, or rather in the living room of the Big House, along with the visitors who keep coming for news long into the night, the farmers of Ayn Chir, the craftsmen from Marsad, the messieurs from high society and the archimandrites appointed by the bishop. They all enter in silence, all hierarchy is forgotten for a moment, they sit wherever there is a free seat, a monsieur from the majlis next to a farmer, an archimandrite next to an old carpenter, and they listen to the news whispered by their neighbor. And finally, on the evening of the third day, the door to Wakim's room opens and Helene comes out, her eyes haggard, supported by her daughters and by Curiel. She passes in front of the assembly that has turned to stone and disappears into other rooms, like a tragic abandoned queen waiting to embark on ships that will carry her to her desert realms, to her arid hopeless estates.

PART THREE

THE TIME OF EXILE

16

ONE OF THE operating rules of the zaymat, that traditional form of political and clan-based status that was overhauled in modern times, is that it is hereditary. Generally, the title is inherited by the oldest son of the deceased zaym, through implicit consensus within the clan, or otherwise by one of his brothers. But if the position is left unclaimed, another member of the clan can seize it. In that case, the precedence between the families is reversed, and the family of the new zaym becomes the senior branch of the clan, while the one that let the zaymat escape them becomes one of the junior branches. That is what happened after Wakim's death. As for the reasons that prevented Elias from preserving the position he should have inherited, all the reports confirm that this had to do with the subsequent endemic lack of money, a lack that also contributed to the gradual dilapidation of the property and the dispersal throughout the world of Wakim's sons.

However, between Wakim's death and his sons' emigration, approximately six years passed, which were, in a most curious paradox, those that saw the most decisive growth of citrus cultivation across the Middle East. In other words, the financial difficulties that Wakim's sons inherited from their father at his death should have been mitigated by this most favorable economic development. If that didn't happen it was because of something that I always suspected was lying beneath what was left unsaid, under a whole series of allusions and Freudian slips, in the formidable silence that weighed heavy on all the Nassars' stories about that period. I might never have known anything about it, about what it was exactly, were it not for my father having revealed the details, a short time before he fell quiet forever about his past, during the period when he would shuffle packs of cards to pass the time, setting them down, picking them up again, then setting them down for good, as if what he really wanted to keep his hands busy with was actually a pen to write all of this down, he, the last survivor of this long story, who never stopped asking me with a cunning air, whenever I asked him questions, if I wasn't trying to write the history of the Nassar clan. And that is how I discovered that what compromised the restoration of the property and led to its ruin was a fearsome machination committed by Gebran Nassar, in which he used Wakim's third son, my future uncle Charlus, the one whom for this very reason the family members among themselves always called the "scandalous brother."

But let us start at the beginning. In the beginning, it was not Gebran Nassar who struck a blow at the integrity of the estate, but the family council, which brought together Helene—in deep mourning, in black from head to toe for two years—her two elder sons, her brother-in-law Selim, and Gerios Nassar. Selim becomes something of the Richelieu of the estate, Helene's counselor and regent. This man, who always lived in his brother's shadow, as his traveling companion, would now give his last performance as a soloist. Up until then, all he ever did—once his phase of adolescent snobbery was over—was seek to deserve the ease and fortune that his brother offered him, by doing his part in the work on the property. He attended to the accounts with the precision of a banker, supported his brother during all the events of the war, and shared his exile. In short, he was Wakim's most faithful ally, knowing with certainty that his brother was working toward what he himself must have always considered the greatness of the Nassar family, but he remained content, as time passed, to contemplate this emerging greatness from afar, as if in fact, after long consideration, and with advancing age as well, he had noticed that all of this was profoundly exhausting. After a while, the only pleasure he found was in long hunting trips with Camille Callas at the foot of Mount Hermon, and in the purchase and sale of Arabian horses, transforming himself from a devotee of his clan into a devotee of his own person, a kind of distant and distracted dandy who was bored in Beirut society drawing rooms. And yet he apparently had a few affairs with married women, but he preferred his mares. He acted rather boorish toward his mistresses, and despite his extraordinary elegance (one of the only details I ever knew about him was that he never wore the same suit twice and that he had a whole collection of ivory pommeled canes) and despite his great beauty, women all ended up avoiding him and looked at him as mares might look at a wolf. On his return from exile, he takes the pillage of his collection of hundreds of suits and canes with good humor, and consoles himself of no longer being able to buy horses by joining the new racing club with Habib Fayyad's support. At Wakim's death, then, he has to take things in hand, under duress.

As for Elias, the oldest son, he is now twenty-four years old and has a little mustache that looks as if it is painted above his lips, giving him a slightly priggish appearance. He is always stylishly dressed and has something in his eyes like the power of crystallization, a capacity to shift from the most complete distraction, from widely scattered thoughts, to an abrupt and powerful concentration, which surprises and unsettles everyone he talks to and makes him rather disconcerting. But since Wakim's death, his gaze appears to be more floaty, following thoughts that no one can exactly localize, including his brother Michel, the second son in the family, who is simpler in his appearance, and at eighteen years old modestly still has no beard, always looks worried, and pays less attention to his dress and more attention to his manners, which makes him exceedingly courteous, to the point of shyness. And yet, from what I always knew of him, Michel was not at all timid. He could read the attitude of the men around him as if from a book, held no illusions about anything or anyone, and hid his skepticism behind his extreme politeness. But in this first period after his father's death, he is just as incapable as the others of saying where his older brother's thoughts are wandering, and during family council meetings he does much the same thing, listening without saying anything, and this silence from the two brothers is prodigiously irritating to Gerios—Gerios, who mutters more than ever now, who is old and no longer has a care in the world except (he says) to live a few more years and see his son grow up, and who doesn't know that he will attend his son's wedding, after extraordinary adventures (or maybe he does foresee it, but knows that he is still going strong, yet complains because, as a rule, that's what people his age do). When the muttering stops, Elias looks at Gerios with his magnificent gaze, dispersed and vaporous, and smiles at him, and Gerios has the impression that he is being mocked. Michel, sitting by his side, takes him by the shoulder and whispers some pleasantry in his ear, and one can be certain that at that moment, if the two brothers are saying nothing, it is because there is nothing left to say, that the decision that needs to be made is to sell whatever is required to pay off the huge debts that Wakim left behind.

So they sell large sections along the boundary of the Pine Forest where the oranges were said to have a musky flavor because of the proximity of the resinous trees. This is a terrible amputation, the start of a process that no one would have ever believed to be possible. But there is still quite a bit left, and for a year or so, let's say, things are still alright. It's not the splendor of Wakim's time, but it will do. Elias and Michel go out to tend to the land in the mornings and then get dressed to walk into town, just as their father did. But sometimes Elias has obligations. For during the first two years after Wakim's death, the Nassar house at Ayn Chir continues to receive visitors and bearers of grievances. They now come to see Helene, and she receives them, sitting up straight in her chair, all in black except for a little touch of white in the lace handkerchief in her right hand, with a faraway look in her eyes, to the point that she makes them feel ill at ease, as if their causes were nothing compared to her own grief. But very quickly she shows that she actually is listening, that she sympathizes, and she promises to do what she can to find a position for this man's son, or to help that one settle a dispute about a few trees with his more powerful neighbor. And every time, she hopes that her oldest son will be there beside her, for he is the heir of the zaymat after all. And sometimes he is there, to satisfy his mother. He listens with a frown, observing the visitors as if they were twenty yards away or they were talking to him from the other side of a mountain. But that gives him an air of somber concentration that the visitors like, it's reassuring, it makes him appear trustworthy, and that's what a leader is for them, a man who appears thoughtful and concerned. Then Helene charges him with taking care of the requests and sends him off to the bishop, who is friendly toward him but intimidating, so he doesn't know quite what to say to him, or to Habib Fayyad, same outcome, or to Curiel, because he has connections to the high commissioner of France in the Levant, and there Elias feels more at ease, almost at home, and takes the opportunity to smoke a cigar and tell the latest stories about the family to their friend. Then if the request depends on the bishop or Habib Fayyad, or if Curiel considers that one should consult the high commission, the petitioner is satisfied and the reputation of the Nassars is saved. But if they need to grease the palm of an official to obtain a favor, if they need to use a middleman who has not been given anything for a long time, then it is more difficult. To begin with, thanks to Selim knowing Wakim's connections well, they can still lean on the men who are in the family's service. But when those they can rely on can be counted on the fingers of one hand, things become almost impossible. And also, if Elias is not in the position, because of his youth, to go see Ibrahim B. at any hour of the day or night, or to whisper a word in Thérèse de F.'s ear, or to ask either of them to intervene in favor of his clients, as Wakim used to do, then that means that the zaymat needs someone else. And in the meantime, when the supplicants pay another visit to inquire of the progress on their affair, and the Nassars are forced to say, two times out of three, that it has not yet been settled because of this or that, it comes as no surprise that they leave feeling disappointed and that they turn to other zayms, and of course especially, for men have short memories, to Gebran Nassar.

This slow and irremediable erosion of the zaymat of Wakim's branch of the Nassar clan, which reflects its straitened financial position, is consummated, let's say, in 1924. From that time onward, there are almost no more visitors with requests for assistance. The connections have evaporated, Wakim's family turns in on itself and looks after the land, which is still generous. And yet in 1925, the family council decides to sell another section, on the western side. But the effect of this sale is nullified because in the same year, just before the harvest, there are two or three unexpected downpours of rain followed by nasty hailstorms. The orchards are utterly devastated in a matter of three days. The fruit is so watery that it goes soft, then the hail finishes it off by battering the flesh apart. The family has to sell more land, and in 1926, according to all accounts, the Nassar family become gentlemen farmers, as it were, putting on a good show with their lifestyle and their fine clothes, the afternoon tea parties that Helene organizes after she comes out of mourning, and the visits she continues to make to Edwige B. and Thérèse de F. But all that is nothing but a forlorn smokescreen. And while the last-born child, my future father, goes to elementary school at the French lycée, and Khalil goes to the Jesuits (which might explain his ease with Cornelian definitions), anyone who is impressed by these educational choices forgets one thing: that the boys have to walk to those schools. They go there together, in their uniforms, their hair combed down, their shirts ironed, all clean and smooth like sons of a good family, with their shoes polished to a high shine, even if they do end up covered in dust. And the following detail will leave a mark on my father for a long time, namely that one day on the way home he tears open the toe of his boot. He tries to keep going but little pebbles get inside it, he stops on the side of the road and sits with his foot close to his heart and tries to close it up with elastic bands and then starts walking again, but even that doesn't work, so then—and he will tell me this story a hundred times (and I started to hear it from the age of ten, the same age he was when this occurred)—"so then I stuck a piece of wood into the gaping mouth of my shoe and I walked like that until I got home, wearing a kind of leather beast devouring a bit of pine wood."

So they go to school on foot, and at the edge of the forest, they take a path leading to the Damascus road. My future father enters the Lycée playground, while Khalil continues on toward the Minims school, and on the way there he has a memorable fight (he knows his Corneille, but is also a battler, and one day he gets seriously beaten up and comes home that evening covered in bumps and bruises, with his clothes in shreds). On the way home, if they are not walking, they take the tram that goes up the Damascus road. And that feels strange to them. Not that they miss the good old days, which they don't even remember. But at the French Lycée and the Jesuit school, some children are dropped off in automobiles, driven to the front door by chauffeurs in livery, or in buggies or carriages, and among those who arrive in carriages are the children of Gebran Nassar.

"It wasn't envy," my father told me fifty times, "but they had such an arrogant attitude. And misplaced, too. When we left school, Gebran's carriage would rush past us with one of his children inside it, I can't recall which one, and he would give us a big wave. Not the kind of wave you make to your friends—hey there, bye, guys, see you tomorrow—nor even a thumb to his nose with his fingers waggling, like a child—ha ha, there you are on foot, you little people, my dad has a carriage. No, it was a stiff, brief wave, as if to say, farewell, my dear friend, like an aristocrat condescending but remaining polite to a bourgeois he despises. And the worst thing about all this, what always annoyed me most," he would repeat, "was that we had a carriage too, even better, a coupé."

Yes, the Nassars of Ayn Chir (that's what people start calling them now) do have a coupé, a relic from splendors past. Except that the coupé is not used to come and collect the children from school. Not that they are being thrifty, or that they don't have a horse anymore—on the contrary, there is a magnificent horse, the last one that Selim would ever buy. But from a certain period onward, the one who is always using it, and who couldn't care less about picking up his brothers, is the third of Wakim's sons, Farid, my future uncle Charlus. Maybe in fact, at the very moment when the two younger brothers are walking to school together and being snubbed by their second cousins, he is already like a marionette in Gebran's manipulative hands, unknowingly, unconsciously leading his family to catastrophe.

Whatever the case, sometime around 1926, my future uncle Charlus—who of course is not really called Charlus—already has Charlus's insufferable character. Although he is only twenty-three years old, and is incredibly handsome—a fateful detail—with that attractiveness that proved to be the downfall of the Nassars and which his brothers and sisters always mentioned with cold fury, restraining their rage, according to the tacit pact that meant that none of them—except my father, who revealed this to me (and I realize this was one of the last stories he told me, and that as the last surviving sibling he had almost unconsciously waited for all the others to die and to be at death's door himself to tell it at last, just as the last member of a line of craftsmen must reveal the secret of his guild, which would otherwise disappear along with him)—none of them ever talked to their descendants about this famous affair, of which their brother's attractiveness and fine manners were the immediate cause. In all the photographs from his youth, it is obvious that his beauty came from his eyes, eyes with a dark gleam that gave his fine, hard, and virile face a curious obscurity, as if he was returning from a journey alongside Theseus and had seen terrifying things. Much like his brothers, he had his father's erect posture, which he heightened further with the majesty of his gestures. For he always added an imperceptible touch of ceremony to everything, including to the most ordinary daily activities, as if each act was a detail of royal protocol in his eyes, and his life a series of theatrically composed moments, all of which turned him into an extremely obsessive person, and also gave the impression that there were simple things in life that he just didn't do. I was surprised, for instance, when I knew him in his advanced age, that he was able to go and boil two eggs and serve them up to himself, or to go get an orange and peel it onto a plate set on a napkin on his lap. I think he saw these gestures as almost a kind of magnanimity on his part toward everyone around him, like an aristocrat who deigns to bend down to pick up a fruit fallen from a crate carried by an old peasant woman passing by when he happens to step down from his carriage.

In short, he is a handsome man, most definitely ceremonious, and undoubtedly a snob. And for a twenty-three-year-old, that concoction means he is a young man always dressed to the nines, with his hair slicked down and parted on one side, who spends his days in cafés, consorting with slightly untrustworthy men who treat him like a prince, or taking little promenades on the new Corniche at Raouché, where he exchanges glances with women in crinolines wearing enormous hats that seem to be devouring their hair. After a while he sees them again at the Fayyads', since he is friends with Halim's son, and at the home of old Edwige B., who enjoys his company because she loved his father and is flattered to have such a seductive young man as her guest. Soon women start going where he goes, and relationships bloom. Contrary to what his shadowy demeanor might suggest—that air of having gone to the underworld and of observing you from those depths, or of constantly comparing you with those who are more important and more interesting than you are—contrary to all of that, Farid is frivolous, carefree, and even a bit of a ruffian. But he is a good conversationalist, he knows how to please. When a woman is introduced to him at the Fayyads' or Edwige's, he kisses her hand like a Frenchman, then pretends to continue the conversation, whereas in fact he is only speaking for the beauty who has just come into the room and to whom, one step at a time, he gradually turns. He never speaks to her one-on-one. He keeps up the pretense of gallantry, of being a refined man who does not want to cause embarrassment, but he knows just when to say the words that make women dream, and then he leaves them to those dreams, doesn't insist, lets himself be devoured discreetly by their eyes, takes his leave with another kiss of the hand, and it's like wine, he decants it once, twice, or more according to the vintage, and when he considers that it is ready, or that it is time to taste it, then he pulls out all the stops, makes pointed compliments, asks questions about topics that bore him but he knows will serve his purpose, offers to take them home, to meet for a stroll on the Corniche, and after all that, he has his tasting.

Not only of the grands crus of the bourgeoisie, either. He often treats himself to delicious little local wines, the salesgirls from Orosdi-Bak (and for that purpose he makes incessant shopping trips, comes back to exchange an item, delays looking at another one to the next day, all that for the attentions of a young salesgirl he waits for at closing time and takes for a ride in his carriage, and especially, in secret) or nurses at the Hôtel-Dieu hospital (maybe he first came with one of his lady friends from high society, and comes back to have an invented shoulder pain treated or because he forgot his snuff box, but in fact it is for the delicious bloom on the face of a young nurse trainee).

All this therefore explains why he has all but confiscated the coupé for his own use. He has it hitched in the morning and, after a walk around the boundaries of the orchard, but a very cautious walk so that he doesn't get his shoes dirty but still appears to take an interest in the property (according to my father, he never went very far into the orange groves and didn't even know what they looked like), he comes home with his cane under his arm, lights a cigarette, and, once the carriage is ready, takes off his hat with a wide gesture, settles in, and off he goes. And often he isn't seen for the rest of the day, which no one complains about. No one asks him where he's been when he comes home either, since they don't want to create a pointless squabble or be the target of a disagreeable remark, for he can be abrupt and insolent, reserving his gallantry for his admirers and his rudeness for his family.

His sisters, who secretly adore him, avoid him and hardly say a word to him. His two older brothers look at him without seeing him and talk to him laconically. As for the two younger brothers, he is the one who doesn't see them, who bumps into them when they come near him, whenever they enter the vital space that is required for his ego to spread out. All this lasts until the day of the famous slap in the face he gave to the youngest child, a slap that still resounded in my father's memory seventy years later, when all this happened long ago, and his brother had owed him almost everything for decades, including, by that time, a carefree old age. He told me this story several times, and I always had the feeling that he was trying to give me all the information required for me to form an opinion, at a time when my uncle Farid was a role model for me, I loved him, and he spoiled me like a grandfather would a favorite grandson. My future father received that famous slap in the face because he had the impudence to say in front of everyone, one evening in 1926, when he was no more than twelve years old, that someone had seen his brother Farid in a hansom cab with a beautiful lady. The person who saw him was a Nassar, who held a little bar in Marsad at the time. He then eagerly told my father about it, as if it was a funny story, when he met him a little later in one of the lanes of Marsad.

"That idiot," my father told me ten times, "that idiot told me about it and seemed so amused by it and to think it was such a remarkable thing that I couldn't help repeating it proudly when I got home that evening."

So he repeats the story he heard, with all the innocent enthusiasm of a little kid who has something to tell the grown-ups. The Nassars are all, or almost all, gathered in the large living room, which is still very presentable even though, if you look carefully, there are a few wobbly arms on the chairs or chips on the edges of the tables. And there, in the large living room, my father—my future father—enthusiastically comes out with his little story ("Abdallah Nassar saw you this morning, you were with a pretty lady in a hansom cab, on the Corniche. He saw you, he was in the tram") and then immediately Farid, who is sitting in an armchair next to the chair where my father is proudly making his little speech, tuns toward him and gives him the famous slap in the face, with a stiff, flat backhand, and reminds him that he doesn't like people talking about his business. He probably didn't like the fact that his little adventures were being revealed to his sisters, and especially to his mother, for whom, like all his brothers, he always felt profound respect. But this time his mother straightens up abruptly, like an echo of the slap on my future father's cheek, as the boy leaps up from his chair and escapes into the bedrooms, and she shouts something like: "Farid, what's gotten into you? Are you crazy?" while Blanche tells him with contempt that he is "nothing but a savage," and Linda runs off to console my father. And Farid, perhaps a little ashamed of himself, frowns and pouts and decides to retreat without giving any explanations (that's not his way). He stands up and is about to leave the room when his elder brother, who is a few steps away in front of the window, comes over to the middle of the room, with a look of terrifying concentration in his eyes, stops him, and grabs him by the shirt collar:

"That's enough, this time. I've had it with the way you carry on. And I'm not the only one. Next time I swear I'll break every single one of your stupid canes over your head."

Of course Farid tries to defend himself and to get away, he struggles, pulls off Elias's shirt, but Elias doesn't let go, quite the opposite, he jostles and pushes him toward the middle of the living room, as if preparing to give him his promised punishment right there and then, in front of everyone. But at that moment Helene and her daughters are on them, and pulling them apart, and shouting at them, and all this is obviously rather unpleasant. In fact, Wakim's children always had painful memories of this period, which could have been peaceful despite their material difficulties, but which was poisoned by Farid's bizarre and uncontrollable lifestyle.

About that lifestyle, in fact, the involuntary report my future father made that evening was not the only account that reached the Nassar family's ears. Other echoes arrive at the house, brought by ladies coming to take tea with Helene, or by Habib Fayyad, who knows lots of things through his son, or by indirect and ill-intentioned witnesses, people from Marsad, Nassars who come to visit Helene, who sit down and are served something to drink, who are perfectly amiable as they prepare their little dose of venom and, while they are preparing to inject it into their host's life, talk nonsense or ask for news about Selim, Elias, and the other children (and they reach their goal little by little), about Catherine and her children, about the Farhats in general, then the Callas family (they move away only to come back stronger, distracting Helene's attention before committing their lamentable act), and then, as if they had just remembered it, "Ah yes, by the way, tell me, Helene, apparently your son Farid" (ebnik Farid)—and they unpack the story they have in mind and which brought them here in the first place, about how Farid is seeing a Boutros daughter (and there are two subtexts here, the first, of no importance, is something like "and you didn't tell us about it," and acts as the sugarcoating for the second one, the venomous allusion to the incomprehensible financial resources that allow Farid to go out with such a rich girl), or that he was seen in a jewelry store with an unknown girl (the same sort of poisoned candy, with a little additional perfidy, the mention of the "unknown girl," in other words someone who is not of your social status, or maybe of nobody's status, who knows . . .), or that he is betting on the races with the Fayyad son (no more poisoned candy here, the venom is served neat). And no matter how much Helene already knows, or expects the worse, or uses an effective antidote ("No, I didn't know, he never tells me anything, but he is free to do what he wishes, may God protect him"), she always ends up being sincerely troubled and this becomes her main worry for months on end. She sees how Farid comes home with new suits draped over his arm and boxes of new shoes, she notices his canes, his ties, his powder and hair oil, but after all, he might just be able to afford all that at a pinch (a very hard pinch) from his share of the yearly income from the orchards. But the rest?

And then one morning, after the visit of a lady from Msaytbeh who tells her that Farid was seen at Tufenkjian's, she decides to find out what's what. She sets out in the carriage, taking Michel with her, leaving him at the door as she enters the Tufenkjian store, then Mzanmar's, in the new city neighborhoods, and on the way home she is silent and somber because she has just learned what she had feared: that her son has enormous debts. Michel, who understands all this very well, does not say a word. And because his mother knows his discretion, she doesn't bother recommending it. He holds his tongue and she is grateful. But that is not the only secret he will share with her. For he knows, because he knows his mother, that she will take on the whole lot, that she will pay off all his debts. And indeed, with the money she set aside at each good harvest, at each good deal with the wholesalers, with this sum that ended up being rather large, and that she will increase even more by borrowing from old Curiel, to whom, just this once, she tells a little lie ("You know, Émile, I have a poor man in Marsad, an old carpenter who was always very loyal to Wakim. He needs a helping hand, etcetera," and Curiel hands out the money with no questions asked), she goes and pays off all of Farid's debts. She is then broke but relieved. Finally, one morning, she asks Farid to come talk to her, and, sitting on a rocking chair on the balcony facing him as he leans on the wrought-iron railing with its curly, spiraling motifs, she tells him everything, "I found out, I went and saw them, I settled it all, don't worry, no one knows anything about it, but promise me," and he is flabbergasted, speechless, and sits down on a stool next to her, takes her hands into his, thanks her, apologizes, promises, gets a little teary-eyed perhaps, but he is undoubtedly sincere, and then Linda comes and joins them, and the other sisters too, along with Michel perhaps, and it all finishes with an idyllic tableau where Farid is standing behind his mother's chair, his hands on her shoulders, and at that point he probably decides to stop being an idiot.

But that's not as easy as it sounds. Not being an idiot is difficult when you have a mistress waiting for you every day, when you are invited to lunch with the Boutros family one day and the Rayes family the next. And so, very quickly he is at it again, not because he is inconstant or incorrigible, but because he can't change his habits all at once, he can't leave the circles in which he has been moving, and he can't live in that world without making the required libations—of clothes, cigars, rides in the coupé, and gifts for the ladies. First he tries to be clever about it, to tighten his belt, to pretend he has forgotten his cigar holder (and he borrows one from Shakib Fayyad), or to make original little presents that don't cost anything and that are well received, such as his little conjoined-twin clementines. But that can't last, it's like wanting to live on a sloping roof, and so he is soon at it again, swearing to himself that it is just this once, and just this other time, and then suddenly, when he is at Tufenkjian's one day, the whole sky falls on his head when his request to "pay a little later" is politely refused.

When my father told me all this, or at least when he whispered it to me furtively and with regret, as if such an old story still needed to be kept hidden, or to be shared only with caution so that it didn't fall into indiscreet ears even though everyone involved was long since dead, when he told me this story as if he was breaking the last seals on secret documents, he insisted quite clearly on the fact that the "embargo" (that was the word he used) imposed on his brother was due to Helene's actions. I vaguely sensed that he was hinting that, if she had acted otherwise, things may have turned out differently. The fact of the matter was that Helene, when she made her round of paying off Farid's debts, gave strict instructions or at least strong advice that her son should not be given any more credit. This must have been very embarrassing for her, which proves that she had no confidence in Farid, unless, on the contrary, she thought he would obey her and would therefore never find out that she had given such an edict. Whatever the case, she must have felt she had no other choice, that she would not be able to cover a new series of debts, and that she would then have to bring this to the family council, which would create another scene among the brothers that she absolutely wished to avoid, without realizing that she was, in fact, setting up the mechanism that would destroy everything.

Because of course Farid has no intention of letting himself be treated in this way. To begin with he throws his weight around in the stores because now the credit has all been repaid, after all, then he shrugs and reminds himself that there are other jewelers, other hat and cane stores. But when he notices that the main suppliers where he shops (and he can't very well go elsewhere without losing face in his own eyes, for these stores are the same stores where his fine friends shop too, and also, let us not forget, he is very picky and set in his ways), so when he notices that the main stores are refusing him credit, that he can't buy anything anymore, not even by getting angry, nor by joking nor making threats, he understands that he is caught in a trap, and then all it takes is for one amiable salesman to tell him, either out of malice or in fact as a show of sympathy, that it was "your lady mother (*elwelde, sitt Hileni*) who requested this" for him to lose his bearings completely. "And then," my father muttered on that day when he told me the story, "and then, instead of thinking that he might go to work to pay for his purchases, he starts acting like an appalling boor at home, as if he has been deprived of a fundamental right, the right to ruin us all." And so he sulks, in a rage, and slams the doors of the Big House until flakes of paint and plaster fall from the ceiling onto the worn upholstery of the living room furniture, and doesn't talk to anyone anymore, and throws his knife and fork onto the tablecloth when he has finished breakfast, and if he doesn't actually throw a tantrum, it's because his mother is there and he still has some self-control. But it is clear that he considers himself the victim of a huge injustice, and since he was always—even much later when I came to know him—extraordinarily selfish, he finds it unbelievable, unimaginable, outrageous, scandalous, that he should be thus deprived of his daily pleasures, even if those pleasures lead everyone else to rack and ruin. And finally, when he is rushing down the front steps one morning, he finds himself face-to-face with his brother Michel, who is bringing up sacks of oranges into the house with a laborer. They are sidling up slowly, and getting in Farid's way, and so Farid is impatient and demands they let him through. His brother tells him to get lost, and Farid answers impertinently and then they are fighting again, but this time it is quite spectacular because it is happening with the most sensible and pragmatic brother, who calmly grabs one of Farid's arms, as if this was something he had done a thousand times and had become a habit, and twists it up behind his back and pushes him down the stairs and quite a way toward the front gate, saying that if it's so important for him to leave the house, he might as well go and never come back, and no matter how much Farid struggles and shouts, he can't break free, and when Michel finally lets him go by pushing him forward headfirst, he loses his balance and lands flat on his face. Helene witnesses this scene from the balcony and is mortified, for this is certainly not the fine behavior she expects. But that evening, they put the pieces back together again, and Blanche takes care of it: Michel is ready to make up with Farid, who mutters an apology because he knows he was being stupid. And then there is a calm spell for a few weeks, and it is no doubt in those few weeks that Gebran Nassar makes his appearance onstage for the final act.

17

THE REAPPEARANCE OF Gebran in the story of the Nassars of Ayn Chir takes place on the occasion of his ill-fated chance encounter with Farid at a famous jewelry store in Foch Street, one of the gleaming new thoroughfares in the updated version of Beirut. Let's say it's at Tufenkjian's, just to keep it the same. When Gebran reappears in this story, he is a powerful man. He acquired considerable wealth during the war, when he was one of the members of the generalissimo's inner circle, then, like a well-oiled weathervane, he became one of the most influential men at the beginning of the French Mandate. This is a well-known fact, just as it is a well-known fact that his position as a zaym was strengthened by Wakim's death and the declining position of Wakim's sons. So when he steps into the Tufenkjian jewelry store that day in 1926 or thereabouts, he is at the apex of his power, he has built up a real estate empire in Beirut and its outskirts, and everyone calls him Gebran Bey. And that is how he is greeted by the staff in the jewelry store, with a bow to Gebran Bey here, and a bow to Gebran Bey there. Farid is already in the store, in a light-colored suit and a lavaliere. His hat and cane are on the counter next to him, and he is in the process of choosing, let's say, a pocket watch when Gebran Bey comes in, also wearing a light-colored suit and a lavaliere. The manager of the store organizes the reception of this important man with a series of little frowns and imperatively raised eyebrows directed to his employees, and of flowery salaams addressed to Gebran, and it's like Marcel Marceau's famous mime act, a play of wide, affable smiles (which can be seen by those standing in front of him) simultaneously with thunderous glances (that can be seen only by those a few steps away). The raised eyebrows bring an armchair forward, the frown packs away a bundle of watches a clumsy salesman has just opened up, an intimate atmosphere settles in, the other employees become distracted, as if it were impossible to do any work at all in such a significant presence, and that is what makes Farid turn around. The two Nassar men recognize each other, greet each other courteously, after which ("do have a seat, if you please, Gebran Bey") Gebran sits down, sets his tarbouche and his cane on the counter ("leave them, leave them, we'll take them for you, here, look after Gebran Bey's things," but Gebran doesn't want them to do this, mutters a few words and does put his tarbouche and cane on the counter), and asks to see, I don't know, maybe some diamond brooches.

And it is while he is examining those diamond brooches of all shapes and sizes in velvet cases, as they are being solemnly presented to him with little whispers—as if diamonds could be sold only with soft voices—that Gebran hears Wakim's son's voice raised in protest and also (lower, ponderous, embarrassed) the salesman whispering many a "your lady mother" and "our house can no longer offer you credit." Farid, offended and wild, calls over the manager, who is in an impossible situation, for the one making the scandal is a Nassar but the significant person sitting a little farther away and who must not be disturbed is also a Nassar. And it is finally the latter Nassar who saves the situation by standing up and approaching Farid to have the reasons for the disturbance explained to him. "What's the matter, Farid? Can I help you in any way?" The salesmen want to say things diplomatically but Farid spills the whole story and Gebran announces that he will cover everything from his own account, and all they have to do is put his nephew's purchase on his own bill.

Let there be no misunderstanding: this is not at all a calculated move on his part, not yet. Gebran Nassar's only concern at this moment is probably just to save face, to avoid appearing as a miser or someone incapable of a kind gesture toward a family member. It is mostly this urgency that makes him act. Which doesn't stop Farid from waiting for him outside, pacing up and down Foch Street, and it is when Farid goes to thank his uncle as he comes out of the jewelry store that Gebran shows the so-called magnanimity by which my father, the one time he told me about this affair, explained his attitude. Once the ceremony of thanks on the sidewalk is over, Gebran takes Farid into his carriage and interrogates him about the family, about the orchards, about Helene, and then, out of pure altruism, in a princely gesture, he declares that henceforth, and until he can pay the money back, Farid can put any purchase he likes onto Gebran's account.

Let there be no misunderstanding here either: this is not, or not yet, a devious calculation. Grand gestures are always pleasant; generosity without expectation of return is satisfying to the ego, especially when it allows one to show one's power to one's rivals. And it is possible that Gebran's generosity was motivated by only one hope, that it should reach Helene's ears, just that, for the simple pleasure of a delayed act of vengeance. But his calculations would be disappointed, for in fact Farid tells no one anything about it, and especially not his mother. However, he does make the most of the license given to him by Gebran, and throws himself into an unprecedented series of purchases. To begin with, of course, he thinks that it is only just this once, then only this other time, then only "one more time, then I'll stop," for each time he has the sense that he is being implicitly kept by a man who is traditionally detested by his own branch of the family. He has a strong sense of betrayal along with a feeling of indecency. But he cannot help himself, just this once, then one more time and then I'll stop, but he doesn't stop, he buys suits and ties and hats (300 pounds), an embossed gold pocket watch (270 pounds), a pearl and diamond necklace (356 pounds), and all of this with the greatest of ease and without credit ever being denied him as long as he pronounces Gebran's name. He sees this as an encouraging sign. One evening, at a ball given by a French countess, he does give his uncle a short, not entirely complete report of his spending, explaining that he may have slightly abused his generosity a little (*slightly* being already something of a euphemism at this point) but that he is prepared to pay it all back, and Gebran minimizes the situation, "Take your time, Farid, there's no rush, really." And there again, maybe for the last time, he is sincere. But the following day, or two days later, he receives the bills and measures the extent of Farid's extravagant spending. First he is angry, then he prepares himself to give the brainless idiot a cold and humiliating dressing-down, and he comes up with a way of pressuring him to make him pay it all back. But then he suddenly calms down, thinks it over, has an idea, and that is when, at that very moment, in his house, in his living room, with the bills in his hand, or in his carriage, where he can hardly read the details of the same bills because of the jostling, or at his desk, that is the moment when his diabolical plan comes to him, he sees it, he senses it, he frowns and taps his pouting lips with a finger or two and finally feels an inner illumination.

You have to admit, as my father said, that in this whole story it wasn't Gebran who was the tempter. Or at least if he was in the end, it was only because Farid himself was the creature who would lead the tempter into temptation, throw him a line, and encourage him in his role. "If Farid hadn't been so stupid," my father said, "he wouldn't have provoked Gebran's appetite. When you meet a crocodile, you don't wave around a piece of raw meat. When you meet the devil, you don't talk to him about the apple."

The very day of the illumination, or maybe the next day, Gebran goes to settle Farid's debts, asking to have Farid's name put on the bills and his own name on the receipts. And he proceeds in the same fashion for several months, patiently calculating the sums that Farid has lost count of: a pair of diamond earrings (213 pounds), an engraved silver cigarette lighter (56 pounds), a gold enameled snuff box (72 pounds), ten ties (28 pounds). Of course, he knows perfectly well that at this rate, it will take a long time for the sums to mount up to something requiring a raid by the bailiffs at Ayn Chir. Because of course that is his plan, revenge against his Ayn Chir cousins, punishment in the form of a seizure of their land. There's no way of knowing how his thinking developed about this, or whether he settled on this goal all at once or little by little. Maybe at the start he just wanted to have the interest working for him, so that Farid would have to pay twice the amount he loaned him. Then as Gebran gets to know Farid a little better, he discovers that spending money is a vital necessity for him, that his "spending capability," as my father called it, makes Farid buy things not because he needs them but out of pure aesthetic sensibility, for the pleasure of the gesture, of making a choice, of setting his sights on something, and then of getting that something for nothing, for a few banknotes or even just the sound of a name. Farid has a kind of irrepressible fascination for the way an object passes from an indeterminate state, as a product for sale, to the precise, pure quality of an individualized item belonging to him alone. And in this fascination, which culminates in the pleasure of giving presents to women (the delectation of inscribing their naked skin with the sparkle of a ring on a finger, a pendant on an earlobe, a row of diamonds on a milky-white neck), I think that Farid—my uncle Charlus, my scandalous uncle—was literally a poet. And then what the more prosaic Gebran also noticed was Farid's imperative need to show largesse, to give without stinting to the poor, to beggars, to café waiters, to grooms, to give money so that doors are opened for him, and his order is brought immediately. In this generosity there is undoubtedly a desire to be recognized, but also the wish to please, to delight, to create happiness for the beggar as well as for the woman or the mistress of the day, and this creation of happiness is not motivated by altruism but by a pure aesthetic desire, as if he were spreading rays of light around himself. As Gebran discovers this and while it remains all but incomprehensible to him, he ends up changing strategies, or at least expanding his ambitions, and in this affair he actually becomes an entrepreneurial middle-class usurer, faced with a kind of prince from ancient times who is lost in the new world of commerce and consumerism.

But of course it would take years for Farid's expenses and the interest to amount to a reason to let the bailiffs and lawyers loose on Wakim's orchards, and while Gebran is a usurer who knows the virtue of patience, he is not sure that his little game will last long enough, and so he decides to accelerate it somewhat. According to what I could make out from my father's account, Gebran made use of a simple stratagem to do this. Instead of settling Farid's debts in one fell swoop, he staggers them out and uses credit himself to pay them back, which is outrageous. And in doing so, he doubles their amount. "He managed to compound the interest," my father explained. "He paid the interest on the credit for the original sale and then it was on this amount, which was already almost doubled, that he calculated the interest he would charge Farid. In other words, each object that Farid bought cost him around three times the original sale price. And he never even realized it. Except when the disaster was consummated." And when I sought an explanation for this remarkable lack of attention, my father made a gesture, repeatedly batting the air up and sending it over his shoulder, as if to say that only Farid was capable of something like that. "He never even asked to see or check the bills, he blindly trusted Gebran. It really is a mystery."

Now that I come to think of it, I don't believe it actually is a mystery. And moreover, I don't believe that Farid necessarily trusted Gebran. I think the truth resided in

Farid Nassar's imperial character, in the fact that he never worried about money—I mean about the materiality of money, of exchange, bills, receipts, all those trivialities, that commonness of the world that is what the hassles of gaining an imprimatur are to poetry. My father always told me that his brother hardly ever worked, even when they all had immigrated to Egypt, and that when he did happen to do so (as an official on the Suez Canal for example), he never knew how much he was paid (or, in fact, even why he was paid), and blindly spent whatever he had in his bank account and then relied on his brothers and especially on my father, who endlessly supported him without receiving so much as a word of gratitude in return, as if Farid believed it was his due, like the obligation a vassal owed to his prince. And I myself was always fascinated by him as a very old man, in Beirut by that time, when I saw him in my father's stores, sitting not like the master of the establishment (which is what he was, in fact, since my father paid him a share of the income from those stores to support his daily lifestyle) but as a guest or a client who is being asked to wait. He used to smile amiably at the customers, sometimes helped one or other of them to get a bolt of cloth out from a shelf or to unwind the fabric (but only out of pure kindness rather than to help out my father and his overworked salesmen) or would join them in seeking out the brand or size or price, exactly as if he was trying to understand the incomprehensible prose of a medication leaflet, when he was in fact directly concerned by it all, since that is what he lived off.

So when I come to think of it, I am certain that the truth lies not in Farid's trust in Gebran but in his incapacity (or his supreme boredom) in reading an invoice or doing any sort of accounting. And Gebran discovers all this little by little, is incredulous, but makes the most of it. So let's say that as soon as Farid receives some money, for example from his share of the clementine harvest, he goes to see Gebran to repay his debts. And Gebran, who has been waiting for this moment, knows that he has to play this tactfully. He asks Farid to take a seat, goes and gets all the bills, and puts them into my future uncle Charlus's hands for a while. These are only the receipts for the first repayments Gebran has made, and Farid is supposed to balk at them, at the very least, but he says nothing, and in fact is rather surprised at the relative modesty of the amounts involved, but thinks that this is probably because Gebran is able to get fantastic discounts or something like that. He asks no questions, since a Nassar, and he in particular, does not ask for the details of bills, but just pays them and that's that, and if the amounts are low, well then so much the better. And maybe he doesn't even leaf through the receipts, many of which are typed on letterhead paper. So he pays, and Gebran accepts the payment. But that will be the only time he does this, and if he accepts the payment, it is only so as not to arouse suspicion in Farid. He then takes his nephew for a ride in his automobile, and talks about himself, his children, his past, the allegedly good relationship he had with Wakim. Then the two men set out on foot to wander through the streets of Beirut, which is in the process of becoming a kind of little Paris, with new buildings in the neo-Ottoman or Art Deco style. They stroll along Weygand Street and Foch Street and Gebran asks Farid questions about Helene and the oranges and the future, playing the role of the confidant, the friend, acting in a fraternal or even paternal manner, and the goal of all this pretense is to downplay any importance given to the question of money, to reduce it to a mere detail, to almost nothing, "come now, between relatives, between friends who understand each other so well." And it ends up working. Farid lets himself be convinced by Gebran's apparent disinterest in his expenditure, and takes the usurer to be a royal prince like himself. This is where Farid, that disagreeable, intolerant, and self-assured man, shows his incredible naivete.

In any case, from that point onward, Farid starts spending even more liberally, putting onto Gebran's account, as if it were his own, items such as a diamond necklace (354 pounds), a five-carat diamond ring (421 pounds), a hunting rifle with mother-of-pearl inlay that he would never use (116 pounds). The relationship between the two men becomes quite close, obviously. Farid, who is too haughty and too selfish to burden himself with a real friendship, perhaps takes Gebran as a role model. When he meets him at balls, or at afternoon receptions with petits fours on the terraces overlooking the sea, where people have loud discussions while the butlers serve tea and cakes on silver platters whose gleam in the sunshine makes the pigeons fly away into the trees all around, or when they meet on the Corniche and walk together for a few steps, with their canes under their arms and their luxurious lavalieres around their necks, Farid cannot avoid telling Gebran that he used his name again, but that this would be the last time, that he will repay him soon, and Gebran, again, says his famous words "Oh goodness, Farid, don't worry about it, take your time, there's no rush," and Farid thanks him with a wide smile or a few muttered words. If they are at a ball, they drink to each other's health, and if they are on the Corniche, they walk a bit farther and chat amiably, and Gebran points to a seagull in the sky with the tip of his cane or maybe, already, an airplane from the postal service approaching the airport that was recently constructed in the sand dunes to the south of the city.

And curiously enough, Farid's attachment to Gebran will only be further encouraged by the rest of the family. For it would be naive to think that this connivance would not be noticed at Ayn Chir. Everything is scrupulously reported to Helene by her visitors with their cunningly distilled venom, the debts, the strolls they take in town, the rides in Gebran's Panhard, or the fact that the two men are seen defending the Nassar colors together at the balls, as if they were from one and the same clan. Helene, who listens patiently to all this as she does her embroidery or fans herself, pretends not to know anything about it all, or to despise everything that is said, and that is surely in fact the case to begin with, until the day her own children start confirming the stories. Linda because she saw Farid and Gebran together in town, Elias because he was asked in a store where he went to buy a hat whether he wished to pay for it himself or put it on Gebran Bey's account (whether this was malicious or innocent, he couldn't say). To begin with, Helene resents her children for stabbing her in the heart with all this, she fumes at their unkindness ("Even if it's true, don't come telling me about it"), and it ends up weighing down the atmosphere in the house. Helene pretends not to hear, not to want to know or see anything, while the others, especially the daughters, make snide remarks in Farid's presence, implying unpleasant things. But we know that Farid is not one to put up with remarks or contradiction, and even less with anyone meddling in his affairs, especially when he is in the wrong. He turns aggressive and even vulgar. To any direct questions, such as, "What were you doing this morning with Gebran on Maraad Street?" or "Your friend Mr. Lentil Soup didn't invite you to go hunting?," he answers tersely: "What I was doing was taking a stroll and listening to him tell me about his life, if you must know." Or "Yes, he did invite me, but I'm not going because I have a date with the fiancée of a French captain, like it or lump it." But the daily assaults are so insidious and persistent, according to my father, who told me about them even though he witnessed them only as a silent and baffled spectator, that they end up literally throwing Farid into Gebran's arms. Which means that Helene finally comes out of her reserve. One morning she calls Farid to her bedroom, where the four-poster bed that once imparted ceremony to sleep is now starting to need refurbishment, and she demands an explanation for his friendship with such a detestable and dangerous man. And the way Farid answers makes her blood run cold, for it is in the same falsely reassuring words that Wakim once used:

"Don't worry, Mother, it's nothing really."

But she does worry, of course she does. Overcome by a terrible intuition, she asks Farid whether he has an acknowledgment of debt. Farid starts laughing and replies no, of course he doesn't, that's not what this is all about. When in fact what he does not know is that he did sign an acknowledgment of debt, but without realizing it. Let's imagine how one day (maybe it was in a café on the avenue de France, across from the sea looking like a vast eyelid shimmering with thousands of silver coins, or maybe it was in the car, the Panhard bouncing over the cobblestones of Gouraud Street, and the choice of these incongruous places is a deliberate one to put Farid's suspicions to sleep or to distract him) Gebran gives him a few documents to sign: "Insignificant paperwork. But the tailors" (or maybe his pretext is the milliners or the shoemakers) "always have little notes to sign." And Gebran pulls out a receipt, then an invoice, then another receipt, and Farid signs them all apologetically: "I should have taken care of all this, Gebran, I'm embarrassed, now you're acting as my secretary." And Gebran laughs, "Oh don't worry about it, it didn't cost me a thing." He signs and it is as if someone had poured arsenic into his whiskey without him knowing it, for among those deposit notes and invoices there is a document on which are listed strict acts and imperative articles, with mentions of lawyers and bailiffs, of short payment terms and ferocious injunctions, and Farid signs it without seeing it, without reading it, he signs underneath the mentions of seizures and prison terms, then closes the cap on his golden pen and leans back into his chair while praising the sunshine in this early spring (or leans out of the window of the Panhard to watch a pretty young woman stepping out of a Ford Model E), after which he declares that he has just been paid a share of the new orange harvest and will soon come around to repay Gebran, but Gebran replies as usual that there is no rush, and the debts accumulate—a diamond necklace (735 pounds), a six-carat solitaire (537 pounds), which after Gebran's manipulations turns into 2,205 pounds (for the diamond necklace) and 1,611 pounds (for the solitaire). It all becomes astronomical, but it doesn't stop there.

"The situation must have lasted a year or so," my father said. "Then Gebran found an idea that brought everything to a head." That idea was apparently a woman whom Gebran threw onto Farid's path.

"And don't come telling me that this is all nonsense," my father attacked before I even had the chance to reply, with that little contemptuous look that he sometimes had when he thought he was being unnecessarily contradicted and he knew that he was right anyway. "Don't come telling me it's subjective or whatever. Or that Gebran Nassar was not capable of such a thing."

"Come on now, your brother was always surrounded by women. You can't tell me that the one he was seeing at the time was someone Gebran had made to measure."

"That's exactly what I think. And 'made to measure' is a good way to put it."

So let us suppose that this creature was thrown by Gebran onto Farid's path. When I wanted to know who she was, my father made an irritated gesture and declared in a tone that broached no reply:

"I can't remember. It doesn't matter in any case. She was gorgeous, obviously. But I'm not sure I ever even knew her name."

And this was so untrue that a few minutes later, when he was telling me the rest of the story, he had a moment of inattention, and whereas up until then he had talked about that Eve by calling her "that woman" or "she," he pronounced a name that in my surprise, and because whenever he mentioned her he lowered his voice as you do when saying the names of devils or demons, I was not able to catch, but which remained imprinted in my mind like a familiar form, something like "Amelie" or "Emilie." Try as I might to go through my memories, among the innumerable names that constituted my father and his brothers' feminine onomastic treasury (for they were all skirt chasers), among all the Sonias, Olgas, Simones, Denises, and Jeannes, I could not find a trace of an Amelie, or an Emilie. It was therefore about this Amelie or Emilie that I conducted my last inquiry before starting to write this story, when my father was already dead, but it was all in vain because, among the oldest members of the clan, not a single person could recall ever having heard that name. All that I can now say is what my father told me about her, the sketch he drew of her. And he told me three things: that she was beautiful ("Obviously she was beautiful, otherwise she would have been of no interest in the whole story"); that she was the daughter of émigrés ("Her father died in America and she came back to live in Lebanon"); to which he added a spicy detail that I often wondered about—why it had stayed with him, and what formidable novelistic talent suggested he give it to me—("She loved money and smoked very long, thin cigars"). That was probably the image he kept of her, if he had ever seen her, that is. In any case that is the detail that I use to imagine her. The long, thin cigars, together with the love of money, evoke a stereotype of a woman with elongated eyelashes and huge hats, a little plump of course (that's how they were supposed to be in those days), pale, milky, with eyes that rest on you like a feather, eyes that always despise you, that pass over you as if you were nothing, and tie your belly into knots, force you to look again, and then the feather turns into an arrow, Circe bewitches you as she draws on her long cigar, but not too much (that would look vulgar), as if it was just a way of playing with her scarlet lips or as a simple accessory held between two fingers to emphasize the suppleness of her wrist and the delicacy of her fingernails whose bright color, contrasting with the gleaming whiteness of her skin, wrings out your heart for good. So let us say that is what happens to Farid, to that arrogant, contemptuous ladies' man. He is petrified when he first meets Amelie's gaze (let's say she's called Amelie), and the second time too, one evening, in a drawing room over dinner or a dance. And let's say that when he decides to approach her, according to one or other of his usual stratagems, she sends him packing, by answering in English that what she is hearing is completely unintelligible to her, and she turns away with a disappointed expression, but in the way one is disappointed not to be able to give a coin to a begging child because one has no small change. Of course Farid, who is left standing there in full view of quite a few people, tries to regain his composure, but a moment later he hears the same Amelie chatting away in Arabic with another guest (with an English accent, to be sure, which makes her sound like the people from Keserwan, but still, she does speak the language very well), and he is gripped by a violent rush of indignation. Everything around him, the faces and the objects he sees, all seem to decompose and explode in his face in sharp fragments. He flees out onto a terrace, and there the fresh air smelling of the sea or of the gardens, or the cool of the jacarandas, appeases him as he leans on a railing, his shadow projected onto a stand of distant trees by the lights coming from the reception rooms, and he gets a grip on himself. A guest talks to him, but he feels as if it is from the end of a long corridor, but he makes an effort, he concentrates, he replies, and little by little, there he is, back to his old self again. And then of course, he has only one desire, to take revenge, because he is not in the habit of being tossed aside like that.

The next few days, he tries to find out where this Amelie might be, whom she visits, where she dines, lunches, and takes tea, so that he can go there too and do something to wound her, to show her he despises her, to say a word to her, one from which women do not recover and for which they never forget you and swear revenge in turn. And in the meantime of course, he can't stop thinking about her, and along with the social injuries he wishes to inflict on her, he also dreams of the physical injuries too, he dreams that she has become his prey, that he subjects her to terrible acts that are in fact nothing more than the expression of his desire boiling over and becoming unbearable, which means that when he finally does see her again, one day or one evening, his heart goes wild, he can't breathe, and when at last the occasion presents itself for him to be arrogant toward her, or ironic or contemptuous, he does no such thing, because just as he is sharpening his sneer or a snide remark, she is the one who speaks first (with her accent that stretches out the words and then suddenly hardens, like a rock in a silk stocking) and says a friendly word, or talks about a common friend, or someone he reminds her of, or goodness knows what, and of course then his rage is immediately transmuted into something like slightly embarrassed courtesy (which is rare for him), and when he finds himself alone an hour or two later, he is no longer dreaming of violence but of torrid passion with the singular Amelie, and this is how he embarks on his final episode with Gebran Nassar.

Let us suppose that it is at precisely this point of the story that Gebran intervenes. He does not, strictly speaking, conceive of this creature, Amelie, as a war machine against Farid. He is not the one who injects the poison of love into Farid's veins, no, Gebran only jumps on the moving train, he seizes control of this nascent love and steers it in the direction he wants, hijacks it and throws it onto catastrophic tracks. To do so, all it takes is for him to draw Amelie aside one day and ask a little favor of her. And if he is certain she will accept, that is because he has some kind of power over her. This is undoubtedly the key to the whole affair, and what made my father say, and maybe everyone who knew the details about the affair say too, that Gebran "created" Amelie. He must have some kind of ascendancy over her, either she owes him something because her father received a favor of some kind from him (money loaned with no interest, a generous lease of land, paying for Amelie's school fees), or else something compromising happened to Amelie (in her past, a secret marriage, consummated in America, which forced her to find refuge in Lebanon, where she hopes no one will find out) or to her father (some shady business that obliged him to emigrate, or the fact that he is in prison back in Chicago, for unpaid debts or some such, and not dead as she claims). He has a hold on her, either because she owes him something, or because she fears him, or he is blackmailing her, whatever it is means that he can ask her a favor, and this favor is almost nothing at all, "on the contrary, Amelie, it might be a pleasant game for you," and it is simply to make Farid give her as many presents as possible, and expensive ones:

"Do whatever it takes, sulk, make demands, insist, make scenes. He is madly in love with you, you know it, everyone knows it. It'll be easy for you."

"Of course it'll be easy, Gibo," Amelie replies. "If granting favors was always like this, life would be wonderful. But I don't understand what use this is to you."

"Not much, my dear. Just to make him spend money. Don't worry, he has plenty. It's just a little revenge thing, between uncle and nephew. A friendly little lesson I want to teach him."

And so let's say that Amelie accepts because she has no other choice, and that it's nothing to worry about anyway, and because she thinks that it is in fact just a little lesson, of the kind that elders teach juniors to make them aware of the dangers of overspending, of wasting money and family assets. And so she sets to it. Her relationship with Farid becomes notorious. They meet over tea at Edwige B's, at the Grand Theatre, at her friends' five o'clock parties, and Farid obviously gives her presents, without any need for special recommendations. But after Gebran has intercepted their relationship, Amelie becomes significantly more affectionate, more jealous, more demanding. And Farid doesn't need to be told twice. "He lost his head," my father told me. "He would go completely mad, lose all sense of reality in an absolutely outrageous way. But he was madly in love, and because *she* was so beautiful, and had many suitors, and *she* made him think that others could give her more expensive, always more extravagant presents, he started acting like a Sursock or a Bustros." Everyone at Ayn Chir knows he is in love, of course. He doesn't appear at home very often, he doesn't speak to anyone, and that suits everybody just fine. He changes his suit three times a day and goes out in the coupé. But what no one knows is the scope of his spending. And that's to be expected, for there is no way they could: diamond necklaces and solitaires as big as a fist are things that are purchased discreetly. Farid is carried away and no longer sees the ground about to crumble beneath his feet. No doubt when he is in those boutiques where he buys the fatal treasures, in the muffled silence, under the gaze of the salesmen, as cold as the diamonds themselves, distant and attentive, as if they were judging him, in those moments when he is looking at a selection of stones of varying clarity, no doubt just then, before he makes a choice, he has terrible misgivings, and maybe the image of his mother appears to him. He sweats imperceptibly, his breathing grows labored. But when it is done, when the dreadful moment of the price being announced and the purchase being approved is past, he feels euphoric and grand. When he leaves the store, he feels as if he is walking with a giant's steps, like a master.

He thinks about Amelie, and his joy grows even more pure and makes him feel even lighter.

But it is still inconceivable that, except in these moments of ecstasy, he doesn't entertain horrifying doubts. When he is alone, when he lies down to sleep in his bedroom in Ayn Chir, or when he is woken by a noise in the middle of the night (the monumental cracking of one of the colossal Berouti cabinets), but also at many other times of his idle days, he must break out into cold sweats thinking (as he must, from time to time) about how he has absolutely no means of repaying his debts. One morning, he finally decides to go see Gebran to set things straight. But Gebran is not there, he is on an inspection tour of his properties and leased land. In the following days, Farid realizes he has become feverish. At home, he notices he no longer dares to look his mother in her eye, as if it were the eye of God looking down on Cain in the tomb. When he goes back to Gebran's house in Marsad a second time a week later, he is told that he is not yet home, even though he obviously is, since his Panhard is parked in front of the porch. A dull sense of dread grips him. That evening he is in a sullen mood, he is rough with his younger brothers, no one dares to ask what the matter is, and he goes and locks himself in his quarters without saying a word to anyone. The next day, he has a rendezvous with Amelie, and before he goes there, he decides to make a little purchase, nothing too extravagant, a peccadillo, but to his stupefaction, he is refused credit. "It goes on Gebran Nassar's account," he insists. It's no use. He gets angry, that makes no difference. He climbs into a taxi and makes a mad dash to Marsad. His hands are shaking in the car, and he needs to hold fast to his cane to stop them. When he arrives, Gebran receives him, to his great relief. But the relief is short-lived because, after Farid makes his usual promises ("Gebran, I'll pay you part of what I owe you as soon as I get my share" and he must feel a bit like an idiot), Gebran throws off his mask. I do not know what appears underneath it, what kind of expression Judas has on his face when he says what he does to the man he has so viciously deceived, but in any case, he tells him to repay everything, that it has all gone too far and now he needs to settle the whole lot, in other words the loans and the interest. Farid thinks he must have misheard the part about the interest, but he doesn't raise it, that's not how he operates. And yet Gebran says he considers it a good thing that the matter is now clear, and he slips in an allusion to the acknowledgment of debt with open credit, doing so in a by-the-by way, exactly as he did when he made Farid sign the acknowledgment that he slid between two trivial pieces of paper, and as if it was all agreed between them. Petrified, no longer hearing clearly, no longer seeing straight, without trying to understand, Farid asks for a delay ("Just until tomorrow," Gebran answers, "that's all I can do") and leaves, in a state of complete disorientation. He still goes to see Amelie, who lives, let's say, with her aunt in Zuqaq al-Blat, but is told that she has left for Damascus and will not be back for three days. His head gripped in an excruciating vice, Farid wanders through the city, then along the Corniche, and at that point he is no longer thinking about Amelie. As if the violence of the shock has paralyzed some of his feelings and galvanized others, Farid can think only about his mother, she occupies all the space in his mind, his head, his brain, which is buzzing and horribly amplifying the sound of the waves crashing against the seawalls of the Corniche. He does not go home to Ayn Chir before two or three in the morning that night. Everyone at home thinks he is out partying. But he leaves before dawn. "He did the same thing the next night too," my father told me. "We were worried. Then the gendarmes arrived, and he was nowhere to be found. The next day they came to announce to my mother that her son was in prison."

I will not linger on all this, I won't say anything more because the clan erased the memory of it with such relentless insistence, and because in some ways they were right to do so. What I will say, on the other hand, is that the day after that sinister announcement, Gebran Nassar appears at his cousins' house in Ayn Chir. He is received in deathly silence, Helene demands to be left absolutely alone with him in the large living room, and by the time he leaves she has handed over more than half of the orchards in payment of Farid's debts and in exchange for the promise that her son will be let out of prison immediately.

18

IN A PARADOX that will never cease to surprise me, the irremediable decay of the Nassar estate at Ayn Chir started at the very moment when the extensive cultivation of orange trees started to replace that of mulberry trees, gradually but systematically, sometime around 1925. The Nassars had been pioneers, and just as they were leaving the stage, citrus trees were starting to cover the land on the coast of Lebanon and all over the Middle East. And yet, when I asked my father once or twice to explain what was left of Wakim's land before his brothers' emigration and then his own, I discovered that it was still quite a substantial amount. But it was no longer enough to provide for the needs of a large family. And the yields were never very good anymore. They had to constrain their lifestyle even further, and I think that Wakim's sons, who had accepted being something like slightly strapped gentlemen farmers, could not accept becoming simple peasants.

In the beginning of 1925, Michel accepts a position on the staff of Habib Mattar, who imports marble and ceramics, and from time to time he brings back magnificent samples of polished marble, green, yellow, blue, moiré, and he has all sorts of projects for laying it in places in the house where there had never been any before, in the bedrooms or the pantries, which made his sisters laugh ("You'd do better to fix the wardrobes, a door almost killed me the other day when it fell on me." "And the ceiling is flaking down on our heads . . . here, look, another bit just rained down"). As for Khalil, who is barely seventeen, he sells all sorts of gadgets in the Corm stores and shows off by bringing home a sewing machine, for example, whose transportation to Ayn Chir requires a horse and cart. He has it brought into the house, proudly sets it up in the middle of the living room, and fusses over it as if it were a car—in fact it does have chrome trim and a whole clever mechanism of delicate cogs and settings. But he doesn't let anybody else use it, only he is allowed. He sits in front of it as if it were the cockpit of an airplane, with his sisters and his mother crowding around, and after wetting the threads between his lips and carefully poking them through one hole to the next ("This whole enormous machine," Blanche scoffs, "and you still have to go blind looking for the right holes"), he finally sets down a piece of fabric. At last, with the flywheel or the pedal, he starts up the mechanism, and then the needle, that minutely fine extremity to which the whole contraption delegates all its power, starts frenetically hopping up and down with a soft purring noise, running over the fabric and inscribing it at a fabulous speed with a long line of red stitches on white fabric, and then everyone is amazed, even Blanche the miscreant. My uncle also brings home a gramophone one day, a box topped with a kind of monstrous flower opening up from a spiraling stem. Everyone looks ironically at this strange beast, this music box with its extraordinary outgrowth that my uncle brought home only for show, to impress everyone, not for the music, because since there is no electricity yet at Ayn Chir it is completely useless. And so the gramophone serves as a giant ornament in the middle of the living room for a week or so. My father brings his playmates, the children of the farmers of Ayn Chir, to see it as if they were going to the zoo to look at animals from the jungle, to pet them and boldly put their hands in the beasts' trunks or ears. And during all this time Elias looks after the orchards. But that requires only a few half days of work per week, even with no laborers, which allows him to try his hand at a few things in business, and of these few things only one has remained in living memory, of which I collected a scrap long ago, the day my father explained to me, when I hadn't even asked him anything about it, that the slightly homespun-looking fabric that he still sold in the 1960s was almost the same as one his brother had imported in huge quantities forty years earlier. I was around fifteen at the time, I wasn't at all interested in textiles or the Nassar family history and couldn't care less about that snippet of memory. Today I realize that my father was actually talking to himself, putting into words the fond recollection of his older brother that was brought back by that bolt of cloth. A long time after that, when I was about to start composing the story of Wakim and his sons and doing the last pieces of research, one of the descendants of Habib Fayyad told me that his father (one of Habib's sons) had started a household linens business that later became prosperous, in a partnership with Elias Nassar and Antoine Melki. This information gives a plausible reason for Elias's departure, which remained rather obscure to me for a long time. The only explanation ever given to me before that had to do with the considerable impoverishment of the Nassars and his need to go find something to do elsewhere. But you don't just up and leave for America without any support, without even an idea of what you are going to do there, without a cousin who has gone on ahead and called you over, unless of course you want to start out shining shoes, according to the well-known cliché. However, Elias's departure could have had something to do with the business he was starting up with Fayyad and Melki.

To begin with, let's imagine he mortgages a plot of what is left of the land on the estate, with his mother's assent, and that he uses that money to buy a share in the business importing English cloth. After that, for months on end, the only thing anyone talks about is the "boat" on which all the hopes of the Nassars of Ayn Chir are loaded. Then the "boat" is in port and Elias on the dock, in a suit and hat, standing next to Fayyad and Melki, amid the bustle of the dockers, his eyes fixed on the cargo that is being clumsily transshipped onto boutres. Then raw silk invades the house, replacing the samples of marble and the gramophones with their inert trumps. It is everywhere, on piles on the divans, in rolls in the hallways, and the stuff is much less exciting than the mad little needle on the sewing machine that writes so prettily on fabric, but these heavy rolls are what hope in the future is made of, which means everyone loves them, almost cuddles them, handles them with great respect. Helene even shows them to her visitors. And this rough silk is indeed a manna from heaven. It is sold by the roll to storekeepers, who give it to the convents and orphanages in the mountains, where the nuns or the children being taught crafts make *very nice little things* with it, handkerchiefs or placemats embroidered in all different colors, which the storekeepers take back and sell for high prices because they are "sewn by hand." It's not a fortune, but it allows the family to fix up a few plots in the orchard that were a little tired, and to restore the furniture in the Big House, and sort out the ceilings and repair the roof. And if Elias Nassar still leaves after that, it is probably for something to do with this new business, either that he goes to visit factories on his own account or for his associates, or that he decides to work alone, to introduce a new product into Lebanon, and leaves to go prospecting with a determined spirit of adventure and maybe one or two letters of recommendation in his pocket. In any case he leaves, and in the annals of the Nassar clan he leaves for America, whereas those same Nassars, whenever they spoke of him, were more likely to associate their memories of his first period of emigration with the city of Manchester. In fact it was always a kind of curiosity for me to hear my father tell the story of his two brothers' emigration, in terms so vague and imprecise that the names of cities and continents might as well be those of distant galaxies, and then suddenly, in the middle of these vast geographical generalities, to see the name of Manchester invariably appear, all clean and tidy and indubitable, like a daymark in an ocean of approximations. One day when I was asking my father to be a bit more specific, I remember he grumbled as if I had insulted him, that it wasn't all that complicated, that Manchester was the city where the factories were, and that those factories sent the goods that Elias bought from them over to him in America. After that he added a significant fact, namely that Elias later brought his brother Michel out, because he couldn't be everywhere at once all by himself.

So, in all likelihood, Elias first leaves for Manchester, and in his mother's mind, and his brothers' and sisters', he leaves for a few long months, but he will be back. Nevertheless, the whole family gathers to take him to the port and there, on the deck of the ship, they take a photograph, unsuspecting that this would be the first in a series that will see each of the brothers, one after the other, standing in the middle, which means that he is the one leaving. With each photograph the number of boys is reduced, until the last one, where it is the youngest, my future father, who is standing in the middle, with only women around him. But, for now, it is the oldest of the brothers who is leaving, and everyone thinks it is only for a few months. In the souvenir photograph, he is therefore the one in the middle, looking extremely dapper, but with a flat, distant look in his eyes. Helene is proudly standing by his side in her strange hat that looks like a helmet, the girls are in skirts and high heels, Farid is pouting (but that was always his pose in front of the camera), and my future father, who is twelve years old, is standing between two of his sisters and already has that incredible resemblance to Arthur Rimbaud, with his wide forehead and timid, watery look, which seems to slide discreetly toward the camera lens, but in which there seems to be some kind of incomprehensible reverie. The family takes up the whole width of the photograph, and in the background, there is a mast with a mess of ropes and canvases in front of it, along with a lifesaver on which the name of the ship is undiscernible.

So he leaves, and that is the beginning of the great dispersal of Wakim's sons throughout the world. He leaves and I do not know what he does. No doubt because in Manchester, through luck or chance, tenacity or mad faith in the future, he raises the stakes, explores, takes options, and six months later, instead of him returning, what comes back is a letter in which he gives instructions that Helene, in all confidence, decides to follow blindly. She sells the mortgaged plot, mortgages a second one, and sends the proceeds to her oldest son, just as Michel, called over by his brother, is getting ready to leave himself. And again, feeling something like incredulity, like a waking dream, the clan all goes to the port for the photograph, the second in the series. Michel is in the middle, staring at the camera so insistently that he looks ill at ease. Helene, at his side, is wearing the same hat but also a coat (which means it is winter and this makes me think she must have worried about her sons at sea for weeks on end). And then there are the girls and boys: Linda is leaning toward one of her sisters, my father is curiously touching his earlobe, Farid has the same pout, but his refined elegance indicates that he has not yet worn all of the suits he acquired in his glory days.

At that time, departures were followed by long silences. The silence that followed the departure of Wakim's second son lasts at least a year, during which the two sons travel, do business, work at jobs unknown to the inhabitants of Ayn Chir, just as the forces that govern us often work beyond our knowledge of them. And when one or other of the girls, one evening on the balcony, sighs, "We miss them so much, what can they be up to?," Helene, in the shadows, declares that they must be patient, that the boys know what they are doing, that all will be well. After a year, an envelope arrives, either from Manchester or from America, New York, maybe Chicago, with stamps with the effigy of George V or the Statue of Liberty. The letter is dripping with the usual turns of phrase, *we miss you, we embrace you, how is such and such doing, and so and so,* and then there is some encouraging but extremely vague news, which is all but undecipherable for anyone seeking to understand exactly what the brothers are up to over there, *we are doing well, thank God, we have reliable friends in the textile factories in Manchester, America is the land of plenty.* Then other letters arrive that attest to their presence sometimes in America, sometimes in England, and this can only be a good sign, even though no one has any idea at the time that what is carrying the brothers forward is the formidable flow of prosperity dashing the world toward the abyss, and that by going farther and farther west, they are heading into the heart of the volcano. But to begin with everything goes well, and the proof of it is that at the end of the second year, money starts arriving in Ayn Chir, quite a lot of money, in fact. This is in 1927. More comes in 1928, and even in 1930 when the source has already dried up, when the Western world has come crashing into the wall of the Depression, and that last sum of money to arrive is like the fossil light that men see when they look at a star in the night sky, when in fact that star no longer exists and hasn't for a very long time.

But before that date and that last transfer, life flowed on at Ayn Chir. At least four years went by, about which I have a firsthand account, my father's, for whom this was the time of his heady youth, of his first clear and personal memories. It is a difficult time, of course, with the absence of the two brothers, the great financial uncertainties, and Helene's terrible anxiety. The period, also, when the Big House is constantly making it known that it isn't being looked after properly. The tiles fall off the roof when there are strong gusts of wind, water pours inside like a fountain every time it rains, putting the furniture in danger, and then the walls start peeling. As for the railing of the grand staircase, exhausted from having sacks of oranges or charcoal propped up against its delicate arabesques, it starts bending over and finally gives way along one whole side, just when Father Callas comes to visit, supporting himself on it as he climbs up, and he almost falls ten yards below. But it is also a period when there are great joys, such as Blanche's wedding that can be celebrated with great ceremony thanks to the first sum of money sent by the two brothers, and this wedding is a whole story in itself, because Blanche is in love with the son of Gerios Nassar, who is younger than she is. He loves her too, that is certain, except that Gerios can't believe this, doesn't want to hear anything about this marriage because "he could never imagine that one of Wakim's daughters would marry his son," my father told me. "It was reverse snobbism. And I think he had some doubts about his son's sincerity." And so Gerios decides to send his boy to one of his cousins on his mother's side, to work in an African country where this cousin is apparently the friend of the Black kings reigning at the crossing of several rivers. The son protests, disappears for a few days, comes back, but his father doesn't back down, so the boy is shipped off. Blanche is a mess, crying all the time, she is even disappointed when a letter from her brothers arrives, because she thought it was one from her boyfriend, and finally, four months later, it is not a letter that arrives but the boyfriend himself. He simply made a return trip on the ship, refused to set foot on the ground in Africa, but in order to prove that he really went there, he brings back a carved ivory flyswatter that would remain a celebrated trophy in the annals of the Nassar clan. Faced with this tenacity, Gerios accepts the idea of the marriage, comes to see Helene about it, almost apologizing, and Helene gives him a good scolding and then the children are married in a lovely ceremony that would be the last grand occasion to be celebrated at the Big House.

My father would retain a fond memory of this, and of everything else, because he never knew the Big House in its days of splendor, when it had hundreds of visitors sitting inside, nor the days of the clementines, the visit of the mutasarrif, and the hunts in Keserwan, the time of heroes or the time of zayms. He lived through the time of the house's slow ruination, the orchards' irremediable decay, and the absence of men. But for him those were still golden days because it was the time of his carefree youth, in which he knew his first stirrings of love (notably for the daughter of the French general in command of the area of Ayn Chir, the lovely Diane, whom he sees on the street on his way home from school, whom he follows and who lets herself be followed, to whom he offers flowers one day, at the corner of a road, in the middle of a path, and who accepts them, and who impels him even to ask Farid for advice about his clothes, and to spend all his pocket money on tram fares so that his shoes are not dusty when he comes home from school, and this is his most enduring adolescent love, a love that he would decide inconsiderately to engrave forever in the memory of the clan by making Blanche, who is expecting her second child, promise to call it Diane if it's a girl, and Blanche, who would do anything for him, does call her daughter Diane, a fact that Diane, one of my innumerable cousins, would tenderly hold against him for the rest of her life), a period when he has great fun with the sons of the farmers of Ayn Chir (they steal tarbouches here and there, one from a customer at the café on the Damascus road, one from an uncle who left his on the trunk when he came to the house, then they sneak into Baclini's son's place, crawl to the well, and throw the tarbouche in, and the purple dye slowly turns the water red, to the point where Baclini first thinks that someone has thrown a slaughtered animal into his well, then that a whole herd is in the water, then that someone has cast a spell on it, and he goes looking for a Bedouin woman, just as his father did long ago, and all this is a punishment from the children, because Baclini is miserly and shoots on sight when anyone goes near his oranges) or with his nephews, Catherine's sons, who are the same age as he is (they spend days together in the huge hackberry tree at the entrance to the Pine Forest, they literally live there, organize meetings, poetry slams, zajal sessions, or throw pebbles on the heads of passersby).

But throughout his adolescence, he still misses a father figure. His two older brothers are gone, Farid is not a role model, and Khalil is not much older than he is. So he turns to symbolic figures, such as the abadays of Marsad who love Wakim's children out of fidelity to the memory of their father and who often arrange curious pastimes for them, especially for him, my father, the youngest and their favorite, such as that famous incident when Baz Baz hijacked a cart loaded with watermelons heading up from Basta to Marsad (Baz Baz forces the driver to steer his horses at walking pace on the tram tracks, blocking all the trams behind them for several long minutes, and I can imagine the trams rattling, with their antennae swaying, throwing sparks and high-pitched blasts from their horns to no avail, while Baz Baz, imperturbable, keeps chatting with the worried driver and winking connivingly at my father sitting next to him, having offered him this little adventure in memory of Wakim). And it is probably this absence of a father that makes him so sensitive to his mother's anxieties, that pushes him to rise to challenges in which he wishes to show himself as master of his own destiny and whose success gives him the impression that the world remains governable through the will of men. When for example he learns that the fees for the French lycée are a considerable strain on the family budget, he gets it into his head to obtain a scholarship for the next year. He becomes studious, concentrated, his Rimbaldian face becomes serious and worried, and he does get that scholarship. Then he rests on his laurels, spends a year lazing about because it is free, such that he doesn't get a scholarship the following year, and he has to start all over again with the concentration and concern, and it works a second time. He gets one last scholarship, for the year of ninth grade, the last one he would get, because after that it would be his turn to be in the middle of the photograph, in a suit and hat with all his sisters around him, looking more like Rimbaud than ever, with a terribly somber expression as he rather unwillingly embarks for immigration to Egypt.

My father abandoning his education at sixteen certainly marks the lowest point of the Nassars' fortunes in those leaden times. This takes place in 1931, and at the time everything had gone awry again for reasons that escaped me for a long time, until I realized that this was directly caused by the Depression of 1929. I never heard my father or my uncles talk about the crash. However, in order to explain what happened, they did tell me about the bankrupt factories in Manchester and the unsalable stocks of goods in America. This is all translated into letters with bad news arriving at Ayn Chir in the envelopes with the effigies of George V or the Statue of Liberty (*we are all well, thank God, but the Manchester factories are having some difficulties these days because of the economic situation and we will need to trust in God*, then *All is well and our health is excellent but the overall situation is very bad, we're having a few difficulties with the stock, but with God's help and your prayers, it will all come right*), then into the interruption of the money transfers (*We hope to be able to send the money we promised very soon*), and finally, one morning in 1931, into the announcement of the departure of Michel for Brazil. My father follows all this quite closely. He reads the letters, with their bundles of disguised bad news. He especially reads the worry on Helene's face, notices her moments of panic when there is money to be spent on repairs to an old pump in the orchards, or to buy a dress for Linda, who insists on always looking her best. He guesses that his mother is counting her pennies, that she now accepts Khalil giving her his salary, whereas to begin with she was happy for him to keep it for himself. All this—which leaves its mark on my father, and for a long time, since he would still be talking to me about it constantly fifty years later, when he had achieved freedom from want, but would still have incomprehensible feelings of insecurity and fear of the future—all this pushes him to redouble his efforts to obtain another scholarship from the French lycée, but it is at that period that Egypt suddenly enters the conversations of the Nassars of Ayn Chir. There is talk of easy work in Alexandria and on the banks of the Suez Canal. Helene starts mentioning one of her cousins whose husband has done well in business over there. She makes her parents give more details about it when they come from Qattine, while the inescapable Émile, Uncle Curiel, who comes to the Big House every morning, has his own stories to tell about his friends in the Canal Company, at Ismailia, to whom he could write letters of recommendation.

My future father listens to all this without saying a word. These plans do not threaten him directly, or at least that is what he thinks because he is at the lycée and his grades are good, very good in fact, as his brothers and sisters would always remember them. But even as he quietly searches his mother's face, even as he grows pensive and no longer sings zajals in the sycamore at the entrance to the Pine Forest, he knows that the sword of Damocles is not dangling over him but over his brother Khalil, who is continuing to work at Corm's and bringing back new products to show the family at home, notably the famous Dodge that he parks at the bottom of the steps of the Big House after announcing his arrival with a few blasts of the horn starting in the Pine Forest, and in which he would later take his brother, my future father, for a ride.

Two months later, bearing letters from Curiel and the invitation from Helene's cousin to board at her place, Khalil leaves for Egypt, and this is the occasion for the third photograph on the deck of a ship, almost as if it were the same one over and over again, except that this time Helene seems to have aged and is not wearing a hat. Blanche is not there but the other girls are, as well as Farid. My future father is crouched in front of his brother who is leaving, holding a boater in his hand, his expression is disdainful and distant, he seems to be glancing sideways at the world, with distrust, in the same way that you keep an eye on a suspicious pedestrian walking beside you in the street and who might be preparing some kind of misdeed. Because of this photo, that is the expression I imagine he has during the remainder of that year, when he is somber and not gregarious. He gets a scholarship. And while he completes an excellent and pointless year in ninth grade at the French lycée, with his pensive and disdainfully grand airs, and his concern not to get dust on his shoes when he arrives at school in the mornings, his brother Khalil manages to find his feet in Egypt quite quickly. I don't know how he was able to get a job so easily there, thus justifying Egypt's reputation as an unmatched land of opportunity. But what I do know, since it is part of the Nassar family heritage, is that a few months after his arrival in Alexandria, he is hired by the Singer stores and six months later he is the head of sales for the Suez region. Five months after that, he sends a letter to Ayn Chir (with a stamp with the effigy of King Fouad), where he tells of his success (*With God's help I found a very interesting job that will allow us to face the future with confidence*). But he doesn't send the money straightaway because he needs to find a home himself over there, and at that point there is almost despair at Ayn Chir. The two sons-in-law help Helene and her children but the situation quickly becomes unmanageable, until the solution to all this arrives in a letter from Alexandria.

I don't know what turns of phrase were used in that letter, I never really wanted to know in fact, but what I do know, and what remained vivid in my father's memory, is that Khalil proposed that his brother Farid and my future father come join him in Egypt, adding no doubt, among other grand effusions, that there were wonderful opportunities for work all around him, that he would be able to find them something to do at Singer at least. The letter is given to my father to read, and he asks if this means he has to leave school. Helene, who is on the verge of tears, sincerely allows him to make up his own mind ("Do what you think is best, you know our situation, but you also know what's best for you"). Three days later, after being silent during all the mealtimes and systematically avoiding being in the presence of his sisters or Helene, who is discreetly searching his slightest expression and gesture for fear that he will do something stupid, three days later, then, he announces that he will leave for Egypt.

He is allowed to finish the school year nevertheless. I will say nothing of the regrets that my father felt about having to abandon his studies, which he was still telling me about decades later, in an endless soliloquy, when at that point everything had been recovered, when he had succeeded, he, the youngest of Wakim's sons, like Joseph the son of Jacob, in transforming his exile into Egypt into a triumph and had contributed to straightening out his brothers' situation before helping them to come home too. Let me go straight to the end of the story, to what would be the prelude of yet another one. In the middle of 1932, the Nassars are once again in a photograph on the deck of a ship, and it is Farid who is in the middle of the picture with his mother and sisters, so well-dressed that you can't tell whether he is emigrating or going on a cruise. My father is in the photo too, crouched in front of Farid, with his boater on his head and an almost amused look in his eye, it's hard to say why. After that, for the rest of the year, he prepares for his departure. Like a hero who knows he is undone, but who makes his last battle the most magnificent one he has waged, he passes his ninth-grade exams with high distinction. It's almost a provocation, a way of giving his mother and sisters a bad conscience. Then I imagine he says goodbye to his schoolmates and spends hours with the sons of the farmers of Ayn Chir talking about Egypt. He also talks about it with his nephew, Catherine's son, and all of them declare that they would love to go with him. They tell him what they know about the place, as if to encourage him, and he listens in silence during their walks in the lanes of Ayn Chir, which are now all lined with orange trees, and where the darkness is so dense at night that the stars seem to be raining down on the rustling leaves.

And finally, the day comes when he is the one in the middle of the departure photograph, with his mother and sisters and nieces, standing in front of a great mast, in a muddle of ropes and buoys, on a ship whose name I do know. He is holding his hat and stands a head taller than his mother, who is already a little stooped and considerably aged, with her hair pulled back in a bun, and he holds her close to him, with his arm around her exhausted shoulders. Two hours beforehand he must have left the Big House of Ayn Chir with its legion of women, and turned his head to gaze one last time at the facade with its three windows like a beacon, its shutters askew and its acroteria cracked, unaware that he would be back in twenty years' time to restore the whole thing from top to bottom. A little earlier, in the nascent dawn, he may have gone out onto the balcony looking out over the orchards to see the sunrise. Let us lean on the balustrade with him, to see what he sees there one last time: orchards stretching into the distance, three-quarters of which no longer belong to the Nassars, forming a vast carpet of green, above which birds chase each other, leaping and swooping and chirruping, and into which they finally plunge. Let us turn to look, one last time, toward the road, where an automobile is passing by, whose passengers are surely craning their necks toward the Big House. Beyond the road, on the horizon, the mountains are turning blue, becoming diaphanous, and the sun behind them gives them a crest of light before its rays come to rest on him, still standing there on the balcony, still leaning on the balustrade. Let us join him as he deeply inhales the air smelling of apples, and listens to the sounds of the house waking up, its shutters squeaking, water tinkling into a basin, the front gate opening as Gerios's son comes in to visit the vegetable garden with his father. Now that the day has dawned, let us review with him the images of daily life one last time, the visits from ladies in crinolines who are served tea in Limoges porcelain with a green striped pattern, the wives of the farmers of Ayn Chir whom Helene receives in her bedroom, the mailman bringing the letters and being invited in to sit for a while in the living room, little Diane who goes missing one day and who is found asleep inside the massive Berouti sideboard, in the bottom of one of the huge stoneware fruit bowls, Curiel's piano being carried up the steps to the house by ten men and set down in the living room so that Linda's musical talents can be expressed, her voice continuously rising in the limpid air but which falters as it reaches high C when it meets the sound of a bus horn or a donkey braying, and Linda then sighs in her usual way.

And in this last inventory of days, with my father, who is still standing above the orchards, let us once again review the thousand little nothings that make up the eternal warp and weft of daily life, the laborers calling out in the orange groves, Curiel, who doesn't want to climb the steps shouting up from the bottom, those steps my father used to leap down four by four on school days, a seagull coming to rest on the balustrade of the balcony, Helene returning home from mass on Sunday with her embroidered black scarf thrown back over her shoulders, or Helene playing solitaire while she waits for lunchtime, the sound of the crockery being set on the table in the great silence of midday, the scent of bay leaves and white soap in the sheets and towels in all the wardrobes, the smell of orange blossom, jasmine, and gardenias wafting in through all the windows, the front door all too often left wide open, the breezes blowing through the house, the huge curtains at the three arched windows that swell, and swell, and swell, until their hems, like delicate fingers, playful and mischievous, brush over a bonbonniere or a Daum vase on a table set a little too close, and as they deflate and recede toward the window, like a child toward his mother's skirts after a scrape, they send it carelessly crashing to the ground, where it shatters into pieces. And now all this is said, now that he is leaning on the ship's rail an hour after departure and the mountains of Lebanon have receded below the horizon, and as he turns away and looks straight ahead, let us also look into the distance where, in twenty-four hours, the new lands of exile will rise into view, let us look with him toward the land of the pharaohs, of the viceroys and khedives, toward Egypt, and let us imagine, with him, that this is where everything must soon begin all over again.

GLOSSARY

abaday: a hit man, a neighborhood chief, and a popular hero within a religious community.

abaya: a wide garment made of camel hair.

abouserra: a navel orange.

dunam: a unit of area equivalent to one thousand square meters.

kaak: a kind of bread with sesame seeds, baked and generally eaten with sumac powder.

kalpak (Turkish word): a high-crowned cap.

khwaja: sir, monsieur.

kombaz: a masculine robe.

liwan: the central room of a house, open to the exterior on one side.

Majlis Millet: a council managing the civil affairs of a religious community.

mashrabiya: wood latticework window.

matlic: deformation of the French word for metallic. The smallest-denomination coin in circulation at the end of the Ottoman Empire.

mejidieh: silver or gold coin bearing the name and effigy of Sultan Abdulmejid.
miri: land tax.
moghrabiyeh: dish of small balls of flour served with chicken and meat.
mouchaa: agricultural land belonging to the village community.
mugarasa: contract by which a peasant can acquire, after a determined period of time, half of the land which he has planted in trees.
mutasarrif: governor of the mutasarrifate.
mutasarrifate: governorate. The word is almost exclusively used to describe the governorate of Mount Lebanon between 1860 and 1920.
narghile: a water pipe for smoking tobacco, a hookah.
rotl: unit of weight worth two hundred and fifty grams.
samsara: activity of the simsar.
seroual: baggy cuffed pants.
shawish (Turkish word): sergeant.
simsar: middleman, broker.
sitt: lady, madam.
sofragi (word of Egyptian origin): a servant who serves at table.
tarbouche: a red felt cylindrical hat, similar to a fez.
vilayet: a province in the Ottoman Empire.
wali: a governor of a province in the Ottoman Empire
waqf: mortmain assets, or a service managing mortmain assets.
yuzbashi (Turkish word): captain in the Ottoman army.
zaym: clan chief and dignitary who plays a political role.
zaymat: from *zaym*.
zajal: a popular poetry form, poetry in vernacular language.